THE DEVIL OF ASKE

The House of Aske, once elegantly beautiful, now stood remote and decaying after years of neglect. Ruled by the iron-willed Old Madam of Aske, the Aske family too seemed crossed by a streak of decay and madness that the villagers blamed on the 'Devil of Aske'. But in spite of a maleficent fate that had destroyed the family, one after another, for generations, there was one man who was haunted by the house and family of Aske—to own both was Simon Carden's obsession. He had enough money to restore the house; he had won the hand of the beautiful but vague Ann Aske. But even the darkly handsome Simon, with his enormous wealth and determination, was finally no match for the brooding and malignant evil that surrounded Aske, and it was left to the woman who loved him to try to help him escape from it.

The
Devil of Aske

A novel by

PAMELA HILL

ST. MARTIN'S PRESS
NEW YORK

Contents

To
E.M.W.C.McC.

Prologue

THE STRANGER

IT WAS ONE morning, that first morning of all, that I had been out riding with Ann Aske on her new pony. Afterwards the stranger was standing by the house-gate.

Ann was at that time very beautiful, like an equestrian painting of some Spanish princess, perhaps, from last century, except that they were not permitted to ride. Her hair, which was fine-textured as silk, had been combed into loose ringlets and then tied back with a black ribbon beneath her broad hat, in which curled a long feather, exactly the pale blue of her eyes; Ann had chosen it for herself before we left London. Her habit fitted like skin, for her figure in those days was trim and not too plump, and her skin was as it was to remain, a white rose. She had black boots and carried a small whip in her hand with a silver handle, that her grandmother, who was always known as Old Madam, had given her for a Christmas present. Old Madam had, moreover, purchased the pony itself for Ann at the Lammas fair, on the advice of the Aske stablehand, Jonie Braik, who knew his horses. It was quiet to the hand but looked as if it need not be; a tall, good-looking chestnut, that Jonie himself had by now—and he did not often trouble with such things—groomed till its coat shone. We had trotted side by side that morning along the nearer lanes, Ann being a timid rider and I, lagging behind with the old habit on that she

9

had grown out of, and on the short-legged mare, had been thinking how much faster I could have ridden her beast if not mine. But I had said nothing, naturally, and had plodded alongside as always, all our youth together, when wherever we might go I had ridden and walked beside or, more often, a little behind Ann. This was partly because she was so beautiful that everyone wanted to stare at her unhindered, and, also, because I lived by virtual charity in the House of Aske and was to all intents, if not in actual fact, a servant.

It did not accordingly surprise me that the stranger, who was tall and dark, did not notice me at all beyond a brief, contemptuous glance, following on the long look he gave Ann. This latter was, however, not to my liking either; it resembled the casual appraisal of a dealer at a horse-fair, as if he were sizing up the points of a mare for purchase. The black, lambent gaze—he was, as I have said, very tall and dark, dressed in a drab coat with three capes only, and hatless, so that the early sun picked out the colour in his hair, striking blue-black from it like a starling's wing, for he wore no powder—this gaze travelled up and down Ann, as though he saw and assessed her naked. She was stupid, I knew, but such a look must be manifest even to her; and she flushed, but sat there waiting for him to open the gate, as any male creature would unless he were a savage. But the tall man made no movement, only went on standing there, as if he had been carved out of the trees which rose behind him, or of stone. For an instant I had the notion he was growing taller till he was larger than life, a demon; there could be few men so tall. Then I reflected to myself that he was nothing of the kind, only a boor, without the manners to open gates; and strange to the neighbourhood at that, or he would know better than to stare in such a way at the young lady of Aske.

"Will you open the gate?" said Ann. I had been summoning the courage to say it myself, but I am never prone to make my voice heard and, from habit, had kept

in the background. I watched, therefore, while the tall man
went to the gate and unlatched it, holding it open with an
exaggerated bow which made the act more of an insult
than if he had kept still. We rode through and did not turn
our heads, so that I do not know whether or not he stood
looking after us.

"Who was that?" said Ann, after we had gone by. I
replied that I had no idea, but would wager he hadn't shut
the gate. The spring day was, suddenly, colder than it had
been. I remembered the disturbing eyes, dark and glowing
like coals, and the look in them which might have been
hate had he known us, which he did not. How could he,
when we did not know him? For hereabouts, where we
had both spent all our lives except for school, we knew
every least one from the surrounding villages, and he was
not a gentleman, of that I was sure.

"I have a feeling that I know him," said Ann,
nevertheless.

"Perhaps it was the devil," I muttered. She slewed her
pale gaze round at me; she had never been certain, when
now and again we exchanged talk, whether or not I was
jesting. "Oh, Leah, it might well be so," she said solemnly,
her eyes round as saucers. "I had the strangest sensation a
moment ago when we passed him at the gate. Do you
think it could be? They say *he* takes human form, and has
been seen."

"Not in these parts," I said firmly; Old Madam had
instructed me to discourage Ann's fancies, although I was
the younger. To some extent, therefore, I had adopted the
old woman's dry, brisk manner which sat oddly, as I know,
on my almost nineteen years. Ann was twenty-two. It had
been thought all of last year, and several before that, that
she would be betrothed soon to young Fordwoodham, but
there was still no word of this, for money was short again.
I thought, with a shiver against the spring day, of Ann's
only brother Peter, in town at this moment where he lived
like a lord, losing Ann's dowry and more at cards. Old

Madam had not told me all of that. I forgot how I knew.

"The devil is tall," said Ann. "He can grow as tall as a ship's mast." Her soft mouth set obstinately and I did not argue with her. Sometimes, although she had wasted her time at school, Ann would remember a fragment of a verse or ballad we had been taught there. That was where it had come from.

I had forgotten the tall man by the time we rode back to the house and dismounted, and went in; by now, again, I was thinking of Ann. In many ways she was like my much younger sister, but she never acquired wisdom as she grew older; while I, I knew, might often have been a hundred years old. After we had gone back upstairs I passed a mirror on the wall and, as was not my wont, stopped and looked into it. Small wonder the dark glance had travelled on! I was tiny for my age, flat, thin and pale, with squab-like features except for my eyes which, though grey and fine enough to outward vision, needed spectacles whenever I read. My hair was mouse-brown, straight, and my figure straight also, like a child's. My hands are beautiful: but there was nothing else about me then, I knew, even without Ann's brilliant contrast always by, to attract the attention of anyone. No man, at least since I came to maturity, had ever looked twice at me.

A shivering took me again, and I made myself leave the mirror and presently go downstairs to breakfast. On the way I passed the gallery where portraits of long-dead Askes, not my own ancestors, gloomed from their frames, beruffed like those in Aske Church, stout in later periwigs and once, on the last turn of all to the stairs, the pathetic, small head-portrait of Dorothy Aske. She had been Ann's mother and neither of her children could remember her, for she had died at Peter's birth a year after Ann's. The painted features might have belonged to a doll; they had been done, no doubt, by a travelling journeyman, and told one nothing about the subject except what I had heard already, in other ways. And nearby was a portrait of similar size, though painted perhaps five years earlier, of Robin Aske, Ann's uncle who had been killed before she was born, at Prestonpans in Scotland in the 'Forty-five. Robin was young, perhaps twenty, with dark eyes and a rose-coloured coat, the cuffs of it turned back almost to the elbow, and braided. The fine lace at his throat and wrists had defeated the painter. Robin, I thought, reminded me of someone. The conclusion I reached was unlikely, and occupied me for the rest of the way downstairs. Robin, though human, gay and feckless, was like, I had decided, the man we had seen at the gate that morning. But that was impossible or, at the least, coincidence.

Old Madam had come down first as she always did. I had by that time lived at the House of Aske for ten years, but I never grew used to the presence of Old Madam or felt at ease when confronting her, any more than one would do if an ancient, solid stone goddess suddenly confronted one, staring at nothing with fierce shining eyes the colour of emeralds. The eyes were the only bright thing about Old Madam now, since her hair, which had been red in her youth, had faded. It was still thick as grey ropes, and she twisted it up anyhow under her cap. She had grown vast with age, but not flabby; if one had the temerity to touch her, I thought, the touch would make no impression on her flesh, for it seemed less flesh than granite. She was constantly active, in a slow deliberate way, still going on long grim walks alone. She was always alone. I have often wondered if anyone, even her late husband who was also her cousin, knew her wholly before the days when they became mere strangers who shared a bed. Old Madam by now was never late, never wrong, never talkative or emotional; like an oracle in the house, and at the same time its heart. Everything deferred to her. To pursue my own analogy I think I knew even then, though I had nothing yet to go by, that it had not always been, perhaps still was not, a heart of stone. But she was very frightening.

I came into the room and dipped a curtsy to Old Madam and we sat there together at the long table in silence, eating breakfast. Ann had not yet come down and nobody ever waited for her. By Madam's plate today, I saw, there was a letter lying whose red seals the old lady had not yet broken. Later she would open it. It seems hard to believe, by now, that for the space of a quarter-hour we sat there together, and she did not do so; and so I could not know how swiftly, like a happening in a romance or play, the dark man we had just seen would come into all our lives soon, almost at once now, and would not again leave them, or set any of us free of him as long as we lived.

Part I

THE BRIDE

I

MY OWN NAME is Leah. It is not one which ever pleased me as a child, though by now I have grown used to it. Then, I would have preferred to have been christened Rachel, and at an early age—for being a parson's child I was nourished almost from birth on Holy Writ and, having neither brothers nor sisters to divert my dear parents' time from me, the classics as well—I asked my father about it, at some time when his duties about Aske parish, where he was clergyman, left him the leisure. Rachel, Laban's daughter, whom Jacob had loved, had, I knew, been beautiful, because the text said so, and I was not. No doubt this was why they had called me after her less attractive sister, which thought sobered me. My father tried to cheer me in his knowledgeable fashion, giving me reasons for the choice as he always did. He was a thin fine-faced humorous man, a scholar, in a black suit of clothes which always looked the same, and clean linen daily and his own grey hair. His name was Mark Considine. I loved him very much, slightly more than I loved my poor mother, whose asthma often made her ill.

"Granted that Leah was plain," said my father, "which may have mattered in the end less than anyone might think: for she was a woman of great character and resource who never, in fact, received adequate recognition for her services." At this point my mother, coming out into the

rectory garden pale and, herself, red-eyed for it was
summer, and she had the hay-fever on her, said gently as
always, "My dearest Mark, do you think perhaps not
quite yet, in front of the child?" as though I could
hear nothing unless spoken to. My father, who never
made this mistake, smiled in such a way as to let me
know that his smile was for me, although he looked at my
mother.

She was not pretty, as I knew even then, but had a
gentle, refined face and beautiful hands. She had been a
governess in a great house where my father had been called
in to eat dinner only once, as he was the curate. That had
been beyond Steed, thirty miles away from Aske where
afterwards they had set up house in the vicarage for my
father's first charge, and there, after twelve years of
marriage, I had been born to them. Perhaps, as memory
can confuse one a little, the conversation I have mentioned
took place not at Aske but at Steed. I have spent a great
part of my life since then in both places, and in each of the
gardens we had was an apple tree. We used to sit under it
sometimes when the weather was fine.

"Why not yet?" said father reasonably. "Better now
than later," and then he smiled at my mother for herself
and she came and sat down beside us and we all began to
discuss some learned matter. My father and mother were
so fond, themselves, of learning that they included me
from the beginning in all such talk, though it is not even
nowadays necessary for girls who will be expected,
perhaps, to earn a living to know Latin and Greek as well
as I did by the age of nine. That I learned so early to
revere and love book-learning has been a great help to me,
as has the remembrance of these frequent, logical, scholarly exchanges between my parents; they always showed
courtesy to one another and had a respect for each other's
opinions. In this manner I was taught, through watching
and listening long before I joined in, to assemble my
thoughts for myself, and to have a reason for every
opinion, and to continue, as they did, as long as I lived to

educate myself and to keep abreast of events. I have continued in this way ever since and still do, although now I am an old woman and for many years have been blind. But Robin reads to me.

What I was taught, by contrast, never by any means to do then was interrupt, answer back pertly and without reflection, put myself forward or make a noise, or do other, if guests should be present, than occupy myself suitably with whatever material should be available. If there was none I would be expected to sit quietly, with my hands in my lap. As I was small and naturally shy with strangers, it was often possible to forget I was in the room at all. All this, though perhaps in my case it was excessive, might be of more value to other young women than they may suppose. Gentlemen everywhere, no matter whether or not they are clergymen, dislike a loud-mouthed, aggressive, blue-stocking female more than anything; and if my dear father's care of me, and early cultivation of my mind, had resulted in only this in the end, his efforts would have been largely wasted. He told me so himself; it was almost the last thing he ever did tell me, so that I must have been already nine years old when he said it, a long time after that summer's day under the apple tree when I had asked why I was christened Leah.

I had had occasional playmates among the children of the village, the doctor's little girl on several occasions and, once only, the schoolmaster's twins. They came for the day, but they were boys and rough, and my dear mother did not ever invite them back again. I lived my life mostly to myself, therefore, but was never solitary; I was so much in my parents' company that I even learned to speak as they did, quaintly, no doubt, and using longer words than most little creatures of my age, and I played few games and never coveted a doll, and never had one. This no doubt made me seem very dull, and soon the doctor's girl, and the village children, left me alone as they grew older and their lives perhaps more boisterous. But mine was no fairy-tale existence; I kept my feet on the ground, and observed what went on about me, for I had the opportunity of seeing the cottagers in their homes on my mother's visits to them, when she would take me with her. Nevertheless we were considered a little different from the cottagers, and the villagers; they would rise when we came in and when we departed, and the men, if at home, would pull forelocks and the women would bob.

One day when our differences showed up, yet in another way we were all the same, was Sunday, when naturally everyone came in best clothes to church, twice daily. I, like the other children, in a bonnet and round-gown, and flat slippers, would walk, holding decorously to my mother's hand, up the churchyard path and bow, as we were in turn bowed to. The depth depended on the other person's status and on ours; I had already been taught to curtsy lightly to the doctor, more deeply to my father if he should cross our path in his gown and bands, and the wig he wore when he was preaching; and not at all to the villagers, but most deeply of all, very much so indeed, to the Aske family, the squire's, consisting of sundry persons I shall describe shortly. These came, of course, from the great house, rising among its trees a mile beyond Aske village. Although in those days it still meant only roofs and pinnacles to me, and a lodge-gate, I will relate here the brief history of the house, as much as is known before the present century. It had not been heard of before the thirteenth, when there was a tower built there which in my youth still exited behind Aske, roofless and full of bats; later on it became one of the known Yorkist manors, rising with some speed to according grandeur after having arisen from origins now totally obscure. Even my father never discovered these, and he thought that the Wars of the Roses themselves, when they at last razed the great house, must have destroyed all former evidence; this branch of the Askes is not in Domesday Book.

Nevertheless the family had always lived splendidly, though now and then, in the last two or three generations, through gambling and other debts, their means had at times been straitened. But one still curtsied deeply to Old Madam, as would have happened no matter who or where she had been. And here at Aske, as I have said, she was still the magnetic force, the sun and moon, though seldom now seen by anyone outside the family. She was visible on Sundays, but not as much in my awareness yet as later, nor were they penned in their pew, like sheep and all the rest of us, through the service, though the Aske pew was in front. As they always, by custom, arrived last, this would create a stir and rustle among the waiting congregation, who were by then in their places. This, perhaps, created a greater air of importance than even the path-curtsies would have done; I can only remember once going through this latter ceremony for Old Madam, who one day went in early by herself for some reason, her great hoop skimming past. This occasion was not repeated, and the service would never begin till they came.

2

IF I HAD been able to look into the future, how would I have felt on these occasions, when I could see the whole Aske family assembled in view of our own rectory pew, which was at the side aisle? I do not know; it is, on the whole, as well that one cannot foretell events. And yet if one could do so, it might be possible to modify them, at least, if not to divert them altogether. But this is presumptuous, and in any case it did not happen.

Old Madam of course came first of all of them down the aisle always, in her hoop, which was by then a little old-fashioned; leaning, while he still lived, on the arm of her son, the squire, Nicholas Aske. After he died, she leaned on her grandson Peter's. She wore, for all the years

I knew her, the same bonnet on her head; a great black one with a sarcenet blind, which could pull open and shut with strings. She would have opened the strings in the porch and by the time she reached the door to enter, revealed her square-jawed, strong, intransigent old face, not much lined although by now she neared seventy. Her eyes seemed the colour of green water in the shadowed church, and stared coldly out from below hooded lids, like a hawk's; alighting briefly on my mother and me, to see, I suppose, that we were soberly and quietly clad as became a parson's belongings, and then inclining her head slightly, so that the grey pomaded curls swung, once she was satisfied, apparently, that we were. She supported her weight, as Nicholas' arm could not altogether do, on a tall cane of ebony, with a gold top; her gloves were of kid, and she had large, fine hands. Her son would settle her, and then himself, in the front enclosed pew, which like ours had a door which shut after them; and also, unlike ours, high kneeling-cushions done in woolwork and a prayer book with a gilded crest. The house-servants sat in the pew behind.

Nicholas Aske was so much overshadowed by his mother than I scarcely remember him, recalling only a slack man like a bag of flour which has not been properly filled, and contains empty spaces. He had a large white face over which the features seemed to shift, as though they floated on water, and his eyes were like currants. Apart from this list of imagined comestibles it caused me discomfort to look at Nicholas, even then at my age of seven or eight; I would pass quickly along the row to where his two children, Peter and Ann, had come in together behind him and their grandmother. Peter and Ann were beautiful.

There was one Christmas when, besides the Askes who always came, the other branch of the family joined them from Scotland, where the season is not celebrated. Perhaps

I speak loosely in calling these Askes, for they were merely Old Madam's widowed daughter, who had married an Edinburgh advocate, and the latter's schoolgirl daughter by a former marriage. But they always came south at such times, and in my memory are mingled with the rest. They were, however, less commanding to the view than the usual family that day, who still had money to spend on some finery.

First down the aisle would as usual come Madam and Nicholas, clad as of custom. Peter and Ann, however, had been grandly dressed for Christmas, much as Christmas-trees have now begun to be decorated; that time Ann wore a blue velvet coat trimmed with fur, and a little matching, fur-trimmed hat and muff. A hand, tiny and plump as a doll's, strayed in and out of this, I remember. I gazed at Ann Aske as though she were a being from another world, a shining toy or angel; but she was nothing to Peter.

Peter, a cherubic vision then, though younger than Ann, was already taller. His hair curled all over his head in tendrils of pale gold, and he had been dressed like a man of fashion, in silk and lace, with a little chapeau-bras. He would be at that time not quite eleven years old, slim and graceful, with the blue Aske eyes set a trifle slantwise in his narrow head, and his full-lipped mouth pouting agreeably, like a girl's, above a white chin pointed as an elf's. He smiled always, as though some inner secret amused him.

His aunt from Scotland sat by him in the pew; once I saw her slip a comfit to him. Like Peter, she wore rich clothes—I could tell this from their shine and rustle—but everything about her seemed sad and colourless, no doubt because she was a widow. I searched in my mind for such things as I knew about the lady, not many then. Her name, I was aware, had been Sophia Aske, and as she did not resemble her mother, Old Madam, I decided that she must be like her dead father. It was a defeated, rather dull face;

kind enough beneath the plumed bonnet. She had been married when very young to an elderly High Court judge, a law lord, Lord Kintyre. There seemed very little more to note about Sophia, and my gaze roved on to her stepdaughter, who was called Avice.

At this point Avice Kintyre was caught in a yawn, and although she quickly put up her hand to stifle it her eye met mine, and I had an instant's sense of conspiracy, almost as though we had winked at one another, and a brief view of her red mouth and tongue and a row of fine white teeth. Avice, although still at her Edinburgh school, was spoken of as handsome, with a bosom remarkably fine for her age, as I had already heard; this asset was not at present visible under her drab cloak. I decided they wore dull clothes in Scotland; but the colour became Avice's bright red-and-white complexion and her smooth dark hair. She looked kind, I thought; the long eyes held laughter. Perhaps some day I should be permitted to know more of the Askes.

Behind them in the second pew sat the governess and servants, including the one I already knew, Jonie Braik. I do not know how, in my secluded life, I had come to meet this rascal, but suffice it that nobody could live within thirty miles of Aske and not know Jonie. His handsome rake's face had subdued its features for the duration of the service, but broke into creases and smiles later on when, devotions over, the family wished and were wished a happy Christmas on the church steps. I made my curtsy to Old Madam and Ann and Peter, who inclined their heads like two Chinamen, as they had been bidden. That was as much as I saw of them, and we went home to our own turkey and plum-pudding.

That day was somehow memorable, but there was, for me, more of a lasting interest in the Aske effigies, commemorating ancestors from whom the front-pew party assumed itself to be descended. There was a Crusader, who had aroused my father's interest in possible Aske records, but these were sparse regarding that period although we knew, from the tomb, that the knight's name was Sir Ralph Aske. He lacked a nose—it had been hacked off at the time of the Reformation—and must have gone on several enterprises to Jerusalem, for his legs were crossed above the knee. He occupied part of the side aisle as we did. Elsewhere there was an Aske lady in a stone ruff surrounded by so many children she ought to have lived in a shoe. They all, mouse-sized in stone, knelt round their giant mother to pray, and elsewhere again there were brasses, one in memory of an Aske knight and his lady, late-dated and with the figures wearing one a wired veil and the other a shoulder-chain.

All these had become familiar to me, but my father of course was more so. He came in now in his hood and cassock, with the choir preceding; and after that it was as it had always been each Sunday of my life, and as I assumed, no doubt, it always would be; his warm, familiar voice intoning for our responses, my own uncertain pipe in the liturgy and psalms; and my mother's short, dry cough which had lately troubled her, although there had not always been the sound of that.

All these were there, as though all our lives were to unroll like a tapestry, which had its beginning that day, and yet the end, for many, would come soon. The brasses on the wall, the knight on the tomb, my father, Sophia, myself, the rest . . . And there is no one now, except myself, to remember any or all of it.

3

ALTHOUGH IN OLD age one seems to recall childhood very clearly, it is probable that one discounts the passage of time. But the events I will describe now must all have taken place in the space of one year, probably after that Christmas visit made by the Kintyre ladies; perhaps they stayed at Aske, or came down a second time from Edinburgh. At any rate they were with us by late spring, because the apple-blossom was out some time since, and shedding its petals; some I watched fall on Avice Kintyre's smooth, dark hair. She was indeed very handsome, even showy, like a big Scots heifer or shire-pony, with the complexion I have mentioned already, and a summer gown with the new French *paysanne* sleeves, which showed her white arms, a little too thick above the elbows, and her bosom. She was a gentle, placid, comely thing, and said little in those days. She sat by her stepmother, Lady Kintyre, of whom she was fond, and the rest of us under the apple tree; my mother had come out.

We seemed to have several visitors that day; my father and Sir Napier Steed, who had ridden over as he sometimes did from our last charge to say the new parson was a fool, were walking together about the garden, admiring the spires of some blue flowers we had. Bees hummed; the sound comes back to me with that of Sir Napier's short, hard, jolly laugh, which he gave at intervals, and the quiet voice of my father. Lady Steed, who wore an old lustring gown and chip-hat, sat at the far side of Lady Kintyre, the two world-weary women exchanging, probably, condolences with one another about the life they had separately led.

That at Steed was noteworthy. Sir Napier's laughter would not make him an easy husband, and his lady, who I believe had written verse when she was a young girl, had speedily learned to shed all such notions with her marriage; she had borne four children in the first five years, and now here, or nearly, after an interval was the fifth. I did not, for children do not heed such things, notice that Lady Steed was big with the expected birth, but I heard that she had died of it a short time later. I know, in this case, that I have not confused the occasions, because that day in our garden was, as it happened, the first time Sir Napier set eyes on Avice, who was to become his second wife, Steed's mare as the common folk called both ladies, within a matter of less than a year.

The occasion of the Kintyre ladies' visit had been to convey an invitation from Old Madam, long overdue, to my mother to come to Aske on a subsequent afternoon and drink tea. But when this near-royal command had been given and had been accepted in current coin, the converse—this also I remember, for it was the first time I heard of the matter—centred on a discussion of Ann and Peter Aske's young mother, Nicholas' wife, who was long ago dead. Perhaps the state of marryings and breedings, the inevitability of birth and death, were heavy in the garden, especially as the gentlemen were engaged elsewhere for the time.

So they were discussing Dorothy, whose ghost was later to be my companion. Her name, I recall, was always prefaced by the word poor; poor Dorothy, poor Dorothy Aske.

"It was your mother contrived the marriage, without a doubt," said Lady Steed, without tact and with some petulance, to Lady Kintyre. My own mother, who never said much at such times, rocked her garden-chair and got on with her sewing. It was finer than usual, because guests were present. She held it up in a little round wood frame with a gilded screw, which tightened and loosened at will as she moved the work. It was white, meticulous, and clean, like everything of my mother's; her slim fingers, moving over it with the skill and certainty of a great lady's, were redder than they should be with laundry-work, for we had only one maid. They were useful, uncomplaining hands, no doubt happy ones; forever engaged in baking and brewing, mending my father's clothes and mine and his cassocks, and the church-linen. My mother's hands had once been her greatest beauty when she was a girl, but, as she said, what good are hands that lie idle? She was very wise in such ways, but not, except for the hands themselves, in any way memorable; a little thin plain woman with a gentle manner and voice, to whom folk brought their troubles rather than to my father, who was a scholar and therefore slightly

distrusted by them. Nobody remembered that my mother
was also a scholar, and of this she did not, at such times or
at any, remind them.

So I heard as much of the tale then of Ann's mother as
to intrigue me, and afterwards I asked my parents about
her. They did not, as they generally did, explain everything
to me gently and reasonably, in a manner that I could
understand. On this occasion they looked, a little
strangely, as if in bewilderment, at one another, for
instants only; then my father said, "No, Leah. Perhaps
when you are older." It was the only time he ever said this
to me, and so, perversely, I remembered about the
forbidden matter of poor Dorothy Aske.

On the day of Old Madam's tea-drinking my mother
dressed me and herself with particular care. I had a gown
made from the good parts of an old one of her own, of
dove-coloured stuff in which, she said, she had been
married; and as she was a neat needlewoman and I was in
any case small for my age, it fitted without being skimpy
or having had to be patched anywhere. It had a real lace
tucker. I was proud of it and of my kid slippers, which
were new, and my white stockings with clocks. Walking up
the path and, later, the drive of Aske itself I was very
careful how I walked, looking behind me constantly to
make sure I had not scuffed the dust. But it was lying flat
enough on the ground, for the day was cool; my mother
said, I remember, that she hoped it would not rain before
we reached home again in our grandeur.

The great house itself came into view after one had
passed the pond, which had been put in artificially some
years ago and filled with waterfowl who had by now bred
wild, and puddled among the reeds by the edge in search
of worms. On the far side of the water—it was oval in
shape, and extended about half an acre—was a clump of
trees, fairly thick, and among them a little stone folly.
When I saw its pillars peering from between the branches I

grew excited; it was like, I told my mother, the Parthenon although not so big. "Is it an ancient temple?" I asked her. She said it was not one at all but where folk sat when they were idle, and had been built last century.

Then we saw Aske. It is engraved in my dreams still, and I see it yet; the tall old house, built haphazardly over the years of all England, with crow-step gables in front and towers behind, and a lichened roof; small windows marched, like grenadiers, about the top of it, under the high slates, and there were taller ones below, and at the front door two stone animals. I do not know what they were for age had almost obliterated their features, like the Crusader in church. They guarded the steps. There was no flower-garden such as we had at home; nobody troubled with such things at Aske, but behind the house there was a spinney, and beyond that a further rise, and above that again an older folly and, still further on, a deep, deep pit which in the winter would become a pool, sludgy and filled with drifted-over leaves. But I did not know all of that yet.

I do not remember that tea-party, or Old Madam at it. No doubt she was there, but what pervades my recollection is what happened at the end of it when my mother said to me, as we went again down the steps past the stone animals and saw the brooding sky, "I hope that there will not be a storm."

Before it came, which it did, one wonders what would have happened had we all stayed at home that day; had Old Madam not been persuaded against her natural inclinations—she was not hospitable or sociably inclined—to fulfil the no doubt dreary duty of having the parson's wife to drink tea and make small-talk; or had we not gone because of some accident, or even arrived at Aske in a carriage—but we had none, my father's parish was too small, and so was his income. And so we walked home—for Madam would not have thought of accommodating us with

her own carriage or even with shelter—through the rain
which first fell, from the yellow laden sky, in drops which
grew ever heavier; finally it was a downpour, in which we
ran back, as much as we could, and sheltered in the trees
for a while, and arrived home at last soaked to the skin. I
took no harm but my mother did; she caught a chill, then
a feverish inflammation, then took to her bed, which she
should have done much earlier, and died. She was dead
within ten days of that tea-drinking at Aske.

Old Madam was a destroyer, not a creator. I have said
there was no garden at Aske. Sometimes she would go for
walks there in the grounds, pulling away branches or
clearing paths where she thought they were needed. She
was very strong, and removed the cluttered greenery with
the ruthless strength of a man. Most days, however, she
stayed by herself in her own rooms, reading a book, or
stumping about on her various concerns. She had made her
life as, I suppose, she now wanted it; there was both good
and bad in her. I have never thought of her as having killed
my mother.

                                    4

I HAVE NO doubt that I mourned my mother, and—in
spite of all that was later said—that my father did so as
well. He did not weep, or not in my sight, but he was
afflicted and lonely, and for long hours, especially in the
evenings, would sit brooding over the fire the maid had lit,
saying nothing. I learned early to join in his silences. And
so autumn came. My mother had died in summer.

   It cannot all have happened as swiftly as that; there
would be occasions, before my mother died, when Sophia
Lady Kintyre came down. She came, I remember, when
mother was ill, with wine and soup-jelly; she was a kind
creature, not like Old Madam her mother. She meant no

harm then or later, despite the tongues, when she went on coming down to the rectory, and began doing little things for us, such as mending a button on my father's black sleeve; one day she tied my hair-ribbon, and as by that time I had got used to it she must have been in the way of doing such things for me also, but I do not remember anything now, except that the apples on the tree were ripe, and made small sweet fruit.

The marriage between my father and Lady Kintyre shocked the parish by its speed, and the Askes by the difference in status of the parties. Old Madam, I believe, would not even speak to her daughter until the wedding-day, when she relented and was after all present. Perhaps Sophia—I had been asked to call her this, as Avice did, not stepmother which she said was ugly—had made it clear to her indomitable parent that this time, at forty-three, she would marry to please herself.

Before that, when she was a young girl, Madam had forced her to marry, for his money and in spite of Sophia's tears, the dry old judge in Edinburgh, who may have been good enough to her though there were never any children of the marriage. She had clung to his young daughter Avice as a companion ever since, and was pleased that Avice loved my father now, for they got on well together. I too was filled by this time with interested pleasure, for the droop I had formerly noted in Sophia Kintyre's features vanished altogether over that memorable autumn, and by Christmas she was almost like a young girl, sparkling and gay. I can understand now that her love for my father, and the growing possibility of his love for her, was like the sun on a late rose of Michaelmas, for all her life had been lived, till then, without love. And poor father, who at the beginning had been too kindhearted or, perhaps, absent-minded to discourage Sophia, had by the end immersed himself in this autumnal colour and fragrance to an extent which was without doubt looked askance at by the parish.

It was in fact openly stated that my lady had lost no time in throwing herself at the rector's head, when his poor wife was scarcely cold in the sod; or, conversely, that the rector had an eye to my Lady Kintyre's money. This was—the old judge had been a fair-minded man—a jointure, however, which would end with her death but which was not affected by any remarriage. The rest, and reversion, went to Avice.

At the time of course I had not heard of half this, being still busy with my first Greek lessons, which father had begun to give me, and I was anxious to make him proud; and my translations and tales, from the history of Rome and the anecdotes of the classical heroes, who were more real to me than most of the people I met daily. So I was, accordingly, much taken aback at the sight of Old Madam, storming up the rectory path one day from her carriage, her green eyes blazing like twin jewels; she must once have been very beautiful.

My father came out and put his arm round my shoulders, as if to protect me from her wrath, but there was none after all, though he said one thing to her which I cannot remember, so quietly courteous was it, and it calmed her down. All that she said, therefore, between a grunt and a murmur, that I recall, was "She'd better stay at Aske, then, while the pair of you are on your trip," and then she opened her mouth and shut it again, and turned round and was off. I was trembling and hid my face against father's black coat, and he kissed my hair.

"My child, do not be afraid of her," he said, "or of anything. I have always talked to you as to a friend, have I not?"

I could not understand the connections of fear and friendship, but nodded still held close against him; another man would have said, "I have always spoken to you as though you were not a child." I waited, knowing that he had more to say, though not yet what it might be; there have been only two people in my life with whom I have felt this kinship, the awareness that something is there to be said, and at the right time will be. The time was now.

"You have read in the fairy-tales of wicked stepmothers," he told me, "but as you know, Leah, life is not always like a fairy-tale; although it can, perhaps briefly, resemble one."

As he said this his face creased and puckered, giving it a kind of pleased resemblance to Jonie Braik's. I was so amazed by this phenomenon in my father that I heard the rest of his news with less shock, perhaps, than might otherwise have been the case. It was not, anyhow, that the news was unpleasant; but all sheltered children, like adults, have a distrust of change.

"You are going to have a good, kind stepmother," said my father. "Can you guess who she will be?"

I pondered; it certainly wasn't Old Madam. I murmured this heresy, and my father gave a shout of laughter. "No, no," he said. "God forbid, my dear; but you're getting warm. You are very warm. It is Sophia."

"Lady Kintyre? To be my stepmother?"

"Very soon; in the new year, in fact. You are to be an attendant at the wedding, and you will have a new gown. Shall you like that, my dear? You have not had many." He looked sad again for an instant, and I knew that he was thinking of my mother. I could not bear him to look so, and I flung my arms round his neck, and told him that of course I was happy to have Sophia for a stepmother. I learned quite early to overcome my shyness and call her Sophia. Later she came to see me by myself, and kissed me. In addition to what my father had said she told me certain other things, such as that they were going north to Edinburgh for a little while after the ceremony, but that they would soon come back and, after that, we would all live together at the rectory.

"And Aske?" I said to her. "Shall I be permitted to play with Ann and Peter at Aske?" I was aware of a shining memory, two Christmas puppets, passing across my recol-

lection, thrusting out nearer things. But a shadow crossed
Sophia's face. "They do not play very much," she said,
"but of course you may see them."

"Do they like to read books? Shall I lend them some of
mine?" In the new world which was opening before me, I
would give anyone anything. I was already contented at
the thought of the marriage; it had been dull, a little, at
the rectory, when my father was busied with his sermons;
the one servant had small leisure to talk to me, except to say
I was a queer little pitcher and she must get on with the
dusting. Peter and Ann were my own age, or at least only a
few years older. And if they would not play, one could
always look at and admire them. It seemed queer—almost
as queer as I was said to be—that they would not play, and
would not read. For Sophia had also shaken her head over
the offer of books.

She spoke quietly now, having pondered the matter in
her careful, kindly way; I could see that she knew she had
disappointed me over Ann and Peter. "You will like to
have my stepdaughter Avice for a companion, will you
not?" she said. "Avice will be at Aske, where you are going
to stay for a few days until we return from Edinburgh,
your father and I. And then life will be almost the same
again as it has been."

My father had entered the room during the last part of
her speech and looked kindly upon us both, but rather
sadly; I could see that he had not forgotten my mother,
quite differently from the fickle fathers in the fairy-tales
who take new wives. But I do not think, and did not even
then, that mother would have grudged him any happiness.
And certainly he was again happy except when he
remembered her. Afterwards, I was glad of that.

Was God angry, perhaps, sitting up in heaven on a throne,
with eyes blazing green like Old Madam's? I thought of
him, already, as resembling Zeus, with thick grey curls and
a beard; and the Olympian gods, with their human

favourites and jealousies, may have grudged so much
unthinking happiness, such lack of propitiation. Perhaps
the matter was, as they say, foreordained; perhaps it made
a pattern, like the story of Orestes by the end, after much
blood and fear. But that was not apparent to me by then,
although it begins to be so now; only beginning, because I
am human, as we all are, and frail, and I was soon to be
quite alone, till that other came: but not by reason of
having a stepmother, for Sophia was always as kind to me
as she had been to Avice.

It seems odd now for them to have chosen to go on a
wedding-trip, which was not yet undertaken as a rule in
those days, and to choose, of all places, Edinburgh, where
Sophia had lived for so many years with her dry,
unimpassioned old judge. But she wanted, for this very
reason, perhaps, to see it all in new colours, with the man
she loved; to show him the place itself, so full of history,
and the New Town which was by then begun to be built
below the Rock, and the drained place which had once
been a grey stretch of water and would shortly become a
garden-space, with trees and grass. Above the great planned
squares there would be the Castle, jutting up into the
winter sky; my father, out of his happiness, remembering
that I would be lonely, sent me a letter with a drawing of
it and of the steep slope where Bothwell had escaped from
prison where he had been confined early in the tale of his
relations with poor Queen Mary. For such things as
remembering a lonely little girl came naturally to my
father, and for this I and, undoubtedly, Sophia loved him.
I awaited their return with pleasure, not mixed with much
grief at the news, which had saddened the wedding a very
little, that Lady Steed was dead of her child, and Sir
Napier a widower. My father had been grieved at the
death, and had sent a letter also to Sir Napier; Avice
showed it to me many years afterwards. For Avice was to
marry Sir Napier very soon, though no one knew it yet.

Avice and I were attendants together at father's wedding, in gowns of dark-red velvet with fur at the sleeves. I had never had so grand a gown, and, as father had predicted, it was new. I wore it happily, for the first time in my life feeling no longer a nonentity, for the colour, which I would never have dared to wear of my own choice, suited me, with my pale complexion, rather better than it did Avice. Otherwise she was of course very handsome, and so was the bride.

We all threw slippers after them as the carriage drove away. It was not till the end of that day, when I shared a wide cold bed with Ann Aske whom I did not yet know well, that I felt lonely, and remembered my own mother. But I was certain that, as I have said, she would have been glad to know that my father was no longer lonely. Perhaps she did; I was not able to pursue this thought long, for Ann, who was piqued because she had not been the centre of attention at the wedding, said, suddenly out of the darkness, that it would have been better if the dresses had been blue. But I placated her by telling her how pretty she had looked in her own gown, and that made her more agreeable. Ann was never hard to please; one only had to know the right thing to say and when to say it.

I can remember only one thing about that visit to Aske, except the end of it; and that was the sight, that same evening, of Peter Aske on the stairs as we children ascended; he was in the shadows, torturing a cat. The poor beast shrieked so that we heard it when we were far enough upstairs, under our roof; and Ann's maid, who was carrying the candle, let it drop so that we could not see what had happened, and the cat got away. It whisked past us into the darkness like a damned soul, and I remember the black, flung shadows of the relit candle, but by then one could see nothing as Peter had taken himself off after the cat. It all made me shiver, for the upper part of the house was cold, despite the warm feeling we had had downstairs, being well filled with the marriage-feast. I rid myself of this feeling of discomfort in the end, for soon the letter from my father came and I hugged it to me till he should return for himself, and take me back with them to the rectory.

But he never did come back, except for his dead body. At the end of that happy sojourn they were returning, he and Sophia, over the muddy northern roads from which the snow by now was melting, so that they were slippery and more treacherous even than usual to horse-traffic and wheels. I have often thought of the pair warm and enclosed in their coach, aware only of each other and not of the cold outside, knowing nothing of what the next moments would bring, and that is a mercy; it was growing dark on the journey, and shortly a peer of the realm, three parts drunk and holding, up on the box, his own coach-reins while the terrified coachman sat by his orders within, careened past on two wheels at the speed of Newmarket, where he thought he was going, no doubt, and locked with my father's carriage. The speed was so great no one could have slowed the horses, and they reared and slewed round screaming; they had to be shot later, and as for the upturned carriage, there was no sound from it and the hooves pounded it to matchwood before anyone came, and long before that there was silence and a miasma of settling cold from the night, and of coming death.

Sophia had died at once; her neck was broken. My father did not, and must have lingered three hours, they say; not long enough for me to have reached him. I was not told about it, in any case, until somebody remembered to tell me before they brought the two coffins in, to lie in the great hall of Aske. It was thought more suitable than the rectory. They would lie there till the day of the funeral, then thereafter side by side in a tomb in Aske church, nearby the Crusader and the lady with the ruff. It seemed so long since I had first seen those, and yet as time goes it cannot have been very long; and the apple-blossom, when it bloomed again in the rectory garden, would not do so for me or any of us.

It was decided, sometime about then, that I might as well continue to make my home at Aske. I had no other kin, and troubled nobody; it was Old Madam, of course, who made the decision, and said that I could be a companion for Ann and help her, and perhaps Peter, to acquire by my example (for I was still only ten years old) some notion of how to write and spell. They could never keep a governess or tutor; and in any case I was, it was supposed, by now, in a way, a member of the family.

Nobody troubled much about Avice. It is unlikely that she would ever have married Sir Napier had her stepmother lived, and certainly not with such despatch. This second wedding after a funeral took everyone with as much surprise as they were still capable of feeling, and it was got over almost without comment; it was a quiet ceremony, owing to the mourning of the bride, and my red dress, which had to serve again for the attendant, was dyed black and had its fur removed, as unsuitable. So I was again a mouse, and a red-eyed one like the first Leah, for I still could not stop crying for my father and Sophia every time I entered Aske church, till time and habit sobered me.

But Avice seemed content enough that day; I have no doubt Sir Napier may have seemed like a restored parent to her, of which illusion, like his first wife with her poetry, she had soon to divest herself. For parenthood to Sir Napier—it will be recalled that he had sired five children on his first wife—was a calling, and he was to sire eleven more on Avice. This future was mercifully veiled, but meantime Avice had a task on her hands, not easy for any bride; the rearing of a handful of very young stepchildren, from the moment she stepped from the wedding-carriage at Steed Hall, thirty miles beyond Aske, on the morrow. Later I was to help Avice, and she me, in various ways which will be related in their own time. Meanwhile, there was no one but myself, Old Madam, Ann and Peter left of the family at Aske.

5

PETER ASKE WAS a monster. I have already mentioned the cat. I mentioned it again to Old Madam, in fear and trembling, when she found me hunting for it next day. I do not know what happened to it in the end.

"Tell-tale chit," said Madam scornfully, and that was all. Another time she said I was a cry-baby. Nothing Peter did was wrong, and at the time she was fond and proud of him as the heir of Aske. As he was largely left to the care of servants, his grandmother did not know enough about him to have doubts on this matter, and nobody dared discuss the boy with her. Only under the greatest stress—for cruelty to helpless things always raises an unwonted flame of fury and courage in me—would I have done so myself. After the reply she gave I withdrew, like a snail, back into my shell, and seldom emerged again in such a manner. But the matter, of the poor tormented cat stayed in my mind, though as time passed, and the other dreadful things happened, it took a less important place there.

Lectured by Old Madam, even in so few words—she never used many—I became able again, as I had been that first time in church, to see Peter as everyone was expected to see him; a slender, blue-eyed, golden-haired and exquisitely attired angel. He had grown taller, and had a dog he was training that Old Madam gave to him shortly after my information about the cat, as if in defiance of something which may well have been of more importance than myself.

One day she came on me; I was reading in a corner. "Stoop too much," she said. "Hurt your eyesight. Ought to get out more." All of her talk was terse, to the point, and lacking in pronouns. I had risen to my feet and stood respectfully terrified, my knees trembling.

"Well?" she said, as though my silence and respect irritated her. "Standin' there, eyes like saucers; ever speak, eh? Answer when you're spoken to? Manners in my day."

By now I was almost dead of fear; she was so vast, so abrupt, and her eyes were so terrible, shining like the eyes of some wild animal in a night forest of my imagination, from the pictures in my books. I stammered, "I—I—I—" as though my voice had hastened after my reason. Old Madam gave a bark of mirthless laughter.

"Lost your tongue, or never had one, maybe," she said. "Where are Ann and Peter? Ought to get about with them more. Ride a pony."

I felt, for the first time, a creeping of warmth towards Madam; I should have liked to ride a pony, and Ann and Peter, I knew, often did so with the assistance of Jonie, who put on the saddles for them. But they had never invited me. I stammered something of this to Madam, who was no longer listening.

"Give you Peter's old pony," she said, "if you get him some book learning. Can't spell, can't do Latin. You good at Latin?" And she looked at me as if I were a fish. "Y'father," she said, with dryness, "told me that. Knew that himself, if not much else."

I felt the colour rush into my cheeks. Suddenly I became angry; the power of the anger made me bigger than Old Madam. I towered over her, talking down as to a midget.

"My father knew many things you will never know, and never thought of," I said. "He was the best man who ever lived, and he—"

The end of it would have been "He is dead," but I never achieved it, but by then broke down into sobbing, my inflated status having subsided like a pricked bubble.

"There, don't blubber," said Old Madam, not unkindly. She turned on her heel and walked away, her skirts dragging after her. "What do any of us know?" I heard her say to no one in particular; the sound drifted in deep echoes down the corridors of Aske.

Nothing more was said then; but next day, I was escorted to the schoolroom to instruct Peter in spelling, bookwork and Latin, after his tutor had left at noon. I was also taught to ride a pony by the man Jonie Braik, and in a few weeks could manage a quiet one creditably.

It is possible to watch a good, sound apple on a dish change, if it has a bruise or a worm unseen inside it, until the dark patch spreads and when one bites into the apple at last, expecting white flesh, it is rotten. This was like Peter. I do not know what they called the disease he had, except that it may have come of the pox. This was not of himself, for as a man (I learned this later) he would be impotent, but no doubt from Ralph Aske, Old Madam's husband, who had died riddled of the disease itself at forty. It is so common in our families that no one knows it half the time for what it is, and whether it was also responsible for Nicholas, or even for Ann later on, I do not know, being no physician. All I remember noticing one day was that Peter's teeth when he smiled were rat-tailed, and that his breath was foetid.

This may have been one reason; and, also, that he had been conceived in loathing. I know of no disease that this may give except that it is not love, can never be love, and perhaps the fruit of it shows some sign, like a canker, that this has happened. I have heard, and do not disbelieve it, that Old Madam again, after Ann's birth, whipped Nicholas' young wife back into his bed, saying there must be a male heir. It may have been partly because of that; I cannot tell, no one now can. All that I know of Peter is that in boyhood he tortured me, in the way he would do, no doubt, with all weak, frightened flesh which could be in

his power and relieve, perhaps, the urges in his mind that
could find fulfilment in no other fashion. By the time he
reached years of what are called discretion he had none,
and was an imbecile; before that he would have gambled
away his honour and his house. But now, long before all
this, I knew him at Aske better than anyone, for I had to.

At some time, I found out about Peter's puppy. It had
been, like the other dog which by now was half-trained
and savage, so that it was not kept in the house, a gift to
Peter from Old Madam, who said the two might make a
pair to train to the gun. I think that she was pleased at the
thought of Peter's doing anything successfully; he had
made a job of the other, as Jonie Braik himself told her.
This second puppy was still young, and a velvety, loving
thing when I saw it; it would stagger about on its new legs
after Peter, who at first let the little creature grow fond of
him; then he wearied of it. Soon after that it ran away, as
we supposed; I was not surprised. By then I knew that
Peter, like many boys, pulled flies' wings, and the legs off
beetles; the servants also told me—and this made me
sick—that he had sometimes roasted hedgehogs and rats
alive in the ovens, so that they could be heard screaming
before they died. I begged the servants with tears in my
eyes not to let this happen to the puppy; they said it had
not. One day I noticed a heavy, sweetish smell behind a
curtain, and pulled this aside. The puppy was in there,
hanged, by now quite dead, its limp soft body covered in
maggots. Peter laughed when I told him.

"You aren't anybody," he said. The full red lips were
parted and hanging apart, like ripe fruit; inside was the
rottenness, and I withdrew a little, still filled with horror
and loathing about the puppy. "Are you?" he asked, and
drew nearer; suddenly he shot his hands about my neck,
and squeezed. I felt the blood drumming in my ears. "I could
kill you," he said, "I could leave you hanging in your
own hair. It'd be slow. They wouldn't find you either.

They wouldn't even notice you'd gone away from Aske."

Then he let me go suddenly and himself went, still laughing out of the overripe mouth. No one else said anything about the puppy.

I still had to help Peter with his lessons, and sometimes Ann also was present although she was not required to learn Latin. Some days she was absent, for whatever reason; nobody supervised her very much. She was more idle than Peter, but had if anything a little more wit at that time; she would mostly sit yawning in the schoolroom, showing her little white teeth and pink tongue, and playing with her long fair hair. She was good-natured enough, and did not dislike me; I began to be ill at ease with Peter when she was not present. I did not yet know why, apart from the puppy and the tales of hedgehogs and rats. But I found out soon, when I had been about a year at Aske.

6

OLD MADAM WAS doubly an Aske, having married her handsome dissolute cousin Ralph at the age of seventeen. At that time she had been a great beauty, much sought after and wagered upon during the brief season she had appeared in London, which was cut short by her brother's having had to fly the country after the 'Fifteen. He still lived in Italy at the time I first went to Aske, although his inheritance had been sequestered. Madam's dowry dwindled, accordingly, with that and with Ralph's fingers always in her coffers; but she wanted her husband to love her and at the beginning, no doubt, believed that he did. She had, as I said, red hair in her youth, and a skin like a flower, and was tall.

The couple had three children. Robin, the eldest, was conceived in adoration, and continued adored for the first twenty-odd years of his life, when Old Madam was to cut him out of hers. But by the time Nicholas was in Madam's womb, she had found out that two of the village-women were pregnant by Ralph from the same month as herself; after that, something died in her which unfortunately was not Nicholas. He was born, and throve after his fashion, but was never beloved as Robin was until the two boys were grown. There was also a daughter, Sophia.

Madam's exercising of herself in the control of her children's marriages may seem to some very hard; but in those days it was common enough, and by now, of course, money was scarce at Aske. The first act of Madam was to get Sophia off her hands as soon as possible, which she did with regard to the widowed old Scots judge. He not only settled a jointure on Sophia, but advised Madam herself about the use of such money as she still had: for a time, things at Aske may have gone better, now Ralph was dead. I do not know how Madam got hold of Lord Kintyre, for there is little coming and going of that kind across the Border; suffice it that she did, and that he was not altogether a lamentable occurrence, even as regards Sophia; for he introduced his young wife to much learned company, and taught her to appreciate good food and talk. I had all this from Jonie Braik, much later; he knew everything.

Madam was left alone, however, Ralph having died before Robin's majority, with an encumbered estate and a feckless heir. For Robin, though gay and charming, had no sense of what was due to Aske; on the way to repeating his uncle's mistake with regard to the Stuarts, he fell in love with a local farmer's daughter, Hester Carden. Hester's fine eyes and black hair, and her bosom, and even her laughter, were no attributes as far as Madam was concerned; when it became known that Hester was to bear Robin's child, and that there had been talk of marriage between them, Madam sent for old Laban Carden, Hester's father. Between then they contrived matters in a way which will be related; but by then Robin had ridden off to the wars.

He had gone, at the toss of a coin, and with his mother's curse; if he went, she promised him, she would never set eyes on him again and his sons would not inherit. She never did, and nor did they; he was killed in the north, later that year. Madam would not permit his sister Sophia to wear mourning for him.

Her feeling for her remaining son, Nicholas, now changed from toleration to doting, in a way which may seem hard to believe; but he was all Madam had left, and perhaps she felt the need to justify herself and, in any case, save Aske. He must of course marry, and it would have to be, this time, to money; but it was not easy, for evident reasons, to find a rich wife for Nicholas. Robin would have been another matter.

However Lord Kintyre, as he was now, once more saved the day. He had in the north the wardship of a young orphaned heiress, Dorothy Kean. Her portion was considerable; she was fifteen years old, short and plump, a trifle foolish perhaps, but that would modify itself with time; having a white skin, sound teeth and quantities of dark-gold hair. My lord was Dorothy's guardian, and when her schooling should be completed he was most willing to send her down to Aske, to the care of Madam; the girl had no other near kin. The arrangement would, on the surface, permit young Dorothy to be chaperoned and taken about in county society.

But society saw little of Dorothy at Aske. She was put straight in a coach from her school and driven south; it was later given out that she was delicate, and invitations were refused for her all of that year. That this state of things lasted so long is a measure of Dorothy's unusual obstinacy. She was, from all accounts and from her portrait, a gentle, biddable creature in the ordinary way, in appearance perhaps something like a partridge. The repulsion she felt for Nicholas was notable from the outset in one so gentle. She could not bear him near her, any more than some young women can bear spiders or slugs. Such images recur

when one thinks of Nicholas; a maggot of a man, a
currant-eyed white bloated creature, slumped, as I could
remember, in the pew at Aske the year he died, like a used
half-empty sack. As a young man he may have been more
appetising than he later became, but I have no evidence.

Having set her will firmly, poor child, against Madam's,
and refused to consider any betrothal, conditions at Aske
became stricter for Dorothy. Lest she let slip the state of
affairs to friends in the north, her writing-materials were
taken away; she herself was no longer allowed out of
doors. The room in which she was shut up was one of
those under the roof, where we later slept at Aske; it is
difficult to hear sounds clearly there through the walls,
and the old house creaking and groaning in all its timbers
has often seemed, in my own recollection, like human
crying on the wind. It may have been no more than this
which caused it to be said, later, that Old Madam used to
climb to Dorothy's room daily, unlock the door and beat
her to bring her to her senses, as was done in the Middle
Ages. If this was so, such salutary treatment had no effect.
Autumn changed to winter without news of a betrothal,
and soon there would be enquiries from several quarters as
to the heiress and why she was no longer seen or heard of.
Madam decided to act.

After having been so strict—it was, after all, near Christmas, the season of traditional goodwill—Old Madam
became somewhat easier with Dorothy at Aske. She took
her out driving, allowed her pens and paper, and even put
it into her head that she might care to pay a short visit to
an old school friend in the north. Dorothy was so overjoyed about this that she forgave Madam for whatever
there had been and, evidently, thought no more of it. She
wrote to her friend, and in due course received the
customary reply, bidding her welcome before Yule.

When all arrangements had been made for Dorothy's
northern trip (from which it is unlikely that she would

ever come back of her own free will) Madam took her son
Nicholas aside. Carefully, for he was inclined to be sluggish
and slow of wit, she drilled him in everything he must now
do. She herself would, she said, accompany young
Dorothy on a part of her journey, after which the girl was
to be met at the Border by her friends. At about that time
Madam had already ridden off on a day's journey of her
own, to a certain inn on the route where, no doubt, money
changed hands.

Dorothy took her departure by coach in something of a
flurry, because at the last minute Madam developed a
severe headache and could not travel with her, and she was
of course unused to travelling alone. There would, however—and Madam sent a note, scrawled from her bed, with
Dorothy to this effect—be someone willing to bear her
company at a named inn several miles distant, on her way.
The journey meantime would be quite safe, near no
pike-roads, and she had the coachman, who was well
enough armed. Dorothy did not look closely at the
coachman.

The coach travelled on through the gathering dark,
which had come down early and there had been the delay,
and now rain and mist. When she reached the inn Madam
had spoken of the girl was glad to step inside, as the
welcoming innkeeper and his wife bade her, to warm
herself at the fire and take a glass of something to keep out
the cold.

The glass was brought, and tasted of several things
including brandy: when Dorothy had drunk it she felt
sleepy, too much so to want to continue her journey. She
made no demur when the good woman of the inn offered
her a bed to lie down on, even helping her to unlace and
taking off, in the end, her gown for her; once there, and
with a good leaping fire in the room, Dorothy fell at once
into a deep sleep, and did not hear the room door open
again or see who had entered.

So Nicholas came in between the curtains, and deflow-

ered her. If Dorothy made any outcry, it was not heard by
the innwife, who swore next day she had heard nothing.
Also, a wind had now risen, and had driven away the
remains of the mist. It blew all that night, making the
flames leap in the chimney, and Nicholas, who his mother
had told on no account to leave the thing half done,
proved his manhood adequately before morning, when
they all arrived in a search-party from Aske to find the pair
in bed together.

If my father had been parson then, it would not have
happened as it all befell; but old Parson Fosse, who was his
predecessor, had been routed out by Madam late the
previous night. The young pair, she said, had she thought
run off together on the excuse of a planned visit of
Dorothy's to the north: it remained to find them, and if
needed to make an honest woman of Dorothy; the girl
had, after all, been left in her charge. Whether or not the
old parson was deceived—to find Nicholas, now sheepish
and disinterested, in bed beside a weeping and hysterical
heiress at an inn was not in the tradition of lovers, and it
was known already that Madam had tried to use force—he
saw there was nothing to be done, and married them.
Afterwards, with the help of his clacking tongue, there was
a coldness towards Madam in the county; it was still in
existence in my own time, and accounted for the fact that
she had few visitors, even now, when long ago poor
Dorothy, and Nicholas after her, were dead and lay
beneath the same stone in Aske churchyard.

Other legends accrued round Madam after young Mrs.
Nicholas, as she was now known, had been brought home to
the contemplation of her duty to make an heir. So great
now was her fear of Madam—there was no escape, either to
friends or anyone outside, and she had no control any
longer of her money, which Nicholas spent freely—that she
endured her marriage; and by the spring of the second year

was pregnant, and Ann was born in the subsequent November. What part Old Madam played in the subsequent begetting of Peter cannot now be ascertained; anything was possible, except that Dorothy was not fashioned to give birth once yearly. She died when Peter was born, and perhaps was glad to; and the money, which was to have replenished the Aske coffers, was by then largely spent. Nicholas was not generous, as I shall relate shortly, but he was prodigal; there is a difference.

Nicholas died of a kidney disease in that same year I had seen them all in church. No one regretted him, or the lack of his pallid, puffy countenance, as far as I know, except Old Madam, who mourned him sincerely. She had in her way, when there was nothing else left to love, loved him. After that she loved Ann and Peter and, when they failed her, loved herself. She never at any time loved me, nor did I expect her to do so.

7

OTHER TALES, BESIDES the ugly one concerning the young heiress who had become Ann's mother, were garnered at Aske. I heard these slowly, from one source and another, over the years; piecing together what Jonie Braik had told Ann, or Old Madam, now and later, let drop from time to time to one or other of us; later Avice filled in certain gaps, about her family and poor Sophia's first marriage. Ann herself remembered some things Nicholas had told her of, when she was very young; oddly, the tale of Robin seemed to have been his favourite, and of how the elder brother had ridden off with his sword by his side, singing a snatch of a tune, 'Sheriffmuir', with braid on his three-cornered hat, and a white rose, which Hester Carden had given him, in his coat, till he should have taken the cockade in the north.

But that was all Ann knew of Hester Carden.

The rest of it I found out in my own way, not from Old Madam; and this is part of the story. Hester, who was a farmer's daughter as has been said, had no education, for old Carden—his name, Laban, fixes itself in the mind as descriptive of all unworthy fathers, and he left Het with no way of fending for herself should hard times come, then abandoned her when they came—had, together with a non-conformist conscience, irrevocable ideas regarding the upbringing of womenfolk; they must be kept under. Hester's own mother died of this treatment, but she herself, an only child, suffered less at first from all this than might have been anticipated; for she was a resilient creature, and no doubt her easy-going ways would have let her embrace, in due course, the suitable mate her father would have chosen for her in the end. But meantime she met Robin Aske, or he her, in a drying hayfield, crossing their opposite ways; Het had taken a fork to help turn the dried grass in the sun. By the end of that day, or another, they were behind a hay-rick together; all of that summer saw their love, till Robin rode away. Before that, some said he had married Het, who was pregnant, and that Old Madam later destroyed the evidence of it, having bribed the parson. But folk by then would say anything of Old Madam. Laban, however, following on the information he had received from Old Madam at Aske, went home and took down a whip and used it on Het, driving her out of his house. She had nowhere to go, and the news had come, by then, of Robin's death at Prestonpans, in the first flush of Stuart victory. She started to walk up north, to try and find the Jacobite army; there might, she thought, be protection there for her and the coming child.

Hester Carden was a tall creature, with her flashing dark eyes and black hair; later, when she had taken her only wares to market, the customers called her Big Het. Who shall blame her? For there was, by the time she won north, no trace now of the Jacobites; they had gone south to

Derby, by a road further west, and were now in slow
retreat again, to the far north and a place named
Culloden. Het never found them, but in the end she found
a redcoat soldier instead; and the pence he gave her
afterwards bought her a meal.

So Simon Aske—he had been borne in the north, but
afterwards his mother came home with him, like the
swallows, and set up in a half-ruined cottage on the bluff
above Aske, which Nicholas let her have rent-free for
certain favours—Simon knew nothing but that his name
was Carden, and that his father was whoever happened to
be about at the time. One who stayed longer than usual
was an old sailor named Alfred Stokes, who had lost one
arm in a tavern-fight with knives long ago at Port of Spain.
Before that happened he had been of some use with a
fiddle, and still kept it by him, and later left it to Simon.

But I am running ahead of my plan, for of course no
one now at Aske knew that story, and I got it from Simon
myself after he first came to the great house, not so long
after the day Ann and I had met with him at the outer gate
and had thought of him as a dark ill-mannered stranger, or
else the devil. And it was he who, in the end, told me that
and other things, including what had happened, in the last
instance of all, to Big Het.

8

IN THE ORDINARY way I should not have been unhappy
at Aske once the shock of my father's death had been
recovered from by me a little. I was a biddable child and
caused no trouble to anyone, and would not have expected
anyone to cause it to me.

Ann herself, though some years older, tolerated me—
friendship was never possible to her in any deeper sense,
and she had not much conversation. She thought of me, I
believe, in those days as a kind of acolyte, to serve her as

Jonie did although a trifle differently, lacing her gowns
and tying up her hair-ribbons. She was already much
concerned with her appearance. It was this concern which
led her, though otherwise under duress, to submit to a
ruling of Old Madam's that year that because Ann
slouched, she must spend two hours a day seated attached
to a back-board, doing her sampler-work bolt upright. The
latter, which Ann hated as much as the board, was another
matter in which I could help her, for my dear mother had
taught me to be neat with my needle and, besides, I liked
sewing. So I would pick out poor Ann's botchings which
Miss Bray, the governess—she stayed for some little time,
near the beginning—said must all be done again, and would
sew them in myself for Ann. But Old Madam, when she
found out, was against this cheating and said that I must get
out instead into the fresh air, for I was too pale. In this she
was quite right; but I trembled by now and did not want to go.
    The reason was Peter. I forget whether or not Peter had
yet been brought home for all of the year from his school.
He did not stay at it long, and Old Madam went herself in
the carriage one day and brought him back to Aske with
her; I do not know what had been said. But after that he
had a tutor again at home, and help from me while I could
still be prevailed upon to give it. By this time, and after the
puppy, I avoided Peter, and he knew it though he was
slow-witted in some ways, and horribly, swiftly cruel in
others, as though a devil arose in him all of a sudden.
    The tutor would come in the mornings. He was a good,
under-paid young man from a nearby village, and bore his
cross with fortitude for a year, when he moved elsewhere.
He would leave work for Peter to do by himself in the
afternoons, and that was when I was sought out as
before; originally I had been most willing, and we had sat
together in the schoolroom over Peter's spelling and his
Latin. But he had begun to do things which frightened me,
such as thrusting a hand down my dress.
    I had been gently reared. When he squeezed at me and

said, "You haven't got them yet. Ann has," I knew what he meant, but could do no more than flush crimson and try to wriggle away, in deep distress.

"Please, please do not," I said, but he took no notice.

We were on a narrow bench against the wall, with a table in front, and before I had escaped he had indulged in other thrustings which bewildered and shocked me. For a long time I would not go back, but said nothing to anyone; another child might have run screaming to summon help, or even told Ann; but I, innocent quiet thing that I was, accustomed to think of my own affairs as of no importance, suffered it almost wordlessly. It happened more than once; young Peter, godlike, the boy of the house, whose wishes were never crossed, who had a cane with a silver handle, a pony, and silk clothes in which the tenants doffed their hats to him outside Aske church; who was I to raise my puny voice against Master Peter, whatever he did?

But the walks in the grounds were the worst.

I have said that he had a dog, which he had trained and which was savage by now to everyone except Peter. It went everywhere with him when he was out of doors. It was of mixed breed, and would do whatever Peter bade it; it was larger than I by now, and greatly frightened me. As Old Madam had by this time decreed that I must walk about the grounds during Ann's exercise-hours, as she said, to get some colour into my cheeks, I did so cautiously, never knowing when I might meet the dog, and with it Peter; as a rule I kept to the main path. One day, while Ann sat rigid in her board, I was walking alone, muffled in a woollen hood and warm mittens, for it was winter or early spring; I wandered listlessly up and down, counting the waterfowl which dived and puddled in the pond, and wishing myself back at the house. So busy was I with my counting of waterfowl that I did not know anything till I heard a snuffling and slavering behind me; there was the dog, and when I saw it I backed away into the trees, as it blocked my return along the path. The beast chased me, snapping and tearing at my skirts, making me stumble. I heard laughter then; it was Peter.

"Leah," he called. "Cry-baby Leah."

I did not answer. He called off the dog and came up to me and started to pinch me, viciously, all over the arms and body. I began to cry and then he twisted my arm. "I can do other things," he said, "and so can the dog. She can bite you on the ankle, bring you down, if I say so, and hold you there. Shall I make her do that? Shall I? Then you do as I say, today and the other days."

There was the stone folly, which I remembered earlier from that walk with my mother; generally he would take me in there. As a rule he would only nip and pinch me, something in the manner in which he still tortured flies; then after a while he began undoing my clothes. After that, when he had found out what a little girl's parts looked like, he used to handle and thrust at them; by now, I was in so piteous a state of fear that I dared say nothing. I let him fumble, nip and torment me for his diversion, with the dog on guard outside lest I escape; it became a matter of pride with me to say nothing, not to let Peter know he had hurt and shamed me, to walk away afterwards as though nothing had happened. I do not know whether I lost my indoor pallor to Madam's satisfaction, or whether she thought I was looking any better for the time I spent outdoors.

One place I could escape these torments was the library. What Aske had loved his books I never knew; but there they were, and nobody but myself or, at times, Old Madam ever took them down from the long shelves. The place was too near her own domain for Peter to follow, and I spent my happiest hours at Aske among the close-packed volumes, bound with tooled leather so old that it sometimes crumbled, with a dry sweet rich tanner's odour, if one handled a book. Sometimes also there had been worms at these, so that the texts were riddled through with holes the size of a quill. I loved books and nobody seemed to mind my using the library; once or twice Old Madam stumped in, saw I was there and said I should be outside, especially if it was summer; but she did nothing to prevent me and, afraid as I still was of her then, it was my haven and the fear of Old Madam had to be weighed against my horror of Peter.

My father, for such time as he had had, had taught me a love of search in reading, garnering the odd fact and delicately expressed phrase for reference, or for keeping in one's mind. He had also begun to instruct me in the use of the ancient authors in their own tongues, and this I was determined to pursue at Aske. There was a collection of Virgil's works there and some of Ovid, and the poems of Catullus; and with these unlikely mentors I at first struggled, not always understanding the sensuous, full language except by implication. Sometimes it roused a secret feeling in me like Peter's prying fingers could do, a kind of fear mingled with delight. For with the receding of outrage once he was no longer handling me, I felt in my unripe flesh what should not have been felt yet, an awareness that I had somehow given him and myself a kind of perverted pleasure. The alliance between this furtive, unholy joy and the terror I had felt began to mingle in me, as time passed, making me in the end so prudent and timid I was like an old maid by the time I was eleven years old.

But the other things of the mind these books gave me were quite different, satisfying and honest; and so I read in Latin, Greek a little, and of course in my own tongue also, for there was a translation of Aristotle among other things, and although he is discredited as a source of fact his language is delightful.

All this reading—there was much more of it, and had

more practical value, perhaps, than the above—stood me in good stead later when Ann and I went to school. That we were sent there at all was by reason of Peter Aske, and so he did one good thing in his life at any rate, if not by intention.

It was the time of late summer by now when leaves have grown heavy and green, having lost their early feathery lightness; they made a thick screen round the folly, where Peter's hands had grown bolder and my misery worse. While Ann was at her back-board—she was still at it—I would skirt quickly and cautiously round the pond, where the reeds grew high; avoiding the bosky part where the dog, who was called Bran, might be waiting, tongue lolling and fangs exposed; once or twice, by now, Peter had seen to it that the beast had bitten me.

That day again it sprang. Peter was waiting in the trees, and had me by the arm as always, dragging me with him and threatening to twist it and perhaps break the bone if I made any sound. If I had had the wit I would no doubt have risked a broken bone, which would at any rate have attracted someone's attention; but I was by now a scared, helpless puppet, obeying my master who pulled the strings, with the terrifying dog nosing me on. Peter got me into the stone folly, laid me down on the bench there and began his furtive thrustings and exploration; he had, that day, an expression of sly triumph, which had been absent for some time since he had found for himself, upon me recently, that a boy of twelve or thirteen cannot always do the things he would like to do, and he had punished me viciously for this, beating and pinching me about the privy parts so that I had bruises there for a week.

Now, however, he again started to behave like a man, and as I then closed my eyes against what horror should come I did not see what this was; it was a stone, a long sharp stone which Peter had concealed in his hand. He had pulled about and disarranged my clothes as usual, and when I was exposed and naked he shoved the stone up me. The pain was fiendish, the worst I have ever known; tears streamed down my face, I heard him laughing, and he thrust and thrust. Afterwards I was to find that I had bled and that for days it would hurt me to walk; but now I knew nothing except that I was in the power of a devil. I knew, though I could see nothing for my tears, that his face was above me, a leering satyr's with dreadful breath; and that the more I writhed and sobbed the greater would grow his pleasure. But I could not now help myself; the wickedness of what was being done to me was not fully evident to my child's mind. I was only conscious of the pain.

Suddenly it stopped and I opened my eyes and there in the doorway was Old Madam. "Heard sounds," she said, and then fell silent, her impersonal green eyes having taken in what had happened. She raised her hand and caught Peter a blow on his ear which sent him reeling. Then she came over and took out the stone.

I have said a good deal about Old Madam's wickedness, in the pursuit of her own way; now she was like an angel, or a nurse, without fuss. She had been passing, I suppose, on one of her clearing-walks: I never knew, or asked her. She said to me only "Lie still, bleeding'll stop presently," and rearranged my clothes; I did as I was bid, and lay crouched on the bench for a long time, until Ann was sent later to fetch me back to the house. Nobody, I could tell, had said anything to Ann of what had happened; she was as usual, vague and self-interested, which helped me on my sore walk. Nothing more was said and nothing, to stanch my wound of body and of mind, was ever done about me. This is perhaps the best medicine.

Peter's dog was shot, and for the first time in my life I was not sorry for a dumb creature. What happened to Peter himself was however no solace. It was no doubt in consideration for my supposed wish for vengeance that

Madam decreed I should watch his punishment.

"Next Aske," she said, as though to herself. "Degenerate." And when Peter came in and she said again, looking at him strangely, "You were got by the whip and you shall taste the whip, by God," and no one answered her. This is the only direct evidence I have about the story of Peter's begetting, and the only complete sentence I ever heard Madam utter.

At the time I cared nothing for that—wanting only never to have to see Peter, or anyone, again; as it was, what happened would have made many stronger children feel sick. I was put on a stool at Madam's feet where she sat in her ceremonial chair, a carved oaken one with arm-rests like lions' heads, that night when they whipped Peter publicly in the great hall.

The method used was, I believe, common a century ago in great houses where there were footmen employed. It had not been used for some time even at Aske; I think Old Madam may have seen it done in her youth. They brought Peter in and took down his breeches. His grandmother did not speak to him, but sat as usual staring ahead of her, as if carved out of stone.

Jonie Braik bent then and lifted the boy up; he knew what to do. Hoisted like a burden on Jonie's big shoulders, with Jonie gripping his knees hipwise, Peter was flogged with a crop out of the stables, by the second man, who happened to be the groom. It was the position adopted by Russian victims and administrators of the knout, and Peter displayed no more fortitude than those unfortunate wretches. Before the first stroke had even descended he had begun to howl, and by the end—for the groom had a score of his own to settle, and laid on with a will—he was no more than a quivering, bleeding jelly, emitting sounds no longer human. I thought Madam would never give the signal for the man to stop, but in the end she did, and Peter was taken down.

He looked over at us once, while they were adjusting his

clothes to lead him away. I shall never forget the
expression on his face and in the swollen-lidded, bloodshot
eyes; he was like a broken animal. I have said that there
was already some matter in Peter which he had inherited,
which placed him below and beyond humanity, like the
apes; emerging as a kind of mindless lust for cruelty, which
burnt him out later till he was no more than a shell. But I
think that that day, with the loss of his godhead in public,
aided its eventual working. Old Madam herself, who had
briefly had pride in him and had hoped, I knew, against
hope that he would grow up to be a man and an Aske, and
the squire, sat impassive, with masklike face and curled lip,
as though she had been watching the punishment of a slave
and stranger. She could, and had done it before, swiftly
change the direction of her heart's loves; and she was
finished with Peter almost from that day, although she did
not finally abandon him, to supervised madness and
solitude, till much later, after that letter at last came
bearing its red seal.

For myself, it was an end to torment. The conclusion Old
Madam had come to over the episode I have related above,
though she did not deign to explain this matter to us
directly, was to send away Ann and myself to school. The
chosen establishment would need a certain wardrobe, for it
took no charity-pupils; so during the weeks which followed there was a coming and going of mantua-milliners and
much franked correspondence, and we were pinned for
new gowns and each given four linen shifts, and other
things such as Jersey hose and nightgear. There was also
the dismissal of Miss Bray, the governess, who would
accompany us to London and thereafter not return to
Aske, going on to some other situation with Old Madam's
lukewarm reference behind her. I watched the poor
woman shed a few tears as she climbed beside us into the
carriage to leave Aske, and was surprised, for she had never
shown she liked us much; but no doubt the place to which

she was going might prove to be worse and would be, after all, unfamiliar. There is a certain comfort in accustoming.

However, on the way the governess brightened; and told me and Ann, although the latter yawned over it, certain things about the school to which we were going, which was already famous and was called Mrs. Musgrave's Academy. As I spent the next four or five years there, and it was to have a profound influence on my life, I will relate something of what happened at it, though not more than is needed in course of this narrative.

9

THE SCHOOL WAS in a house in a discreet part of town north of the river. I had not previously seen London, or anywhere as large and grand; we did not drive through the squalid parts. I was still dazzled with what I had seen when we were ushered up the steps of Mrs. Musgrave's Academy, with which, I and Ann were rapidly to discover, Mrs. Musgrave herself took very little to do.

If Old Madam had brought us herself there would have been fruit cake and madeira wine, with which such visitors were always regaled on arrival, in the parlour. However as it was only the poor governess, who soon departed when she had handed us over, there was none; and Ann and I, in our new clothes and feeling strange in any case, were left alone with the presiding dragon.

She was not, poor soul, a dragon except in the outward evidence, which was formidable; inwardly she was timorous and rather indolent. Her very appearance served as a good receptive front for the school, which was in fact run in the background with devotion, knowledge, and furious and unremitting hard work, by her sister, Miss Amelia Fish, who being a spinster was inconsiderable. That Mrs. Musgrave herself was a Married Lady—one could not but spell it with capitals—albeit widowed, constituted, as far as I ever found out, her sole claim to give advice on the education of girls. This she gave to parents who came, to the staff, and to the servants, in such abundance that it was hardly ever listened to; I do not however recall that she ever gave any to her sister. Mrs. Musgrave wore a long-bodied frogged gown, of a fashion nowhere prevalent since the days of the Dutch king, and a high wobbling frame on her head from which fell an imposing cascade of black lace: I believe that she had at some point been told that she resembled Madame de Maintenon, which notion flattered her.

She was not, to me, very interesting and I only remember her at all because of her plaintive, carping voice, which never ceased. It may have driven the late Mr. Musgrave into his grave because nobody seemed to have heard of him; the school is still called Fishy and Carp's although most people have forgotten the reason. That is why I still remember Mrs. Musgrave. Sometimes, of course, the girls used to make a mockery of the poor dear and imitate her and the voice behind her back, except when Miss Fish caught them at it; then they never did it again.

I can say a great deal about girls' schools, and I do not want to take up more time with this one other than to state that I came to admire and love Amelia Fish more than any other woman I have ever met, except one. I made of Fishy a friend for life. She was small and spare, with eyes which at first appeared stern and cold behind her spectacles (it was a comfort to me that she too must sometimes wear them) but on closer acquaintance they revealed in their depths a twinkle, which Fishy's friends all knew of; the girls on the whole loved her. Most of these had enough sense to know, even at that time, that to be well taught to the limit of one's ability, even if it meant some hard work, would do no harm even in the marriage-market. This was the eventual goal of most, except for those who, like myself, would have to become governesses. These worked harder, but if any girl were at all lazy, or showed no

interest in her work, Fishy abandoned her to Mrs.
Musgrave.

This happened early on to Ann, who through all our
time together there remained a vegetable. She was fed,
walked—we used all to walk out into the town in long
rows, with a preceptress at the beginning and end, wearing
our scoop-bonnets and grey cloaks, like an assembly of
little nuns—and learned to do her hair, and in the last year
there to paint her face somewhat. Mrs. Musgrave gave the
girls this final instruction, at Fishy's request, and sensibly,
on the whole; saying quite rightly that if the young ladies
were going to do it at all, then it must be done
knowledgeably. She also gave lessons in genteel conversation, fitting oneself for the polite world in such ways as
dispensing tea to guests, and so on. I never knew that
Ann's conversation became any more genteel than it had
ever been, for there was almost none of it. However she
was so pretty that this did not matter, and by the time
Mrs. Musgrave had finished with her she had begun to
look, as I have said at the beginning, like a Spanish
princess, with her long fair hair dressed different ways and
her cheeks rouged a trifle.

I saw little of Ann during those years at school, therefore,
except in the holidays; for, as may be imagined, I was at
my books. It had been assumed from the beginning—Old
Madam had informed Mrs. Musgrave by letter, and in any
case that lady, being sharp in such ways, would have
pinpointed my difference from Ann in the first quarter-
hour we had been deprived of our madeira—that I should
have to earn my living. There is only one way in which a
young portionless female can do this even today, except as
governess. The alternative had never been considered for
me, nor had I considered it for myself. The prospect of
having to be a governess did not, however, displease me,
remembering my mother. I was still more pleased after
gaining a somewhat closer acquaintance with Miss Fish,

who was pleased with the reading I had been doing for myself at Aske.

"The mind," she said to me one day in her terse way, "can compensate for a great many things, Leah, which I have never had and, no doubt, neither may you. It remains with one everywhere, even on a desert island; not that I have encountered such a place for I have never travelled. And now, my dear, the little French essay."

I was to emerge a well-educated young lady from Mrs. Musgrave's Academy. Ann, on the other hand, emerged a desirable one.

Among the more blue-blooded boarders, at the time we first went there, was the Honourable Eliza Fordwoodham. Her honour, which she later lost on frequent occasions about Prinny's London, was kept safe meantime at Fishy and Carp's, which made her discontented there. She ignored me, naturally, but made something of a friend of Ann, who admired Eliza in her unreflective way and was, I believe, flattered by the attentions. These included, in our second year there, an invitation to Ann to spend the holidays at Fordwoodhall, and by some machination of Old Madam's Peter also was included in the invitation, to my relief; he would be of an age with Eliza's brother, the younger, not Fordwoodham. So that summer holiday at Aske I had all of the great, breathing house to myself; its library with my classics, a Book of Hours I had found, and a Dante, in translation; a great herbal with plates coloured by hand, and the virtues listed of the different herbs, some of them unlikely; treatises, fulsome prefaces to dead divines, which I did not read, and the Bible. There was an atlas, and I took much pleasure from the maps. In all such ways I was very happy all that summer, quite undisturbed, and even ate when I liked; Old Madam did not trouble with me.

I mention this holiday because of the other friends I made, lacking Ann. There were, as I have said, few visitors

ever at Aske, because of the talk about Old Madam. So the
place had always, as long as I knew it, been a world to
itself, undisturbed from outside except on very occasional
incursions of the kind such as had long ago killed my poor
mother. Now that I need no longer follow Ann like a little
dog, and perhaps ape her lady's ways, I could make friends
with the servants. This was never a dull occupation for me;
I have always thought of those beings, whom my parents
had in any case brought me up to regard as human, with
their hot-water cans and brooms, toiling upstairs and about
at all hours, as more wonderful than horses, on which so
many of the Eliza Fordwoodhams and others lavish their
affection, but ill-treat their maids. These servants seem to
me to be full of a hidden, pulsating life, a kind of world
within a world, like the world of insects scurrying in a
busy, colourful carpet unseen through the grass where we
walk unheeding. This life never dies, till the servants die
themselves, as many do, at too early an age. Perhaps a time
will come when there is some respite for the hardness of
their lives. They are not much considered, but I got to
know several of them and their troubles, that holiday, and
also their wit which, if they are wise, they generally keep
to themselves. One who did not at any time do this was
Jonie Braik.

I have spoken of Jonie before when he groomed Ann's
pony and taught me to ride, and held up Peter to be
flogged. Where he had come from nobody now knew, or
enquired if they ever had done so; he had been at Aske for
about thirty years. It was whispered—and I believe this
may have been true, for in Gaelic there is a word *breac*,
which means brindled—that he had come from the far
north, in the train of the Young Pretender when the latter
swept down as far as Derby in 'forty-six, bringing his
Highlanders with him after the victory at Prestonpans, and
the taking of Edinburgh. At that point Jonie, when they
withdrew and turned back to Scotland—and this sounds

like him—had seen there would be no more for him in what remained of the matter than a hangman's rope, and had stayed in England. He had hidden in a haystack, they say, and in due course had come and found work at Aske. Others say that Madam already knew of him, and that he had held Robin Aske in his arms when dying, on the field of Prestonpans. That is possible also; for Old Madam permitted him many liberties which are not, as a rule, those of a servant.

He was a large, long old man by now, white-haired and very thin, with the big Highland bones thrusting almost through at knees and elbows. He had once been extremely strong, and still was fairly so, and could pick up a heavy iron bar and toss it, laughing and showing his disgraceful teeth. He was a vagabond by choice, and a rapscallion; I know well he stole, and Old Madam knew also. But it was impossible to help liking Jonie or even—almost as when he had been younger, no doubt—loving him. The other manservants, who made pretence to despise him as a Scot but feared him nevertheless for his strength, left him alone.

He lived alone. He was never seen in any company, but as he had more bastards in the village than anyone else except old Ralph Aske he must have sought and found this for himself sometimes. He lived in a dilapidated cottage on the edge of the wood, where he kept hens and a variable number of cats. Every so often Jonie would have a cat-shoot and there would be yowling for a while, with the popping of the gun like bursting broom-pods, then silence; then Jonie would go out and get drunk. I do not know what he did with the bodies. By now he sat for most of the day by his fire, though he still helped at times in the stables. He had once been a house-servant, but could always do anything with a horse, and had been used to lift Ann on to her pony in childhood, cuddling and teasing her. When all of us were children we were used sometimes, or rather Ann and Peter were, to trail after Jonie on some of his concerns, though not on all of them.

Now I got to know Jonie for myself, as far as anyone could in these days. I cannot recall any notable feature of our acquaintance at the time of which I speak. After it, though, we remained friends, in a manner which in the end bore fruit: but here I am succumbing to the very servant's wit I have been mentioning, with disapproval, formerly.

Ann came home for a few days at the end of that holiday, filled with ecstatic descriptions of Fordwoodhall. This stately home, which she informed me was greatly superior to Aske which was too old, had all been rebuilt in the present century, and had landscaped gardens and an artificial lake, much bigger than our pond, and a Corinthian folly. This may have been part of the reason why the Fordwoodham family remained chronically in debt, so that they had to sell out in a few years although, I believe, they always kept a house in London. This lack of money was to affect poor Ann's life very cruelly, perhaps more than my own; for if she had married young Fordwoodham, who was taken with her, what would have become of Simon's plan when he arrived to commandeer Aske? But I have not yet come to Simon, except for that meeting at the gate, which by now was to happen soon, perhaps two or three years after we had left school.

10

PETER HAD CONTINUED in the acquaintance of the Fordwoodhams and stayed a great deal with the two brothers in town. I found this difficult to understand when I thought of it, which I did not do often. The brothers, particularly the elder who was something of a rake, seemed to have little in common with poor Peter, who by this time was a shambling, backward thing just come of age, without wit or parts. But I found out, and it was Madam's fault for giving Peter money in the first place. They had taught him

to play for stakes that time at Fordwoodhall, and used him
later in this way in town, fleecing him night after night of
all he possessed. For so short a time did this continue—it
was the last and only time Peter had his freedom, before
being confined with a keeper at Aske, which happened
during that same year—that it seemed incredible that even
he should have lost such sums as he did, bearing in mind
the state of Aske coffers; he all but ruined Madam.

When she could send him no more money Peter pledged
what he might expect, in rents from the farms and
tenancies, for two more years; he pledged poor Dorothy's
diamonds, which had been her mother's long ago and were
being kept for Ann to wear when, as was still hoped by
then, she should have become my Lady Fordwoodham. In
the end Peter pledged Ann herself, and the House of Aske,
and all of his inheritance. I mention it here because, with
the swiftness of events following the arrival of the letter,
there may be no more time. Afterwards Peter had his own
freedom taken away, lest he do further harm.

I have had to put all this first, but if it had not been for
that meeting at the gate it would have seemed like
beginning at the beginning and not, like a watershed,
dividing our lives into two parts. For the part which was
still to be lived as a result of that meeting was not sprung
from it directly, though it seems now as if it should have
been; all things, for me, started from that day with the
ponies. But Simon of course had had his plan laid long
before about Aske, and what he would do with all of us
once he was master there.

11

THE LETTER HAD come, and Madam opened it after
breakfast, when she had wiped her fingers on her napkin
and instructed the servants to take away the covers. Ann

had not yet come down. She would, I knew, be doing her
hair, and having no notion of time would be surprised
to find that the table had been cleared; it happened
often. I was thinking of this, and of how Ann never
seemed to learn anything, when I heard Old Madam give a
groan.

I turned round; it was so seldom Old Madam showed
emotion that this must I knew be a matter of great
moment. She had her hand to one side; when I went to her
to see if she were ill, she waved me off.

"Where is—" she said, and her voice, which had
deepened like a man's, came thick; I saw that she breathed
with difficulty. She was staring up at the great staircase
and I saw that Ann had come down, and was standing
halfway holding on to the balustrade with one white hand;
she had combed her hair into side-curls, and they shone
like gold and she wore her new blue gown, which had lace
at the elbows.

Madam's face contracted suddenly till it was old and
wicked as sin, and her voice grew clear again as she called
up to Ann. "You'll take yourself to market, my fine lady.
A rich offer has come." Ann's hand, which had left the
balustrade and strayed to her breast, stayed there; I saw
her breaths rise and fall quickly. She must have known,
even then, that if it was a rich offer it could not be
Fordwoodham's. She went so white that I thought she
would faint, standing there on the stairs; I made ready to
go to her.

"An offer has come, I said," the old woman told her
again. "You will accept it, Ann; it may be the last you'll
ever have. For Aske—"

She slumped forward then and it was she who fell to the
floor, not Ann; the pair of us hurried to raise her, and it
was not till much later, when Ann handed me the letter
which was from a lawyer in London, that we knew what
Peter had done, and that the man's name who had offered
for Ann without even seeing·her, and who was already in

the district and who now by our strange laws of England owned Aske, was called Simon Carden.

It may seem incredible that our separate fates could be so arranged. But at the time of which I write it was often enough done; estates and entire fortunes, gamblers' daughters and even their wives, changed hands at the casting of the dice, or the dealing of a card. Peter had lost, and lost again, and though it could be argued that he was only just of age the resulting lawsuit, which would take years, would cost more than Old Madam had, and we still might lose in the end to Simon Carden.

But Old Madam could not now think of lawsuits. She would never walk again, on her destructive journeys about Aske where she would tear branches down from trees, and pluck out upthrusting greenery by the handful. Her fall had been due to a seizure, and though she did not die of it she took to her bed, and in the end had no more use of a hand and one leg, and her speech was affected. This had a result which could not have been foreseen, even by herself, though she adhered to the decision she had made: and this was never to set eyes on the new owner of Aske, Simon Carden, the son of Robin Aske and the farmer's daughter, Hester. As Simon had likewise decided never to set eyes on Old Madam, the resulting situation suited both of them.

12

SIMON CARDEN HAD arranged to take the name of Aske. This was made known to us in a further communication from the London lawyer, who said also that Mr. Carden Aske would visit us shortly to make arrangements about moving into the house, but did not wish to meet Old Madam. For moments we saw ourselves as homeless and without a roof, but it became clear that this was not the new squire of Aske's intention; he had possibly intimated his avoidance of such a necessity in stating that he would in any case marry Ann.

This was from the beginning a statement coldly issued, never a request; there was no courtship. Poor Ann had hoped with all her heart for Fordwoodham, who had said he loved her and perhaps told the truth. But about then it was announced that Fordwoodham had betrothed himself to an heiress, plain of face but well dowered. That he would never now come and rescue her, that her hopes were dead, made Ann from then on to all intents witless. I do believe she lost her remaining wits the day Simon Carden came into Aske hall with his lawyer.

For her, he had been frightening enough that day at the gate: he was of course that same man we had seen. When he appeared with the lawyer and, between them like a sack, Peter with his head lolling, and a thick-set man stated to be Peter's valet, who remained with him night and day, walking behind—when all this happened, Ann gave a moan and fainted, as she had done on first hearing the news. I did not, but knelt down and ministered to her; looking up, I saw Simon Carden Aske towering above me, a frown drawing his thin black brows together. Evidently he disapproved of his welcome. My rare anger rose up, while I myself continued kneeling by Ann, white as a fallen rose-petal on the hall floor, her hair spread round her like gold and her breath coming thickly.

"Will you be kind enough to fetch a little water, please?" I said crisply to the late arrival. He laughed suddenly, turned away, and I heard him calling to the man to bring not water, but brandy; this applied to Ann's lips caused her to splutter and sit up, and receive the new owner's addresses in the form of a salute pressed on her hand. She still looked as if she had seen a ghost, or the devil; and presently I saw her to her room. Simon Aske took no further heed of us that I know of, and I next heard from Ann herself that he had made her a proposal of marriage through the lawyer. It did not seem a propitious beginning. Meantime, Simon occupied himself with striding about the lower part of the house and also the staircase, with its gallery of portrayed Askes brooding there and on the upper walls. Once or twice he asked me about some of them in curt fashion, addressing me as though I had been a servant.

"Who is the woman with curled hair and a great lace ruff, by the north window?" he said one day. I replied that it was Dinah Aske, who had been removed from the Court of Queen Elizabeth and married suitably elsewhere, and had died of a visitation of the plague in 1609.

"Your information seems precise, if it is accurate," said he coldly. "Why was she removed from Court?"

I knew, but had no intention of telling him at this stage of our acquaintance. "If you doubt my accuracy, sir, there are the parish records to consult," I said flatly. It was perhaps the first time my information on such matters had ever been queried, and I was nettled by it. He smiled suddenly, and I thought for the first time that, provided he was a kind husband to Ann, it might become possible to like him. I was still very shy of men. "Who," Simon Aske said, continuing his inquisition, "is . . ." and he went through them all, the lace-collared cavaliers, the periwigged bucks of the Restoration, a Tudor Aske who had faded somewhat in the sunlight, and the rest: and then, last of all, he paused by the portrait of Robin. "And who," he asked me, "is this?"—and the odd thing was that I knew, by some means, that he knew already, but wanted to hear what I had to say. I decided, accordingly, to say very little.

I told him only, "Sir, that is Robert Aske, who died at Prestonpans."

"That is uninformative. Tell me more of him; was he well spoken of?" Few of the Askes seemed to have been so, in fact, and I did my best for Robin. But I could not, for truth is essential to me, disguise the fact that he had been spendthrift and reckless, and had he not died a brave fine death might have ended as badly as his brother Nicholas. But I did not add this last possibility.

I crept away then and left Simon staring at the portrait, a curious twisted smile on his thin mouth.

Another day, shortly after he had come to live at Aske, occupying Nicholas' old room on the first floor, I came downstairs. Ann was not present; remembering that early time, it seems astonishing how seldom she was with us, and how little interest she took in what was after all her own fate, not mine; or so we thought. Nevertheless already, as I had done at the gate, I had begun to notice things about Simon, apart from his great height, which I have mentioned already, and the way he made himself immediately at home, as though we were the strangers in his house; by now, we were.

I noticed his shoulders, which I could do from where I stood, hesitantly, on the stairs, wondering whether or not to go back quietly to my room. They were broad and strong, and his coat sat on them smoothly and had a velvet collar. He was standing with one booted leg on the hearth, looking down at the logs which glowed and sparked, for there had been an early touch of frost. One hand was on the mantel where the Aske arms are carved, and the other held a glass of red wine which he was drinking. I can remember the firelight glowing on the figure of the tall man, and the finely shaped hand, its nails well cared for and the snowy linen falling at the wrist. I can remember also the dark brooding of the glowing eyes, staring down and not yet aware of my presence. And even at that time, even through my fear of Simon Aske, I said one thing to myself, which may seem strange in my circumstances, situated as I was and without right to question, even, one would have thought, to notice what went on at Aske at all.

I told myself, "He is not happy." And the more I pondered it the more certain I was.

I would still have crept back upstairs, for I had no wish to be alone with Ann's betrothed, happy or wretched. Hitherto, apart from the matter of the portraits, we had not exchanged many words, for at meals the bailiff still came in, and lately also one or two of the tenants by Simon's invitation. The new squire of Aske made free, evidently, with his hospitality, more so than we had ever done in Old Madam's reign when there had been a constant shortage of money and, no doubt, of goodwill. I had the feeling Simon wanted to be known and respected in the district, where it was possible, after all, that some remembered him before he had become as he was now. This I could understand, for he now owned Aske; but why make poor Ann miserable as well as himself? For this she was, as I knew; and not entirely by reason of having lost Fordwoodham.

He turned his head and saw me, on the way back up, and jerked his head, as though I had been a maidservant, for me to descend again. This angered me, as did the whole situation.

"I will come down later, with Ann," I said from the stairs, and he laughed. It was a sound without mirth, and bitter; I suspected that he disliked me, inasmuch as I was of any importance. It was probably that he would have sent me away from Aske, I thought, had I not by now been looking after Old Madam in her bed; to stay here on sufferance did not please me either.

"Am I so dangerous, Miss Leah?" he said. "Come down if it suits you to do so; you will take no harm from me." He sounded indifferent, and for this reason, probably, I grew more angry.

"You've harmed others," I said. "Is Ann happy? Have you asked her? Have you asked Old Madam?" My boldness, in speaking in such a way, shattered me already; but the thing had been said. He raised an eyebrow and sipped at his wine. "Old Madam's happiness is no concern of mine," he replied. He indicated the flask and that he would pour wine for me also; I decided that it would be unbecoming in me to drink with him, and shook my head. "If it is no concern, why marry her grand-daughter?" I said. "You have Aske already, and you care nothing for Ann, nothing!"

I had grown scarlet, and he looked up at me curiously. "Have no fear, Miss Leah Considine," he said. "I will neither marry, seduce, or eat you. I am not Bluebeard or even, alas, Casanova. You will not drink any wine? Then leave me to do so, and return to your own concerns, and so will I."

I made my way upstairs again, snubbed as I had deserved; it was the only time I ventured to speak to him of Ann, and the wedding was in three weeks.

Perhaps I have seemed to gloss over this matter of Simon's and Ann's betrothal. This is partly because I know what happened later, and also because I could not then know—how could I have done?—what it meant to him. Thirdly, I could not know either yet, as I was to do later, that Simon in the determination he had to achieve any goal would go towards it ruthlessly, bent on the exercise of his will, and not considering the harm it might do to others and, most of all, to himself.

13

IT HAD OCCURRED to us, of course, in process of all these events, to wonder where Simon Aske had got his money. None of us, including Ann, dared ask him, which is one index of the way we felt; Madam of course was no longer able to do so, except through the lawyer. That that gentleman was satisfied I know, because he came up later and stayed for almost an hour with Old Madam, where she lay in her bed, able to understand but not yet, or not fully, to ask questions.

But she made no difficulty about the marriage, even if she could; nor did Ann. It occurred to me even then that the latter was not being forced into it. There was no one to force her. Peter could not, nor, any longer could Madam; but of course poor Ann had nowhere to go, and no doubt thought she might as well marry Simon Aske as do anything else. Yet I think there was more inevitability about the matter than that; she was like a thing bewitched, and that not happily. No doubt this knowledge had made me bolder than usual with Simon, that day I had stood on the stairs.

However as regarded his income, I was still in the dark, not having remained with Old Madam and the lawyer. Simon could not, I thought, have made his fortune by a series of cunning card-deals, or constant crooked throwings of the dice. Such things will take a gambler so far, no doubt, but not much further; and he will be discredited very shortly in all the larger gambling-hells. No fortune could have been made, or kept, in such a way; and Simon had the air of a man of standing. I had reversed, perhaps at sight of his clean fingernails, my earlier assumption that he was not a gentleman; but he was still too young, I thought, to have followed a lifetime's bent on the stock-exchange, unless by one stroke of excessively good fortune. He had no rich kin; old Laban had died intestate. Perhaps he was in trade; and the more I thought of this the more likely it seemed, because at times, even in those weeks before the wedding, he was frequently away from Aske, returning in a day or two. He could not, in so short a space of time, have gone to London. Perhaps—and here my assumptions grew wilder—he managed an assembly of travelling packmen.

It was Jonie Braik, of course, primed no doubt by the village, who informed me and Ann. As God knows, his information was near enough the truth, as I would discover under a quite different set of circumstances. Simon Aske, he told us with great relish, owned a number of whore-houses, in Liverpool and London. He employed a hunch-backed negro to supervise the girls, whom he had brought in by ship from divers places and whom he always, on the occasions when he was away from home, inspected personally.

After this there was silence between us on the subject at Aske.

Simon had already made changes. He began to receive the farming-tenants himself at set times, mostly in the mornings after he had returned from his ride. (Ann and I no longer rode out.) He had a small room downstairs which he had taken as his office. He dismissed the bailiff, who had not been efficient and whom Old Madam had kept on as he had been there since Ralph's day, and never argued with her. He now received a pension, and Simon in a short time had the estate-business at his finger-ends, and I believe saved himself a great deal of money.

All this took time; but Simon did not spare that, any more than his own guineas, from whatever source. He ordered items, paint and mortar for pointings, such things, and new ladders for the workmen to mount and to maintain the fabric. Some upper windows which had been broken as long as I could remember were mended, and the roof had new slates. If all this was for the wedding, it was also for Aske; which took on, after so long a time of neglect, a shipshape look, as sailors call it, and lost its abandoned, half-forgotten air in which it had dreamed for two centuries. None of the roystering Restoration bucks, or Nicholas or his father before him, had spent a penny more on Aske than they could spare from their debaucheries. I had always loved the great house, and it seemed to me that a redeeming feature of Simon Aske must be that he loved it also.

Later, with the fabric clean and sound, Simon brought in new furnishings; rolls of fine velvet, hollands and French brocade, of a yellow colour, and heavy silks, and a carpet containing all the tints of the sunset, that he had picked up, he said, somewhere in India. But I did not think that he could have made his fortune with the East India Company, for he was too young; nor have been there as a soldier, the other reason for any unknown young man's adventuring there. I brought myself in fact to address him on the subject, coldly for I disapproved of his whore-houses, but could not tell him so, yet felt that he ought to be made aware of my disapproval. He may have noticed it, but made no comment; merely assuring me, courteously, that he had never been in India at all, which made him out a liar.

Ann took no interest in the furnishing.

It may be thought, hearing all this, that I was narrow, and that my education, though formidable for a woman's, had been too much out of books; this is possible. I had never, quite certainly, encountered anyone like Simon before. For one thing he was a man, and my knowledge of these creatures had been limited; except for my father, Sir Napier a very little, and Peter if he might count, and Jonie Braik, I had not known any men. And Simon was indubitably one; it was manifest in every line and movement of him, in his deep voice, his height (and I was a dab) and his hands, which though shapely were much larger than my own, or than poor Ann's. I had to describe him, in detail, to Old Madam where she lay on her bed, for although she would not see Simon for herself, nor he her, her curiosity was as strong as the next woman's. When I described the strength of his hands, and the way I had seen him take up a piece of roof-lead for the workmen and twist it into shape, with slim fingers as strong as a vice, Madam said "H'm," and was not displeased, I think, at having a proper man at last in the family. But I, in spite of myself, pictured those hands touching Ann's body, as they must do on the marriage-night; anyone would have thought that I, not she, was the poor sacrificed bride.

But no bride was I. And for Simon to have done other than ignore me, as he did on first coming to Aske, would hardly have been possible. I was an insignificant thing, and he was—as, even in my dislike, I admitted—personable. His black-avised colouring, thin brows and slim, erect height, the hands, and the general air of a *grand seigneur* to which, I was certain, he had no real right whatever—had not his mother been, they said, a farmer's daughter, and his father not even certainly Robin Aske?—would have earned Simon admission into, very nearly, the best society, particularly as he seemed free with his money. But I still told myself I did not like him, or despite the money that he should marry Ann, and the reason was—as I in some confusion could tell myself, even then—his power over us all. It was present in everything he did, making success where there had been failure, or inefficiency; a force from some hidden, infernal source within himself, so that at times he seemed to burn with a dark flame and frightened those nearest him, not least myself. Yes, it was power indeed, I knew, of a diabolical, implacable kind; he would certainly be able to exercise it upon poor Ann.

14

ANN, THE BRIDE, wore a dress made of white satin, high at the throat and narrow at the wrists, with eider edging there and on her close, narrow cap. There had been no wedding at Aske since Avice Kintyre's to Sir Napier Steed, seven or eight years previously, and that had been in mourning; so everything now was to be undertaken splendidly, and the house itself had been made ready, as I have described. Everything was bustle, as it were in spite of the bride, who seldom left her rooms; the white dress stood, like a ghost, on its lay-stand with two mantua-makers working on it, right up till the last week when Ann came out and submitted to be pinned and fitted.

She was in a kind of daze, I thought; when the flowers arrived later from the bridegroom she fingered them absently, as though uncertain what they were for, and pulled off some of the petals. But she was not otherwise

like an unwilling bride; although her cheeks were ashen, so
that the rouge they put on her that day sat like two garish
patches, staring below her eyes, which were glazed, a little.
Yet she had never from the beginning complained, wept,
or fainted. No one but myself was ill at ease concerning
her. She was, on the whole, considered fortunate although
she had lost her noble lover, and everyone here knew the
groom's origins. But he had seemed to overcome them, and
his industry and address were already making him respected in the community. His wish to take the bride's
surname by a customary legal arrangement was understood. Everyone came to the wedding.

My own dress was, by the order of Simon Aske who
paid for everything, to be of rich stuff, but it was nothing
notable on me. I did not mind, for all I wanted to do was
creep into a corner; the wedding filled me with terror, for
Ann's sake, and I had no wish that anyone, not the
formidable groom or another, should cast eyes on me
twice. I need not have troubled on that score; all eyes
would be for Ann. When she came into the church there
was a gasp of indrawn breath for her beauty, though she
now seemed a wax doll rather than human.

She went through her part in the ceremony without
faltering, though we could not hear her responses; not so
the groom, whose voice was firm and clear. He wore dark
clothes, as though to make himself a foil for the bride's
whiteness. At the end, when he must kiss Ann, he bent
towards her and did so hard and with full certainty; but
from where I was standing nearby I saw that her mouth
had fallen open, so that he kissed her teeth.

This made me shudder, but as, as far as could be
ascertained, Ann had ceased to feel anything for herself, I
tried to look with interest at the other guests who had
come to the wedding. There seemed no figurehead without
Old Madam, who lay in her bed at the great house; some
would visit her afterwards, and Ann had been taken up
first to her room, to show her grandmother the wedding-

gown. But many were there, including the villagers who
filled the church to overflowing, and called blessings on
the bride as Ann went out. Behind them stood the last
bride from Aske, Avice Steed, with her husband; Avice
wore wine-colour, which did not suit her, and was big at
that time with either Bertram or Mary, I cannot recall
which; she had borne children yearly since the wedding
and must return early to the vociferous batch at Steed.
The rest would linger at Aske following the feast.

The ceremony had taken place in the evening. I had an
idea this had been done, as it often is, in order not to have
an overlong entertainment of the guests. Simon Aske's
aspect was taciturn, as if already he hated everyone and
everything concerned with Aske; he had said little in reply
to the toasts. Sir Napier Steed's facile jollity, which never
failed on such occasions, began to seem almost intolerable;
all along the supper-table smiles, to me, seemed forced,
and there was to be no dancing afterwards. The reason
given was no doubt the health of Old Madam, half-
drowsing upstairs in her bed; as soon as the bride and
groom were bedded, I was to go back to her. I longed with
a sick apprehension for the time to pass, waiting till the
signal, which was when Ann rose to leave the hall, came
for myself and Avice to go upstairs after her and undress
her in the bridal-chamber.

That had already been decked, like everything else, by
order of the bridegroom; and this had been done in so
particular a fashion that I had begun to wonder if Simon
Aske might perhaps be a little mad. Ann no doubt may
have wondered this also, but a glance at her face now made
me realise that she was beyond anything except fear.

The room had been darkened, as though it were already
a winter's night. It had been lit completely by white wax
candles, like a bier; on the bed itself, which had a great
tester above it carrying the Aske crest, was to be spread
the Flemish embroidered coverlet used even before the

days when Madam herself was a bride. I had seen it taken
out of the chest where it lay by custom, and shaken
carefully to clear it of moth; an odour of sandalwood, old
herbs, and damp came from it, that I had likened to a
smell of death. This smell was now all through the room.

Were my own nerves a fool's, on that night? I could
only pray, by now, that Ann would remain beyond feeling,
as she had been all day; or, somehow, that things would
mend.

They did not. In friendly enough fashion the pair of us
undressed the bride; when Ann was out of the white gown,
clad only in her shift, she looked young and defenceless,
even with her rouge. It would have been customary to
dress her hair again with flowers, which were as a rule lying
ready in a jar on such occasions; but the groom, again, had
said that this was not to be done. We combed Ann's hair
out smoothly. When she was placed ready in the great bed,
in its shadows, she looked small, lonely and wan; we
beckoned, with a clawing of doubt at the heart, the guests
to come in, and bring the groom with them. They came;
and I saw a face to which I had, I realised, paid little heed
that evening in church; it was young Fordwoodham's, and
he had consoled himself with wine. He was able, accordingly, to greet the moment with insouciance; like all the
rest, he must kiss Ann, and did so with a mouth which
looked pink and wet, all wine and saliva. In the moment
before they all began to leave Sir Napier, who had
remained for the feasting, flung one of his coarse jests, like
the old-time stocking.

"I'll wager we all come back within the year, sirs, for
the christening! To work, and make the heir!"

They raised a straggling cheer, and stumbled out; I had
stayed by Ann. She had hold of my hand where I stood
next the bed and for the first time that day, or in long,
spoke to me as if she knew who I was. "Don't leave me
with him, Leah," she said. "I'm afraid."

It was no more than a whisper, but the bridegroom

heard. I saw the glitter of his eyes as he surveyed me where I clung to Ann; his mouth had set hard, like a trap.

"Go now," he said, again as though I had been a servant. And I went, and left them alone together; what else could I do, I who had no power and no standing at Aske?

I cannot recall what I thought of all that night, watching by Old Madam, who slept. I did not sleep; and the memory which recurs to me is a later one, and cannot have happened then. Robin told me only the other day of a history lately written purporting to be a romance but founded on fact; they say it happened in Galloway in Scotland, last century. It concerns a young bride who was forced to marry against her inclination, to please her strong-willed mother, and on her wedding-night went mad, and tried to kill the groom with a knife she had concealed, and later she died. But nobody had forced Ann to wed Simon Aske, nor, I knew having put her to bed, did she have any knife. And Fordwoodham was a sot, and unworthy of a tear from Ann, or from anyone.

Nevertheless I trembled for Ann; it seemed to me, in that silent house, that I heard her cry more than once, as her mother might have cried unavailingly against the storm beyond the inn where she lay drugged, with Nicholas upon her. And when at last my eyes closed to feign sleep which still did not come, I saw an image behind them; not Dorothy, nor Nicholas, but the thing I had myself seen that day, and which had summed up for me, in a kind of access of wickedness, the whole pretence of this forced joy which could never be real. I saw Ann's mouth fall open again as it had done many times in our lives when she had not been listening, or paying much heed to anything, and as it had done today at the ceremony in Aske Church. I saw the bridegroom's ruthless mouth then, placing a kiss to bruise the flesh, and awaken her, had flesh been there. But what he had kissed were her teeth.

Next day, heavy-eyed and greatly afraid as I was, I crept out and over to the bridal-rooms and tried to go to Ann. They told me—the one who answered my knock was Prossy, the woman Simon had brought here lately who had a terrible, ruined eye, and she seemed to me now like an ape of hell, guarding Ann like Proserpine—they told me Ann was to see nobody that day, and I went away. I knew well the order to keep me from her had been the groom's.

15

I HAVE OMITTED so far to mention Prossy, who had arrived at Aske in the weeks before the wedding, with her arrival masked by the bustle of preparations. It would not have been possible, either for me—who at that time sought for any adverse matter to weigh against Simon, and justify the dislike and fear I felt—or for anyone who once looked on that poor creature to imagine that she might be Simon's mistress. Among the many things which were said against him later, I never heard that; not that a mistress has never been brought by a man into his house at the time of his wedding. Some cruel acts of that kind have been known, with a crying bride left solitary in her own rooms after the marriage-night which gives away her fortune, and the groom, having done his duty, roystering it all away upon his harlot, or several of them, thereafter. This is not unknown in the history of England, but it did not happen at Aske. Simon in any case, as I afterwards found, was at that time trying to make the best he could of his marriage to Ann, and had she been as other women I daresay things might have worked out differently. But she was not, and they did not. And, meantime, unless Prossy were Simon's mistress I could not myself think why he had brought her, for there were already servants enough at Aske.

She was a tiny thing, ageless—we never did know her age

to the end—and skinny, as I was, but differently; she was a
skeleton who had by chance the merest skin dragged over
the protruding bones, no flesh, so that the cheeks had
stringy hollows like an old woman's. She was livid in
colour, with a diseased whiteness like, I imagined, the leper
in the Bible white as snow; but Prossy was no leper. I did
not then know what her illness might have been, which is
as well; it was the pox, and she had been a child-prostitute.
This state is not, at any stage of life, undertaken always for
choice, but for the most part, unless with very high-paid
madams or royal mistresses, to make enough money for
food. And she had paid; for however Prossy's thin frame
was now nourished, and they all ate well enough in the
servants' hall at Aske, she would never again look like
other people, if indeed she ever had. For she would seem
to have been almost born diseased; the sight of one eye
had by now been completely destroyed, and had an ugly
ring of inflamed humour within the very eyeball. The scabs
and afflictions of the poor that I had seen in my
childhood, on my dear parents' visits to these, hardened
me now in my ability to look on Prossy without showing
disgust, or repulsion; but one of the maidservants at Aske,
I heard later, vomited when she first saw her, and none
would eat alongside her. I wondered a little that Simon
should have put her in attendance on Ann.

Part II

SIMON'S TALE

I

I MAY MENTION here a thing which at the time seemed unimportant, but helped to reverse my opinion of Simon Aske, perhaps, in the end; it was that Prossy herself, like a young girl in love, would hear no single word in his despite. I cannot think that Prossy can have loved Simon except in the way any grateful, half-destroyed creature will lick the feet of the hero who, like Perseus, flies down on wings of rescue from some monster. Certainly Prossy thought of Simon as such a hero, or angel. I do not remember how the subject came to mind so early, but this is the way it may partly have happened; I used to sit with Ann later in those first days of the marriage, finishing the sewing-tasks with her on curtains and the like; they had all to be sewn with wooden rings, and hung on square frames over the beds and windows. The task had not been completed by the time of the wedding in Aske church, and occupied us in fact all that first winter. The curtains were of very rich material, the yellow brocade I have mentioned, or else another, a heavy linen sewn by hand all over with silk threads, sequins and such things, which caught the light. I was not used to handle such fine, exotic things, and exclaimed about the cost of them.

I had meant nothing, and Ann's fair head did not even raise itself, but she got on with her sewing. Only Prossy, neither housemaid, drudge, nor lady's maid, but by now perhaps all three, raised her head; and the sad eye looked on me with, I saw, reproach.

"He's got a right to spend his money as he chooses, hasn't he?"

I was dumb, never having been answered in such a way by a servant. Ann opened her mouth and then shut it again, like a fish, but still said nothing. I had already noticed that she showed no dislike of Prossy, and tolerated the poor creature about her, to help her dress. I said nothing more; my own place in the house was not such that I could reprimand anyone, but I remember the episode as giving me some idea of the way Prossy regarded Simon Aske, though not yet the reason.

I was by now mostly occupied with the care of Old Madam, which no one else would fully undertake. Although she was helpless they were all afraid of her, her sharp tongue and terrible lizard's eyes; and she was heavy, an inert and solid weight, which I could not lift unaided without one of the maids, who helped me. Old Madam could no longer perform her functions without help, or eat unless she were fed with a spoon from a cup. She would never again leave her bed, the physician said, but might live for many more years.

She liked to be read to; so I undertook that, and the other things, as well as I could; after all, she had sheltered me at Aske. For this reason I had not yet left it after Ann's marriage, to become a governess in another household as I had expected, by now, to have to do. It all left me little time for the sewing on of curtain-rings, and I did not, unless at such times, see anything of Ann except in company at meals.

One day it had been much like the other days; I had waited till I was sure Simon Aske had gone out of the house, or to his office to the tenants; then I used to spend a few moments with Ann, before rejoining Old Madam.

The latter would sleep between nine and ten of the clock, when she would take a posset, not without some mumbling in her speech. It would be clearer at times than at others; I could see the intelligence undeterred in the green eyes, but the effort of making herself understood sometimes tired Madam, and soon she would fall into the snatched sleep of the old, rather than doing so at night, when I was much awake with her. I waited accordingly till she had drowsed on her pillows, then went out and down to Ann's rooms.

Prossy met me at the door that day and informed me Ann could see no one. This had happened before on several occasions by now, and I no longer doubted Simon's agency; he had, evidently, objections to my uninterrupted intimacy with Ann, and this angered me. I determined to ask him about it, braving his own anger or orders, perhaps, to leave Aske. Meantime I must go back again to Old Madam, and so I made my way back there by the upper staircase. On my journey, hearing my footsteps echoing on the floors and stairs, I felt the unaccustomed company of ghosts, though it was broad day. Except for the devil, a madman, an old woman awaiting death, and myself, and the servants, who lived now at Aske?

In this state, which is like a kind of heightened perception brought on, I knew then, by a series of wakeful nights, I traversed the seldom-used upper corridor of Aske, near Peter's rooms which I did not enter. Up here the morning light seemed to thicken and change as it filtered through the squat, regularly disposed casement windows. They had been let into much older walls, some of these four feet thick and built in days when the women of Aske, who stayed at home, must accustom themselves to the chill from the stones, which struck at me now like the grave. I could not rid myself of the remembrance that this was the part of the house where Peter was confined with a warder, and that he had once been the silk-clad heir of Aske with the world before him. I did not often come this way.

Presently I found I had reached the end of the long corridor, and for some reason turned and looked back over my shoulder. There, across a dozen slanting rays of dusty light, stood the devil, looking at me. It was Simon Aske.

The sight shook me out of my fancies; how much of a fool was I, I thought, mistaking dreams for reality, putting a false identity on anyone? It meant nothing more than that he must have come in when I was at Ann's rooms, and had not cared to meet me, and so had come up this way and so had I. I no longer cared whether or not he thought my conduct strange. I was aware, chiefly, of great weariness as we stood there looking at one another down a stretch that seemed less of space than of time. The light shone, as it had done that first day at the gate, on his dark hair. He did not move, or speak to me.

What did I feel for Simon Aske? What was he to me, other than Ann's husband?

That he had some feeling also I knew, then: I knew it, or else he would not have remained staring at me, now that we were alone here with no witness except the dust. He would not so have discounted all courtesy to survey a plain, defenceless, shy young woman who avoided him. It was, I realised, and the certainty made me afraid, the same look he had given me earlier, that day Ann and I had met him when we had been out riding on our ponies, and he had seen Ann and looked her up and down, where she sat, with contempt.

Did he still hate Ann? Why had he married her? Was it that she was only a mare, to be bought and bred from? An Aske, to fashion him his heir?

And I thought, then, that I had found the reason. I turned away, the blood coming up into my face and neck, and left him standing motionless; we had given no greeting to each other. I did not know how long he stayed where he was. I went straight back to Old Madam's rooms and shut the door, and with it shut out the cold of the stones and of death and madness, and my own fancies.

But the matter of why he had made the marriage stayed to trouble me, although that same day, as if he had known of my weariness, he sent a second servant to aid me with Madam and allowed me leisure for a night's sleep. This refreshed me, and I would like to have spent more time with Ann in the coming days now that I was at least partly free; but often, as before, I was prevented from going to her. If it had not been that I had convinced myself of Simon's lack of personal regard for Ann, it would have seemed to me that he himself preferred, as a husband, to be her comforter and companion, and was jealous of any other. But he seemed to spend little time with her, and never by day, for I often saw him striding about the house or the estate, and always alone. I did not think Ann meant anything to him but what I had thought of that morning in the upper corridor, and still did; a mother for his son, a name for his namelessness. Such things, after all, happened every day elsewhere. But to ally oneself deliberately to a woman one disliked, as though to mortify her flesh and one's own . . . why, why? And what had poor Ann ever done to wrong Simon? She could scarcely have been born when he left Aske as a child, a boy, whenever it was; I realised I did not know when he had gone, or why. But, in any case, to make Ann a scapegoat even for some fault of her family was an ugly thing to have done; I wanted no part in it that did not side with her; I would not be the man's ally.

About that time, I went out to the stables to use some of my new leisure on the old pony. Ann's chestnut was not now in the loose-box, and on enquiry I was informed by the groom that it had been sold. The thing puzzled me, for she had seemed pleased enough with the animal that time we had both ridden out.

I happened to see Ann some days after that; she was
walking in the grounds and so was I. I hastened to her, and
we met by the pond with its reeds, which I remembered
well enough from childhood but no longer avoided; there
was no danger now from Peter.

"Why, Ann," I said, and kissed her; she looked pale, I
thought, and stouter, a little; could she already be going to
have a child? The feeling this thought aroused in me was
curious, as though everything were suspended in me, not
Ann, pending further knowledge. But she was not; she told
me that later, after I had asked about the pony.

"Did you not want him any more?" I said. "I thought
you liked him," and I remembered the habit she had had,
and the hat with the feather; would she never wear them
again?

Ann looked about her nervously, almost primly; I could
see Prossy in the distance, and knew she had been put to
follow Ann. The discovery shocked me in some manner I
could not name. I did not like the way Ann looked, waxen
and almost fat; it was unnatural. Nothing was natural
about this marriage. I heard her break into quick, furtive
speech about the pony.

"*He* won't let me ride it," she said. "He says it may
delay the heir." She laughed a little, but there was no
mirth in the laughter. "There isn't one," she said, "but he
talks of nothing else; that is, when he speaks to me at all.
Leah—" And then, for a moment, she was Ann again that I
had known, blue eyes cognisant, looking back over her
shoulder to ensure that we had, for the space of some
moments yet, privacy. "He comes to me every night, and
says nothing," she said. "Not a word, at night with me in
bed, and gone by morning. It's like nothing I had ever
imagined, when . . . sometimes, I think he doesn't know
I'm there. And yet, there's my body." She gave a little,
coarse, unfamiliar sound. "Marriage!" she said. "It's—"

But I did not need to turn my head to know that Prossy
was now at the pond's edge; she stood respectfully,

waiting. "He sets her on to watch me," said Ann, as
though Prossy had not been near. "Is he afraid I'll get out,
and have another man's child? I must give him an heir, he
says. An heir for Aske."

She turned half facing Prossy at last and made a
contemptuous movement of the lips. "That bitch was his
mistress once, did you know?" she said. "Imagine it; with
one eye."

I watched them go together. Some revolting change, I
thought, seemed to have come over everything with the
change in Ann. Even the pond looked obscene, as though
things swam and crawled unimaginably beneath its surface.
I escaped quickly from the sight of the pond, lest this new
horror bring back the others, the inward one from my
childhood, which had itself happened not far away.

Once back at the house I shook off the feeling. I made
myself go down to try and find Simon Aske. It was better,
I thought, to face the devil, if devil he was, and to try and
find out what was wrong with Ann.

                              2

WAS IT ABOUT that time that men began to call Simon
the Devil of Aske? Did they, then and long after,
remembering lovely young Ann in her bridal gown, blame
him for ill-treating her and keeping her prisoner, later
driving her mad? Did the sight of the changed, waxen face
yet warn them of that last? I do not know; nor do I even
know where Ann's madness came from, except that it did
not come to her from Simon.

I shall have more to say of all this; but in the meantime,
even now that I suspected Ann's state, I was concerned
with my own also. For I can think of no sudden or notable
instance, other than those I have related, which altered
and, in the end, transfigured my feeling for Simon Aske.
To say one day that one dislikes a man, and the next that

one loves him, is the reasoning of a fool. Perhaps I was and
am such. I do not, in such ways, know that either.

Had I met Simon in the ordinary way, without Ann,
would we have ended by loving one another? I have asked
myself this also, and found no answer. Inevitable as our
love later seemed, it was not likely that a man such as
Simon was then, rich, personable, intolerant a little, in
search of a wife to suit his own anticipated needs, would
have chosen me, poor and plain and insignificant as I was,
at once, forsaking all other. Nor could I ever have taken
Simon from Ann had they been happy together. I know
that, nor would I have tried to do so.

Did I in fact try? Did I set myself in his way, or—this is
the way I felt it had happened, rather, and that my hate
and even loathing had dropped away or snapped suddenly,
like a rotten tree-trunk, and in its place there was already
growing a strange, new, uncertain feeling, like a tender
green stem without support, till it hardened in the air? This
was my feeling for Simon, liking first, then love. I am sure
of it, and that I did not set out deliberately to filch him
from Ann.

But already to others he was the Devil of Aske. That
there might be a curse on Aske could have occurred by
now to almost anyone given to the contemplation of such
things; Peter's madness, later Ann's, the remembrance of
Nicholas himself, the marrying of Dorothy; all the hate
and coercion, lust and greed and fear, could have com-
bined in such a word. Many young people have married
without love, and grow used to and, even, fond of one
another with accustoming, and the coming of a child; but
it had not happened in that way at Aske in the last
generation, nor would it do so in this. And the roots of a
curse could have grown from that, embracing the mindless,
half-destroyed thing Peter now was, and later Ann. I do
not know, and there was also the other reason Simon
spoke of.

He spoke of it first that day I went to him in his office, using a manner which might have made us, had I never learned his own story and had other things been as they should, only lifelong friends; with the friendship, the affection, any married man may feel for and give to a plain, unassuming woman employed usefully about his house, without involving her or himself. Such friendships are very pleasant, and for a while after the day about which I must now speak, and again after many years at Aske, I was to enjoy such a relationship with Simon. But that was not all, and the beating blood, and the beating heart, had their own words, their own time, but not yet, not so soon as that first day I went to him, troubled in my mind over Ann.

He was working at his accounts as he always did in the mornings, and there was no one with him in the office; I entered timidly, again only the young, scared creature I had been, whom Simon Aske could turn out of his house at any time without warning, if I now angered him. That I was by this time about Old Madam almost constantly, and that she had begun to cling to me with the helpless pathos of a sad old child, could mean nothing to Simon even if he had heard of it.

He was seated at the table, wearing riding-clothes; he had come in lately, and the whip lay by his gloves. I let my eyes rest on the slim, vicious thing as I carefully closed the door; his way with horses, his way with women, a whip perhaps. Fear came into my throat and made it dry, and I had already forgotten my carefully prepared speech about Ann. He had risen as I entered, and stood smiling down at me from his great height. He had indicated the other chair, and that I should sit on it, but I did not; how much worse it would be to have him towering over me in that! So we both continued to stand, somewhat formally.

"What is the matter, Leah?" he asked gently.

The gentleness and his use of my name—it was the first

time—unmanned me further, and I told myself that his manners had improved since that day at the gate, when he had not had the courtesy to open it for me and Ann. Perhaps marriage to a lady had—I nerved myself, and burst forth into something like my intended speech. At the end of it I had ceased to feel afraid of him.

"She is sick with loneliness," I said. "She sees no one, except Prossy, and now you have sold the pony. Why did you do that?" And then I blushed like fire, and did not tell him, as I had planned to do, that the Queen of Bohemia had ridden out on horseback each morning of her life, and had had eleven children who all lived. Perhaps I had told him too much as it was; he was staring at me with an expression hard to read, and his lips tightened. He turned away to make a pretence of replacing some of his papers, and I was quite sure now that he was angry at what I had said, and began to tremble.

He spoke then, with his back to me. "My kind little goose," he said, "have you lived all of your life beside Ann, and have never thought what might be the matter with her?"

I began to stammer a little. All our lives . . . we had been at school much of the time, she had been simpler there than I, and she . . . A memory of the hours with the back-board, Mrs. Musgrave's classes, other things, which had partly all our supposed days together separated me from Ann, came to my mind's eye. Had I perhaps never really known Ann? Did one know anyone?

"Ann is insane," he said, "or soon will be. Before she becomes irretrievably so, she must give me an heir."

It was spoken so coldly that I felt nothing for a moment. Then the realisation of what he had said came fully to me, and I recoiled from him. "Precisely so," he said in a dry way. "The notion repels you, as I had expected that it would. That was—partly—why you were not permitted to be much with Ann. As for the pony," he shrugged, "there might be an accident to the beast or to herself; nowadays, she is no longer capable of controlling any animal, even—" But he stopped, and I think he knew that I would not have endured this last reference to Ann.

"Did you," I asked him, and my voice like his own was cold now, and deadly slow, "know this, before you married Ann?"

I looked at the broad, shapely shoulders, set well under his coat as he stood half turned away; for a time he did not answer. Then he said, simply, "Yes. I knew, I think. Perhaps not quite—" Then he turned, and I saw that his face was white and that the close-shaven jaw, long and determined, showed darker against it. His eyes burned, not for me nor anything in the room; they saw into his own memory and mind. "I knew by the time I was with her in the church," he said, "and perhaps before that. But I had made a vow, and must fulfil it. That is my excuse, if I have one, for—the fault. I do not use the word sin, as your parsons would, you see," and the mouth relaxed, a little, into a smile which the eyes did not interpret. "Call us lost together, if you like, myself and Ann. But she has grown worse in the last weeks, possibly as a result of the marriage; an unflattering conclusion as regards myself, doubtless, but true as I see it."

I was filled with pity for him, for them both; even, at this moment, in some way for myself. How could I stay at Aske, knowing this? A thought came to me, then, that I would write this very day to Fishy to see if she could accommodate me in a place in her school, or help me to find some other situation.

I must have spoken of that. He brushed it aside impatiently; he would not let me go, he said. "Your home is here; where else would you find one? With some posse of brats whose ungrateful parents would make your days a misery? And where then? If you were ill, or lacked money, and had nowhere to go?"

I said it had happened to others before. "I know that,"

he said grimly. "It happened once to me. For that reason, I'll not let you endure it, Leah. No, your home is with us, as long as my grandmother lives, and after that, if you choose." I did not at first remember that Old Madam was his grandmother, as well as Ann's. I laughed a little, to release the unbearable tension in the room. "Your grandmother, whom you have never seen," I said. "The Askes!" But his face darkened.

"I have seen her," he said. "I saw her when I was a child. Afterwards, she drove past us in her carriage, splashing my mother's skirts with mud where we walked on the road. I never forgave her that, or the other things."

I did not then ask what the other things were. But by degrees I learned of them, in the friendship we had begun that day. There was another reason for this; I had, he said, spoken civilly to Prossy and had not made her feel, as all the others did, that she was a monster, and unclean. "She is cured now, as far as it can be done," he said drily. What Prossy was cured of, and the other matters, I learned; oh, I learned all of them, and the place to relate them is now, though of course I did not find everything out except by degrees, talking with Simon as the days passed, and winter changed to spring, then summer again, and Ann still had started no child.

3

HE TOLD ME, first of all, the story of Prossy.

"She had a grandam no softer than Old Madam here," he said, having spoken already of that carriage-drive, and later, of what I myself knew already but had not known Simon did, of the way Old Madam had sold her charges one after the other into marriage for money without love: Sophia, Nicholas, young Dorothy, though Robin had evaded her. But Prossy's grandmother had not even sold her charge to the highest bidder. "Prossy was sent out, as a child, every night on to the streets to make money from men. If she brought no coins home the old woman beat her till she was senseless and gave her no food. When I found Prossy first it was on a bitter night with the wind blowing, in a town whose streets had their filth all rimed white with early snow. No one had been about that evening, and so she dared not go home. I was poor then but I gave her some food I had with me; I hadn't money. As soon as I could, I brought her here, as you've seen, to a place of her own. She has, at the least nowadays, supper and a fire."

"Her eye?" I asked. The horror of Prossy's story had frozen my bones, as though I had myself been there on that winter's night; as though the cold were all through me. Nothing I had ever encountered had prepared me for the fact that children were abused in such a way; other children.

"Her eye?" said Simon coldly. "She was given a disease by her customers, which finally destroyed it, as one aspect."

I began to cry.

Without control or volition, the tears rolled from me; my whole body became convulsed with jerking sobs, and I heard him come over; he thought, no doubt, that I wept for Prossy, and I covered my face with my hands to still their shaking. I wanted to shout at him that there were others, besides the very poor; they were not so much alone . . . Suddenly, I wanted also to know more of the boy who had been Simon, what had happened to him, why he was, by now, the man he had since become.

"Tell me, please, of yourself," I said, when he would have comforted me.

That was the way I first heard of Simon as he had been; but, also, he had guessed, in some way, by now, that I had once been hurt and frightened, almost, though not quite, like Prossy . . . He took me, I remember, in his arms, and stroked and caressed me like a child.

"You too, Leah?" he said. "I had not known."

After that, without asking any more, he told me his own story.

THE STORY MADE me feel young and also old. In fact I had not yet been born when it started, and by the time Simon was a footman in the house of Maria Gore I would be, perhaps, seated beneath the apple tree with my parents at Steed vicarage, asking why they had called me Leah instead of Rachel. But I felt, again as with the tale of Prossy, that I had myself been there; and beside me a little black-haired boy running through the night and storm, trying to fend off death, but nobody would come.

I have mentioned Big Het already. Simon could remember the time when they had only just come back to Aske, and he was walking with his mother through the village, taking great strides to keep up with her on his thin, still uncertain legs, and holding her hand. She was like a queen, he thought then, with her head held high, and the black shining hair piled up on it; they walked as if they cared for nobody, and he remembered that his mother did not turn her head, or give any sign, when one of the women called after her for a harlot. That might have been the time they were walking to the great house, to show Simon to his grandmother. His grandfather Carden, a bitter old man whom his mother had pointed out to him only once, after Laban went by one day, did not speak to them and they never saw him again. He died at some time not long after that, quite alone in his house.

Old Madam, the other grandparent, was in the end no better; she had looked at Simon, from a place he later remembered which was immense, dark, and shadowy, with a great staircase rising at the farther end beyond which hung portraits in frames on the wall. His grandmother did not show Simon the portrait of his father; she did not show either of them anything, except the door. "He resembles the mother," Simon heard her say coldly, as though he himself could be expected to hear nothing. How well I remembered that same feeling, as a child!

It was after that, of course, that the world had narrowed for him again, including only the cottage on the bluff, and sometimes Alf and his fiddle. By now Big Het was no longer so much like a queen; her flesh sagged, after a year or two, and she was a sloven, and worse; there were several miscarriages, and Simon used to be sent down to the village by himself to fetch a brew of herbs from the old woman who lived there, to bring them on. There had to be other men, of course, besides Alf, for the money. One of them was Nicholas Aske, who being the landlord did not pay. Simon had by now learned to keep out of the way always, say nothing and stop his ears; this was more difficult when Nicholas came, for the boy loathed him and so, he knew, did his mother. They never discussed this and it was doubtful, from a reasonable standpoint, why the loathing existed, despite Nicholas' dough-face and the air he had of a little-eyed, rooting white pig, and his meanness with money. Once Het said a thing Simon remembered, after Nicholas had gone. "He thinks," she said, staring at the wall where damp dripped down, "that he'll prove to himself that he is a better man than his brother, this way at any rate; but he won't."

Nicholas had ignored Simon after having, at the very first, looked him over to see if there might be any truth in the rumour that he was Robin's son. Simon remembered that, and the way Nicholas laughed later and said that whoever had been his father, he was a little bastard like all the rest. Then Het had said one other memorable thing; holding up her head as she had done in the old days, and looking full at the squire.

"You know well it's other gait," she said, "you and your mother."

She had not told Simon, then or later, what she meant

by that. But he remembered it: it was the only time he ever heard her stand up to Nicholas, for they were very poor, the money was irregular, and here was the cottage without any rent.

Other men came whom he hated less, apart from Alf of whom he was fond. Some of them liked to hear Simon play, beating time with their feet on the floor, an arm round Big Het's waist. They would often wake Simon up, if he had been asleep on the twig-pile, and call to him to get out Alf's fiddle and he would get it and tune up, at the same time rubbing the sleep from his eyes. By the time he was nine years old he could play any tune he had once heard. They would pay him afterwards with a coin for himself, but he always gave it to Het. When he was a man, he used to promise himself, he would earn money fiddling at fairs and harvest-kirns, and give it to his mother instead of her having to go on taking men. But in addition he took pleasure in fiddling for its own sake. It was almost the only pleasure he knew.

Would Simon have made a musician, a great one perhaps? I used to wonder, later, at the sound of his deep voice, which could sing well and feelingly in tune. I thought also that I could hear for myself the small boy's fiddle, the drawing of the bow across its strings to make sounds gay and sad, while his fingers flew, and his black hair fell forwards in an unkempt lock over his sleep-clouded eyes, and his thin body gave itself wholly, devotedly, to the making of music.

But it did not turn out that way. It did not turn out that way at all.

He did not know even at the very last whether or not it had been Nicholas' baby. No doubt Het had not been sure either, of anything except that, this time, the herb tea hadn't worked. She tried other things after that, but still she thickened. One couldn't turn the customers away, and she had to go on taking men up till the day the labour started; then when it had, she lay down on the bed and told Simon to lock the door and go and bring out his fiddle, so they would think if they came that there was still somebody inside and go away. "Play me the tune your father rode away to," she said, and he knew what that was, for she herself had taught it to him, long ago, by whistling it to him; it was 'Sheriffmuir'. Robin Aske had whistled it too, she said, the time he'd come over to say goodbye, with the braid on his hat and a sword by his side for the Pretender, and had asked if she was sure she had the paper quite safe. Later on, she said, she'd been a fool, and had given that to Nicholas for what it was worth to him and them. "They'd taken away your father's lands, by then, for riding north, and given them to Nick and Old Madam," she said, "so what did it matter?" It might, had she thought of it, have mattered to Simon in the end; but Big Het was not far-seeing or provident.

Simon played on and then played other tunes, till it was growing dark and the wind rose outside, and later came rain; no one would come trudging up now, his mother said, and he could stop playing and light the bit of candle they had, for as long as it would last, and then perhaps it would be all over and they could sleep. But the pains were on her now and had already continued a long time, and they had no more candles. The one they had guttered down at last to the size of a dice, of Simon's thumb, blowing sideways in the draught, and then went out, spluttering; the boy went then and got some of the dry twigs from his corner and mended the fire, which gave light for a bit, and then faded, and by that time the storm had risen higher. His mother was moaning by now and for a while he knelt by her, and listened to her and to the storm, hoping now against hope that somebody would come; but on a night such as this they'd all be at home now, he knew, the men, or in the tavern where it was warm. No one would come here tonight, and he knew now Het needed help; in the end, gasping, she asked him to go down after all and fetch the old woman.

"Tell her I'll pay when I can," she said. "It's not going to come by itself. Not in time, anyhow; I'm done, or very near." And she babbled something to him about the paper she'd given Nicholas, and Madam had taken it, and had made them tear the other page out of the parish book. It all meant nothing to Simon, everything now was a matter only for fear, and he knew that perhaps this time his mother would die.

He ran out into the storm as she had bidden, not even remembering to put more wood on the fire. Afterwards he wept bitterly that his mother should have been left alone in the cold. But now he ran swiftly at first against the driving rain, determined with all the force of his will to save her, and bring the old woman, no matter what it would cost. He would play his fiddle night and day if it would save Big Het.

The old woman was not in her cottage, which was at the end of the village street. After knocking vainly at her darkened door for a while, he tried others; they mostly, seeing the soaked little dark figure who had come running down from Big Het's on the bluff, shut them again in his face if they answered at all; most were asleep, and it was past midnight. In the end, shouted against the noise of the storm, Simon had an answer; the old woman had gone up to Aske many hours since, and would not be back till morning. The voice, which was a woman's, called on that Mrs. Dorothy had been taken that day with her pains too early, and the child wouldn't come for any of them up there, but Simon had not waited for her to finish. He ran on, for the night was darker now and his mother was still alone and ill up there in the cottage, without any candle and without food and aid. The folk in the other houses he knew would not in any case come out; they would say it was a judgment on Het, and other such things they had said before.

He ran on along the dark road, stumbling often, for it had ruts and potholes, till he came to the gate of Aske where the lodge too was dark and empty; then he continued along the mile-long road he had once walked with his mother. It was smooth enough for carriages by day; now, with the dark, Simon fell twice again and grazed his knees, but got up and ran on, in the storm which still blew; black as the nether pit it was now, black as hell, and hell's devils in the wind and rain; they slapped Simon's face and drove the hair into his eyes, and soaked and beat at his thin little body. He was nine years old, running against death; and at last he saw the lights of the great house of Aske, which was astir, and ran on and found the door open into the great hall, as it always was, and went in.

The hall was empty, though a fire blazed in it. He did not stop to warm himself there, or take time to remember the place itself and the tall, green-eyed woman who had once come and looked at him, then shown him and his mother the door. He went on up the staircase he had seen that day, past a portrait in a rose-coloured coat, with sconces blazing; and along a passage where there were more sconces lit. Then he came to a room where everyone in the house, servants and family, seemed to be assembled. His own breaths were still rasping and at first, with that and the storm, he did not hear the other sounds, that came from the great bed below the tester. On it was a coloured coverlet, bright in the light of many candles which made the room unbearably warm. In the bed was a young woman with golden hair darkened with sweat. She was in labour, like his mother; like Het, she strained and moaned.

Simon was sorry for the girl in the bed, but she had so many folk about her, including the old woman whom he now saw, that she would not lack aid. So he made his way, thrusting through the crowd who took no notice of him, till he could reach the old woman and shake her by the shoulder, and tell her about Het. The old woman turned, and when she saw him she screamed once. After that there was a noise all through the room, and on the bed things happened differently. Simon tried, through the noise and the sounds of birth, to tell someone again about his mother, but nobody would listen or come.

It was Nicholas who took him from the room; Nicholas, in a sullen humour because, after it all, there was only a girl, no son yet to inherit. He kicked Simon downstairs and, following, marched him across the hall by his scruff and the seat of his breeches, and to the door. Simon still tried to tell Nicholas, anyone, that Het was dying, she would die if no one went up to aid her, and for hours now she had been quite alone . . .

But Nicholas paid no other heed than to cast Simon out again into the black night and the storm, aiding departure by a well-placed final kick from the toe of his boot. Then, perhaps, he went back and found wine and drank to himself and to his new-born daughter, who would be called Ann Aske. It was not yet certain whether or not the mother would live.

Big Het had not. By the time Simon limped home again it was early morning, the thin grey light staring in on a cold hearth of ashes. It stared also at Het, who was long dead and cold, the baby dead also, waxen in colour, still lying between her thighs. Shortly Simon went and got Alf's fiddle and carried it, with a few of his belongings wrapped in a bundle, and walked away from the cottage on the bluff. He did not go through the village again. He did not know where he was going. But he had already made a vow, in words not those of a child at all, to be revenged on the House of Aske and to break and master it and every soul in it, including the child who last night had been born: and that if it took him the rest of his life.

Then he started out on the road.

5

I WAS TO know Simon better as the years passed than anyone, and this knowledge I had of what had happened to him after Het died—I do not think even Prossy knew of it—helped me to understand the traits of character that had emerged, perhaps, from the first tender matrix, hardened and asserted themselves, sometimes however still revealing a streak of softness and pity such as he had showed for Prossy and, later, was to do for me. At such times one could glimpse the earlier Simon, the little boy who had handed his coins to his mother and had run later for her through the wild dark. No darkness now, of fear or of the mind deterred Simon; he was flint to Ann, using her as an instrument, almost, of wrath, although he was never physically cruel. But out of the twisted curse and the vow only this remained to do; he had, perhaps, broken Old Madam, but Peter's destruction had been his own and his ancestors'. Nicholas was dead. So, if it signified, was old Laban Carden, whose unyielding, bitter quality showed often in Simon himself. It had been cruel of Laban to disown his daughter, to cast her out in misfortune and leave her to the only fate that could otherwise be hers once they had killed her lover; and he had judged Het also for that acceptance. All this was in Simon too, except perhaps the implacable judgment; he could act swiftly, impulsively, cruelly enough, but could never hold a grudge against a living being always close to him. For he had Big Het's qualities as well; her generous gaiety, her looks and height, her wantonness sometimes, and—I used to imagine I heard her in him—laughter. And he had Robin also, the gay fine father back in the shadows, and farther back again Old Madam herself, with her strong will and her beauty, and the good and bad in her. Add to all this that I loved the many people Simon himself was and could be, and that he would soon mean the whole of my life; where else could I be than at Aske, loving him and saying nothing of it?

Shortly after that first talk we had had he moved his gear
back out of Ann's rooms, though he still visited her. He
would sleep, again, as before his marriage, in the great
upstairs bedchamber Nicholas had once had, and it was
there, in the end, that I would go to him. But that did not
happen yet, and in the meantime I must continue with his
tale.

This part is brief, for I loathe it. After the boy Simon had
walked several miles along the road that day he was
hungry, but had no means of buying a meal. As time
passed he smelled a savoury smell of cooking and left the
highway to follow it. In due course he came on a tramp,
cooking a hare over a fire. This man was Snib—all tramps
in a certain part of the country have this name, like other
men take Bully or Gaffer for themselves—Snib Ray. Simon
came up and asked if he could have the bones of the hare
afterwards, and some gravy. The man looked him over and
asked what he had in his bundle, and if it would pay for a
meal; Simon brought out his fiddle. When the tramp had
heard him play he knew he would give Simon not one meal
but many, for his own fortune was made. So he gave him a
portion of the hare to eat; and when the boy had eaten,
the man stood up and brought out a piece of corded rope
which he had by him.

There are poor children I have heard of in the cities who
beg for bread. Some are child-harlots, such as Prossy had
been, whose small bodies are abused to earn money for
brutal men or women who take their youth away and, if
they have any, their health. Other children's eyes have
been rubbed with acid to blind them, to inflame the lids so
that the ulceration may arouse pity in passers-by, who
throw them a coin; or perhaps their limbs have been
broken and re-set in twisted fashion. Poor scabbed maimed
children, monsters at fairs, who should not have survived
birth, perhaps live on; all these, and other horrors, to fill the
pockets of those who, often, have made them as they are;

this still happens. But the thing that happened then to Simon fills me with so fierce an anger it seems even now like the devil's mark. For that man, whatever he may once have been, however he was as he had become by now, was like those spoken of in Holy Writ, in that it would be better for them were a millstone cast about their neck and they with it, into the depths of the sea. I hope that man is in hell now, in the flames. He beat Simon with the rope until he could neither stand nor run away; he beat him till he was incontinent of his water, and vomited up the food he had eaten where he lay on the ground. Then—and this is the part my mind will not stomach, and yet it happened. The man was a sodomite. He used Simon in this way, up and down the country, for a year; first attached to the end of the rope, then later, when he had bought one, to a padlocked chain.

He also made the boy play. He took him about, up and down the roads in the part farther west than Aske, where no one knew Simon. There was almost nightly demand for playing in barns and, once, at a fair, as Simon had himself planned to do for Big Het. But none of the money now went to Big Het's son, or into anybody's pocket but the tramp's, who had a plausible tale. If Simon had not had old Laban's determined heart in him, and some matter of his own as well, I think that he would have gone on trailing at the rope's end till he died, not of old age, playing at that man's bidding to all comers. He could not shed Snib Ray; he was attached, now, by a long chain made by a blacksmith, one end of it round his waist, fastened there with a key Snib kept always safe about his own neck, inside the soiled and greasy shirt. Snib kept hold of the other end by having first hooked it round his body, so that even while he slept Simon could not writhe free. Snib told the audiences, when after any performance they would go round with Snib's cap to collect the money, that Simon was his son and must wear the chain always, to prevent him harming himself; he took fits, Snib said; look at the way he couldn't hold his water.

Simon, by now a small, defeated, filthy animal, did not say anything. He dared not. Every so often, to keep him where he belonged, Snib said, the tramp would beat him, after they were alone; beat him as he had done that first evening when they had shared the hare together and afterwards, Simon's stomach had cast the food up again on the ground where he lay in his tears.

6

IT WAS NOT, with all the above, until some weeks before his eleventh birthday that Simon could make up his mind to kill the tramp, as the only means of again being free. By then he had grown as cowed as some kicked and beaten lurcher that slinks back to the heel of a brute; it was by far more difficult now, for he was less resolute, than if he had done it just after he left home. He had grown by this time, for with the money he made with his fiddle they fed, and Snib Ray drank, well enough. Simon could not see his own face, which beneath the dirt had grown oval now and pale, except for the sunburn, with a mouth and long lashes like a girl's, fringing the great dark eyes; a woman at one of the kirns had exclaimed about it, and how he was like a little lass. But he saw, like a lass's also, the growth of his own long, slender limbs, like daffodil-stalks, the skin fine as a woman's, and his hands with the slim tapering fingers which were, but only because of the fiddle-playing, strong. He knew all this, and the way he had outgrown his clothes in the year they had been on the road. And fear was growing in him also, deeper than the fear he had of being beaten, of the chain, anything; and it was because of that, because, in himself, he knew he might grow womanish and effete, no longer a boy or, if it went on, with no prospect of being a man either, that he must kill Snib Ray.

He killed him with a stone. When I heard that story from Simon I shuddered, thinking how a stone had joined us in our childhood misery; Peter's stone, and now this. Simon had not used any sling against Goliath. He had waited, planned and again waited through the drunkenness and weary filth—this day of the week when certain men get particularly drunk was once, they say, a Papist fast, and, by now unaware, they mock it—till one Friday; and accordingly Snib that night was as drunk as a pig. They were in a wood, and near by—Simon had been looking for some time now, but here it was, within reach—a large stone lay. Once Snib was asleep Simon reached out his hand, and cautiously, in order not to wake the sleeping tramp, for a jerk to the chain would do so, scrabbled the stone over towards him till it was in his fingers' grasp. He took hold of it with both hands. "Then," he said, "I hammered it hard down on his temple, and smashed and smashed until he was dead. He gave one jerk, no more; but I had to be sure. Afterwards I looked round his neck for the key he always kept on a cord there, and took it out." He had had, he said also, a moment's horror in which he had seen himself unable to find the key, and lying chained to the corpse until it rotted, or they came and found him and took him away to be hanged for Snib Ray's murder. He had thought of all that, and risked it. But the key was there, and Simon unlocked the chain from his waist and stood up. His legs were shaking by now and he felt sick; but he groped to where Snib always kept the fiddle under his own body, as an additional safeguard to the keeping of Simon; he never let the boy have it, or his bow, till they were going to play for money. Simon took the fiddle and bow, turned round, saw Snib's shattered head again and covered it over with leaves. After that he was sick. Then he took the fiddle and, walking resolutely, made his way downhill out of the wood and out of that part of the country. Shortly he found a hay wain and hid in it, letting it carry him wherever it was going; then he rolled off it, still unseen

among the piled hay, and lay in a ditch till night fell and
then walked on, by himself, keeping his direction next day
by the sun, until he was well south of the tramp's country.

"What did you do with the fiddle?" I asked. I had never
heard Simon play, and did not know, until he told me
about it, that he had ever done so.

He looked away for a moment. "I buried it, in the end,"
he said, "and the bow."

I gave a cry, and he made a little, sideways grimace with
his mouth. "They might have known me by it, that is
true," he said, "but that was not the reason. Oh, I saw to it
that no one would use it again; I smashed it first, and then
I broke the bow."

"Why?" I cried. "Why?"

"Alf had left it to me," he said. "He didn't intend that
anyone else should have it. And I—well, I found I couldn't
play it any more. I have never played again."

7

WHAT HAPPENED AFTER that he could not altogether
remember. Time passed, as it always does; he would not
go, for nearly another two years, anywhere near a city, or
humanity very much where they assemble at markets and
fairs. Firstly he was still afraid of being hanged for killing
Snib, and secondly he had no means of knowing whether
or not anyone else, if he approached them, might not be
another such. So he hunted alone.

This in the autumn in England, with berries thick in the
hedges, is not hard. The nights are crisp, but there is
generally a barn or hayrick; and there is enough to eat.
There was even, one year, an abundance of ripe blackberries, and Simon sold some early in the day to a woman
who sat at her booth in a market-town, escaping before the
crowds arrived. By that time, though, he had a chip-basket,

which means he must already have been with the tinkers. They, before they moved north again, had taught Simon, or rather he had learned for himself while among them, how to make these. The tinkers are passive, resigned folk, descended, they say, from Jacobites who took to the heather a generation ago, and the one before. As time went on they forgot how to live under a roof, and never returned to one even after it became safe. They taught Simon to make baskets out of woven strips of birch-bark or soaked osiers, and to make brooms with long handles, which could be sold. He also learned to steal.

But the winter is another matter and Simon, who was still not twelve years old and had always had a roof over him till last year, was not yet seasoned as tinker-children are, for if they cannot live in the open they must die. He took an ague at last and shivered, too hot and then too cold; they left him behind without, perhaps, intending to, and by now he had a lurcher of his own which stayed with him. The two hunted together when he was well enough— he had recovered, by himself, in the end—and when they were hungry stole chickens and eggs, and once spent three whole days in a loft full of stored apples. The scent of these was ever afterwards memorable to Simon; I would see his eyes grow remote sometimes at Aske, eating an apple fresh from the tree, and know he was thinking of the lurcher, whose name was Kit. Kit died the following autumn, while he was with her, for no reason, neither poison nor a gun. She had not been a young dog when he got her.

He was solitary again now for the third time in his life, and this may partly have dictated his next step; it is probably that he had the whole thing planned from the beginning. He had realised, when among the tinker-children who could neither read nor write, that he knew, for Alf had taught him, a little more than they, but not enough to answer all the questions they asked. He also found that he had even forgotten some of what he once

knew in Alf's day. On this realisation, he took himself to
school.

This is not easily done without any money, and Simon
had only what he could make from brooms, baskets and
blackberries. But he went to the door of a lady who merits
description, for she was a legend almost as far as Aske. She
ran a dame-school, held near a village by herself only; her
name was Lolly Pate. Simon, when she opened the door a
crack, addressed her in the ingratiating way of tinkers.
"Would you be wanting any work, my lady?"

Lolly had been going to refuse; Simon had not yet
washed himself. She was a timid, bespectacled spinster in a
man's round cloth cap, which she wore pulled over her ears
for warmth, and pinned under that a grey shawl. Her gown
was long, to hide her men's boots, which she wore because
they lasted longer, and there were mittens on her poor
chilblained fingers. Simon noticed these. "I can chop
wood, lady, for a fire," he said, and smiled, and Lolly was
lost.

"I cannot pay you very much," she quavered. "Would a
meal—?"

Simon ate the meal. By the time it was finished he had
made an arrangement with Lolly Pate about his schooling.
He would, he said, draw water, chop logs daily from the
surrounding woods, scrub floors after school, light fires
before it, clean everything, milk the goat—Lolly to her
terror had one of these, a black one with horns, from
whom with much travail she drew enough milk, sometimes, for butter as well. Simon had never milked a goat
before, but let her believe he knew everything except what
one could learn in school.

However it was, he stayed. He stayed till Lolly had given
him in all she could in the way of teaching, and when he
had drained the last drop of information from the poor
soul, he left. He left with a working acquaintance of
elementary history, mostly Roman, and the use of the
globes (Lolly had an old pair salvaged from her own days

as governess, which had ended in such a way as to make a tale of its own), and how to spell as well as the next man. He also had a knowledge of Dr. Johnson's Dictionary and parts of the Bible, which he could read if he wanted to, and other books: and, above all, and transcendently, mathematics. For Lolly was a mathematician *manquée*, a brilliant brain under the shawl, not only for a woman but for anyone, anywhere. Being one of those underrated creatures, and without money or friends, she had made nothing more of it till Simon came; then he became her joy and, later, her memorial. From doing his first sums on a slate wiped clean with spittle and his sleeve, he progressed, that first winter, to the monetary system, algebra and the theorems, logarithms and the stock-exchange, and before he left they had started calculus, when they came to the end of what Lolly knew.

So he left her. He was now thirteen, and after two years took again to the road. Poor Lolly had now no one to milk the goat (it was in kid, Simon said, and she could sell it) but he himself had a lighter heart than formerly. For during the last school holidays he had nerved himself, braced himself, to go back up by night into the tramp's country and go, for the first time since it all happened, to the place in the wood where he had left the body, its pulped head covered over by leaves. There in the dawn's light were still the bones, drifted over now with more leaves and earth. Nobody had yet discovered Snib but the birds, as was so evident that he could not, by now, have been identified as anyone at all, and no longer mattered.

There was another place to see. On his way back from looking at Snib's unabsolved, clean bones, Simon came to Aske. It was not to the great house, which he would never see again till he owned it; but he passed through the village, and not by the street, I have heard them myself speak down there in my youth about Big Het's varmint, who they remember stole the pears. Simon would not have

stolen pears or anything else while he was at Big Het's, no
matter how hungry they were; he had, for what it was
worth, been reared in the strict tradition of Laban Carden.
But Laban was dead now, and there was, besides, another
death.

Simon slept that night in the spinney beyond the bluff,
from which one cannot yet see Aske. The ground, he
remembers, was white with wood-anemones like snowdrift,
and there were early primroses. He lay in the young grass
and stared at them and heard a dead-bell ring, down at the
church, and it went on till dark had fallen. It was for Mrs.
Dorothy, who had that day died in childbed giving birth to
Peter Aske. The customary rejoicings over an heir may
have accounted for the slackness of the village over its
stored pears as Simon passed through. But what no one
would account for, then or at any time, was the influence
the tinker-boy now lying in the wood would have, in due
course, on the halfling thing Peter Aske would in a few
years be when he was grown, and old enough to get
himself to a gaming-table. And there he would gamble
away his inheritance, his house and, last of all, his sister to
a tall man with dark eyes and hair, a set mouth and good
shoulders, who seemed to have the devil's own luck at
cards, and won and won. Nobody could foresee all that as
Simon heard the dead-bell ring out for young Dorothy
over Aske, at a time when, perhaps, he renewed his vow.

8

SIMON HAD MADE his way to London by November.
For a country boy, who has never seen the city before, to
come to take up some situation, perhaps, which awaits
him, or, in different circumstances, escorted by his parents
to a public-school, or still later society and the gaming-
table, is one thing; for Simon Carden it was quite another.
Although he knew that the city would be where his

fortune must be made, he was not yet certain how this was to be done, except that it would be. He had resolved on that, but meantime he had no money, no friends, and nowhere to sleep. At first, as anyone might do who did not know London, he lost himself in the honeycomb of huddled, dirty streets where the poor lived, though they were not yet as bad as they became later, in the days of the factories and sweated labour, when one could hardly see the sky. But Simon soon found his way out of the poor districts and into the others, where there were wider streets and noble squares, sometimes a lilac tree in a garden and, constantly at all hours except early morning, a coming and going of grandly dressed people. With these, he knew already, his fortune would in some manner lie.

The difficulty was to draw himself to their attention. He was not, or not yet, clad in powder, flowered waistcoats and full-skirted coats, with high-heeled shoes like a woman's, and a hat too small to wear, held by courtesy under one arm. He studied these beaux with interest, and the ladies also, who were as grandly clad if not more so, with towering hair on which perched artificial ships and flowers; many of them nevertheless, he afterwards remembered, stank.

But he himself was in rags, or very near; the time at Lolly's had not permitted of new clothes, and he had walked a long way since then. He was wearing his customary threadbare shirt, which he had washed himself now and again and hung on a branch by a river; a short coat and breeches of homespun stuff; and his shoes, with much walking, were worn away at the soles. He had tied them on with cord from a farm-sack, taken from a barn where he had slept on the way; soon this also wore through, but by then Simon discovered that he could do better barefoot.

This state he saw had its compensations in that, when the rich notice the poor at all, they do it more readily if they have no shoes. Half-naked children, standing begging in the snow-filled winter gutters; slippery urchins diving to hold a gentleman's horse; all these, with chilblained toes bare, made the odd coin, but such activities, Simon decided, are unsteady at best; the most hopeful was street-sweeping. He soon saw them at it once or twice, for the money of course was better in the rich parts of town. They would hover beyond doorways, waiting for some great lady to come out, or else alight from her coach to go inside, guarding her petticoats which were hooped, draped, and heavy with embroidery or fringes, from the muddy space between doorstep and mounting-block. This space was kept clean as a whistle, three seasons of the year, by barefoot children wielding brooms. Simon bided his time, and looked for a stance.

He had meantime found himself a place to sleep, which was called a hide, and this was peopled by others who had what was, by this time, his own rascally appearance. Simon's black hair stood out now, for he had no comb, in a shock round his thin young face; the soles of his feet were hard as horn, and he was starving, though he had already run one or two errands to make a bite. Nobody would, he knew, employ him regularly till his looks improved; but how were they to do so without employment? In the hide, at nights, he thought about it. This was a space of a kind fairly prevalent in large cities, which belongs to nobody interested and can be reached from the street above, by means of a short flight of broken steps, littered with refuse, filth and smashed glass. Simon slept there for a week before he took a day out in the country again, ignoring the clamouring of his empty belly which could have been filled, a little, by further horse-holding, and found a wood and cut himself twigs and withies, and made a broom, as the tinkers had taught him. Next day he went straight back with it to a place he had been watching, which seemed to be nobody's, and where a great many well-dressed folk went in and out, mostly in the evenings. In the meantime, it rained.

He swept the pavement all that day and the next, for it

was still raining, but made less money than he had done at
the horses; the great beaux, although their towering wigs
got wet, had their high French heels to mince upon, and
splashed their full coat-skirts very little, so they were
stingy with their rewards. This, no doubt, Simon thought,
must be the reason why the stance had not been already
taken. However there seemed no other available, and
Simon decided to stay for one more day before going
elsewhere. In the end he was rewarded. A carriage drew up
at last, and out stepped a lady; or at the least, as Simon
put it afterwards, she was wearing silk. This rustled
agreeably, and as she passed by Simon smelled a scent of
violet-powder, and she pressed a coin into his hand, smiling
to display ruined teeth. He had an instant's impression of
childlike hazel eyes; otherwise she was much painted,
getting stout, was perhaps fifty years old and had never
been beautiful. But the coin was sixpence, and Simon was
so gratified he smiled. That smile, as with poor Lolly, may
have been the reason for many things which befell later.
For Simon had kept his teeth, and they were white; and
his charm, after a sojourn with the tinkers and with Lolly,
was now formidable; Maria Gore sensed it at once.

"You're a new rascal," she said. "I have not seen you
here before. Where are you from?" The end of the speech
deviated somewhat from the mincing gentility of its
commencement, and gave away one thing about the lady
to Simon; she was desirous of rising in the world a little
farther than she had done already, and so was he.

Maria, had he yet known, was based on somewhat surer
foundations than her appearance might lead one to
suppose; she was, among other things, a brothel-madam.
She did not live at this establishment, which she owned
and visited occasionally, to ensure that all was well and
that nobody was making off with the money. Maria had
her own reasons for guarding and respecting money, of
which by now she had a great deal; one of her husbands,

the third, had run off some time ago with much of it, but she had now recouped her losses to some extent, and had never risked a fourth husband. Now—though such a consummation could hardly be expected from their meeting that day on the steps—she saw Simon. She said nothing more than she had done, however, and he told her a lie about his origins and made off presently with his broom and the sixpence, with which latter he bought pies at a barrow. But he hoped not to have seen the last of the open-handed old queen—the phrase occurred to him later, not then—and next day again he was back at the pavement-space. Maria did not, however, put in a further appearance for almost a week.

One day Simon found the pavement swept already. It was the day Maria often came and by now, he had begun to think of himself as entitled to the stance. So when the sixpence was filched, at noteworthy speed, by another barefoot individual, a stocky lad with ginger hair, Simon was aware of outrage. Maria, who had of course appeared, knew the boy; said "Ha, Ginger, so you're back; where've you been?" and swept down into her waiting chair. Simon, while gratified that she had not troubled to wait for Ginger's reply, had nevertheless his own score to settle, and did not delay long enough to allow the bearers to move off with Maria. He and Ginger started at once to fight.

"'S my lay," the latter was saying, between punches, with give and take. He was shorter but more solid than Simon, as if there were good cooking somewhere behind him, and he might have been perhaps a year older. There was no doubt that Simon, at the beginning, expected Ginger to win, and had determined to give as good an account of himself as he could, and then perhaps retire gracefully. But in the process a knot of gentlemen, he had leisure to observe, had gathered on the steps. They were laying wagers; some of them began to cheer Ginger on, and others himself. Maria's sedan-chair, as Simon did not yet see, had also stopped in its tracks, and Maria and the bearers were watching, the former standing up, hands on hips below her lavender silk mantle. She did not, she told Simon afterwards, care which of the little bastards won, but it was a diversion; they had gone in, she also told him, to it like the chubs, and she wanted to see the end.

It was at this moment that Simon became aware of his devil, urging him on. The devil told him, coolly and in so many words, that if he could attract notice by winning the fight, it would be a better investment than losing it. He must therefore, the devil said, be or become stronger and more cunning than Ginger, with better footwork than Ginger, with a punch to the stomach, a punch to the face, the nose, anywhere as long as it was hard enough, then side-step out of the way. And so he did; and after a time, with blood running from his own nose and a sensation, beyond pain and quite beyond fear, that his body was a puff-ball, resilient, unafraid, and could fairly give an account of itself, he punched; right into Ginger's midriff, and the other boy doubled up, cursing, then drew a great gasp of breath and again came on. Several carriages had by now stopped, and had disgorged some of their occupants, if male, into the street to watch; the ladies however stayed for the most part in their cushioned places, screaming, except for Maria. It was better than a cock-fight, someone said; by Hector, both cocks were game! And that was, again this time, Maria. She had climbed altogether out of the chair by now and was standing not far off, over the boys, as it were, holding coats; the lavender hood had fallen back from her wig, her paint was garish, and her eyes were shining like a young girl's. "That was a turn-up, hey?" she called out to the men on the steps, as Simon won.

If he had not won, if Ginger had sent him sprawling in the end, what would have happened to him? Would he have

crawled back, beaten and shamed, to the hide, thereafter
to vanish into the obscurity of poverty, the uncertainty of
want, and never more be heard of? I do not believe this; I
think some other opportunity would have occurred for
Simon, perhaps not involving Maria Gore. By then, he
knew his devil, had made his acquaintance, in that fight;
perhaps he had also helped Simon, unknowing, to kill Snib
Ray with a stone. But Maria would, at least, help him
further on the way even than Lolly had done.

She was not herself, or not officially, involved any
further, however, in the meantime; she had remembered
fights weren't a lady's business, and had taken herself off
in her sedan at last after a single brief, picturesque
expletive at the sight of Ginger now, and the sight of
Simon. Then she left word for the latter to be taken inside,
sponged down first, and afterwards fed to keep his inside
where it ought to be, because she dared say it was heaving.
So this was done. Simon was taken—by other hands than
the beaux', who had now dispersed, yawning a little, to
other business—round by the servants' door, not the front
with the fanlight, to nether regions where in short
course—and this had never happened to him before in his
life—a huge, beaming negress, in a turban, gold earrings,
and an immense fichu of French lawn, brought in a tub
and filled it up with hot water. Then she washed Simon in
it all over. He emerged newly white, cleansed and refreshed
so that he hardly felt the bruises, even his rapidly swelling
left eye. He felt better, already, than he had done since
leaving Lolly's. And after that they fed him.

That was the beginning. He did not, however, sleep in that
house or the other one of Maria's yet; at nights he still
went back to the hide. By day, at first, he was employed
in various ways too uncertain to have an official name such
as footman, which later he became. He was too young
meantime for this, and too tall, Maria told him, for a page;
he'd better be a thrower-out. As it happened, this was

never needed, for the establishment, like most others of its kind, was decorous. Simon changed, in the morning hours before he stood on duty by the door, or followed Maria to the card-room, from his rags into livery. This was of brocade, crimson one year and green the next; and they put a wig on him over his hair, which had to be cut as it would no longer comb, and had lice in it. Later it would grow again and be kept clean; by the time Simon became a full-fledged footman he would wear powder, but preferred the wig; it was less trouble and the colour did not show through by the day's end. For the time, all this was his daily wear. He spent much time studying the delicate tracery of the fanlight, from inside the entrance-hall above the door; at other times, although less leisurely, he might survey the young ladies. They would run downstairs and out very briefly, in their off-duty which was in the late morning or early afternoon; they were pretty and demure, in chip-hats, not dressed in any brazen fashion. There was one young negress (she was in fact the daughter of the cook) like carved satinwood, graceful as a slim tree, with dark, liquid eyes; she used always to smile at Simon in a shy way, and sometimes the rest chaffed him about it. They seemed well fed and kept and looked after by the manager, a thin little woman who might have been a mantua-maker or governess.

It was not for some time that Maria Gore discovered her luck, which came to her always when Simon stood behind her at the tables. After that she never played without him there, and the more she played the fonder she grew of Simon. She refused, in fact, a solid offer for him from a marquis, and another from a jaded beauty; had either of them made the offers direct to Simon it is uncertain what might have happened. But although he had his palm greased a little from time to time, and received presents, he perceived that the luck might be of value to himself in other ways than standing behind a chair. He watched every move of the cards he could see, and some that, officially at any rate, he could not. By the end of six months he had a working acquaintance with all hands at a game of loo, and by the end of the year faro and whist. This faculty, allied as it was to the progress he had made at Lolly's, would stand him in good stead when, as happened later, he came to embrace all forms of gaming. For the present, though, the luck was Maria's. She did not forget to reward Simon; if she had, no doubt, he would have left her. Once early on she gave him a guinea, which was more money than he had ever had in his life; the first time it happened he did not know how to spend it, and wandered about the booths when he was free, then bought himself a shirt and hose. Another time Maria gave him comfits in a box tied with blue ribbon, that someone had given her; and, again, a cane with a silver top like a major-domo's, to hold while he stood behind her chair. He did not spend all his gift-money or wages, or eat all the comfits himself by this time; he gave some of everything, in each case, by then to Prossy.

He had been making his way back to the hide one night, carrying the bundle of bread and scraps the cook always gave to him to take away, when he saw a thin, fluttering little twist of rags come up to him in the half-dark, blown on the cold wind. It revealed itself as hung on a framework of bones; Prossy, soliciting. Even at that time, when her eye was not so bad, Simon said, the sight of her shocked him. He had known, or believed himself, to be beyond shock or horror; but he was never beyond pity, and the pity he felt for this child—she hadn't known, she assured him, that it wasn't a man, he was so tall, but now she could see it was only a boy, sorry—made Simon take her with him to the only available place, which was the cemetery, and sit down with her on a tombstone where they shared the scraps. Afterwards—Maria's guinea had not yet transpired—he told Prossy he was sorry not to be able to give her any money. "But I will later, whenever I can," he said. Already he believed in his own luck enough to be able to say so.

They had not done anything that time except eat, which he saw she did ravenously. This made Simon ashamed; she was a scrap of a thing, younger and far worse off than he was. Prossy told him, on enquiry, about the grandmother. Then she offered, as a matter of business, the only recompense she knew for the bread and scraps, if it was any good to him. Simon shook his head, aware of how easy she was to talk to. "I can't," he said, "not yet, at any rate." He could likewise not yet tell Prossy, or anyone, about Snib Ray.

Afterwards—he would often meet Prossy after that, on the tombstone, which had been a Tudor dignitary's, any time his work and her customers slackened and they could both get away—it was usually in daylight—afterwards, when he knew Prossy better and felt less knotted and afraid inside himself, he told her about the tramp. She nodded wisely. "There's some like that," she said. "I know there's some, though I ha'n't never dealt with them; wouldn't stand to reason, would it?" And she smiled, with thin closed lips like an old woman's, up at him. "Let me show you some time, when you feel like it, if you like," she told him. "It's easy; nothing really, and I don't mind if it's you."

It had comforted Simon, as later it was to comfort me, to know that his had not been the only twisted nightmare of a childhood, and also that Snib Ray, as Prossy said so, was not the only one of his kind in the world. After that he did finally, once or twice, establish his manhood with the help of Prossy's thin grateful skeleton of a little body, for nothing of course, as she put it, except the food, on the cold tomb.

Even in those days he realised what she had done for him and would not, as he also told her one day, ever forget her or, meantime, let her go hungry again. And he never did.

After that there was Maria.

It happened long after Prossy had come to Simon's

knowledge in all ways; by then, he was a house-footman at her place in Grosvenor Street. He slept now with two of the others, older than himself, in a little, stuffy box at the top of the house which could scarcely be called an attic, for it was more like a cupboard without shelves. It had hooks on the wall where they hung their clothes, and a corner for the powder-jar and cone, which they must all use on their hair daily and otherwise, somehow, keep themselves clean, for a footman must never stink. Otherwise there was just room to sleep, one broad back against another. But it was at least a roof, and warm, if too warm sometimes; better than the hide, though there was perhaps less privacy.

Simon had been there for over a year by now and was in his fourth year as footman, and although he was still very young he was tall and looked, as Maria told him later and other women, in different words, had perhaps told him already, like Adonis when he was undressed. He had a broad chest and shoulders, white skin, taut narrow hips and his limbs, a young man's by now, were strong, straight and comely. He was, I can well imagine, like a healthy young tree, a sapling; and Maria Gore was running out of health and sap.

She sent for him one evening on some pretext after the card-players had departed. She was in her bedroom, about to take off the red and white stuff from her face, but had not yet done so. She was looking in her mirror, and beyond it saw Simon's reflection as he came into the room, after tapping respectfully on her door first for admittance. He was wondering why she had sent for him; luckily he hadn't taken off his brocade coat yet, or washed out the powder. He was tired, as always at the end of the long day, spent standing; he hoped she wouldn't keep him long.

But Maria seemed oblivious of the correctness of Simon's appearance, of the time, or anything except herself. She went on looking, as if she had never seen it before, at her own face reflected in the glass, the latter's oval shape contained in a gilt frame whereon cherubs pranced in baroque. Below, the table was cluttered with haresfoot and violet-powder, amber and musk in a dozen assorted pots and little jars. But none of these could do much good, as Simon saw the face now; an old trout's, with the raddled lips and cheeks drawing the eye, rather than otherwise, to the wrinkled neck yellow in its fat, running unchecked down to the bosom.

And above it all were her eyes, the sad and, somehow, childlike hazel eyes of Maria Gore. It was the eyes, Simon said afterwards, that made him tolerate her and the situation.

He spoke then, almost as he had done to Lolly Pate at the schoolhouse long ago. "Did you need anything else tonight, madam?" (Would you be wanting any work, my lady? By God, he thought, she would.)

Maria threw back her head then and gave her sharp roar of brittle laughter. Then she beckoned Simon. "Come," she said. "I'm not sure, you know, that I don't. You've known that for a week, lad. Come on."

Afterwards, long after, he told me that he had in the end grown quite fond of old Maria, in a way. She was really a fool with money and everything else, he said, although she tried to pretend she was so hard. He was able to help her about that, and several other things.

There were to be a great many different women in Simon's life, and in his way—always that, only that, perhaps—he was fond of all of them. What interested me also, and was perhaps another manifestation of his continuing luck, was that, neither from Prossy nor Maria nor anyone else, did he catch, then or later, the pox.

9

MARIA HAD HAD, when all was said, three husbands. The first was a widower when he married her, and had been out for many years with the East India Company, somewhat earlier than the time of Robert Clive. He had accordingly made a great deal of money, and was chosen by Maria's parents for her when she was fifteen and he was sixty-two. He probably, though one has no means of knowing, made Maria what she later became. There were no children. Her second husband, after the first had died at last, her own youth being long gone, was a younger man than she, rich also but not, this time, robust. Maria wore him out in five years. After that she had married again, but the third, a gentleman of some address—no one knew much about him even by Simon's day—ran off, as has been stated, shortly with another woman and some part at least of Maria's money. Later on, she heard, almost for certain, that he had died abroad. He never, then or later, resurrected himself for all the careful research undertaken by Henry Gore the lawyer, second cousin to Maria's first husband, who would otherwise have become the old man's heir on the decease of Maria herself and was, naturally, very much interested in what became of her money; he had in fact proposed to her on his own account, as soon as it was circumspect to do so. But Maria stayed free, and moreover still rich; she was, by this time, very rich indeed, for besides the Company's jointure she had two warehouses, from the second husband, which she filled with spoils from the connections of the first; they were at a port, and there was also a smaller place in London for the retail trade. Then there was the brothel, which paid very well and could be developed, and the card-houses, a third one of which was opened in Simon's time and of this, like the other concerns as time passed, he became manager. For Maria, who would not have been besotted enough for such a thing to happen without good reason, reaped the fruits of Lolly Pate's early instruction to Simon. His accounts were meticulous, and as happened at Aske afterwards he saved Maria a great deal in outlay and uncertainty, in such pursuits as employing several men to keep an eye on one another, instead of one man only, who could be trusted. And Maria did not tire of Simon himself, as might perhaps have been expected as the months passed, then the years. It was servitude of a kind, it is true, but by that time he was no longer her footman. And he had by now acquired, thanks to Lolly, Maria, the card-house clients, and other contacts during those years in London, an excellent notion of imports, exports, and the timely retail of foreign merchandise, as there were no enemies then at sea.

I have not at any time mentioned Maria's ruby necklace, though I have spoken of Henry Gore the lawyer, who raised the hue and cry about its loss and, as a result, had Simon transported for theft. It had naturally been a source of some chagrin to the lawyer to see himself supplanted, as it were, in his hopes by a young sprig from nowhere, except, no doubt, the gutter, and who had been a servant. Henry had poked about—the expression was Maria's—in all ways, down at the warehouses, everywhere else, trying to find a flaw in Simon's administration so that Maria might be prevailed upon to dismiss him, preferably in disgrace; the young fellow's insouciance struck Henry as improper, but his accounting was, at the least, too efficient to find any fault, and he seemed to be honest. The business also prospered, but Henry Gore had few hopes of benefit to himself by continuance of the present situation.

The affair of the necklace was, therefore, a godsend, although acquiring somewhat less publicity than the later episode of the same name in France. For one thing, the rubies were not very valuable ones; their setting was interesting, and had been done in India. The clasp broke while Maria was at cards and Simon, retrieving it, promised to have the stones cleaned and the necklace mended. Then, for the excitement of the game was mounting, he put it in his pocket and forgot about it. When Maria asked for it later, it could not be found.

It never was found, and what light-fingered person had

reaped the benefit was never known. Henry, hearing of the
matter and magnifying the lost gawd into an heirloom of
irreplaceable worth—it had in fact not even come to Maria
from the first marriage or the Company's spoils—informed
the authorities. Simon was arrested in the street, as could
happen very easily to a young man who, while having a
flair for figures, had not acquired money of his own, or
not at any rate enough to grease palms on the way. Henry
greased these copiously; Maria was represented as a
besotted, foolish and ageing woman under the influence of
an unscrupulous young ex-footman; the situation was not
without parallel, and when it came to the hearing of
Simon's case the young man was doomed. Maria herself,
by some palm-greasing of her own, in spite of Henry,
probably saved Simon from being hanged; when she heard
his sentence had been commuted to one of transportation
for fifteen years she fainted, and was carried out of the
courtroom an old woman, with no more to live for. She
died in fact within the year, and never played cards again.

Once more, Simon's fate rested with Prossy. Had Maria
had her wits by then, she might have thought of the
answer first; later it seemed simple enough.

This may seem strange, for a poor little scarred ruined
whore has no great wit, let alone influence; any more than
a young man of no connections, who at the end of such a
sentence might have grown hardened and calloused into a
recurrent criminal, as happened with others whose sen-
tences were renewed again and again after first innocence,
without their ever coming home. Prossy knew this, and
determined by whatever means, if it took all she had and
could make for the rest of her life, to save Simon.

She had also saved a bit of the money Simon by now
gave her, the old woman being dead so that it could be
kept safe. She put it all now into a purse and took it,
dressed in the best clothes she had, and veiled to hide her
eye, to a lawyer. Then she laid the purse on his table.
"That's all I've got for now," she said, "but I can make

more. Doesn't signify what it costs, he's got to be brought
back out of that place they've sent him to, for a thing he
didn't do; that Henry Gore's doing, it all was, but if
anything else is needed I'll say I took the bloody thing
myself." And here Prossy, not Simon who was by now in a
ship's hold in mid-Atlantic, had some luck; for not only
had the lawyer she had irrespectively chosen to go to a
deep-rooted dislike and distrust of Henry Gore, whom he
knew, but he was also, as far as can be achieved in that
profession, an honest man of humour as well as wit. He
took Prossy's money, however, and more that she made—
by the time Simon was brought back she was penniless
again, and ill, but said it had been worth it—but he found
the flaw. This was, by great good fortune, due to the
lawyer's own luck in contriving to see Maria for himself
shortly before she died and to disentangle her own
uncertainty and folly. Otherwise it might have sunk into
oblivion together with Big Het's marriage-lines.

I can remember Simon hesitating, for the first time in
his relation of all this, to tell me more, but I insisted. And
when at last he did tell me, I could see at once why he had
been unwilling. But the fact of it brought him home again,
and had it not done so I should never have known Simon,
nor would Aske. So it was worth it, like many things.

He had long ago been brought up from the gaol, where he
had spent four weeks, to the courtroom with eight others,
then afterwards back down to the gaol again. They waited
there till a ship should have space in its hold to take them
across seas to Barbados. Then, for the voyage which would
last nine weeks, they were thrust down into this stinking
hole, close-packed like herrings with twenty-four other
prisoners. Before that, for the vessel's life, others had lived
down there and eaten, slept, and voided into their own
excrement; there was hardly room to lie down. Several of
the men, as usually happened, became fevered and ill on
the voyage, and two died and were cast overboard, with

appropriate hymn-singing. Simon however lived, to land on
the island, where like most of the others he was indentured
to a sugar-planter. There, for a whole year, till Prossy's
lawyer had done his work (lawyers, God knows, have to be
slow to be certain) while the sun grilled down on their
sore, flayed backs, the prisoners, and Simon among them,
worked among the sugar-canes. He came to know many
men there, both black and white; some were slaves. The
overseer was like most overseers, a brute of the calibre
that had once walked the galleys of the Mediterranean.
He whipped the men as often and for as little as he chose,
the owner of the plantation being himself absent for most
of the year in America or England. The scars, which I have
myself seen on Simon's back, would harden with difficulty
until the sun and flies were left behind, when as often as
not they would burst open again under a fresh flogging.
But even so, after the day's excruciating work was done,
and the men had been paid a little, they could talk and
drink rum together in the huts where they lived, and
exchange information about one another and, sometimes
and many months late, word from home. This did not
come often. There were many prisoners on this and other
such plantations, many of them in servitude for life, there
or, a generation later, to Australia. Some of them were
from Simon's father's own time, the 'Forty-five Rising;
these were the fortunate ones who had escaped the rope,
bullets and drowning, or the block if they were of noble
blood. Most were not; many were Highlanders who had
followed a dead chief, and their soft, lilting voices would
sound by night against the cabin-walls, like a sad, old song
whose echoes had almost stilled. There were others from
even further back, from the 'Fifteen and the small
Spanish-aided fiasco four years later; and there was one
old, old fellow, tough as brown leather, from Monmouth's
day, seemingly indestructible as he had been sent out as a
boy of twelve. By now he was like the Apostle John on
Patmos, except for his foul tongue, and he had a long, very

dirty white beard down to his knees, and kept the pay-books now that he no longer worked in the fields.

More than all these Simon knew and grew to respect Samuel Grover, a little hunchback long ago grown dark as a gnome with the sun. He had aided an escaping lord, the brother and successor of the first Derwentwater, who like the latter ended by losing his head on Tower Green. Grover had himself escaped with a life-sentence. He had a brilliant brain—he had been a stock-broker formerly—and when they shared a hut together the two men would talk by the hour about finance, and markets, and the changes that had come everywhere and would continue. Later, to the profit of them both, Simon never rested till he had literally bought Grover's freedom, after much litigation and expense. This could not happen, of course, till after Prossy had at last contrived his own.

The news of this came, as such things did, quickly; he had not known the matter was afoot. One day he was a prisoner, flogged without right of protest, despised, over-worked, enslaved; the next he was free, had been bathed and shaved, and was awaiting a ship home. Maria was dead, he heard at once; the news came with the lawyer's letter. For the rest, Simon was reinstated, and this now meant a great deal; for Maria had left him the warehouses, their connections, all of her own money which was not tied up in the Company jointure and Gore's reversion, and the card-houses, which were also her own. The brothel, as a gesture, she had left to Henry Gore. If he had chosen, Simon could have started others of his own. He did not choose; there was plenty to do without them. He never heard how the girls fared under Gore.

"But how did Prossy contrive it?" I cried. For it is almost impossible, as everyone knows, to reverse a court decision, at least without a great deal more money than Prossy had, or by intervention of the King. And that takes years to achieve, and Simon's purgatory, for one may so describe his spell in the Barbados, had lasted only one.

This was when he looked at me queerly, and hesitated. "It was a matter of form, no more, as it happened," he said at last. "There was—one point, which Henry Gore had not known of and which I myself, I must say it, had overlooked; it had not occurred to me at the time, or even later, that in losing the rubies I was losing my own property. Prossy's lawyer noted that or, rather—for Prossy did not herself know of the matter, of course—discovered it for himself, from Maria, who had not thought of it either."

He was silent then for some moments, and I said nothing to help or hinder him. I knew that he would tell me in the end, and he did.

"Maria," he said, "she—she had married me, you must know, by then, although it was never made public. She wanted, she said, as far as possible to make all right about the will, and leave no loophole for Henry to take everything. Of course she—she was fond of me as well, poor old Maria. I did the best I could for her; it was sad that she died not knowing, or believing, that I would ever come back."

But there were still the warehouses. When Samuel Grover came home he was put in charge of them. Simon looked after the gaming-houses for himself. His luck, which had seemed to desert him for a while, had not, in this way, and never did, though he was careful not to win constantly enough to discourage customers. He did not of course rely on luck entirely but watched his game. He also put a good deal of Maria's money into these houses, introducing certain improvements such as refreshment-rooms, and wall-mirrors and rich panelling before which, in wig and livery as he had himself done, negro pages stood, who also kept an eye on whatever passed. Simon had always a fondness for negroes after Barbados and perhaps from his first warm bath of all at Maria's, that time after the fight on the pavement; he employed them both in the gaming-houses and warehouses, and said they were grateful, honest, intelligent and trustworthy; myself, I expect they knew a good master.

The card-houses prospered, and he met Peter Aske at last there, as has been related; after that, and his own marriage to Ann, he sold them within a few years to an interested party, very advantageously. They had, after all, a legend of luck accruing; especially in the latter years, in course of which Simon had, two nights in succession, taken a hand himself at the cards and dice, against the fair-skinned, slender, weak young man who had been brought in, and who was drunk, a little, by the end of the first evening. His name was Aske, and as soon as he had ascertained that Simon knew what was to be done, and he did it, casting the dice and dealing his own hand till four in the morning, his devil behind him, standing no doubt in the same place as Simon himself had once stood for Maria.

The tale of Simon's childhood, boyhood and youth, and the way he had grown rich, was not made manifest to me all at once, that first day at Aske in the accounts-office. Its relation spread over many years, and was accompanied by a flowering of our own love, and its later decline; a rise and fall of fortunes; everything, in fact, that can encompass a lifetime, or rather two lives. All I knew, apart from what I have already said, about Simon was that he spoke as a gentleman does, possibly from listening to the customers at the card-tables, or later in talk with Samuel Grover; being musical, he would attune himself quickly, and he never spoke as a yokel will, or retained any provincial slur in his speech. This might not have mattered to me, any more than several of the other things I have related. Because I was only a young girl at first, and unmarried, it may be supposed that Simon told me many things I should not have been permitted to hear. But this was partly my own fault for insistence. Latterly I would be able to bring

about several changes, among them one which pleased me
well. It was almost at the very end of Simon's life when I
heard again a sound from its beginnings, namely his music;
he played for us again one day, at Thanksgiving years ago
now, when one of Robin's friends had brought a fiddle in,
and played it badly, and Simon took it away then and played
it, after a shy, uncertain, scraping start, as he must have
played long ago at Big Het's; and soon they were all dancing.

But this would take nearly all of two lives to bring
about. Meantime, I was able to understand why Simon
had, that day at the gate, looked with what appeared to be
contempt and dislike at Ann, whom he must marry shortly
as a part of the vow about Aske he had made long ago; soft
pretty Ann on her new pony.

One day after hearing some of the above I asked Simon—it
was before his son Robert's birth—if he were not afraid of
madness, the curse of Aske, again in his heir. There had
been the sins of old Ralph, and perhaps a further sin-wage
from Nicholas; no one now knew, except as it affected
Peter and Ann and, maybe, the latter's children. But
Simon laughed, in the way he could at such things, if they
were obstacles in the path of his expressed will.

"Even the God of your Bible, Leah, promised only the
sins of the fathers to be visited for a third generation and a
fourth. By the time my son is a man, he will have been
cherished daily, hourly, to guard his inclinations, to cause
him to grow to be a man such as I intend he shall be. And I
have no legacy from Ralph Aske in such a way, nor had
my father, who was clean."

The inclusion of Nicholas' tainted blood was discounted, I felt; everything was, which opposed or modified
Simon's plan. It almost seemed impossible that so ruthless
a will, setting the gods themselves at naught, could do
anything but conquer. But I knew from my classics that
when the gods are made angry by defeat by any mortal,
they take a revenge; and I trembled for the child who was

not yet conceived; how, in any case, could Simon be certain even that if so it would prove a son? But he had determined on this also.

10

THE JESTING PROPHECY Sir Napier Steed had made at the wedding however knew no fulfilment that Christmas, nor yet the one after that. In the third year Simon began to take his wife to visit physicians; one in Bath, two more in London. They prescribed everything for the ailing creature that would justify the bill they charged, but without result; Ann was bobbed in the waters at health-springs, wearing a linen turban and smocked gown; she swallowed medicine both of bitter herbs and sweet, possets and purges and aphrodisiacs; she was taken to an Austrian hypnotist who had come to England. None of them did any good, and in the end the nerve-racked, exhausted wretch was brough back to Aske, where, in the summer following that in which Simon had at last given up all treatments as useless, the oldest one of all, that of nature herself, worked very well now that Ann was allowed to be at peace again. In the fourth year of the marriage, accordingly, she was proved with child.

Immediately, Ann once more started to be far from well. By autumn, and after it, she was still feeling sick in the mornings, and before Yule her ankles had swelled. The swelling, through all the months of pregnancy, increased over her body, more so than should have been the case; some say it went then into her brain. Certainly she was never whole again in mind, though her body came back again to some semblance of its former self, after the child had been born. I think myself—but I am no physician or midwife—that no doubt Ann's unwilling harbouring of Simon's seed reflected itself firstly in a like unwillingness to conceive by him, and later, when the thing was done, in a dislike of his unborn baby, which none the less grew in

Ann to her discomfort and distress. She began to have headaches, such as I myself had often and whose pain and dolour I know well; but I had never made the sounds Ann did, hunched in her chair or, as the time drew near, lying on her bed altogether with the curtains drawn, saying the daylight hurt her eyes. I tried to have sympathy with her and to help her, but Ann herself made this hard; she knew nobody, or acted as though she did not, and lay about idly, a great white bloated thing, almost monstrous, long before term. There was none of the softness and expectancy of a mother about her; what the labour itself would be like I dared not think, or that the child could be like other children, when even its mother had no love for it. It could have been said I shrank from the coming birth as much as Ann, except that by then she no longer seemed to foresee it, or even remember anything. By the eighth month, she was having to be fed like Old Madam, with a cup and spoon, and pap only, for she still vomited up all solid food, and wine was forbidden to her by the physician.

But the labour itself, though it was the first I had seen and should perhaps have terrified me, was less appalling than I had expected, though Ann no doubt suffered pain. But the thing that happened in course of it was abominable, and I, who by that time knew a part of Simon's story, shiver yet when I think of it and can understand, more than a little, why folk outside called him the Devil of Aske.

I have said that he had already insisted, with particularity at the time of his wedding, on a certain Flemish coverlet over the bed for his marriage-night to Ann. This was called a birth-quilt, and had been used at Mrs. Dorothy's labours, in the latter of which the poor girl died. It was to be used again, of course, at Simon's order, now for Ann's. I thought myself that, with the whole house filled with new, sweet-smelling furnishings, the old musty article, with its sorry memories, should have been burned or put away. But Simon twice asked about it and to have it put over Ann. While the poor soul heaved and strained beneath it in the middle stage of her labour, with the tears running down her face, Simon came in.

He stood by the door, as he had stood that day long ago, in this same chamber, the night of Ann's own birth. I have never seen so hellish an expression of triumphant loathing and revenge on any man's face; even now, half a century and more afterwards, as I sit here, it still comes to me in my darkness and makes me hate the man I loved. The candles blazed; his eyes glittered in the light. He seemed taller than life; for instants I wondered if my rational beliefs, to which I have always firmly held and in which Miss Fish herself had encouraged me, were folly and the older, darker things such as witchcraft and spells, ill-wishing on toad's blood in a dug skull on a black sabbath, or whatever the jargon may be, were reality. I felt my heart turn over in me for fear, and as for poor Ann, I was glad she was as good as blind by now and could not see Simon standing there. The servants, like assistants at a sabbat or coven, were moving about the room, fetching and heating water on the fire. This blazed up, for it was winter's end, and the shadows magnified themselves, dancing, on the walls. When I looked again for the Devil of Aske to tell him to go, he had already gone. The moment of his full revenge for Het's death, if that is what it had been, was over.

Afterwards it was I who took his son to him. I was still angry; I wanted to say to him that it was no imp of hell, no succubus, but a large, quiet boy baby, normal as far as one could see in spite of his parents. I said nothing like this, of course; I crept mouselike to where Simon was, and showed him his son, and took the child away again; before that, he had smiled down at the red-faced creature in the shawl; later it would have fair hair and blue eyes. "He is an Aske, and my son," said Simon. Later he went back into the room and kissed Ann on the forehead. I had helped to tidy her a little and to moisten, for the first time now it could be done, the flaccid lips with wine; later on she slept. And a little boy running, running through a bitter night of storm, the black hair plastered into his eyes, blinded and afraid, could go back again by now to the place whence he had come, his task completed.

The baby was to be called Robert, after Simon's father. Robert grew and thrived, although he was never as active as other babies, and gave no trouble. He was a large, blond, placid child, who would be slow in learning to crawl, walk, speak, and read. But all this happened long after the christening, which took place when Robert was a month old and was, as it happened, the last of the great traditional feasts which had commemorated births, weddings and the coming of age of heirs, at Aske since the Middle Ages.

Long trestle tables were set out on the newly shaven lawn, and in case it rained there was a great tent. On the day itself we were all, except for Ann, up early, decorating the tables with green boughs and candles. The feasting for the tenants and the village would go on till night, and there was to be dancing afterwards. Even the wet-nurse, who had been found for the baby, helped; she was a big fair-skinned, plump thing from a nearby farm, whose own baby had died, so that she had plenty of milk. It was thought, and had been discreetly stated by the physician, that Ann would be better not to nurse her own child lest her humours fail to settle. In fact they were frightened that her very strangeness, which had grown more notice-able since the birth, would be exacerbated by child-nursing. It was hoped that she would play her part in the christening-ceremony without mishap, and for the occasion Madam had lent the Aske pearls, which by rights were Ann's in any case. But Madam had only mumbled that she herself would never need them again, which was true.

I had not expected to be able to leave Old Madam for the ceremony itself, but she professed so much curiosity to be told about it afterwards, mumbling at me that the maid could see to her perfectly well and that later she'd sleep, and I must go, that I agreed though I had no wish to. I have never liked public occasions and display, and this one, like the wedding, seemed to me to hold the seeds of sadness rather than joy. Simon I knew felt as I did; he went about grim-mouthed, supervising and altering each item, driving the servants to distraction. Even the details of what Ann was to wear had been worked out by him, as though she had no interest or say in the matter; and, indeed, she had not. I could begin to understand by now, knowing Simon a little better, that he must take this way of escape from near-madness of his own; otherwise he might have been close to it at times with Ann.

She came, however, into church docilely enough, comely in her silk gown although she had put on a good deal of flesh since the birth. I remembered that her mother had been a plump young woman and it was evident that Ann would take after her, like many small-boned people; though for all of our youth together she had been slim as a reed. I wondered if, when Ann should be old, she might acquire the solidity of Old Madam; would Ann, as she was now, as she soon would be, live as long? The thought chilled me, though I had little more notion than I had ever had of what might be taking place behind the blue eyes, in that childish brain. It still governed her body that day; looking, if anything, bovine, placid as a cow, she proceeded up the aisle where she had been married and saw the godparents, of whom I was not one, hold and give the responses for the baby in his long lace robe. Robert Aske did not cry when the water was poured on him; he never cried. The robe he wore had been lent by Old Madam, like the pearls. It had been worn by her sons and her husband, that husband's father and his father also; which took one back to the Civil Wars, and any preservation of christening-robes from before that time is, whatever anyone may say, in my opinion doubtful. My father's successor handed

Robert back again, having kissed him, and the party went out of church to the christening-hymn.

Afterwards we all rejoined one another in the lawn tent and later Ann, by now holding the baby for herself, made a slow progress, with Madam's pearls milky at her throat, round between the tables to show the tenants the new heir. The sheen of the pearls and the quiet good looks of Robert having been commented on, to the exclusion of Ann who did as she was bid, closely followed by the nurse, she then returned to the high table, concluding that part. I had not dared to hope that it would be achieved without mishap, and let out an inaudible breath of relief, as did some of us. A faint, sour odour reached me as Ann passsed by, leaving me saddened; she had lost, with other things, her fastidiousness. She sat down and began to eat.

There was a grèat deal of food, much of it served as must have been done in mediaeval times, with a great boar's head in jelly on a platter, its tusks replaced; lavender fish-cakes, roast meat hot from the ovens and dripping with gravy, which the men carved at side-tables; basted birds, cakes baked with whisky and sherry and fruit and many dozen fresh eggs; lengths of white bread cut into manchets, fruit syllabubs and, everywhere of course, flowing ale and wine. I looked at the Devil of Aske chatting amicably with his tenants and thought that, whatever anyone might say, they knew him now as a good landlord; he grudged no hospitality, and there can have been nothing like the feast at Aske since long before the days of Nicholas. Perhaps it had been rivalled at the time of Madam's wedding, as a red-haired and lovely bride of seventeen.

I left the green boughs and lighted candles and cut cakes, and the débris of the feast, as soon as I could, and hurried back to Madam as I had promised. The fiddles were striking up already for the long reel and I knew she would hear them where she lay, upstairs in her room, and perhaps remember when she had danced down the lines with Ralph her bridegroom last time fiddles had sounded in the grounds of Aske.

But she would have none of me yet for long; she wanted
me to get back to the dancing. To Madam, I was a young
thing who ought to want to kick up its heels; it was useless
to persuade her that the crowd would be drunk by now
and very merry, and that I would be happier with her in
her room. The fiddles scraped far below and from the
window, looking out, I could see, against the bonfire
which had now been lit up and leaped orange into the
night, the flinging dark shapes of the reel. Meantime,
Madam wanted something.

"Fetch it, 's i'th'drawer," the poor lips mumbled. "Then
go back. Young people dance."

She wanted some matter brought from a drawer in her
French chest, against the wall. After some searching and
handing her first one wrong thing and then the other, she
lost patience with me, and wept with the easy tears of the
helpless old. Finally I found what it was she wanted; it was
a long folded paper, finished with a seal. The sight of it
caused Old Madam's face to change and she stopped crying
and a thin large hand, like a claw, reached out eagerly; I
left the paper with her, and went back presently to watch
the dancing, as she wished me to do.

Simon was by the bonfire, no dancing and still deep in talk
with his farmers. I thought that on the whole, very few of
them still thought of him as Big Het's varmint, or her bastard; he was the squire now, the owner of Aske and husband
of Mistress Ann, and had fathered the heir. His cup should be
full, and perhaps it was. He smiled when he saw me, and
extended a hand. I suspected that he was a trifle flown with
wine; his cheeks were flushed, perhaps only with the bonfire.

"Come and leap over the flames with me, Miss Leah,"
he said, "then we'll tread a measure."

I was terrified, and shrank back; nothing, he should have
known, would induce me to let him lead me out there,
among the ribald crowd and their shouting, which sounded
now as couples leaped across the fire. I made the excuse

that I must get back again to Old Madam; she was not very
well, I said. This was a lie as far as I knew; but I wanted to
get away from the open space by the bonfire, where our
two figures were lit up darkly against the blaze, and cast
long shadows. "May I see my grandmother?" Simon said
unexpectedly. "I have never seen her since I was a child.
Perhaps tonight is the time to do so, when all's mended."

"Maybe," I said. I did not know whether Old Madam
would agree to see him. Together, and in silence now, we
climbed the stairs to her room. The house was dark, silent,
and empty of servants, who were all out at the bonfire; its
bright flares illumined the windows inside with a peach-
coloured glow, growing fainter as we climbed.

When I came into the room, Old Madam was lying very
still. On the counterpane near her hand was the long
folded paper I had given her. She had broken the seal, and
folded it back to reveal a name written there in script
which was as infirm and scrabbled as a spider's crawl. The
name was Simon Aske.

Then I fetched him in.

Later, he let me see the paper. She had prepared it some
time before; with great labour, writing it at times when
perhaps I had been at church, or away briefly on concerns
such as this afternoon's visit to the tent. There was
writing-gear always kept by her, but I did not know she
could still use it. There was no date.

This is my gift, it read. *I can give you no other, nor would
I. But now I am old.*

*You are the son of Robin Aske and his wife, Hester
Carden. I had them destroy the paper of marriage when he
left to go to the Pretender, and would not heed me.*

*You are the heir of Aske. But I shall be dead when you
know it.*

Guard Ann from herself.

                                    Maude Aske.

Part III

JONIE'S TALE

THE YEAR CAME to its end again in a flurry of snow, and there were further changes in Ann's mind and body. Inasmuch as they can govern one another for the better they now did so, with her, for the worse. I used to meet her some days, wandering aimlessly about the house and grounds, as though they were nothing of hers, and I a stranger. She took no interest either in the child Robert, who lay in an open calèche and was driven about in it behind a docile, doctored white goat Simon had bought, whose fleece was combed daily. Looking at the placid, fair child, in colouring like the Askes, bowling along in his little carriage, the new day-nurse by him, both of them warmly wrapped against the cold, I felt pride for Simon. I was glad he had his heir; it made everything, presumably, worth while.

But not for Ann. Ann had the few, fixed notions of madness; she had once desired to marry, and it had not been to Simon. Perhaps that stubborn recollection of things as they had been before the cloud settled on her mind made her, some days, like a nymph in a glade when the sky briefly clears. At any rate, one afternoon later in spring I was walking, as I often did, past Jonie's cottage to take the air. I was thinking about Ann, Simon and myself, and what if anything was to be done, and I walked on some way farther than usual into the woods. There was an older folly there, less frequented than the one down in the pond-garden and overgrown, half-crumbling now into ruin: it had been built in the time of Charles the Second. It was being used again now; I saw Fordwoodham come out, fastening his small-clothes. I still knew him after five years. He glanced furtively about, did not see me where I was standing,· and went away.

I knew Ann was in the folly.

I did nothing, for one does not at such moments, except to turn and walk quickly away. To come upon Ann, and tax her with unfaithfulness to Simon, was not for me or anyone. But the thought of it, of those two in the folly, coupling like animals without knowledge or care for themselves, for others or for the future, sickened me. I went back to my own room and stayed there, and all the rest of that day did not come down. There seemed no reason to tell Simon of what I had found out, or of seeing Fordwoodham in the grounds of Aske. Then a notion so fearful that it made my senses reel came to me; was Robert Simon's son?

I do not know how often the thing happened between those two, but for as long as it did so Ann seemed, of course, a little brighter. Then she grew dull again and I assumed, with the coming of autumn, Fordwoodham had gone back to his wife; cuckolding is a seasonal matter and a folly, or a summer-house or the open woods, revealing in its leaflessness and lacking in fires. No doubt I seem hard on Fordwoodham, but at the least he had known what he was doing to a woman who by then knew almost nothing. But Ann knew some things still, and one day I found her with a concoction of herbs, which she finished drinking down and then grimaced, and looked sideways at me; I had the impression of a dull hostility, and wondered, not for the first time, what Ann felt about anything she might know concerning myself and Simon: yet at that time we were still not physical lovers.

Her lip dragged up then and she tried to smile. It was a
furtive, conspiratorial echo of the times we had known as
children, and made me aware of a dreary inner sadness.
The herb tea, I knew from its colour, contained smut. This
grows on tainted rye and is used in abortions. Some of my
horror must have shown on my face, and Ann began to
cry. The tears ran down her face without hindrance and
she let them drop on to the bodice of her gown, which was
already stained with that and dried food. Poor Ann. I felt
shame rise in me, as though I, not she, were the harlot,
which no doubt I was, in my mind; so who was I to judge
Ann?

I tried to go to her and wipe her face, but she pushed
me away. "What else is there?" she said, and followed this
with what was almost the last coherent statement I was
ever to hear from her. "Simon hasn't . . . hasn't come at all
since the baby was born. He won't ever come back. I'm
glad of that, at least."

Then she turned away and before she took up her
aimless trailing again cast back at me, over one shoulder,
and with the hostile look renewing itself in her vague eyes,
as though a stranger had had enough courtesy, "He never
liked me." Then she went outside. I never learned what
happened with the herbs, except that there was no pregnancy.

2

I WOULD NOT have told all this to Simon, but in any
event another matter occupied my mind about then. Not
having any belief in timely coincidence such as had
happened on the night of the christening, it had sometimes
occurred to me to wonder how Old Madam came to die so
pat. The quiet manner of her death had caused no
comment; the physician, whom I had had Simon fetch at
once—although I knew well she was dead, I had no wish to

be murmured about as the one who had finished Old
Madam off conveniently—the physician had held up one
hooded eyelid, which we had placed by then over the dead
eyes, and shrugged a little and said no more. If it were not
that I myself had been the last to see her, and that the
maid—who was so much afraid of Madam even when
helpless that she would have brought her anything she
asked for—had been out at the bonfire and dancing, I
would have been certain Madam had died of taking some
noxious drug. Yet how could she have got hold of it?

The burial also took place without comment, and this
was no more than need have been expected; there is
nothing remarkable about the death of an old woman who
has been helpless for four or five years. But I was unhappy,
and had it not been for the discovery Prossy made some
time after the funeral, I might well have grown into a
melancholy with that, and the other matter of Ann,
besides my own troubles; for now that Old Madam was
dead, of course, I had overmuch time on my hands.

Prossy had come in, however, one day with a mysterious
look, and beckoned me. I went with her a little coldly; I
dislike familiarity in servants or, in fact, in anyone, and I
was not yet fully aware of the part Prossy had played in
Simon's history. Moreover she had never acquired the
obsequious ways, the miss-and-madam manners instilled
almost from birth in those who will see service in a great
house where their parents also, most likely, have done so
for a lifetime. But I was to be glad both that I had gone
with Prossy, and that she never, by word or look, was
made aware of these unworthy thoughts of mine.

She opened her hand when we were alone and showed me
two small pellets, of a greenish colour, lying in her palm. I
was not certain what they were, but it was evident that
Prossy knew. Still saying nothing, she beckoned again and
led me upstairs to Old Madam's room. It was in process
now of being tidied out, the mattress shaken and hung in

the sun, the curtains sent to the laundry downstairs and the carpets beaten below in the yard. But the bed was still there, gaunt and uncompromising without its hangings, and to this Prossy led me. It was a tester-bed, of course, and had been made probably in Holland, early in the seventeenth century; its hangings, when they were on it, had been of blackwork, and it had carved posts with cherubs' heads, which stared censoriously out from the dark wood, between flower-swags.

"Stands to reason you wouldn't never have thought of looking, Miss Leah, would you?" said Prossy. "*I* knew, though; don't ask me how I know all I do."

She stood for an instant regarding me with her old-wise smile, and the dreadful eye; its inflamed iris had grown no better since she came to Aske, and never would, and she was as thin as a skeleton. She turned now and pressed the nearer post on the bed, about the shaft's middle where a cherub of particularly stern aspect located itself. "Whore's trick, this is," said Prossy. "That's how I know. In the bawd-houses, them that's in those, they keep things in there, see, so's to reach for them easy, in the dark maybe, or first thing next morning: haresfoot and the like, or maybe more." She winked. "You got to be able to think quick, in them places. Old Madam, she knew a lot of things. There's enough pills in there to kill a coal-horse, even yet, and she'd laid them by all ready for herself, I don't doubt, long before she took ill, knowing she'd use them sometime."

"What are they?" I said, dazed; I was no longer inclined even to underrate Prossy. I could picture Madam's large clawlike hand edging up, inch by inch, to the place . . . "They're foxglove," said Prossy, and leered. "That's a pink flower grows here in hedges, like a peal of church bells. It's bells all right for them as takes more than the doctors say they should; I ought to know. I got some for my old woman when her heart was bad." The alarming, elfin grin appeared, which was seldom seen at Aske; I felt as Aladdin

might have done had his genie proved of singularly
outlandish appearance, although performing its tasks
almost unbidden. And I knew of no reason why Prossy
should have done this for me.

"You've always been kind to me, Miss Leah," she said,
when I stammered something. "If there'd been talk about
yourself having done away with her, which there wasn't,
but it might have been—well, I'd have said I did it, maybe,
if I couldn't ha' thought of anything better. But I thought
I'd look, and sure enough here they were." And she
showed me again the small, square aperture which had
revealed itself in the hollow shaft, behind the cherub,
whose stern eye concealed a spring in its protrusion. I have
never been able to witness certain church-faces without
remembering that cherub, and the way its excessive
godliness concealed an undoubted knowledge of many
bedtime secrets from a remote, probably Dutch past. A
great lifting of the oppression from my senses came to me;
I knew, now, how Old Madam had died, having long ago
got ready the letter for Simon, and the pills, and known
when to take them, though she could not have foreseen
that in that very hour he had felt he must see her again,
after so many bitter unforgiving years. Would it have made
her endure life a little longer, perhaps, now that it had
become such a travesty? Perhaps not; she had hated
Simon's mother, and Simon for Het's sake, perhaps also
Robin's; the ways of love which has changed to hatred are
very strange.

All of this I knew would have been readily understood
by Prossy, standing there. It was only by the way, and no
more to be spoken of than anything else, that I knew also,
with as much certainty as one may ever feel, that Prossy in
her own day had given her grandmother all the foxglove
pills she possibly could, and at once. From what Simon
had told me about that old woman, this is understandable.

3

ONE REASON FOR Old Madam's decision to put an end
to herself may also have been due to the fact of Peter's
death in that year, which I have forgotten to mention. He
had for a long time now been confined to one separate
part of the house near the old tower, with his keeper for
the time; these changed fairly often. One who had already
stayed for longer than was customary was called Stephen,
and was a muscular young fellow without much in the way
of speech or other resources; the task was hard. His only
desire seemed to be that he should have regular hours off
to visit the ale-house in the village, during which time
Jonie Braik deputised for him. Jonie, I knew well, when I
gave the matter any thought which was not often, would
be unlikely to carry out his duties towards Peter with any
great care. I knew, for instance, that he was casual enough
to let the poor creature wander about the corridors by
himself, leaving the door from Peter's own separate
apartments unlocked: I had twice seen the white, vague,
considering face at some upper window on my return from
my walks, in a part of the house where Peter would not
have been at all had the door been kept firmly locked and
bolted as it should. It was like Jonie to be uncaring about
such matters; I lay awake both nights for a long time,
thinking of Peter, who I nevertheless knew was a vegetable
now and would never harm me or anyone else again.

But he could still harm himself. No one knew what
really happened, in such mind as remained to him, by the
end; for more than a year, I afterwards heard, he had had
delusions, mixtures perhaps of failing memory and failed
ideas; some of these had even in their day been grandiose,
and Peter by now perhaps imagined himself a person of
great, of mighty consequence and would stare wordlessly
and royally at his true subjects, the chair, the chest and the
bed, sometimes falling upon them and hurting himself.
Prossy said afterwards she had heard thuds and whimper-

ing sometimes from where she slept, though not clearly at that distance and with the thickness of the mediaeval walls.

Persons of consequence wish to climb again after a fall, the steps of a throne not being the final ambition; and poor Peter was no different from the rest. One time when Jonie was, or should have been, in charge of him the poor fellow got out and, wearing his loose felt slippers, wandered out and through an upper casement and across the slates to the old part-roofed tower, among whose sparse lichened slates he stayed poised for a while, thinking himself, no doubt, Christ raised to a high pinnacle by the devil, and shown all the power and glory of the world. I can still think of Peter up there, with above him only the sun, his rival, and below all of us like flies crawling. And at last, with a great, imperial beating of his wings he sailed down, strong as Lucifer, once more among men; but there was only a flurry of bats disturbed in the roofless tower, down which, as though it had been an open well, he hurtled, and plummeted down head first and broke his neck. They found him that same evening, after Stephen returned from the ale-house, for at first it was not even noticed that Peter had gone.

So they buried the one-time heir of Aske in the tomb where, later, he was joined by Old Madam, and after that nobody ever mentioned him again, with two exceptions.

Jonie Braik had escaped lightly, as he had always done since the days with the Pretender; I believe that he had been with the great house now so long that it would not have been thought possible for Aske to stand on its foundations if Jonie left it. He must soon, however, in the nature of things retire, and he did very little nowadays, if indeed he ever had. He spent most of his time with his cats in the small cottage he had lived in from the beginning, on the edge of the wood that rose behind Aske, its thatched roof darkening greenly now that Jonie no longer had the strength or inclination to renew it each seventh summer.

(Later Simon was to improve this cottage and lay on slates, and for many years the new coachman and his wife lived there, for they had a growing brood of children and had become too numerous, all of them, in the end for the quarters above the stables.) But in the meantime Jonie, who was still there, began to ail; it could almost have been said that he did so from the day of Peter's death, except that he had never seemed to care for Peter as he had for Ann.

The reason for that became apparent, as it happened, to me in the same week Jonie decided he was dying.

He did not die this time—in fact, he was to live for many more years—but in the convincing manner of the Highland old he developed second sight, went fey and clutched his innards, as though they gave him vague but constant pain. No doubt they did; I believe Jonie died in the end of a cancer, which can be a slow business and must have been with him for years. Now, however, hearing he was ill, I went over with a bowl of broth to him from the kitchens.

He was sitting outside the door, not in his bed at all. I set down the bowl and said to him, "Jonie Braik, are you as ill as you say you are?" for I knew how to deal with him ever since that summer alone at Aske so long ago, and I took the other chair. His face broke up into a kind of grimace which admitted the discovery and at the same time revealed more charm than I have seen on many a handsomer one, showing the stumps of his teeth which had all, those that remained, gone yellow.

"It is a sickness of the heart," he said. His filmed eyes stared over at Aske beyond the slope, where the chimney-stacks, except for the kitchen end, had no smoke rising from them on this warm day. Jonie's hens had by now edged forward again, being tame, and were pecking about our feet, and would have taken the bowl of soup for themselves had I not retrieved it, which I did, and handed it to the old man. "Drink that," I said, "and your heart will mend." It was nonsense, such as I always talked to

Jonie; despite the fact that he was a scoundrel and everyone knew it, I found it, as I have said, impossible not to love him. Watching him now feed himself from the bowl, slavering over it as the old do, I stayed beyond repulsion and tried to picture Jonie as he must have been when a young man. He would be tall—his limbs today, in hodden trews and coat with long woollen hose pulled well over the knee even on this summer's day—were thin now but still very long in the bone, and had once been powerful. I remembered how strong Jonie had been even in my childhood, when he had used to toss me and Ann with as much ease as if we had been two oranges, up in the air on to our waiting ponies.

He spoke now with reproach, having finished his broth. "It is not the heart in my breast of which I speak, but the heart in my mind." It could not, I thought, have been better put, and I have always remembered it; for which one of us but has a heart of the mind? And it can break.

"Tell me, then, Jonie, about the heart in your mind, and why it's sore."

"It is not so sore for Peter," he said, for he had never called anyone master. "He was," he added, "no son of mine."

He had set down the empty bowl and I had taken it and had replaced it in my basket before the full strangeness of the words he had spoken came to me. I turned to him again and said "But, Jonie, Master Peter was Mr. Nicholas' son, not yours." I thought he must be getting childish. He had sons enough, God knew, and daughters as well, scattered through the village and beyond; but the analogy as regarded Peter Aske seemed far-fetched if not disrespectful. But he shook his grey head and said, with the obstinacy I knew well.

"Nicholas may have fathered him, but if that is so it will be the first time it happened. He was an Aske, oh, ay,"—and he went on to depict, in one somehow intel-

ligible phrase in the Gaelic, the habits of all male Askes
and what they went down to do in the village—"but he
never got any of the women bairnwise for all of it, save
only Dorothy at the last, the poor young bitch."

"Mrs. Dorothy, Jonie," I said rather helplessly, obeying
the injunction laid on me from the beginning, so that it
was now second nature, never to permit familiarities to
servants, even those of as long standing as Jonie. The very
nurses, as I knew, who had reared a child from the month,
and stayed with the family for perhaps two generations
afterwards, spoke of each charge as Miss or Master, boy
and man, girl and woman. And Ann's mother was dead,
which made her the more vulnerable. I had to defend
Dorothy Aske even though, as might happen in the
process, I offended Highland pride, which is a thing never
again to be forgiven. Jonie had several such enemies. But
the answer he made was no declaration of undying war; in
a way, I wished that it had been.

"It was not Mistress I called her, in the days when I
got at her in the linen-closet, and she fidging fain before
the end. Fair hay we made between us o' the clean linen,
all that summer, Dorothy and I; and never a soul knew."

At the end I was to walk away still in a state of shock;
afterwards I could remember his eyes, and that they had
lost their filmed look and were blue, the colour of spring
water in a lake. Aske colouring, blue eyes and golden hair,
and Nicholas who had never got a woman bairnwise. The
linen-closet.

I knew the latter fairly well, from the door. It was still
used for clean linen, which lay there smelling of lavender
and rosemary, which the maids were taught to put
between the folds. As an assignation for lovers it would be
ideal, whenever no one wanted linen; it was in a place
below the roof and never locked, and beyond it was the
attic with warning of footsteps on the wooden stairs. Not a
soul knew.

Dorothy's answer to Nicholas and his mother. Ann's revenge on Simon. Nothing in the world was as it seemed, and in the meantime—

"Jonie, are you—" But I stopped halfway, and did not finish; he was not, this time, I knew, telling anything but the truth. He had decided he was dying, and had wanted to shrive his soul, and had waited till I should come along with my basket and the bowl of broth. I took his hand now and held it, as if he were dying indeed; the skin was hard as polished wood on the palm, and, on the back, burnt brown with the sun and the hard work he had always avoided. "You had better tell me about it, Jonie," I said, "and then, mind, I must use my judgment." For young women then, even unmarried ones, were not as prudish as they make themselves out to be these days, unconvincingly.

"Once," said Jonie, "I was better than I am now. I was a fair-haired chiel, tall, with a lily skin like a lady's. And at the beginning, when I first came here, I was not put to the outdoor work at all. I was Madam's footman."

The thing he had finally told me, divested of such trimmings, pared itself down in my dazed mind even as I returned to the house after listening to him; Ann must be Jonie's daughter. He had himself described with pride how he got Mrs. Dorothy, loathing her husband and, till Jonie taught her better, any man's touch at all, with his child; and how poor Dorothy had then, under persuasion from her prudent lover, let Nicholas again achieve that state which might have, but hitherto had not, convinced everyone that he was the father of the coming heir. Only when that came it had not been an heir at all, but a girl, and then Dorothy . . . by this time I could see her, poor little plump, trusting, outraged bride—by then, already seduced under the experienced footman's hands (he would be, I thought, twenty years older) turning again for revenge or solace, perhaps conceiving his second child,

perhaps not. Recalling Madam, who could hardly have
failed to suspect what had been going on under her nose,
one still wondered about that. But meantime other aspects
concerned me. Poor Dorothy, hiding away upstairs from
the fumbling pursuit of her pallid, loathed lecher of a
husband, seeing the cupboard as a haven, perhaps, not
knowing, after she had first gone inside the door, that
there would be that other quietly closing, then standing
firm behind it; what had Dorothy's escapade done to
Simon now, although it was all of thirty years ago? For
sorting out the people and pieces like chessmen on a
board, as I was, what troubled me was Simon himself in all
this matter.

He had married Ann solely because she was an Aske. If
she were not—if the tale of that premature birth at Aske
long ago was misinformed in such a way, the only way to
matter to Simon—then he himself had been grossly
deceived and mocked, whether or not deliberately.

Had Madam known? Could she have known of it, and
had she laughed to herself, knowing that Simon knocked
always now at a closed door? And, with her green eyes
that saw everything, knowing her son's wife had quickened
with child to a servant the year previous, when the child
fortunately proved a girl, had she—I had heard of this
before—taken strict steps, the time Peter was conceived, to
ensure there was no further doubt?

They had all been punished, in the end; poor Dorothy,
Old Madam, Nicholas, Ann, Peter . . . the sins of the
fathers . . . except Jonie. Jonie had suffered nothing, rascal
that he was. He must have made a fine, manly lover; I was
glad Dorothy had had her summer among the linen, at any
rate. But for the rest—

Ought I to go back to Jonie again, and ask him more?
But in the wandering of the mind that he had begun, or
could assume, he might not remember. Yet suppose he did,
and told others? What if it all came back to Simon by
other lips than mine, and he went then and did bodily

harm to Jonie, or perhaps even to Ann? For he had never liked Ann, who had so unwittingly deceived him, and had borne him, now, at last, a son who was no Aske, perhaps doubly not; but of that other matter, that Robert himself might be the son of Fordwoodham, I would never tell Simon at all.

But he need never have married Ann. In the end I went upstairs and flung myself on my bed and beat my fists against the wall. When someone came in I said I had a headache, and as I was often known to have these they asked no more questions and left me alone. I did not want to see anyone. I wanted time to think, among other matters, about the truth, which was that now I too was deceiving Simon. Should I indicate to Jonie that I thought Simon should be told, and that I must tell him? Or should I, for Jonie's sake· and Ann's, even for Robert's, say nothing, and let a child inherit who was not an Aske at all? Did that matter?

It mattered, I knew, to Simon. It mattered more than anything in the world, his world, that he had so lately and with such pain rebuilt. And for that reason I could not, I thought, tell him yet, and must myself bear the burden.

4

FOR WE HAD grown in tenderness.

I must speak of it only as a part of my story. Knowing Simon by that time as well as I did I could still have believed, with the calculating streak that was in him, that he might have made some plan coldly to seduce me, now that it was evident all was not, and would never be again, well with his marriage, and Old Madam was dead. In that case I would have been no more to him, or to anyone, than a poor young governess of the kind so frequently and briefly abused by an employer, possibly some squire or great lord whose children she may have in charge. In such a case, perhaps by the use of threats to lose her her situation if she does not yield, it happens, and afterwards, when he has wearied of the connection, she is abandoned, often with an unborn child, and in despair of ever finding another place. But that was not, or not quite, my story. Moreover Simon could, had he chosen, have found some willing young woman, of greater physical attraction than I possessèd, at one of the nearby farms. There were also, by now and regrettably, several successors to Big Het in the village itself, as the new parson, unlike my poor father, cared nothing for the moral welfare of his parishioners. But Simon took no advantage of that situation either, and instead this is what happened, about the same time as the events I have been relating.

It started over the parson, as I have been referring to that gentleman. Uncaring as he was, he preached a fine sermon, and I always went to church. I sat by myself in the Aske pew, as Simon never came himself; he had never been religiously inclined, and after the early days of his marriage, when he had been wont to come in at times with Ann on his arm, in her wide hat and silk gown, he stayed away. I would walk down and back on Sundays from Aske as a rule, for the distance is not great. One day it rained heavily while we were in church, and hearing, above the psalms, the patter begin on the roof, I felt some dismay. But I need not have troubled, for, on my emergence, I found Simon had sent down the Aske carriage for me.

This was very good of him, and I went in at once to thank him, on my return, still wearing my cloak and bonnet. He was in his small office, where he spent much time even on that day of the week. He looked tired and strained, I thought, with shadows about his mouth that I had not noticed previously; it was at the height of the trouble with Ann. He stood up courteously when I came in, and I found myself dwelling on his great misfortune. She had lately begun, at meals, to miss her mouth at times when shovelling food to it, and lately he had arranged that a tray of covers should be sent to her own rooms, where Prossy served her. We contrived, the pair of us, well enough at each end of the long table once food had been set down; we were by now very easy together in conversation.

He enquired now about the sermon, having discounted my thanks. I disapproved of his idle manner of speech about such matters, and replied, as I believe, from under my bonnet.

"If you desired to know about the sermon, sir, you should have come to church, as you are the squire."

He was still standing, and walked over to me; his expression was a mixture of amusement, determination, and a certain air of boding no good, and he no longer looked tired. He whisked off my bonnet, untying the strings and setting it on his writing-table. Then he removed my cloak.

I had not protested, as his purpose in all this did not immediately reveal itself, though no doubt it should have done to anyone more worldly wise than I. As it was, when he picked me up, and carried me to a high shelf, I decided that matters were going a little too far for propriety. I had begun to struggle, without much result, and to beg of Simon to put me down, but he would not. My chief fear was still that the servants would open the door to come in and tell us dinner was on the table. I tried to make Simon understand this, and at the same time—for he took no notice of me—observed a large Bible, tooled and bound in leather, which nobody had used since Cromwell's day and which located itself, as such things will, for some reason among the dusty documents and rolls of the estate-office. It had been placed now on the high shelf out of Simon's way, and he perched me upon it. I sat there helplessly, for it was not possible to jump down to the floor without great loss of dignity. I saw that he was laughing.

"Now I can punish you," he said, "and you will not be able to run away." He went back to the door and turned the key and put it in his waistcoat. Then he came back again and started to kiss me. I was at first very much surprised, and then in increasing confusion.

So it began. After he had kissed me well on mouth, eyes and face—I was reminded, through the swirling uncertainty that had come, of nothing at all, and did not know who I was or where—he stood back, and regarded me gravely. I was as pink as a peony by now, and cross; I did not know what to do, except to beg him again to put me down, although I did not now expect him to obey. He lifted me to the floor at once, however—he was very strong, and made me feel light, I remember—and said, with his hands still on my shoulders, "I would not have done so, Miss Pewface, but dinner's served. Otherwise you'd know more of me, Leah, and you will."

His voice had deepened, and I closed my eyes—I could not help it—and swayed on my feet for a moment. He said then, "But now, you little, frightened, prudish, learned and agreeable mouse, shall I tell them to send up your dinner, because you will want to go up to your little, narrow bed, and have the vapours, will you not, and not come down to table? Shall I?" And he took my chin in his hand, and forced it up, but I jerked my head away. I was glad he was so sharp-set; but how did he expect me to eat? My heart was beating wildly, and how, I now asked myself, did he know my bed was narrow? His weight, if he were on that, would—

I do not know what I said about dinner. Later he had it sent up to me by the little new maid, who brought in covers. "The master says you took a dizzy turn after church, Miss Leah," she told me, eyes wide with interest rather than distress. "Shall I fetch the hartshorn? He said I was to ask."

There would be only one thing for me to do now, I knew, and that was to leave Aske. I had had, after all, no real excuse to stay after the death of Old Madam, except that I had told myself Ann might need me; but I knew, none better, that she did not.

He had come upon me before, I remembered, at the time of Peter's death. I forget who had told me of it, for I had not myself, thank God, found the crumpled heap down on the stones of the tower, or seen the shape covered with a cloth afterwards as they carried the body away on a disused stable-door. The informing of Old Madam then, which they left to me, had been nothing, for she had never either asked for or accepted comfort; but the resulting feeling of horror and death about Aske brought my childhood memory of fear, involving Peter, back again strongly. It was cold, too, by then, with no sun to melt away the prevailing greyness and mist, so that everything was in a mood for funerals. I hid myself in a passage, not wanting to go past where the coffin stood between its candles, down in the great hall where Peter himself had not been permitted to remain now for many years. Pressed against a cupboard, I stood trembling, and in this state Simon found me. He came to where I stood and took me in his arms wordlessly, holding me close. Since that other day not long before when he had told me something of his childhood, and I had told him something of mine, the relationship between us had grown and already defied boundaries; it was nothing unnatural that I should be in his arms now, like a child with its mother, when we were alone. At other times it would be days before I spoke with Simon other than formally.

"What is it, Leah?" he asked, as I stayed close against him. "It's Peter, is it not?" Whether he thought that Peter newly dead had brought back some golden memory of him as he should have been I do not know; but the horror burst open in me, like an abscess, and relieved itself in tears. The flood stilled my earlier trembling and I wept; great sobbing tears, the difficult wrenching of which from deep inside me brought, in the end, a second access of shaking all through my body, so that I clung as fast to Simon still as if he had been a rock and I drowning in the sea. He knew, of course, when he thought of it, that I could have no remaining affection for the poor crushed thing on the stones; not even earlier, when we were children, when we . . . And then, he had guessed; I knew it as he grew taut against me, and his arms tightened almost as though to crush memory out with renewed hurt. "Leah," he said. "It was Peter who . . . ?"

"Yes," I whispered, "with a stone." And now that it was spoken of my sobbing changed to hot, healing tears that flowed down without sound, except that I was still trembling like a leaf, and he took me to one of the rooms and we sat down together for a little while, and then he sent me back to my own. That was all, and not even the trailing figure of Ann at the door and the survey of her vague eyes, if it had happened, would have induced in me any sense of guilt or impropriety. But the episode had tightened the ties that already bound us, so much so that, later, the improper business taking place upon the Bible which I have mentioned was less shocking than it should have been, for a gently brought up young woman from a parsonage who hoped, in time when other matters should somehow have arranged themselves, to become a governess elsewhere in some respectable household.

It is a fact that between those who love truly there must be truth, and it no longer seems, thinking of it all now, that there could in the end have been any other decision for me than to tell Simon what Jonie Braik had said, though I never did tell him about Fordwoodham. I can recall how it befell; it was after breakfast, because two letters had come in for Simon that day. One was from Italy, and bore a foreign frank and seal; the other was from Ann's physician, who had been consulting another in London.

Simon handed me the second letter wordlessly, his face

dark. I read it, and was filled with pity and horror of fools; the consultant physician, a person of some eminence about Royalty, was a believer in the efficacy of repeated natural events for women. The madness, which was he said of a kind he had met with previously in numerous instances, particularly following a first pregnancy, could be put right at least partly by a second and decidedly by a third. The cure, he ventured to state, was in such cases certain, as he had observed it himself in a duchess and others.

I folded the letter and handed it back to Simon, saying something of the misguided folly of such a cure. I was horrified when he failed to respond; he had some faith, perhaps induced by the little he knew of their practices, in all physicians, and this man's name was certainly very famous. It appeared that Simon now entertained the notion that Ann ought to bear him a second child, and thereby perhaps cure herself. I exclaimed, and drew away from him. Had he forgotten that miserable initial pregnancy of Ann's already, and the swelling and sick wretchedness, headaches and sharp crying and blind, incessant pain?

"She is an Aske," he said, and his mouth set obstinately. "Robert will need a companion." I was still silent and he went on, as if he were reciting lines learned by rota, "The physicians say all of that need not happen a second time; it's a fancy of women."

"Are you a monster?" I cried at last, the cold look he gave me drove me to further frenzy. Then I screamed out like a maenad, as is not my wont, "She is no Aske, she's not, she's not, she is Jonie Braik's daughter," and thought it might save Ann.

He believed I was raving at first, of course; of a prey to pique of some kind at the thought of his returning to Ann even for the time. When he saw I was in earnest he came over at last and seized and shook me, till my teeth chattered, and then cast me away from him and I fell

against the table, bruising my cheek. He did not come over
to see what had happened or, perhaps, notice; he stood by
the window, the light against his head and tall figure so
that the face could not be seen. I crept away, and much
later, from my room, saw him go out alone and over to
Jonie's.

I had no fear now, despite Simon's recent violence to
me, that he would hurt the old man. The reason was one
which may seem odd or insufficient to those who do not
understand, as everyone cannot, the feeling between
myself and Simon at this time, a mixture of love and
teasing awe, terror and sometimes almost hate. But
whatever it was it meant a bond between us, and at some
time there had been a thing said that day which would save
both Jonie and Ann. It was while I had stammered replies
to the questions he had been asking afterwards precisely,
painfully, about how Jonie Braik could have become
Dorothy's lover when he was so seldom inside the house.

"He was not in the stables at first, in those days," I said.
"He was the footman," for so Jonie had told me himself.

Simon stopped then. "He was the footman," he said,
and added as if to himself, "So, once, was I."

I never knew what he and Jonie said to one another
about the matter. Simon did not refer to it again, or to the
other one we had discussed by reason of the physician's
letter.

5

IT WAS THAT same night that I went to Simon's room for
the first time, and anyone who wonders at this after he
had shaken and ill-treated me that morning, and caused me
to bruise my cheek, must do so in their own way. I had by
now forgotten about myself and my bruises, and was
concerned only with Simon.

For I loved him. I loved him so much that only now,

when I had myself brought down the edifice he had erected for himself about his marriage and Aske, did I go to him; I could have done so, I daresay, earlier. But I had no notion of myself as a temptress, and he was Ann's husband, despite everything. Now, though, in every way except a divorce by way of Parliament, he was finally free of Ann. He would never divorce her, I knew, because she was vulnerable, being mad. Simon's mind worked in such ways. Mine did not work at all, for the moment of which I speak, except that I knew that, by now, the man I loved would be alone and in much need of comfort, which perhaps I could give. And so I went to him, at an hour after everyone had gone to bed and the house was silent.

I did not scratch timidly at his door at once, but waited outside it. Now that I had crept down, in my shift, to where only a door separated us I was again trembling and afraid, and it was very cold; my heart beat wildly under the thin stuff of my shift, and my teeth chattered. I stood for a long time regarding the panelled wood of the door, the same through which Dorothy had by force been sent in to Nicholas, and I knew fear, and the increasing cold in my bones. If he did not want me, how should I feel? He was no longer, as earlier he had again become in my mind, the little orphaned boy, in need of comfort, whom I could perhaps cherish, but a man grown, with a man's full need of a woman. Was I such a woman as he could ever want, small and inadequate with my sticks of trembling limbs and thin flat body? He might not desire me at all.

He must have sensed in the end that someone was there because the door opened; Simon stood there in his shirt, a candle by him. "Why, Leah!"

He was not angry, I thought. The relief made my teeth chatter like castanets. He took me inside, still shaking uncontrollably, and put me in his bed and then came in and put his arms about my body and drew me close,

warming the chilled flesh. "You are frozen," I heard him
say. "You are like a little frog," and then I began to laugh,
and cried and laughed against him; as a comforter I was
worse than nothing, and it was Simon who comforted me.
I still had rigors, shivering now in his warm bed like
someone with an ague, and my teeth were clenched to
make them behave themselves and my knees took over the
function they had had so lately of knocking together, so
that with it all I could not yet speak.

He warmed me. He would not make love to me and
when I said, at last, a thing about it Simon soothed me,
stroking and comforting me like some small wild animal
caught in a man's hand. "No, Leah," he said, "you are not
ready," and then he lay there with me close in his arms as
if to hold, and make me warm again in them, were the
only things that mattered; dimly I wondered that he
should be so little concerned with himself and with
everything else that had happened that day. He seemed
not, as I had expected, downcast or defeated; he was like a
man who has had good news, and has perhaps altered his
plans; how could I know that this had already happened,
so soon after the confirmation of what I had told him
today about Jonie and Ann?

But I did not by now think greatly of that. His hands, as
Peter's had once done but very differently, soon found and
touched the places in my body that were for no one else;
like a healing and benison, so that my mind, which had
been filled with brief and sudden fear again, grew calm.
"Sleep now," he said, and gave over caressing me till I slept
against him, which I did soon. I had not said one word
more about why I had come and I knew he understood,
and would always understand. I have always found it
difficult to explain such things in words.

In the morning, very early, I awoke first, I raised myself
on my elbow and looked at Simon asleep; the hard mouth
had relaxed, the profile was haughty, remote a little with
the dark eyes closed in slumber, and he needed a shave. I

loved him; my whole body ached with my love, and it was, I thought, like looking at a sleeping giant or hero. Barbarossa under his hill, Arthur, the Trojan Hector. I would never love any other man, I knew; my whole life, for good or evil, was Simon's now to do with as he would, and my body, one day soon perhaps, when I was ready, as he had himself said, but not yet. I slipped out of his bed now and cautiously, in the grey dawn, made my way back along the cold flagged corridors of Aske and to my own bed, where I lay for an hour wide-eyed. No one of the servants had seen me, no one could talk, and pass it on to the village, that I had spent last night in the arms of the Devil of Aske, and had emerged a virgin, except for Peter and his stone.

6

HE CAME TO find me later that day in the library. I had been sitting in my accustomed place with a large volume taken down from one of the shelves, trying to fulfil my daily hour of Greek. I heard Simon come in, and anything I had taken in already, which that day was not much, went out of my head.

He came up behind me and kissed my neck, then removed my spectacles which I had been wearing to help me with Herodotus. "I want to tell you about the letter from Italy, Leah," he said. "Come." And he led me to the place by the window which had seats of cushioned hide, and was secluded, and we sat down.

The letter had contained the following information, and it was like the Greek fate which pursued us all at Aske that it should have come at the very moment Simon's carefully rebuilt world had fallen about him. To rebuild yet again, in a different fashion, I should have known would be his aim, not being of that humour which ever admits defeat. It was one of the things I loved and, possibly and in another manner, feared Simon for. I myself might have hoped, after the previous night, to have some hand in the rebuilding, in a way which I knew could not mean that I would become Simon's wife. That I did not greatly care may perhaps be due to the early death of my parents, before they could instil correct notions in me.

This is as may be, and although Simon now, on our seat together, held and caressed me in such a way as soon made my face burn with confusion and my heart pound almost as it had done outside his door on the previous evening, I knew, even half listening in this way, almost at once that I was not the chosen instrument of the new plan. This appeared instead to be a little baby, whose name was Melissa Aske and who had just been born in Rome. She was the youngest child of the son of Old Madam's only brother, who had lived for many years as an exile in Italy after his part on the losing side in the 1715 rising. He had married, very late, a merchant's widow there, and they had only one son who in course became a wine-merchant. I listened to all this whenever Simon's hands permitted me concentration, and I gathered from his discourse that the name of Aske, in the male line, still persisted in the far-off city of Rome, though in trade as is common with the expatriate Jacobites. "So you may read your Italian for such little time as we have left, my love, not Greek," he said, and teased and kissed me, not explaining further except that we would be leaving for Rome together very soon. Nor did I ask more; such joy, in an unholy fashion, had risen in me at the thought of, for whatever reason, going away with Simon by ourselves that it was some time before I took in the rest of the tale, when he had sobered also.

Melissa's father had died, Simon said, with almost all his family, in a plague of Roman fever, which comes in in summer from the Campagna marshes. "This one poor little wretch was saved because, being still out at nurse, she was

beyond the city walls, and stayed there till it was all over."
The partner in the dead man's wine-shop, whose name was
Giambattista Giorgio and who had written the letter which
had arrived at Aske the previous day, had himself sent a
messenger to the young nurse, who lived out in the
country, telling her to keep the baby with her till he
should send again. She would be paid, he had added. By
now, at the time of writing, he had brought the nurse and
baby back to his own house near the Piazza di San
Silvestro, where they at present were.

He had been looking, he also said, through the effects of
his deceased partner, who he already knew had no kin in
Italy either of his own or of his wife's, who had herself
been an Italian. He had found among other things a letter
from Old Madam to her long-dead brother, the baby's
grandfather, written a lifetime ago. Was it possible that
there were still some of the child's kin at Aske in England?
He had written, hoping that perhaps they might be found,
and would want some news of the deaths, and of the
remaining child. A human note now sounded through the
formal, stiffly translated wording of the merchant's letter.
Signor Giorgio was himself without children, and his wife
had died long ago. He had grown fond of the little Melissa,
and if it was wanted and her relatives agreed, would keep
her with him always, and would bring her up suitably and
make her his heir. But he had thought it advisable to make
enquiry first of the father's folk, if any should be still
living in England.

Something, although I have no belief in premonitions,
made me shiver a little, and Simon kissed my hair absently
and murmured, "Still, be still, little mouse," and continued in his plans regarding the baby Melissa. At the same
time he patted and stroked me all over so that my body,
which was by now grown all in one blush, a rose, knew at
last a sweet inward yielding, and I remembered Jonie's
saying about young Dorothy; fidging fain, he had said,

he'd got her that time in the linen-closet, and if he had not
done so Simon and I would not be here now. Fidging fain,
that was what I was, or I supposed so; I would have lain
down, I knew, at that moment in a linen-closet with Simon
or, if he had asked me, on the library floor. But he hardly
heeded me all this time; he was still thinking and talking
about Melissa, and his eyes had grown bright and secret as
they would do when he was far away, planning some
irrevocable matter. And seeing this I was afraid.

"Why need you take her?" I said, when I was able. "She
is more than half Italian, and the merchant seems fond of
her and would treat her well, and, he says himself, make
her his heir." I was already, as I knew well, jealous of
young Melissa Aske, and this before I had even seen her.
Soon, though, I should do so; and again the thought of our
journey together to fetch her home drove most other
things out of my head. "She will come here," said Simon
flatly, "and later marry young Robert. She is—can you not
understand yet, my darling?—an Aske; there is no doubt of
that, after all the other doubts there have been. It puts the
matter ahead by a generation, no more; my son and
Melissa, inheriting Aske for their children. Their children;
my grandchildren, all Askes and all mine. And you will
also be that last, very soon now, Leah."

He would have turned to me then, but I still murmured
about the fantasy, as it seemed to me, of his plan; it could
not be for twenty years more or less, I told him, and perhaps
young Robert would have notions of his own by then, or
possibly even Melissa, if her will held out against her
upbringing. For a little girl to have a strong independent
mind did not, however, I knew, happen very often if she
were carefully reared, for most upper-class young women are
brought up to submit to the notion of planned matrimony,
though not perhaps from so tender an age. It was Robert I
felt for, our acquaintance having progressed, to some
extent, already when I sometimes walked by him and the
nurse with his goat-carriage. The more I dwelt on the

infancy of these two children the more absurd it seemed. "This is not the Middle Ages, when they would bring a child-bride into a husband's house before the age of five," I said crossly. "How rigid you make your plans! One day, perhaps, they will betray you." Then I bit my lip, feeling that I should not have spoken in that way to Simon yet, with the discovery of Ann's parentage still fresh, as it must be, in his mind. But I could not think of Simon himself as sane with regard to Aske, or his own will.

He did not answer, and instead began to rumple me. He turned me deliberately from a rose to a fire, kissing, dabbing and teasing till my already excited, too obedient rogue of a body almost succumbed to the rising tide which engulfed it; I was soon no longer able to think of or remember anything, not Melissa, not Robert, only Simon, hardly myself . . . Why, if he hadn't taken me last night, did he do everything but take me now? I cried out something of the kind from my increasing shame and confusion; and he only laughed. He was enjoying me, I now knew, as some quite separate plan of his own.

"Why, my startled heart? why? If a little, frozen mouse crept into my bed one night out of the cold, would I frighten it so that it would never come back again? Wait till we are on our way to Rome, Miss Leah; then, you shan't sleep so sound, I promise you."

And that was how I came to leave Aske next day, in a plain cloak and bonnet and with very little gear, in a coach and, alone beside me on the journey which would take us both to Europe, Ann Aske's husband. And I had no regrets.

Part IV

ROMAN SUMMER

I

SIMON HAD TOLD me, even before we had caught the Channel packet from Dover some days later, that I would never have earned a living as a *fille de joie*. Whether or not it was true that I might have been all things to him that earlier day on the library floor, the reality, after the first night we spent together in an inn on the way to a westland port, from which we would take the coach-roads south by reasonable stages after Simon had concluded his own business there, was far otherwise. I tried to think of reasons, or excuses; Englishwomen, I told myself, in particular those who have been genteely brought up, are not perhaps adept in love, or not at first; and I knew I had made a sad botch of our primary excursion into passion.

In fact there was less excuse for me than for others of my kind, although the seduction of a prim little parson's daughter, who at times wore spectacles, might have seemed to many men a more formidable assignment even than bringing home a very young baby, almost unaided, from the Italian peninsula. I understood however that he had hopes of making some arrangement to bring the nurse also, for a little while, with us back to England, till other provision could be made for Melissa. But for myself, I had betrayed even my knowledge of the classics, which should have sustained me. I knew, after all, of the beauty of Helen and the havoc she wrought in Troy; and the delicious fate of Psyche after having been deposited, by her zephyr, in the bridegroom's home on a very high rock, away from everyone. I had read about Persephone and her successful ravishment by Hades, and Andromache and Dido and those improper loves of Zeus, Leda and Ganymede; and yet I had failed to repay Simon for his—as even then I realised—undoubted patience and kindness with me, in our bed at the inn.

It had been partly the room there, I knew; everything in it reminded me of poor Dorothy, and what had happened to her that time with Nicholas. The recollection of Dorothy was contained even in the bed-curtains, which were of dark, serviceable stuff and when drawn made the space we lay in together as dark and close as the tomb. That Simon was entombed with me, and that I was in his arms, as after all I had been most happily that other night at Aske when I had slept against him till morning, meant little; he had become, as I was miserably aware, a stranger, one who demanded and did to me what I still understood hardly at all, and was afraid of. Even in the close warmth I shivered, and grew rigid as if it was cold, though a fire blazed, as it had done no doubt for Dorothy, making shapes that flickered beyond the drawn and muffling curtains. Later I begged Simon to draw them apart a little, but still could not sleep; I lay and watched the orange square of the firelit wall, wretchedly aware that I had disappointed Simon, although it had not all hurt as much as I had expected. I knew I was a fool, and said so once aloud.

He answered at once from where he lay by me in our bed and I knew that he also had stayed awake. "You are my own love, no more yet," he said.

No more yet. But at least he was not angry, any more than he had been the time I waited outside his door: and in this knowledge in the end I slept.

He had already promised to show me where much of his

money was made and as we travelled westwards I felt that
he was watching me, with amusement somewhat evident in
his expression but, perhaps, I thought, he felt uncertain
about my plainly-dressed appearance; we would buy
clothes, he had said already, in Paris, but meantime I knew
I still looked like a governess. I sat with according docility
in the carriage and we said little to one another; Simon
himself was handsomely clad, in a dove-grey coat with
great upturned cuffs which had gold embroidery on them,
and a tricorne beaver. His hair was black as a crow's wing,
and pomaded; he had always disliked powder since the
time at Maria's, and never now wore it. He could have
made an escort for a queen, I thought, instead of myself,
plain and dull as a boxed pigeon in my closed, upholstered
seat; I saw heads turn to stare as we drove together
through the streets of the port. The prosperous houses, set
in wide streets and squares, most of them new-built, we
soon left behind; the streets grew meaner, and I thought
we must be coming to our destination, the house of shame
Jonie had told me of. The whorehouses, as Jonie called
them and as I still thought of them, proved to be a long
line of huts alongside the open wharves. Great ships, with
their sails furled, lay beyond in the clear water. As soon as
I saw them I knew that something was wrong.

"Simon, they're warehouses," I said, "not —"

"Yes, my love. I am sorry you are disappointed. Can
this be kept from our friends at home, do you suppose?
For the Devil to be a merchant, other than in flesh, would
sully my standing at Aske and elsewhere quite notably."
As so often, I was uncertain whether he was jesting or not.
It had all been said in the carriage, and there was no more
time to ask concerning it; we had drawn up, and out of the
door of the nearer hut a little hunchback came, bowing
deeply and obsequiously, like a troll out of the earth-lined
hollows below hills. He aided me, with the air of a *grand
seigneur* and as if I myself had been a duchess in brocade,
from the vehicle.

This was Sam Grover, the manager of the Gore warehouses. I knew him at once from Simon's tale of the Barbados. He looked better now, I thought, than he must have done then; he had put on flesh, and looked contented, at this moment, beaming with happiness at the renewed sight of Simon. The pair of them plunged into an immediate discussion about the delivery of certain bales, and I was escorted and left for a time in the tiny, ledger-crammed office, talking to the clerk. The conduct of business, the checking and receiving, and, after I had given him leave, the scratching, once again, of the young clerk's pen, went on unceasingly; in the near distance, there came the occasional hail of a tall ship. I watched it all till Simon came back again with the manager; it was a part of his life, I realised, that I had not known of, as there were no doubt a great many other parts of him still unknown. I had noticed also that here, as formerly, they spoke of Simon, and addressed him also, as Mr. Carden.

The warehouses were filled with bales and wooden crates, opened at times to reveal foreign wonders; rich shawls, heavy with embroidery in white or coloured silks, and printed India muslins, smelling of the sandalwood chips in which they had been packed. There were odd, eccentric things for rich folk here to buy; hookah-pipes, with glass bowls like a witch's globe for old men to sit over, inhaling cool smoke up through the water; and snuff of various kinds, and spices, and tobacco itself, close-pressed in broad fragrant leaves as it had left the plantations. The shop-keepers who would retail the goods were in and out, exchanging courtesies and snuff, but with their nostrils twitching knowledgeably also as regarded the purchases, which were displayed by Grover, the packers, or the negro porters who came past, from time to time, bearing bales or baskets on their heads, and grinning pleasurably at sight of Simon. He seemed well liked by those he employed, and I felt my heart constrict my chest with pride of him. If only they could hear at Aske about all this! But it was evident that the Devil, and the Squire, and merchant Carden did not acknowledge one another. Perhaps Prossy knew them both, I reflected; she was alone now at Aske with the baby and Ann, till we should return with Melissa.

One of the ships had come in and it was arranged that Simon might take me on board, where I stepped cautiously past the huge furled sails, and coiled ropes the thickness of a woman's waist. We watched the merchandise brought up and later drank tea and rum by invitation of the captain. While we were doing this the great vessel rocked gently, like a cradle; I thought, while I sipped my laced beverage, of all the myriad ships at sea, carrying goods without let. Their sails flung out in my mind like mighty wings, with the brown men hauling at the ropes and singing sometimes, as I had heard them do today while yet another ship came slowly into port, gulls wheeling high and whitely about its masts. The air was tangy with wind and salt when we emerged from the captain's stateroom, and the sun had come out above the sea, making a bright dazzle to the horizon. Afterwards we went back to the warehouse and Sam Grover, still bowing in the French manner, caused me, on leaving, to be given a flat parcel. I opened it back at the inn.

"He worships you, that little man," I said to Simon. He had been like a dog wagging its tail at sight of its owner, and the clerks and porters, also, I thought, as though Simon had been a king or great chieftain, come on a visit. I told him and he laughed. "Grover was with me in the Barbados," he said, again, as though that explained everything which no doubt it did. I closed my eyes against the thought of the brutality which still occurred in such places. I had seen, by now, the scars on Simon's back, long, white and as healed as they could be: but they would never leave him.

In the parcel was a shawl, of heavy silk the colour of ivory, having embroidery thick upon it and long close-knotted fringes at the edge, like queen's hair. They swung richly as I gasped, lifting out the lovely exotic thing from its wrappings.

"It is very beautiful," I said. "Why did Mr. Grover give it to me?"

"He did not."

"Then you—oh, Simon!" For I had never owned anything so beautiful in my life. He draped it round my shoulders. It proved to be as warm as wool, with a cherished, sliding sensation whenever I moved. "I shall take great care of it," I said, "and never put it on except on special occasions." I stroked the embroidery, which was of strange birds and flowers, with my fingers. Suddenly my feelings overcame me and I turned to him. "Oh, Simon, Simon!" It was all I could say; like the clerk at the warehouse, I seemed to have very few words.

"Oh Simon, Simon!" he mocked. "Do you love me?"

"Yes, oh, yes, I do, only I am so much of a fool—"

"Then I will make you pay for the shawl now." And it slid to the floor. I had already forgotten to take care of it.

Afterwards he said, against me, "Are you happy, Leah?" and, this time, I was able to answer more coherently; I even tried to choose my words. I told him I had never been as happy since I wore a red velvet gown beside Avice at my father's wedding, and it had fur on the sleeves, and since then I had never—

"There is certain to be a red velvet gown in Paris. We should be there in about four days, I believe."

"Oh, Simon, you know I did not mean—" I was distressed, for it did not seem right for him to spend much money on me; I was not, even yet, I knew, value for it. That was when he told me about the *fille de joie*. And when I remembered about that I was aware of a kind of fear, both for my own inadequacy and, also, of the hidden power I sensed in Simon himself, which he had not made fully known yet lest he frighten me.

2

IN PARIS, WE quarrelled. He had bought me the red
velvet gown and other things, among them a plain gold
ring. This I refused to wear, although he tried to put it on
my finger.

"To be a hypocrite is worse than anything," I said. "I
am not your wife; I am your mistress." The statement
seemed reasonable to me, but Simon was angry.

"Are you?" he said with sudden bitterness. "You do not
even know how to begin to achieve that state." And he
turned on his heel, after a few more words by us both, and
went out. He did not come back all of that night, and by
the end I had sobbed myself to sleep; in the small hours of
the morning I awoke and saw him moving about the room,
pouring water into a basin. He knew I was awake and
spoke without turning his head.

"Go back to sleep," he said, "it is still very early." He
sounded no longer angry, but I gave a sob; then he came
over. He smoothed the bed and kissed me, but only my
hair; matters were still not as they should be, I thought,
between us. In the end I slept again, miserably, waking
with a headache; and later in the morning we left Paris,
which is stated, erroneously, to be a city for lovers.

At Dijon there was a wine-tasting, and Simon made me
drunk. This had the desired effect, I believe; I do not
remember it. Several things had however become crystal
clear to me at last while the rest of the world, by contrast,
remained a blur. I remember little more except his
laughter, close against me so that I knew we were again by
then in bed; next day, in the coach going further south, he
told me that I had recited Ovid at him, but I had no
recollection of it.

"How could you have known that it was Ovid?" I said,
for I was aware that he had learnt no Latin from Lolly
Pate. I was certain both that Simon was deceiving me, and

that he was still laughing. I was still, I knew, in a state not quite usual, not perfectly composed; I wanted to touch him all the time, and had to restrain myself. "You told me," he said, regarding Ovid. "You instructed me, in fact, fairly well."

I had clasped my gloved hands firmly together in my lap, to keep from reaching out and stroking his sleeve, as though it had been a cat. I saw that he was still in a state of badly concealed amusement and blushed a little, and looked for help to the landscape beyond the carriage window. No doubt we would soon come to some mountains, as this was Cisalpine Gaul. I did not say it aloud; I must already have given him a great many classical allusions, from what he had implied.

My hand now separated itself from the other, without my volition, and stole over to his sleeve like a straying, inconstant mouse. He caught it and bit the fingers gently, then kept hold of the hand, in a strong clasp, while the carriage rolled on to the south. "That's better, my girl!"

To say that my initiation stretched across Europe may perhaps seem to be taking matters rather far; but the journey did not in any case seem a long one. Soon there was the sight of the Alps rising in early morning, like pink spun sugar beyond our inn-window in the sunrise; then later, beyond the mountains, the speech grew higher, harsher, Italian, having a timbre something like the sharp flavour of the grape-skins in their own red wine. This flowed for us all down the Plain of Lombardy, through Turin and great palaces, and by that time I had, surely, been fashioned into some kind of instrument for his pleasure, a little; and had learned the sweet wanton moaning of deep love soon, for he taught me well.

In such a way we came, at last, to our first sight of Rome, with her spires rising out of blue mist in the summer distance and a great dome, like a promise of perfection, floating among them like a bubble.

3

THE DIRECTION GIVEN by the wine-merchant to Simon in his letter proved to be a high, narrow grey house with an antique Roman mask incorporated in one new wall, staring out eyelessly. There was the shop entrance at one side, leading to a cool, dark inner cavern wherein, among mingled scents of stored sunlight, dust, and wine, bottles hung in straw cradles from hooks or beams, like hams at home. A fat man of perhaps fifty-odd years of age came out, rubbing his hands together in pleased excitement; he bowed, like Sam Grover at the warehouse, repeatedly over my fingers, as though his whole life had been spent in waiting only for this moment. Afterwards he led us into the house. Signora Giorgio being long dead, as he had told us in the letter, he had a housekeeper, who appeared briefly and thinly in black, then vanished after leaving a tray of wine.

Signor Giorgio served us with this and pressed upon me a plate of small sugared cakes, which because of the heat had begun to melt and in any case I did not feel like eating them. The sun in Rome is like everything else, either there or not, and when present hearty; my clothes, which Simon had purchased for me in Paris, were not light or loose enough and so again, here already, he had bought me further delectable gowns, thin enough for comfort, with a wide hat and innumerable pairs of fine white gloves. Every lady wore gloves out of doors in Rome, no matter how great the heat, and mine grew limp and soiled thrice daily, when I would change them. The dust was everywhere. We had already found out a thing which intrigued us in our separate ignorance of such matters, namely that the new Pope was quite unlike the Reformation ogre of my childhood, being young, handsome and sartorially inclined. His shoes, which were of traditionally embroidered satin, revealed shapely feet of which he was proud, and he used to sit with one extended to the ecstatic view of those ladies paying their respects at audiences. His wig was curled and powdered, also of much elegance. He was a builder, and had already in his brief time as Pontiff expressed the intention, which accounted for some of the dust, of making Rome the fairest city in the world. My own soiled gloves and our constant changes of clothing were one penalty exacted by the already changing skyline, and sounds of hammering were everywhere.

Signor Giorgio—with whom I was able to converse a little as my Italian, originally instilled at Fishy's, had been of some use since our arrival—presented me with the usual compliments, then went straight on to business. The *bambino* was very well, had grown, and we should see her presently. "She still has the nurse," he explained with some apology, as though it were unusual, "and she is, how you say it, not, not—" He had broken into sudden English for Simon. Many of the shopkeepers in Rome spoke it, particularly in this quarter which was near the Palazzo Muti, where the Pretender lived when he was in the capital.

Tact now became requisite. The nurse had milk, oh, yes, a great deal! "That is the main requirement, surely," said Simon, who was growing bored. He downed his remaining wine, which I knew was too sweet for him, and, concealing impatience which might well be to see the baby Melissa, though perhaps not, stood up, and waited firmly till our host rose also. "Yes, yes, *signore*, I understand, you are consumed! We will go up now," and we went. The Italians either, like their sun, are furiously active or else idle. The stout form preceded us, with an apology, up the outer staircase at a speed which left me breathless.

The stairs were narrow and of wood, ascending from a side-door which mirrored the shop-entrance, at the other side of the house-front. On the first floor, again sideways, not unlike the coachman's place they had over the stables at Aske, was a room. A young woman sat in a chair there; she made no attempt to get up, as she was nursing the child. Her dark eyes roved incuriously over us both and then returned to Simon, where he stood looking down at the baby. I did not like the expression in the nurse's eyes; it was evident, I told myself, that her present occupation did not sufficiently fill her mind. The baby itself was like all babies and had a fluff of dark hair on its small head. Later we found that it had dark eyes and a powerful yell. When the nurse Teresita—this was her name, as Signor Giorgio informed us with his flourish, as though it had been a concerto—took her breast away, we heard, for the first time, the voice of Melissa.

"*Piano, piano*," cooed the merchant, clutching his wig in what, I could see, was entirely theatrical deprecation: he evidently enjoyed the noise. "She is strong, it reveals itself," he explained happily. I could see that he was very proud of his own exploit in having saved Melissa, as well he might be; she was full of life, it oozed from her mouth in milkily expressed fluid and, I thought, from every pore of her. I kissed her, as was expected, and the sweet smell of the milk came up, making an island of warm, animal closeness in the austere little room. It was almost bare, uncarpeted as they were here, by reason of the heat; it held only the cradle, a table and chest, the single chair, and a bed against the wall. I wondered where the young nurse had come from and where her own child was. Haltingly, I asked her.

"Dead, *signorina*," she said, and looked me up and down. The title, I knew well, was an insult; she had seen through my pretence and, no doubt, my left glove. I did not like her. I said that I was sorry to hear about the dead child and turned away, looking out of the window while the men finished their talk and made tentative arrangements with Teresita about travelling home with us to England. I did not look forward to the journey back. But I myself had no more notion than Simon of how to care for a young baby on a long journey, and Melissa would have to be fed. So there it was; but we were not, in any case, leaving Rome yet. We had by now found an inn a little way out where there was a small, airy upstairs room, smaller than this one, with outside the window a vine which rustled charmingly and gave shade, and when one looked out beyond it there were the Apennines.

Simon was still talking to Teresita with Signor Giorgio as interpreter. She seemed to have made no difficulty about the journey. "Will your husband agree?" Simon wanted to know. "Will he not mind your leaving him, perhaps only for a little while, and you will be returned, when —?" He spread out his hands, leaving Signor Giorgio to deal with the provisos. Simon was vague, evidently, about the length of time it took to wean a baby. So was I.

Teresita replaced her large breast, still expressing milk a little, inside her black dress, like fruit into a bag. "I have no husband," she said deliberately, in English. She was now looking full at Simon, and as though she saw him naked, and smiling with a dazzling display of white teeth.

I found myself blushing. I felt myself grow scarlet all over in the oppressive little room and I wanted—how much I wanted!—to leave with Simon and get out, both of us, again into the air. I would use discourtesy, if necessary, to get him away from this woman. I would even fight. I would —

"We will go now, *grazie*," said Simon admirably, adding that we had an appointment.

"I noticed the nurse put herself forward somewhat," I ventured by way of conversation, once we had made our way downstairs and out into the sunlight, and had parted for the time with the signor.

"Unblushingly so. I prefer blushing ladies." He was looking ahead and not at me, and tucked my hand into his arm and again took my fingers, correctly gloved as they were, into his clasp; and thus, with joy between us, we made our way along the growing, gracious streets, the wide piazzas of modern Rome, and the sudden vistas nevertheless of a broken row of pillars, a shattered fountain, a stone mask in a wall, as the old peers through the new. I added primly that the baby would be very handsome. "No doubt you will contrive your plan about continuing the Askes."

"Damn the Askes," he said suddenly. "Are you fidging fain, my darling? Shall we go home?" For that phrase of Jonie's, which of course I had in the end told Simon (how could I keep silent about anything now?) no doubt explained my blushes at the merchant's house, and everything else. And Simon loved me, I thought, joy surging in me like a shower of unbidden gold; me, not Teresita with her breasts like melons and her hips like porpoises, and her flashing smile and other advertised wares. Together we walked along the Roman pavements as though we did not touch the stones at all, but only air; it was a quarter-mile to the inn and on the way, in a shadowed archway, we came on a pair of coupling lovers. We did not, I told myself, have to hide in an archway or make love on a tomb, as I had also seen happen here, or in the street. We could go home—the inn, for the time, was home, wherever Simon was, to me—and, once there, we would mount to our cool vine-shaded room and he would undress me and then himself, and we would go properly to bed no matter what the time of day. And so we did, and I forgot for a while about the baby Melissa and how we were to get her to England and when we did, marry her in the end to young Robert whether he liked it or not, and whether to take the nurse in the meantime or ... ah, Simon!

Later I said to him, "What if I were to give you a child of your own?" for, as I knew enough by now to know, in all our dealings he had always been careful not to get me with child. But his lifelong plan for Melissa seemed impractical; so many things, any number, might happen to prevent matters from falling out exactly as he wished, though nothing in the world, I knew, would turn him from his notion that, once he had set his will on a thing, he could enforce it despite the whole of Olympus, ranged against him. But at my own solution he looked grave.

"Would you bear my child, Leah?" he said. "Would you, my darling?" And I knew, with a faint withdrawal once more into myself, that he thought of me as by now, no doubt, with his will in all things, I had been made; a toy for delight, not to be strained or broken, not for everyday, only for gentle, considerate usage such as I had had, again now; not at any time to be permitted to interfere with sterner matters such as plans for Aske. Damn the Askes; he'd said it himself. And that little baby, whose life was already planned for her, was to be shipped home, and Teresita as well, for her milk was good and one could not change a baby from one nurse to the other without upsetting it. The baby. I began to laugh suddenly. When Simon and I, with Melissa, returned to Aske together, the village would say the child was mine, and that we had gone abroad till I should have borne it. But now Simon would not even give me a child when I asked for one.

Things were to turn out differently from almost all of the above arrangements. Meantime Simon still showed no inclination to leave Rome, or remove the baby from her present place, though he now paid the merchant for Melissa's keep and Teresita's wages. This meant he had to be absent sometimes, seeing to such matters and consulting Signor Giorgio. I learned to accustom myself to all this, beginning—and it was not difficult, even without the interest I had in such subjects from the time my father had induced me to share his own love—to know Rome for myself. I often went out unaccompanied now when Simon was elsewhere, as it was possible, with circumspection, for a young female of breeding to do, especially in late mornings when pursuit by gallants is at a minimum, though in no city can one hope entirely to escape it, whatever the time of day.

4

THE PIAZZA DI San Silvestro was always crowded with foreign visitors hoping to catch a glimpse of the Pretender and his young German wife, who had briefly returned to Rome from Albano. The visitors stayed also to gape at the flowersellers' booths filled with asphodel, roses and melon-flowers, the old church which houses the supposed upper jaw of John the Baptist, and the carriages with yellow wheels and patient, fly-ridden horses and mules which would in due course, when everyone had gaped long enough, bowl some of them away in hooded, ill-sprung, straw-smelling discomfort down the Corso. Sometimes instead they would linger on to gape further, their hats stuck round with flowers, if it was the time of carnival, still wearing last night's gay attire, by now limp and dusty in the heat, with their masks dangling from their hands and their revealed daylight faces puffed and wan; travellers use more licence when they are abroad than in England, and once I saw a man turn to vomit into a handsome old Roman basin, the flowers in his hat nodding sorrowfully. But others among the English were pleasanter, in particular the Jacobites here who had settled down, many of them, into local trades, with whom we ourselves dealt as shopkeepers. There were also the tutors or upper servants to great houses, accompanying young sprigs of the nobility on the Grand Tour to ensure that they did not overreach themselves. The sprigs themselves haunted the Piazza only briefly; they had been warned before they left home on no account to meet, except by unavoidable accident and in that case without speaking any English to him at all, the Pretender. The cold, watchful eye of Sir Horace Mann, the British Ambassador, was everywhere; I never encountered that personage, but I believe he sent home meticulous reports of every single happening concerning young visiting Britons who might, although it seemed unlikely these days, be personally reminded of an ancient loyalty. It seemed to me extraordinary that the government at home should still be watchful of the fabled charm of an elderly, disappointed drunkard whose travelling days were done, although I believe he always kept a box of gold coins under his bed ready for return home if called for. But the call would never now come, any more than it would do so for Sir Francis Drake awaiting his drum-roll, or Barbarossa or King Arthur. We were in a new age, for which the absent young noblemen were, one presumes, being fitted in some other manner than by taking the sword for the Stuarts.

The remaining crowd, which could be thick, jostled me one afternoon when I had stayed out by myself somewhat later than usual, for Simon was away on prolonged business connected with letters of credence for conveying the baby and its Italian nurse home. I had put on my chip-hat and, with a light gauze scarf over my shoulders and muslin gown, made my way to the piazza, which with the old church opposite was one place women might frequent by themselves without being pestered. I wandered into the church out of the day's heat and, in the sudden welcome darkness, surveyed the gleam of silver votive-offerings on their velvet cushions, and smelled the doused incense about San Giovanni's altar and, as before, looked at the grisly panel depicting his head on a platter, carved into the stone walls.

A scuffling sound made me turn, sharply feeling for my purse; but it was only that in one of the narrow side-passages to the smaller chapels, always unbearably stuffy with their dust-laden curtains, a stout lady of discreet appearance had fainted. I came to try and help her, and knelt down and loosened her laces, which were tied too tight about her fat, sweating torso. The relief made her open her eyes, which were a pallid blue, and she

said a word or two in English. I assisted her to a seat,
fanned her somewhat with my handkerchief, and offered
to fetch water from the source outside where it dripped
into the Roman basin. But a second lady—they were, both
of them, of the appearance and dress of my own kind at
home—had appeared, searching and fussing nervously;
unlike the first, she was thin, and wore a plain straw hat
and gown of serviceable stuff, not too retentive of the
summer's heat. Her gloves I noticed were immaculate, but
bore small darns. She sat down by the other, and
ministered unto her; from what I gathered now, they were
related.

"My poor dear Milly, my own poor sister! There, I will
fetch the water myself; this young lady has already been
much too kind." But I went, of course, to fetch them the
cool fine water of the Roman spring, carrying it back in a
shell such as is always kept there. Poor Milly drank, giving
a hearty gasp which showed that she had recovered for the
time. By now we had, of course, progressed further in our
acquaintance, as happens whenever the English meet
abroad although they are by far more reticent at home. It
turned out that they were indeed schoolmistresses, not—as
I would have thought, the type being unmistakable—from
England itself but from Florence, where for some years
now they had together owned a small and select finishing-
school for the further instruction of young ladies.

"It is particularly for those who wish to become
proficient in some language not their own, for example
Italian or French," poor Milly's sister, who was the elder
and *éminence grise*, told me. She added that poor Milly
(the adjective was so frequently applied in conversation
that I still use it, although that lady was not, by now, an
object of particular sympathy and in fact managed very
well for herself, like Mrs. Musgrave, most days), was
troubled at this moment by the failure to appear of a
governess already hired from England, who had been
promised overland by way of Berne but who had not

arrived, although they had now waited in Rome a week before hearing that she had found a situation nearer home.

"It is a serious matter for us, and at this time of year they are not easy to find, being all engaged already," said the elder sister, who was always called Miss Coke Green and never Miss Eustacia. "Our young ladies return to us in early autumn," and she looked me over hopefully with the bright eye of a speculative bird, as if to imply that I seemed most suitable and would almost be taken without references.

I lowered my eyelids and, in what I knew to be a thoroughly mendacious manner, murmured that I had not, as she evidently supposed from my appearance, conveyed a young charge here, but was staying in Rome with friends on a visit of pleasure. At the same time a dancing certainty, renewing in me the joy in which my whole body now daily, nightly pulsed and had its being, told me exactly the expression which would arise on the good lady's face were I to say, as I longed to do, "Dear madam, I cannot consider your offer because I have a lover who fills my days with delight and my nights with tenderness, and the whole of my life now, here or anywhere is for him." But I did not say it, and instead took her direction with, as I said and meant it, the intent of letting anyone know who might suit them, had I encountered such a person, which was unlikely as things were.

We parted, shortly after that, with the expressed hope of perhaps encountering one another again in Rome, or should I ever come to Florence.

It was Miss Milly who said this last, a trifle wistfully; I liked the absurd creature. I liked them both, though Miss Eustacia made me feel as deceitful as, no doubt, I was; she had a fine pair of clear grey eyes, not unlike Fishy's, and their direct gaze caused me to see myself for the first time as, in fact, I really was, here in Rome; a kept woman. But by then little cries and flutterings heralded the arrival of the *carozza*, which would take them back to their

Colosseum inn (the food was good, the beds were clean, everything was very English, they said, and one could even order tea). For they had found, shortly before leaving, that my name being Considine meant that I was the daughter of an old acquaintance of Miss Coke Green's; for she had known, though not well, my dear father when they were both for some time in Worcestershire, many years previously.

I would almost have driven with the sisters to their destination, having found this out; as it was, I thought I might perhaps try to see them once again before they left Rome in a few days' time, after making further attempts of their own to find a governess, of which they were not very hopeful. But Simon was to meet me shortly now at the place where the Pope was planning to erect a great obelisk at the top of a flight of new steps, from which one could see a fine prospect of Rome; we often went there, despite the pinkish dust which settled on everything, to watch the builders' progress and to drink cool wine at an inn, nearby the steps.

I could not know under what circumstances I was to meet the two sisters again. I could not know quite yet.

5

I AM A Whig.

Like the other visiting English in Rome, I contrived to have a glimpse of the Pretender, in the same way as one visits the catacombs there and John the Baptist's withered maxilla. It is not that I am unsympathetic to Charles Edward Stuart, merely that, had he kept an eye about him, he would have known when the times had gone by, and might perhaps have accepted the throne of Corsica, which was once offered him in his youth, and have done very well there among that proud fierce people. Instead, he caused much death, heartbreak and misery, and himself

ended in a wretched state, though at the time I speak of he
had fairly recently taken a bride, and still hoped for a son.
We saw them one day in their carriage, driving in past the
leprous patch of stone where the royal arms of Great
Britain had till lately been seen above the palace-entrance,
but the Pope, who was their landlord, had at Sir Horace
Mann's urging taken it away, and also the clashing salute of
Papal Guards. All this no doubt made Charles gloomy, and
he brooded in his place beside the young wife, whom
everyone had turned out to gaze at and cheer by reason of
her youth and her golden hair, seldom seen in Rome. It
was worn on a high frame, and I thought I myself might
beneficially acquire such a method of wearing it.

Simon used to waken me in the mornings with his light
swift kisses, honey-sweet, a shower of living butterflies felt
above the opening rose which had been sleep. It would still
be very early, before the heat of the day. This fact gave us
pleasant exchanges; I said the Italians always transacted
their business then, taking after the old Romans, who
would partake of olives and corn-bread, and some wine, as
the sun rose, and then receive visitors, which we would
not. "The sun," Simon would say, "has risen long ago,
little sluggard, and has been shining in on us for many
hours." The light soon grew dark-gold in our room, coming
as it did between the dancing vine-leaves beyond the
window.

He kissed my stomach, then laid his hand, with the
slow, considering gesture I loved, under my inconsiderable
breasts, raising them a little, kissing each separately, as he
said, to make them grow. I watched the sunlight, on his
hair and body; I was drugged with fullest happiness,
amazed as always when Simon showed how much he loved
my body, which I had never thought of as likely to appeal
to anyone; a thin flat white thing, with limbs like
celery-sticks, which could deceive me in the dark and glow
by now and respond and tremble, as though the flesh itself

were royal in a royal bed. But by day there was no such illusion, for me at any rate. I murmured against Simon now almost resentfully; it seemed extraordinary, a little wasteful, for his glorious, pagan nakedness to expend itself in contemplation, however godlike, of so poor an offering. The adoration I myself had for Simon could not fully express itself in flesh. It could not even do so in words, which were inadequate like everything else of mine. He listened to me for a while and smiled, his mouth travelling over my breasts.

"They are absurd, like two halfpence," he said. "Why do I love you? Because, with the precision of a good little governess, you can tell me—"

"Don't." I did not, at this particular instant in time, wish to be reminded of governesses.

"Don't, don't," he mocked me. "Why are you like a little frightened bird always, after all I . . . no, my tremulous one, my sparrow, I said I loved you because you can tell me with certainty what the ancient Romans had for breakfast. None of the others knew. And now lie quiet for me again a little while, my darling darling . . . "

Our modern Roman breakfast was, with the ineffable tact of all Latin races, left outside the door and the tray was never collected by anyone till midday. It was always fruit and coffee, the latter contained in an earthen pot. The smell of coffee-grounds lingered agreeably about the inn all day, cloying a trifle, in the southern manner, for down here they added no herb to it, to render it bitter. There was no bitterness about anything.

Later we would go out, I in a different one of the many gowns he had brought me. I had never had so many clothes and trifles, and never would again. We had found them together in the grand, baroque centres near the Cancellaria and again in little booths below the Vatican wall, where the dark secret arcades house treasures of lawn, velvet and silk; once we found a Venetian mask for me there, with a fall of black lace. On the open booths of Santa Susanna there would be jewellery, beads and trinkets of mosaic, earrings of turquoise and sea-coral to hang in one's ears; or cameos carved at San Paolo, some new and some old, all exquisite. I had shifts of transparent lawn edged with lace, that Simon swore he had bought for me personally in a convent, where they made them. He put the shifts on me one after the other and then took each one off. Other times we would dress up grandly to go to a masked ball or summer carnival, he in a domino whose colour, I remember well, was yellow. I was glad of this because it meant I could not lose Simon in the throng; everyone else wore black, red or lavender. I had always this fear of losing him, and perhaps never finding him again; later, on our way home, I would walk close held in the crook of his arm, gazing up at his eyes' glitter behind the slits of his mask through the slits of my own, and clutching his fingers as an extra safeguard. Then again we would hire a carriage and visit the Apennine countryside, the great lake glooming slate-blue under its hills, and the catacombs nearby Rome where martyred skulls waited piously on shelves, and Simon stole one; I never knew what happened to it. And always, always, after visits to famous churches and gloomy palaces, shrines and ruined temples and the Colosseum, with its seething market inside like ants in a heap, and the Tiber itself, rolling yellow where Horatius had swum long ago, we would go home gladly in the end and make love. Everything converged towards and sprang from that, both at the day's end and its beginning.

One day I, who had again been noting the grand ladies dressed in their latest fashions on the Corso, decided, next time I had an hour or two alone, to obtain a hairdresser. The Pretender's wife was not the only one to wear her hair this year on a frame, very plain and unbecoming to the face, but high as a church steeple; I though the arrangement would give me the height I needed. So when Simon was off somewhere—about the baby, I expected, for she needed a good deal of arranging for although we had not yet, being too greatly entranced with ourselves and with the place, made any real move towards returning to England—on such a day, I caused one of these persons to be sent for and brought to the inn. He washed my hair and dressed it, charging a great deal for that and for the frame itself, which looked like a lobster-pot. The finished result was startling, but very fashionable; it did not therefore matter that it would be uncomfortable when one lay down, for one could not demolish it without the constant services of a lady's maid. I asked in my halting Italian how I was to put my head down on a pillow without disarranging everything, and an explanatory volley greeted me which I could not wholly understand, but whittled down in the end to one final answer; I must also purchase a pillow of wood. The edifice itself need then on no account be taken down until the next visit of the hairdresser. He sold me such a pillow, shaped like a box with a bite out of it, and costing a great deal, and went away.

I then dressed myself, in some trepidation at Simon's reception of a wooden pillow, in my other remarkable purchase, which was the only one I felt would do justice to the hair. It was a completely circular cloak of Venetian brocade, fashioned so as to act the part of an unbelted gown. I had seen the ladies patrolling on the Corso in these, and they had the benefit once shared by farthingales of revealing nothing at all of the true state of the wearer's figure. I turned myself about before my mirror in the inn, still a trifle uncertain but on the whole pleased; one must change with the times, and the tower of hair would at least enable me to walk out creditably with Simon, alongside whom I had hitherto trotted like, I told myself, a small undistinguished dog, below elbow-level.

Simon came in then and caught me at this mirror-pastime; and burst out laughing. Then he seized me and dismantled all my expensive hair, taking out the pins and throwing the frame out of the window. The tirade that followed started in amusement and ended in increasing anger; how had I dared to make a spectacle of myself and him; what did I imagine I looked like now, a whore? "And that cloak needs a midwife," he finished coldly. "Did I not tell you never to wear it in my sight? Leah, Leah, what does it matter what other women make fools of themselves at? If you were another woman and not yourself, would I ever have loved you?"

And he whipped off the Venetian cloak and threw me on the bed and, for the first time and as though he were still angry, made hard love.

Was it next day? The day in question must have been long, for I became two people in it; one hour I was in a glow of love and happiness, and then ... But I must, surely, remember the last time we were together and the way in which, after Simon had gone out, I suddenly felt I could not endure the time without him till he returned, and went out and followed him where he had gone. I remember that I had not let him make love to me, saying I had a headache and that I would lie down for a little out of the sun, and he could go alone. And then, yes, that was it, after he had left me with all tenderness, drawing the curtain so that the light would not hurt my eyes, and moving quietly about the room before he left, I lay on the bed for a while, then after all followed Simon; as soon as he had gone, my head had felt better.

It did not trouble me again even in the sun, which as usual was blinding in the hot afternoon. I had dressed quickly and plainly in my *feuille morte* gown which had a white lawn tucker, and tied the wide hat Simon had bought me over my hair. Its brim was the only shade in the dazzling streets, which were deserted; I lost my way, being a fool with any direction, and was some time in finding the house where the baby stayed; it was Sunday, and after noon there were no shops open and no one left about to ask. But I found it in the end and, after trying the locked shop-front, went swiftly, gladly up the stairs; how surprised and glad he would be to see me!

A light burned, with a small steady flame, behind red glass; it illumined some saint's shrine on the wall of the staircase. Otherwise the house was empty and quiet, too quiet, I thought. Melissa did not wail or make the sounds babies do, showing there is one in the house. Perhaps she was sleeping.

I opened the door carefully, lifting the catch without a sound lest I wake Melissa. She was asleep, I could see now, in her pearwood cradle over by the window; the barred shadow of the casement fell across her face. It fell also across the nurse's bed, against the wall furthest from the door. The bed held two people; one of them was Simon. Under him was the girl Teresita, and she was naked, her breasts like great filled creamy gourds beneath his hands. Her eyes were open and she saw me.

I closed the door and put the latch down again and went out, as quietly as I had come, into the street. The sunlight was still blinding and I walked quickly into it. It had not yet occurred to me to wonder where I might be going, or to tell myself that I would never again go back to the inn.

6

AT SOME POINT I found myself in a church; it was not San Silvestro. The furnishings and arrangements were however much the same, and there was a life-sized Pietà by the altar. A sound of sobbing came from near by and I saw the prostrate, black-clad figure of a woman in deep grief; I envied her her feeling and that she could find release in tears, and in a lit candle. The chapel was filled with an oppressive sadness, as though generations of heartbreak had knelt there.

I went and sat down and, not to make myself conspicuous, knelt; I still felt nothing and knew that what I wanted was time and peace to think, not pray. It was not for some time that I was able to tell myself that I would never pray again. For the moment, like a little hammer knocking at the back of my mind, came the awareness that I must get away, and never see Simon again; I must get away.

Simon. I had not been able to satisfy him physically and he had gone to a whore.

The plain, ugly words rising in my mind recalled something, some memory. After a time it came back to me as the voice of Ann, that day by the pond long ago. *"There's still my body,"* she had said. *"Marriage!"* and then an expression of loathing. Ann had disliked Simon from the beginning.

Ann. Moralists would, no doubt, say that I was being punished now for having gone away with Ann's husband. Ann, who herself had lain down with Fordwoodham later and had dosed herself to void his child. They would say, naturally, that Ann had been punished also. We had all been punished, except Simon of late.

Punishment. Already, this meant that I must not see Simon again. I must not lie in his arms again. I must forget that I had ever lain in them. I must go away.

The English ladies. They had had a school in Florence and had wanted a governess. Till the other day, they had still lacked any such person. Florence was some way from Rome.

There was a sacristan in the church. I knew he would speak some English; they mostly did. My mind was clear and cold and calculating now, no more a little frightened bird . . . don't, don't. A bird, caught once in a beguiling net, but now I was free. I was free.

The sacristan spoke English, as I had expected. He no doubt earned a coin or two by showing tourists over the older part of the building. No doubt he thought I was such now, and he should have his coin. "Can you tell me," I said carefully, "of a cheap convent where I can find lodgings? I am staying at an inn which is too expensive, and I wish to change it."

For it would all have to be done very carefully, this about the English ladies. They would be less likely to give me the situation were I to appear, dishevelled and shocked, with a white face and no luggage at the door of the Colosseum inn. Everything must be done with circumspection, from my convent, giving them time to consider the matter if they wished to do so. But I was Mark Considine's daughter, and no doubt my poor father would serve as a reference. I would say, with truth, that I had parted with my friends and had decided to stay and look for a situation while still in Italy.

A precise little governess . . .

I still had a certain amount of spending-money, although it was Simon's. As soon as I could, I thought, I would return it to him. The other things he had bought me, every one, I would leave behind at the inn; he could give them to Teresita, if—I thought with sudden vicious-ness—her huge breasts would stuff into the bodices.

The convent the sacristan had recommended as suitable for an impecunious English lady was situated in the Via Antica, and I had to spend further sums on a *carozza* in order to arrive in a decorous manner there and, also, to avoid the possibility of meeting Simon on the streets. The familiar smell of horse-flesh and straw, the jogging of the unsprung vehicle, jolted me almost back to a realisation of my true state; by the time the convent was reached I was shaking through my whole body and could hardly step out and up to the door, where there was a heavy iron rasping-pin. The portress who appeared presently at the grille spoke no English and had, after I had stumbled through the process of asking for shelter for a few days, to

go and ask higher advice; I waited on the step, watching
the stones of the street down which legions had marched
to Pompey's wars; worn as they were, they were puddled
now, for after the great heat it had begun to rain. To my
relief, the portress reappeared soon and opened the heavy
locked door, revealing a whitewashed stone passage with
scrubbed tiles in a strange old pattern, having each the
consular fascia in yellow on bright blue. One remembers
such things at such times. I followed the portress, watching
the flapping of her black skirts and hearing that the rain,
which is brief at that time of year, had stopped.

The convent belonged to the Ursulines and the small room
they gave me was cool. I had explained, as well as I could,
that my baggage had been sent on to another destination
and that I should be lodging here with them for a few days
only, till friends should come to take me away. What I
should do if the friends failed I could not yet think. My
calm plans, made in the midst of shock, deserted me in the
execution from the moment the door closed and left me
alone, with the portress's footsteps growing fainter along a
second passage which led to the enclosed quarter. As soon
as she had gone I knew I would have to recall her; I had to
find some means of obtaining writing-materials, and to
send a letter to Simon and, also, to the Englishwomen at
their address in Rome. In the end all this was accom-
plished.

The letter I wrote to Simon was quite short. I told
him—in case Teresita had not, I thought—that I had come
to the house, and had seen him with her. I said nothing
more regarding that. I told him also that I had made
arrangements for a situation, that I would be well looked
after, and that he was not to trouble about me further or,
on any account, to try to find out where I now was. I said
nothing about my clothes or other gear and truth to tell
did not care, or ever know, what happened to them.

I sent that letter, and the other to the Colosseum inn,

off by special bearer that same evening, lest, firstly, the two sisters should be departing for Florence early on the morrow, and secondly because I knew that, by now, Simon would have returned to the inn and, not finding me there and perhaps already knowing why, might think I had drowned myself in the river or committed some other act of folly, if he heard nothing from me before morning.

In the morning, he came.

It had been announced to me by the nun that a visitor awaited me in the convent parlour, and I hurried upstairs behind the portress, thinking it was one of the English ladies, who had certainly called very early in response to my letter. The passages, and other rooms, like my own, were whitewashed and the reflected light was of a bluish, luminous quality. It fell on Simon's tall figure, standing by the window.

He heard my involuntary, indrawn breath; I would have turned and gone unseen out of the room, but the portress had already closed the door. He came swiftly across the expanse of floor towards me, saw my expression, stopped, turned white about the mouth and said, in a voice which told me he had not slept any more than I had done, the previous night, "In God's name, Leah! I was walking the streets, searching, till your letter came; I asked everyone . . . "

"How did you find me?" I said coldly. "I asked you not to try to do so." My mind still was cool, separate and precise; a governess. I even found leisure for surprise that the sisters had no objection to male visitors; they had appeared to think it quite customary, and no doubt it was.

Simon had made an impatient gesture. "I asked the letter-bearer, naturally," he said. "What kind of fool do you think me? That letter—"

"I was the fool," I said. "I am cured now."

"Leah—"

"Leave me, please. I haven't—I don't want—"

Abominably, my control was deserting me; his very presence made me babble, as I had used always to do in the end, in bed. No more bed, never that, not even the thought or memory of it. A convent room, a narrow room in a girls' school. The remembrance of the school strengthened me, and reminded me that on no account must the two ladies, if they came, find Simon still here. "Please go," I said again. "There is nothing more to say; I have made my arrangements, as I told you," and I turned to the door.

"Damn your arrangements," he said, and placed himself in the way so that I withdrew, not yet able to bear his nearness; it would have been so much easier to yield, I knew even then; but nothing could ever be the same. He sensed this, I think; he had grown very white. "So you would shed me as if I were a worn-out coat," he said. "Can you, my gently reared little madam, perhaps try to understand a little? You were . . . " and his voice dropped, to the tender, caressing note I knew well, and my heart throbbed and responded, in spite of everything my head knew. "You were as I so often told you; a frightened bird, one that has been hurt, and I . . . Leah, men are animals, no doubt, too near the earth; I am a worm, if you like. A worm for the bird." He smiled, and again my heart wrenched round in me. To forgive him everything, go on, even if it were not quite as before . . . but one would never know.

"One would never know," I said aloud, "which whore you had been with, or were going to, every time you were restrained with me. Did you tell Ann these tales, when you first married her?" For I had a wish to wound him as I had been wounded; it was unforgivable of me to mention Ann, and his face darkened with anger.

"I went to a whore that time in Paris," he said. "Did you know that? Do you—even yet—know why?"

I did not answer. Presently he said, "I would not constrain you. Do you still prefer that I go? Is that your certain wish, not to see me again?"

"Yes."

"Have you money?"

"Yes."

I did not see him go, at the last, for I had hidden my face in my hands. An hour and a half later, in a flutter of joyous anticipation and consent, the two Misses Coke Green arrived to take me with them to Florence.

7

THE VILLA FIORI had been at first rented, then later purchased, by the two sisters as their financial position improved and their school grew modestly successful. The house itself was not in the first quarter of the residential city, though within walking distance of most of the sights. From it one could see a short stretch of the River Arno, but it was possible for the attention to be given instead to the small garden itself, which was filled, for the previous owner had been an exile, with English roses. They bloomed by now in a kind of adoptive luxuriance, seeming, I thought, to grow in a larger, brighter form than at home though with a less sweet scent. I did not see them till next morning, for it was late when we arrived in the carriage.

I had indulged in further mendacity in order to explain my red eyes, for I was, I told the sisters, unaware of the whereabouts of my luggage, which had been sent on mistakenly with that of my friends who were returning to England. To this Miss Coke Green, who was a businesslike person, offered to advance me a little of my salary, the terms of which she stated at once. Miss Milly said excitedly that they could furbish me with such necessaries as I should need until my own gear was returned. Had I not been my father's daughter, I doubt if even these two good souls, the elder of whom was shrewd, would have behaved as trustingly in all these ways to a stranger without any baggage. However I had relieved a pressing worry for them, as they had been quite unable to find a replacement in Rome during their stay. I would also have been enabled to pay the convent and have a little left over, but—my feelings when I discovered this were hard to describe—Simon had already done so for me, on leaving. This was the kind of act he could perform which made it impossible not to love or, depending on circumstances, hate him implacably. I found, as the carriage rolled towards Florence with myself wedged between the two ladies, Miss Milly very voluble so that there was no need to talk, that I could not, by any means, implacably hate Simon, even now, only a day after we had parted. As the days passed I was to hate him less and less.

The school was for young ladies aged not less than fourteen years, being intended not to give them the rudiments of an education but to finish this, as far as is necessary for entry into the polite world. It was, if anyone likes, a kind of glorification of Mrs. Musgrave's classes, with considerably more appeal to the intelligence. For such a purpose Miss Coke Green herself was particularly fitted, for like my mother she had been a governess in a great house, and since then had continued to improve her mind by reading, which she still did when there was time. Although she was in appearance the frailer of the two sisters, the whole enterprise in fact rested on her shoulders; for Miss Milly, who was eight or nine years the younger, had developed a chest-condition which made it advisable for her to live out of England. This I heard, but unless the air of Florence had meantime alleviated the condition, Miss Milly had very little wrong with her chest, wherein were located an excellent pair of lungs if one might judge from the voice she used when teaching classes. I heard from another source that the real cause of the sisters' leaving England had been that Miss Milly had been jilted, and had broken her heart and had almost died, till Miss Eustacia took her away. This version gave me a fellow-feeling for her.

My own quarters at the Villa Fiori were cramped, being no more than a curtained cubicle shut off by this means from the girls' dormitory. Miss Coke Green apologised for this, and said with truth that there was no more room when all the pupils were present. The little house, with its kitchen-quarters and laundry, the classrooms and office and a withdrawing-room, very large but which it was necessary to have for the purpose of impressing visiting parents and to display the harpsichord to advantage, was on two floors only. It looked asymmetrical by reason of the fact that an inner court, not unlike a Roman atrium, ran round three sides and had a pillared arcade where the young ladies could sit to do their painting and embroidery, out of the deleterious rays of the sun.

I did not show my dismay at sight of the cubicle, which seemed to promise very little privacy; but they had been so good to me already that I would not complain. I went to bed there after supper on that first night and fell asleep at once; the young ladies would not return from their holidays for a day or two, when some might be expected to arrive by the coach-load.

8

MY FIRST NIGHT at the Villa Fiori had been comfortable, for I was tired. Before I drifted off to sleep I had pictured the dormitory lying beyond my curtains, still empty and pale in the light of the risen moon. Soon each narrow bed would be filled, and with the arrival of the full contingent of young ladies there would be responsibility for them and, I feared, little peace. But now it was all my own and I lay and remembered, then again the next night, by now as though it belonged to someone who had died, my summer with Simon. With the prospect of security I now had, I could forget him, I told myself; in working for these kind souls who had, most fortunately and opportunely for myself, employed me without asking questions of a variety I could not answer, I need surely find no difficulty in transforming myself from one person to another, perhaps even to the young woman of rectitude I had once been. In the midst of this praiseworthy resolve I would fall asleep and would not waken till morning.

The sun would be shining on the roses when I awoke early and their scent, which is supposedly at its finest in England about noon, came tentatively already here like a promise of sweetness; but the dew had dried out on the petals already, as it would not have done at home. I thought of the English exile who had lived here, walking among his roses and thinking of England; like him, I must try to forget it and Aske, and everything I had known or been. I washed and dressed speedily in my cubicle and went down to breakfast. Miss Milly in those first days would be waiting, a broad smile on her still drowsy face; a teapot sat before her and she wore a morning-wrapper and cap.

"My sister has already breakfasted," she would say, then ask, as she always did, if I preferred an English breakfast? "My sister and I always enjoy it as a good start to a working day," and then the maid would appear with covers containing eggs and bacon. At first I fell upon this gladly, and Miss Milly watched in some amusement.

"You are exactly like the girls, some of whom will arrive by the midday coach tomorrow, my sister tells me. That is a little earlier than we had expected, and they eat tremendously, in spite of remaining as slim as yourself, and the resulting food-bills—oh, dear me, you know I did not mean *that*, Miss Considine!"

Nations, and individuals, have risen to a height and fallen, when the time came, correspondingly low. The fall of

Rome occurred, I believe, more by reason of imprudent taxation than from the attentions of Attila. That I taxed myself, or was taxed, in many ways at the Villa Fiori is quite true, and I would have expected to feel hungry at mealtimes. But while I ate well enough, unlike most young ladies in contemplation of a broken heart, I put on no flesh; in fact, I grew thinner. Miss Milly noticed this, and fussed over me for a time like a stout, motherly and rather foolish hen, until the young ladies left her no time for it, and for that I was grateful. For by that time I had no appetite for food, especially in the mornings when the very sight of eggs and bacon made me feel sick, though later, if I had not eaten any, I felt hungry. By that time, I should have known also that certain lunar courses of women had not visited me, and it is perhaps incredible that I did not; but the pressure of my work was by then heavy and constant, lasting well into the night hours so that by the end, without time to think of myself too much, I fell into exhausted slumber behind my curtains. That it was almost a full three months, the whole of one term, before any lack of this kind was noticed by me may strain belief, but it was so; my own downfall in the end being due to what I had so enthusiastically fallen upon in the beginning, to wit, the English breakfast.

But meantime I must describe the young ladies. I will not attempt, though it would not be dull, to describe them all. They were the same variety, in talent and social standing, that had been met with at Fishy and Carp's, for the most part rich rather than well-connected, or their parents would not have sent them to the Villa Fiori in the first place. The English did not come from England, for there are schools there already near one's home, despite the attractions of learning a foreign tongue in its own country, a practice which has since grown much more fashionable than it was at the time of which I speak. But that there were many English here nevertheless, and not a few Scots, was due to the fact that, thirty-odd years before, the parents of these girls had supported the Pretender and had come afterwards, having evaded the hangman or the block, to lifelong exile in Italy and France, after the fashion of Old Madam's brother in the previous rising. Their lands and money having been sequestered, they had to think of ways to maintain themselves, and on the whole did this with some success. Some went into the French King's army, but others, and the Scots especially—being hardheaded and shrewd and owing to the poverty of that nation—had long accustomed themselves to the idea of apprenticeship to some profession or trade, even if of noble blood which many of them originally were. Often, when they had prospered, or to help them do so, they had contracted marriages with Frenchwomen or Italians, possibly the daughter of the firm to which they were in the first place indentured; and it was the children of such marriages whom I taught now, and they were sent less to perfect their Italian than to learn properly spoken English, for every Jacobite dreams of again returning home. They and I benefited one another mutually in this way, and I was able to perfect my Italian at the Villa Fiori.

I liked them, on the whole—I had been in some terror, less evident with my other troubles occupying me than it might otherwise have been—about teaching young women at all, as they had poise, address, and were in many cases impudent. The worst was, and I must now dwell on her a little, a girl with light eyelashes named Cornelia Fraser. I try not to give way to unreasoning dislike at first meeting anyone, especially a child of sixteen; but the fact remains that my first impression of Cornelia proved to be correct, and she was to cause me much misery. She was pretty enough, and would always get her own way by ingratiating manners when she chose; but she did not choose, or not often, with me. She was sly, cruel—she used me, as is sometimes done with young instructresses who work for pay, as a kind of whipping-post or target, or butt; I do not know the best description, except that constantly, and without warning, she would at all times be ready with a vicious little knife to twist in me.

This did not make itself fully manifest at once. In the meantime, I had tried to overcome my initial terror and was, in many ways, beginning to enjoy my work. The times I liked best were those during which I could myself become, in a sense, a pupil among the rest, for Miss Coke Green herself was a remarkable woman. I can well understand that she and my father, when they had met briefly years before, would each of them remember the meeting for life although they never met again. She had a mind which was avid, precise, scholarly and, in the true sense, catholic. She would investigate every new thing she heard of, adopting or else dismissing it as suitable, or otherwise, for her girls; this standard applied to everything, and she spared herself no trouble in the matter. This led to one of my greatest pleasures, for she would sometimes invite me to go with her to a picture-gallery, to inspect some exhibition of paintings as perhaps instructive, while it stayed on view in Florence, for the girls at the school. Later she would take them to it, provided she had made certain there was no matter in the galleries which the girls' parents might later call in question. This search sometimes warred with Miss Coke Green's own preferences, and she said to me once, with a little half-completed gesture which in anyone else would have been a shrug, "I myself would have preferred them to view the Rubens for the flesh-tones, if nothing else, but old Mackenzie would come and remove those two girls of his at once, for he's a Presbyterian, and I dare not risk it." So she would conduct the girls in the end, and myself when it could be arranged, round head-portraits, which were remarkably fine, and Dutch renderings of assembled flowers, fruit and dead game. There were also the Italian primitives, on which she was most knowledgeable. As I had never seen anything of such a kind either in my brief life at the rectory or at

Aske, where the portraits were, I now realised, second-rate, I took full advantage of the instruction. Even my poor father cannot have known such pictures existed, and the state of his ignorance, had he realised it, would have grieved him. But almost more than the beauty and interest of the paintings themselves I was entranced with Miss Coke Green's exposition of them. I regard those hours as a part of my life which, however briefly, was most profitably and gladly spent, and the recollection of the swift Arno, the arched bridges and slender campanile, and the crisp, autumnal air of Florence which sharpens the mind and leads to question and challenge in a way the inert summer heat of Rome can never do, is one of pleasure for me.

But I must return, however unwillingly, to Cornelia.

9

I TAUGHT THE girls languages, as I have said, including French which was of great importance, as it was then the universally spoken tongue in polite circles. Italian until recently about then, with the advent of Alfieri and other modern poets who had begun to write in it, had remained neglected and almost rustic. We were in some little difficulty therefore with regard to the acquisition of books which would be of practical help, and meantime I did what I could in the way of conversations with the girls, in French, Italian and English, whereafter all of us, including myself which I think encouraged them, wrote the new words and phrases we had learned in this process down in small notebooks, with the spelling as accurate as I myself might ensure. This method of instruction should not have been as formal as it became by the insistence of Miss Milly, who kept an occasional eye on the proprieties as she understood them. Going by the polite usage current when she was a girl, which must surely even at that time have been out of date, she insisted that, when any young lady asked a question of a teacher, it must be prefaced by the phrase 'If it please you,' replacing which by anything less pedantic was not allowed. Young Cornelia, who as I have said was my tormentor in every subtle way, seized upon this formula to cause me many painful moments of embarrassment. She would take particular pleasure, having found out that I blushed very easily, in making me do so; asking about the meaning of words which, I suspected, she knew perfectly well, although she should not have done so as they were always improper ones. That I myself knew the meaning and could, therefore, be embarrassed, which as a young unmarried instructress should not, or not always, have perhaps been the case, caused great secret delight to Cornelia. Her source of pleasure I knew continued private and furtive, as to give us both away would have ended it; so she tortured me, in such ways, to the end. I do not know what happened to her after she must have left the Villa Fiori, presumably by the summer of the following year.

One of my duties included snuffing out the dormitory candles last thing at night, leaving only a single one burning behind my curtain. When Miss Coke Green or Miss Milly, as used sometimes to happen, had done this they would see personally that each girl was confortable in her bed, and kiss her on the cheek before applying the snuffer to the taper. I was much too shy to do all this, and never attempted to; nobody minded, but Cornelia pretended she did, and though she never succeeded in forcing me to kiss her she made my life a torment over it, saying, as I would reach the long snuffer over, "Why won't you kiss us, Miss Considine? Do you not like kissing young ladies?" And there would come, from the other, till now quiescent beds, a titter; it is no doubt all meant less than I thought it did, but it unsettled the dormitory again, and by the time I had once more quieted them I was myself so disturbed that I often could not sleep. It seemed to me that Cornelia directed her wit more and more—and I realised by now that this was possible—in a way which might mean that she had seen me at some time with Simon in Rome. That she had not openly mentioned this already meant, I knew, that she could, if she chose, make matters even more difficult for me than they were already. My misery over the whole thing grew so incessant that, to end it one way or the other, I asked my employers one day where Cornelia's parents came from. The father, Miss Milly told me, was a dealer in furniture and upholstery, and had recently, she added with pride, installed new furnishings for a part of the palace at Frascati, where the Pretender's brother, the Cardinal of York, was bishop. Frascati is only an hour's ride by coach from Rome, and this in itself answered my question, and made my life as regarded Cornelia a hell. She knew this, naturally, at once, and spared me nothing.

"What—if it please you, Miss Considine—is the meaning of *fille de joie*? What—if it pleases you—is a gigolo? What did you do before you came to the Villa Fiori, Miss Considine? Were you teaching someone?" A titter again here; the young ladies were well enough instructed in other things than those the Villa Fiori tried to teach them, and one of the troubles here was to keep them from exercising their knowledge to the detriment of the onion-seller, the farmer who brought round daily milk and the dancing-master, always a target. "What—Miss Considine, if it please you—is the meaning of *enceinte*?"

That was the very last time; but before that she had finally made me so angry that I lost control. I had endured her impertinence because, as she and I knew well, I had to; but one day I had had more than I could stomach and said coldly, in the hearing of all the young ladies in her class, "Where can you have been, Cornelia, not to know such things? All the others here have learned of them long ago, and understand them well enough to make of them a matter for no great wonder. If you need fuller instruction on such subjects should I perhaps ask Miss Coke Green to begin a children's class, solely for yourself, I fear, and have it all more fully explained to you?" And then, taking advantage of all the sudden incredulous hush of silence, I gave them all, very viciously, a written translation of a part of the *Purgatorio* into French. My sudden metamorphosis from a mouse to a lion brought in the exercises, neatly written and in time; but there was one drawback, which was that I myself was not yet quite proficient enough to translate the whole thing with entire correctness. This was a sharp lesson to my self-esteem, so briefly trimuphing.

But Cornelia's last knife-stab followed even that.

It must have been a full week later, during which she had been very quiet; but I myself knew, by then, what was the matter with me, and I was sitting now in my cubicle, where with my candle I often had to work late into the night, the care of the young ladies not allowing for much correction of their work by day. I had corrected till my eyes ached, and to ease them I had taken off my spectacles and laid my head down on my arms. I was in an access of loneliness and misery, and thought of Simon; I knew by now, with hardly any doubt at all, that I must be with child, and afraid of the future as I was, the worst part was to have betrayed Miss Coke Green, whom I should soon have to inform. I trembled at the thought of this, and at the same time was filled with a perverse joy; for a part of Simon was, however reprehensibly, still in me. I remembered again his careful, tender usage of me, designed, as I knew, to prevent the very conception which must in spite of it all have taken place, that time I had made him angry with the hair-frame and brocade cloak from Venice. I remembered all that, and other things besides, and for a time was far away from the cubicle in the Villa Fiori, with a number of young ladies supposedly asleep beyond my thin curtain. I must have murmured pleasurably, I suppose; and when I opened my eyes at last, there was Cornelia regarding me, in her nightgown.

I had no idea how long she had been standing there. "Are you perhaps ill, Miss Considine?"

Her face was a mask of discreet triumph. The loathing I had for her rushed up in me, like vomit; I stood up on my feet and blazed out at her, forgetting the sleeping dormitory outside. "How dare you invade my cubicle? You have no right to be in here at all, Cornelia, and you know it," I finished; I do not know what else I said. "Go back to bed and to sleep, and do not ever do such a thing again." Then my head gave a lurch of agony and I put up my hand to it; she regarded me with slow, considering interest, and did not move. I said no more to her; by now I was sick with pain.

"You *are* ill," said Cornelia with enjoyment. "I should perhaps go at once to fetch Miss Coke Green or Miss Milly, but—Miss Considine," she said then, "if it please you— what is the meaning of *enceinte*?"

It had to come, of course; the sisters would have had to know at some time. It happened over the English breakfast, as I said. For days now I had forced down only a part of this, sending the rest back untouched to the kitchens. I had not liked to ask, as I daresay I could have done, for some fruit instead, such as many of the girls took in the morning. I did not want to draw attention to myself by causing trouble. But Miss Milly must have noted the return of my daily plate; she came over on one occasion to fuss and ask, as Cornelia in her way had also done, if I felt ill, and were the eggs quite fresh? Perhaps I would like a buttered egg, as these were known to be less heavy on the stomach? If so, she would tell the cook.

But Miss Milly did not tell the cook. What she did at that precise moment I never knew, for I did not see her again. I know what I did, however; over the breakfast-table and in front of all the young ladies, including Cornelia; Miss Coke Green had already gone to her office. I was not actively sick, I am thankful to say, until later, when I was alone; but in the meantime the thought of a buttered egg, and my resulting nausea, misery and headache, overcame the desire to remain unnoticed at all costs, and I slid into a faint across the table.

Miss Coke Green saw me alone in her office, later that same day.

She was seated, with a quill in her hand and her ledger, as always, open by her; she had been writing in her small neat hand, and she finished the word and then laid down her quill. The ensuing silence should have been alarming, no doubt; but for me it was, by contrast, sad. She looked me in the face with her direct grey eyes, and herself flushed a little.

"Miss Considine," she said, and from the lack of surprise and shock in her tone I suspected that she had known, or had an idea of the possibility, for some time, "you are going, are you not, to have a child?"

It could not after all have been put to me in any way which would cause less embarrassment; and I was overcome, not so much by this as by shame and regret at having caused them both, even for so short a time, grief, for this by now I knew was what it meant for us all. I began to stammer something of that; they had been so kind to me, and I had deceived them, though at the beginning I had not known its extent.

"You know our position here," said Miss Coke Green. "My sister and I have put all we possess into this venture; if it should fail, we are ruined."

I said I knew that, and that she need have explained nothing to me. Many employers would not have done. A word, a hint of looseness—which after all my conduct had been—and parents, icily appearing in their carriages, would remove every single pupil from the Villa Fiori within hours and days. It had happened elsewhere.

"I understand that you wish me to go," I said. "I will do so tonight." But she held up her hands.

"No, no, to depart precipitately would cause talk; we
will arrange matters." She rose, and began to walk up and
down the little room; beyond the window one could see
the roses, and the Arno. "You must think me a cold,
unfeeling woman, as I know," she said. "Ours is a
relentless situation, Leah," and this time she had forgotten
to call me Miss Considine. "In our profession we are not
permitted softness or grace, not even, one would think,
natural functions," she said. "One breath of suspicion that
all is not as it should be with the body, although the mind
is filled with riches ready to impart, and—but, in any case,
my dear," she said with great sweetness and dignity, "we
know well, my sister and I, that you are not, and
never have been or would be, a bad or an abandoned
woman."

She struck her hands together and let them fall. "Is he a
married man?" she asked baldly. I was impressed by her
grasp of probabilities.

"Yes," I said, "he is married," and remembered the
travesty at Aske. No relation of such circumstances would
however help me, or the Villa Fiori, at this or any other
moment. So I kept silent, and I think she was grateful for
this. She was by now making plans.

"You must leave here almost at once, of course," she
said. "Perhaps a letter, sent by courier, about illness at
home? Then if you left before the end of term it would
seem less remarkable. We shall miss you very much. You
have been more than we hoped, or have ever had, in the
way of caring for the children, teaching them in a way
which interested them and caused them to learn something, even that Cornelia." For Miss Coke Green, being an
excellent preceptress, knew her charges. "You had your
troubles with her, I am aware, and so will the—the next
person." I did not know, and knew she did not either,
where the next person would come from or, in fact, if
anyone would come so great a distance at all. I ventured to
ask if there was any help I could give, even by letter or by way

of finding anyone in England; but she looked at me sadly.

"You must not even write, Leah," she said, and then, "Have you friends to whom you can go?"

I said I had. Thinking of it all afterwards I realised how kind she had been; others, I knew, would have turned me from the door within the hour. But she saw that I had enough money to support myself at least for the journey back home; and even offered, though guardedly, to tell any enquirers that I had taught French and Italian with proficiency. This could not, I knew, include any reference as to character. Miss Milly was not in evidence, then or later, being busied no doubt with the classes I might no longer take. I never saw her again.

I left next morning, while the classes were again in progress. Miss Coke Green herself appeared on the steps to see me off, and lend credence to the tale already circulated that I had had bad news from home, and might even, at a later date, be returning to Florence. But I knew that I would never return, any more than Eve returned to Eden; rightly, after she had sampled the tree of forbidden knowledge, she was forever cast out.

Where was I to go? The question had exercised me during those last hours in my cubicle at the Villa Fiori, quietly assembling my few things (a single valise would hold them, which at least spared the expense of carriers on the journey) and in the end, knowing of nowhere else to turn, I had written home to Avice at Steed. I had told her everything, discreetly phrased in case the letter fell into the hands of Sir Napier, who would not be discreet. I knew that, but had no means of predicting his other reactions or if he would forbid his wife to have anything to do with me. I said to Avice that I had not time, which was true, to wait for her reply; I expected to be back in England by a certain date, as I was leaving at once, and should in the end await her in a hostelry we knew of in the near by town to

Steed, if she should wish to see me. The town itself was too large for gossip, I thought; I did not mention that there was nowhere else to go and that if Avice failed me, for whatever reason, I was lost. The future otherwise was a terrifying blank, and I could not yet think of it.

The stage-coach bore me northwards and on the journey, while I pretended to sleep (the Italian passengers called out about me to one another, for an unaccompanied female is always a source of interest to them, and no doubt they thought I was a servant), I began to think of my baby. The joy I had felt, on becoming certain that I carried Simon's child, had deserted me for a while in the shame and regret of the parting with the Villa Fiori, but by now had returned. I began to think of him—it would of course be a son—and as he could not be called Simon, which would have inconvenienced everyone, I decided that I would give him my father's Christian name, Mark. Mark and I travelled companionably together across the Plain of Lombardy and over the Alps, without mishap as far as Dijon; then, perhaps, the memory of my own tipsy performance last time there with Simon saddened me, and I spent a wretched night; in the morning I felt ill. I was not yet short of money, as good Miss Coke Green had pressed on me, while leaving, an extra month's salary, which was most kind of her and I was glad of it. So I lingered at the inn and, next day, took a later coach, which got me to Paris where, once more, I rested. I took a third rest before crossing the Channel, and achieved this, in the end, with no more than an ordinary bout of seasickness; but I was in a fairly wretched state by the time I reached England, and worse when I got to the arranged place where, I had said to Avice in my letter, she might, if she wished to do so, find me. I was later in arrival than I had expected, with the additional halts I had had on the way; I found no one waiting and no letter, and if she did not come, I thought, I would solve my own problem by dying of misery. My discomfort was beginning to concern me, for it was some time now since I had left the rolling coach. I lay down on my bed in the room I had bespoken, and waited in case Avice should come, while one after another a clock chimed the hours from a steeple outside my window. By eight o'clock, I had never felt so ill.

Avice came. Later I found she had come twice already. She took one look at my white face and called to the maid to dismiss her carriage, saying she would stay with me. In her kind arms she held me, sponged my face and body, and, afterwards, brought me wine. For it was afterwards; after I had lost Mark, in a sliding weakening access of blood and pain, ending in nothing but wretchedness, failure and fear. For I am a coward, and even the memory of the pain I had endured made me cry. Avice was very kind to me; discreet, knowing exactly what to do (she had much experience) and asking no questions then or later, for which I was more grateful than I can say. She took everything in charge, told the inn people I had a flux, and that she would be staying with me for a day or two till I should be improved; and she stayed. She never left me for a single instant; and when it was time for us to go, she saw me helped into her own coach, settled me in it with my feet propped up by cushions, and said only, "Now, my love, try to doze, for it's a dull journey, though short. When we are back at Steed I shall put you straight to bed in your own room, and you are to stay there as long as you wish, until you feel quite well again." That was all; but it was enough, more than enough, and the tears of relief, gratitude, and weakness rolled down my face all the way to Steed, on the appearance of which, looming among its great elms, I dried them.

It occurred to me at this same moment to look at Avice, where she sat opposite. I had not even noticed—

such had been my state—that she also, as was customary, could expect another child very shortly, and I hoped that she had not overtired herself by her constant attention and great kindness to myself.

Part V

MELISSA

I

IN MY TURN, I was to sit with Avice through that labour
of hers and three subsequent ones, and after that, when
the death of Sir Napier on the hunting-field had put paid
to others, I stayed on at Steed for five more years. It may
be wondered why I chose to reside all that time so near
Aske, if I did not wish to hear of it, or, perhaps, encounter
anyone who lived there. But at first, as I have said, I had
nowhere else to go, and later, as so often happens, I found
that I had grown tentative, uncertain roots at Steed. I was
averse to tear myself up a third time, particularly as it
seemed they wanted to keep me there. I had always been
prone to stay where I was, like a parrot on a peg or, as I
was still shy and unforthcoming at this time, a dove on a
secluded branch, perhaps; not any smaller bird, for the
analogy would have troubled me, remembering Simon as I
used to do often, oh, very often in the night hours.

At first I had been disturbed at the fact that only thirty
miles separated us, whether because I hoped that I would
see him again, or that I hoped I would not, is uncertain.
After having miscarried of Mark I had lost what looks I
had had, and never regained them. Although I knew that
Simon would never be likely to learn about the lost child,
which knowledge would have brought him at once to me, I
had, perhaps, a wild sweet hope that this might happen;
but I would not tell him, and Avice did not, and told no

one, not even Sir Napier, what had occurred. And as time passed, and Simon never visited Steed and never wrote, although it was unlikely by now that, in a country place, he could fail to know that I was with Avice, I lost this hope. After all, it was I myself who had told Simon I never wanted to see him again. I heard that he was at Aske now with the two children, Robert and the baby Melissa, whom he had brought back that time with her Italian nurse, who had now gone away (this was a certain balm to me). Ann was still the same, no worse, as they said; but she would never be better. Prossy now looked after her in one of the lodges.

In fact it had been Sir Napier who had informed Simon I was at Steed, at a date early enough for the latter to have supposed that I was still at the Villa Fiori. They had encountered one another at some shire-meeting, doubtless held over the fact that Steed is hunting country and Aske is not.

"That girl, ye'll know, little filly whatsername, parson's daughter, she's with us now". This was what Simon heard and, commendably, disentangled to identify myself and that I was now at Steed. He asked how I did and was informed, being all Sir Napier knew to the contrary, that I was as fit as a fiddle. So he did nothing more except to honour the request I had made him that he should not try to see me; and it was not, accordingly, for many years that I heard the exact words Sir Napier had used to him. Meantime, he neither visited at Steed nor, for reasons I shall relate, was himself visited at Aske, except by Sir Napier once or twice a year. At the time we again encountered one another we were by far more formal that we had ever been, and exchanged no anecdotes of the above kind as we would once have done. This went a long way towards again breaking my heart, which had perhaps begun to mend its cracks a little over the busy years at Steed.

2

AVICE WAS LIKE a cow. I say this not in any derogatory way of that dear woman, for she probably saved my life at the time I lost my baby and, thereafter, was always sweet and kind to me. But a cow, which is a sensible, productive, good mother, seldom showing traits of viciousness and being moreover of consistently handsome appearance, seems to me very like Avice. And though at another time and place these virtues might have wearied me, at the period of which I speak I was extremely glad of them.

I do not think that anyone asked me to make my home at Steed so much as to let it be known that they had assumed that I would do so. This was pleasant, and, in some endeavour to repay that kindness and the other I have mentioned, I did what I could, and in many ways it was not a great deal, to ease Avice's lot. This could not be easy, and had never been since her wedding-night when—as in the frank way she had she informed me, one day when we were talking together over our mending of the boys' shirts—Sir Napier had lost no time in getting her pregnant at once. The eldest daughter, Sophia, had been born nine months to the day after I had worn my black-dyed, denuded attendance-gown for Avice's wedding at Aske. Since then poor Avice had either been breeding, nursing or in labour, with very little respite over the years; he was, as she also told me, back again in her bed within the week of each birth, but by now she'd grown used to it. "He's like a great boy, in ways," she assured me, for she was fond of her loud-mouthed, red-faced squire and would not have heard a word in his default; but to me the great boy, by now a family Jehovah who thrashed his children and his dogs with equal impartiality, and thought of all women only as needing a baby a year to keep them out of mischief (he may have been right) was a bully, drunken, undisciplined, narrow-minded, inconsiderate and lustful, and I did not like him. I will give Sir Napier his due inasmuch as

to say that he did not return my dislike, for his godhead
remained quite naturally unaware that this existed. He
barely, I believe, realised that I did so, although I occupied
a room in his house for nine years. At the time I first went
to Steed there were children of all sizes, babies in milky
plenitude upon the nursery floor and sometimes the stairs,
or occasionally the flagstones nearby the kitchen fire if
the cook had been asked to lend a hand in some crisis, as
she occasionally was. Servants at Steed had to display a
versatility beyond their usual occupations, which was not
very good for them; it would not have happened at Aske,
where everything had remained in its proper place since
Old Madam's day in this fashion. Here, nothing could. The
two girls, by now of marriageable age, of Sir Napier's first
marriage. Dinny and Cis (their mother, it will be remembered, was a poetess by desire, and their baptismal names
were Diana and Cecilia), were already set in the pattern
they would follow as horse-loving spinsters of a kind
particularly to be found in the hunting-shires, and were
out every day in all weathers; they could give, as a result,
very little help to anyone. Otherwise, Steed was a medley
of hunting-crops and abandoned boots and guns, the latter
kept greased and well cared for; and small boys' coats and
frilled shirts to be mended, lying about on tables and
chairs. There were also bottles, leaning towards one
another after Sir Napier's daily refreshment, which started
at four o'clock when he came home from the hunt. There
would by then be great game-pasties put out, roasts of
meat congealing and sliced into; everybody ate when it
suited them. This was necessary owing to the habits of the
hunters and to the fact that little children, at least until
they can stand up by themselves, must be fed and put to
bed early. The rest of the household roystered well into
the night, and were up at dawn and out again with the
horses. Sir Napier, being monotonously faithful to his
spouse (a diversion or two would at least have kept him off
her some nights of the year) slept with Avice in a wide

curtained bed on the first floor, between midnight and
dawn when fires were again lit. The servants began this
work at four, which would include stoking and laying the
house-grates and the great ovens, and heating water with
which they later toiled upstairs to our rooms, carrying it
there in brass cans. Once the hunters had gone out the
business of the day, the baking and cooking and mending
and lessons and pony-riding and hoop-and-ball games of all
kinds, everything in fact except reading for pleasure which
was never to my knowledge done by anyone at Steed,
could begin.

3

I HAD HELD on to my own privacy as precious to me in
the few hours of daily respite from Avice's throng. As the
children grew older I began to take them for lessons, and
as no reasonable governess had ever been known to stay
more than six months at Steed Avice was, no doubt,
grateful to me.

Sir Napier did not notice; provided the boys could stay
in the saddle, breed sons in due course and hold their wine,
that was as much as he expected of them. Of his daughters
he only expected two things, silence and needlework. For
a little girl to be seen sewing and, therefore, keeping out
from under his boots and from mischief meantime, suited
Sir Napier no doubt very well; and in the diligent pursuit
of this exercise—we had made, by that time, slippers for
Papa, with embroidery in coloured wools, which he wore
with some pride when at home, and samplers the least
shaky of which were hung on the schoolroom walls and,
once, on the staircase—it its pursuit we found pleasure, for
I loved it myself and taught the little girls to enjoy it for
its own sake and not as a punishment. I was therefore
surprised, one day, to find Mary Steed, the step below
Bertram and the one above Barnabas, Stephen and Kate,

and the baby (Young Napier, Sophia and the older glories were removed, some of the time, by now to schools, aunts to be visited and other such places) in tears over her sampler, on which she had been executing a house with trees.

"Why, my darling, what is wrong?" I asked her, but she turned her head away. I was afraid, and proved to be right, that she was in that state of wordless terror children achieve when they are not encouraged to exist other than in silence. I asked Avice about it and to my relief she told me the trouble at once.

"Mary is having nightmares," she said. "I wondered if—" She darted a quick, almost shy glance at me, and said no more for some minutes, diverting the talk instead to Bertram who, she stated, was a great grief to his father. As Bertram was a quiet little boy who spent his time saying and doing nothing at all, and appeared harmless if not enterprising, I asked why, and Avice told me that also; Bertram, she said, was afraid of horses. This crime would only be paralleled at Steed by incest. "He won't mount," she said, "although his father bought him a pony; Barney rides it now. Napier is afraid Bertram may never hunt; he's whipped the child till he can't sit in a saddle or anywhere else, but that's no help and Bertram wets his bed every night, and nurse is at her wits' end with him, and so am I." Avice raised, with a suddenly lost and helpless gesture, her face towards me; I could see the remains of her once pretty, high colour, now a mass of minute broken veins which made her cheeks look scalded. The coming event sat as usual under her thickened waistline, and would arrive in a few more weeks. I resolved to help with Bertram if I might, though my own bravery with horses is not notable. I asked also if there was anything I might do about Mary and her nightmares. Children, I knew well, had these if they were afraid; but of what use to tell that to this poor harried woman? Avice brightened, however, and her face flushed plum-colour with relief.

"I did not like to ask it of you, Leah," she said, "but Mary is fond of you; all the children are, and you give up so much of your time to them already, but—I wondered, dear, if you would perhaps let Mary sleep in your room with you? Only for a little while, till she is over the trouble. I would not," said the kindly soul, "have you disturbed for always," and she went on to make a speech of gratitude for all she said I was doing for the children, which touched me very much so that I made my own speech of thanks in reply.

I accordingly rescued Mary from the conglomerate night-nursery that same day and thereafter, at nights, she slept with me in my bed. I had known an instant's unworthy regret, no more, at the invasion of my prim, solitary room, but how could one refuse? They had grudged me nothing at Steed, and at least, I thought wryly, they had not visited Bertram and the bed-wetting on me. With him, I hoped also for success, but it would take time; as far as Mary was concerned, the cure was easy and fairly quick. She had the nightmares again at first, once or twice, in my bed; I got my arms round her so that when she waked, she would know I was there, I told her. I told her also that I often had bad dreams on my own account, which was not quite the truth; my bad times came before I slept.

"Then if I scream, Aunt Leah, you wake me, and if you scream I'll wake you," was Mary's practical solution. All of Avice's children were good little souls, tough and resilient like all bloodstock, if one must keep to the analogy of horses; soon I cured Mary.

Mary stayed with me thereafter, and soon Bertram also came about. His trouble was initially helped by the fact that in the stables there was a disused pony-carriage. Sir Napier was applied to for his permission, which was given; and thereafter Bertram and I, and later one or two of the others, made lengthening excursions in it behind a docile, trouble-free old pony. I told Bertram, this time, the truth in that I was not very brave or expert with the reins and needed a strong, manly arm to take them from me should I fail. This accustomed the small boy at least to the near prospect of the pony's buttocks, jogging along at an easy speed in the nearer lanes and then, as we grew more proficient, the far ones. I remember how I felt my eyes prick with pride the first time Bertram drove the carriage entirely by himself; soon he was on the pony, by which time (he told me) he intended to become a hunting parson. I believe he did so in the end, as younger sons are encouraged to take up the calling; I know that I had a letter from him some years ago when he was ordained, and that its spelling was dreadful.

The last time I ever saw Sir Napier was on the day Avice had gone into labour with her eleventh child at two in the morning, and I was sent for to be with her and he, as was customary, moved out into his dressing-room. He was up and out to the hunt as usual later, and when I met him as I was returning from an expedition to the kitchens for hot water. I expected him to be out of temper at the disturbance, but he was not; on the whole, he displayed more amiability than I did. I had been awake with Avice for the remainder of the night.

He greeted me sociably, slapping his whip on his thigh; he wore his pink coat, the wig cheerfully askew on his head, and his boots on. "I hear," he said, "young Bertram's a devil with the reins now, eh? A Jehu, is that it? Good, good," and he passed on, and out into the yard, where the horses and grooms, and Dinny and Cis and the rest, stood waiting. I heard them, directly after that, set off with a happy clatter and shouting of confused orders and much cursing, as they always did.

I did not see the return. By that time I was still upstairs with Avice. She was long in labour, more so than usual, and I feared for her as I thought that, this time, she was exhausted. Her face now was like candle-grease in colour beneath the sweat and tears; she had strained incessantly for many hours and still the baby would not come, and then it did so all at once. I handed it to the women and returned at once to Avice, trying to persuade her to drink a little warmed wine afterwards; but she turned her head aside.

"Where is Napier?" she said. "I didn't hear him come up." Nor had I, although the hunt had returned an hour ago. In the ordinary way he would have been here by now, to drink a bumper of wine to the new baby and force a mouthful over Avice's lips. I went out and came back again. There was trouble also with the afterbirth and when that was all over she was still tense. "He has not come," she said again, "and something has happened, I know," and she began to cry; the tears rolled down of their own volition as though she had no strength either to produce or stop them. Nor had she, on this occasion, any milk either; it was almost the end of her. I postponed what I must tell her, having hoped to be able to wait till she was a little stronger; but she would have had to know soon. Sir Napier was dead. He had broken his neck at a fence; I heard the details later. They had just carried him in.

In the end I told Avice. I can remember the way she took the news; she stopped crying and for a long time said nothing, I was uncertain whether with shock or relief. But it was neither; presently she said, gently from where she lay in the aftermath of suffering, "It was quick, you say, Leah? I'm glad of that. He could never have endured pain; he used to roar like a bull if a needle pricked him," and then she cried again a little and, after that, slept.

4

SIMON RODE OVER to attend Sir Napier's funeral, I believe, but I did not see him or anyone else, as I stayed

upstairs with Avice. She took a long time to regain her
strength, but now that she was, for the first time since her
marriage, able to garner this, she was soon herself again
and, perhaps, more. Her natural habits of social exchange
reasserted themselves, now that she had more time and less
to do with the constant babies. She spent, even in that first
year after her mourning-season, a great deal of time away
with two or more of the children, seeing friends in the
nearby shires or, once, the Kintyre relatives in Scotland.
Later, of course, we began to receive guests at Steed other
than members of the hunt-meet. I believe it became a gay
place by the time Avice's young daughters were of an age
to find themselves husbands. However by that era I had
left.

One of the places to which they began to take
occasional jaunts was Aske, and although I never went
with them I was, despite myself, kept constantly informed
of what now passed there. Of all this I shall have more to
say when recounting Prossy's visit to me, which took place
about then; but before it I had already had a brief
encounter with Avice on the subject of why I could never
be prevailed upon to go with them all to Aske. It would of
course have taken a very incurious woman not to try to
find out the reason; but, no doubt, though she had kept
her own counsel, Avice had always suspected it. Perhaps
she thought it was time things were mended; at any rate,
she spoke of it one day.

We had been sitting together in the garden, ourselves
mending, as I have said already was a frequent occurrence
with us, the boys' frilled shirts, to which their tree-
climbing and other propensities did no good; I often
thought that, like a crowd of young monkeys, they could
as profitably have run about naked. Avice was saying that
she had thought of driving over again to Aske on the
morrow, taking some of the children to play with young
Melissa; and she asked, as she always did, if I would not
accompany them.

I shook my head and made great work of threading my needle, holding it close to my eyes. These were short of sight, as they had always been and did not improve as I grew older, but they were not quite as bad as all that. Avice's own eyes narrowed, as I managed to see, and she drew a breath as if to speak, did not, then again changed her mind.

"Leah," she said, "it—that time you came home to us from Italy—it—it was, had been, Simon, was it not?" She had never before, in all these years, asked me concerning the father of the child. I did not answer, which in itself was a reply, and she nodded and went on with her sewing.

"He looks well," she said, as if we spoke of a stranger. "I met him again the other day, at the Wynmalens'. He has altered very little, I think; older, naturally, as we all are. He had the little girl with him, and Robert, of course. Robert has grown tall. He looks, I think, like Ann."

I closed my eyes against the sun, which had grown too bright. Avice did not mistake my silence for discourtesy; she went on to talk about other things, and next day they all departed without me to Aske, as I had wished.

But I was not always to be left in such peace over the matter. As a result, no doubt, of the above visit Prossy wrote, a few weeks later, in a careful round hand I did not know, to ask if she might call over to see me on her annual day's holiday. She could be given, she said, a lift by the carrier until the last four miles, and would walk the rest of the way if it was fine. It was, and she came.

It was some years since I had seen her and she had not grown uglier; she looked, in fact, much the same, not older for she had always been old, and now, with the bonnet she wore having a veil in front, which she could draw down to disguise her eye, she was like a timeless, sad black gnome. I sat her by me and let her talk, which she had come to do.

She did not speak at first of Simon, but of Ann, which was understandable as she spent all her days with her. Ann was no better, and had fits now sometimes, so that Prossy needed help; she had grown, Prossy said, very stout.

"She'll wander out," she said, "if I let her, which I sometimes can't help but do. *He* never comes near, not that she'd want him to. But there are times when you've got to turn round, aren't there? Then she'll get out by the door, and walk about in the woods and places, talking to herself a bit, and crying sometimes. It's as if she'd never been right in her head since that young lord, the one as used to come, went away." Prossy had been told nothing about Fordwoodham, I knew; but she was sharp. Sometimes, she said, it was difficult to find Ann, because she hid away, like a child playing truant, from anyone following her. "And I'm not as young as I used to be, and them brambles can tear something cruel. Once I didn't find her till after dark, and had my own task getting her back home; but I didn't tell *him*, he said I never was to. Out of his sight, he said she was to be kept; well, she's that all right. He's not so much at home, now, these days; not since the Italian piece left that he—" She swallowed, looked sideways at me out of the good eye, then began again. "There's the business, always," she said. "He's away a lot on that. And when they know he isn't there, the children come out and torment my poor dear when they can. Cruel, that young Melissa is sometimes. I chase them off, but that one won't heed me or anyone, though Robert will." Prossy did not yet use obsequious prefixes, but that no longer troubled me. What did this, after she had gone, was the image of the stout, draggled figure among the darkening woods, tormented by children one of whom was her own son. That haunted me, and the picture of Melissa, whom I was already not disposed to regard very evenly, was unpleasant. And Simon was often away . . .

I held up my head long enough to drive Prossy back for most of her way afterwards in the pony-cart. We took two of the children with us perforce, because they would not be left behind, and in any case I dreaded hearing more from Prossy if we had been alone. I drove to where the last hill began to ascend before the turn of the road that would lead one to see Aske, slumbering like a towered and gabled dream in the distance. Above me was the bluff where Big Het's cottage had once been and where Simon had later lain among windflowers, hearing the dead-bell. I set Prossy down there, as I did not want to see Aske, and said that the pony would not manage the climb as he was getting old. "He will, he will," chorused the children. They could not understand why I would not drive them all the way so that they could see Melissa. Melissa was the most enchanting, inventive, exciting playmate who had ever lived; when might they invite her back again to Steed?

That would have to come, of course. Meantime I had felt that it might, that day, be the last time I saw Prossy. I was right; she had always been a bag of bones, and the subsequent winter killed her. I remember how we stood looking at one another that last time, at the bottom of the hill; she knew well why I would go no further. At the last minute, instead of giving her my hand as I had intended, I leant over from my place and kissed her. She was pleased, and I said, "God bless and keep you, Prossy, for all you've done and are doing; look after him," and then I turned back to the reins. But before that I had caught sight of the gallant wink, out of her good eye, for me; and she said, as we set off, "Prayers, well, I should think we was beyond those, wouldn't you, Miss Leah? But there's some as is past praying for, others not." And she jerked the blind over her eye and went trudging uphill again towards Aske, and that was the last I ever saw of her.

Afterwards I went back upstairs to my own room. Mary was not there, but I knew she might run in at any minute; she had grown pretty and confiding, and would want to climb on my knee and tell me all of the day's doings, and I could not listen yet . . . I took myself to the closet and locked the door, and there wept in the only place nobody would be likely to come and disturb me. I stayed for some time, then dried my eyes and endeavoured, as I always did, to ridicule myself out of it all; what did I expect from my life more than it had, and I knew it was by far more fortunate than some? A little, ageing governess in a round-gown and linen cap, and sometimes spectacles, and here I was howling in a closet because I had lost a handsome man to handsomer women long ago. For that was what it amounted to, and I might as well face up to it and get on by myself with what was usefully left of my life. Simon knew I was at Steed, had known for years, and had not come over except for the funeral; he had not once written, or, so far as I knew, enquired, and was evidently done with me, as much as I had said, that time long ago, that I was done with him. That we had both obtained our wish in this respect should, after all, have consoled me. But it did not. I wept again for a full quarter-hour, emerging finally to dab my reddened eyes with witch-hazel so that I would be in a fit state to appear later when the children were having their supper.

5

I HAD KNOWN that it would be impossible to avoid asking Melissa back to Steed, as we should not, either of us, be permitted to forget the matter. There was no doubt that, now that the chastening hand of Sir Napier was removed by death, the children were growing a trifle spoilt. They ruled their easy-going mother, and without any doubt they ruled me, though I continued to play the part of strict governess as convincingly as I could.

Melissa was to be brought over, at last, with Robert to spend the whole of one day. Although I had not set eyes on her since she was a small infant, I knew exactly, from my charges' ecstatic descriptions, what she looked like now. She had flying black curls, the running-speed and endurance of an Arabian pony, her eyes were like treacle toffee (this from Bertram, who was in love with her), and she had many things these children had not, and which I would never have encouraged. Melissa had coral necklaces, more gowns than she could wear, of China silk and velvet, sprigged muslin and hand-made lace; she wore earrings; her very aprons were French, and had little pockets (this was Kate, who pestered me for a pocket on her own till I made her one, in the end, of gingham) and her slippers were of real bronze kid or scarlet morocco. Of the character contained within all this splendour I knew little as yet, except that Melissa was a born leader in games and afraid of nothing, not high trees or boys or, presumably, bulls in a meadow. And this was all I knew of Melissa except what was in my own heart, until I saw her again.

That day she came, I saw her. I saw her almost at once; she was brought to me where I sat in the garden, in our sewing-place, for it was summer. Avice was away seeing to the food which was to be set out by the maids; every day, at Steed, had to be a kind of mediaeval banquet, and two or three guests made no difference. Two or three, I had supposed; for Robert and Melissa would be brought, no doubt, by a nurse or *gouvernante* or some other person with whom Simon would have made arrangements. But they were not brought by these, but by himself.

I had not expected it. If I had done so, I would have hidden myself away for the day, saying I had a headache. As it was, they caught me there beneath my tree, he and Melissa. He led her to me by the hand, wearing her French pocket and sprigged muslin as she was, and as tall, by now, as his elbow. I let fall my sewing and stood up, words deserting me. Except for a lock of grey at his temple he was the same, and I—I knew I was not.

After some moments I saw that he too had grown older, as Avice had said. It had not been possible to notice certain things till he came closer, the child still by him, clinging to his hand. She swung on one slippered foot and regarded me in what I could see, even then, was hostile fashion; her dark eyes were enormous, exactly as Bertram had described them, and she had long sweeping eyelashes. She was a beautiful little girl.

We stood regarding one another, for the first time since that parting in the convent-parlour, years back. We remained grave and formal, middle-aged strangers, perhaps acquaintances. The experience was very painful to me. Presently I said, to break the silence, through stiff lips, for something to say, "Is Robert with you?"

"No. He did not come." His voice was the same; how could I have forgotten it, or thought that that would alter? "He has a stomach-ache," said Melissa. "I kicked him. He is in bed."

The silence had broken and I should have been grateful to her, and was not, and watched her smile up at Simon; the smile of a child who knows it will never be punished. My mind reacted like that of a governess; I longed to slap Melissa, hard. I said I was sorry to hear about Robert, and Simon smiled.

"He will recover," he said. "Run along, my witch." He patted Melissa on the sprigged-muslin behind, but she stayed where she was. "I don't want to," she said roundly. She had not, except for that one telling upward look, taken her eyes off me since they both arrived. I could see that she had assessed me, in the first half-minute, as what in essence I was; a dowdy old maid, but with some partly glimpsed, not to be encouraged alignment, no doubt from some former time, with Simon.

I may perhaps add that neither at that meeting, nor at any subsequent time in all my dealings with her, did Melissa address more than the minimum of words to me. No doubt I was an object of contempt.

There likewise seemed nothing more for us to say to one

another, Simon and I, except as concerned trivialities. I could not yet talk of these, and after the children had come running up and had dragged Melissa away by force, which at least got rid of her, I felt panic rise. He sensed this, no doubt, and himself began smoothly, easily to lead me into talk; asking courteous, everyday questions about how I fared, and was I happy at Steed?

Happy? The word can have a thousand meanings, as I could once have told Simon in several different ways: but now I did not. We moved away shortly, at my instigation, to where the children already played, noisily running and shouting about the great front lawn as they would never have done in Sir Napier's day. I exclaimed in some way about this; and he looked down at me kindly.

"You have your hands full with them, Leah, I don't doubt," he said. "I am glad that you are happy here. I—I have my own compensations in such ways."

And his eyes followed Melissa where she ran about, frilled petticoats twinkling about her kicking ankles till she looked like a star; she was wielding a cricket-bat, not the way it should be done, and chasing Barnabas. They were all extremely wild, had a glorious day, and in the evening the Aske carriage called for Melissa. She departed in it like a queen, alone except for the footman and coachman, and everybody saw her off except myself, for I had withdrawn upstairs. Simon had gone long ago, that same morning, back to Aske. He had only come over, he said, to bring Melissa. I thought bitterly that it would have been better had he not come at all. No doubt, like Avice, he now thought it was time to gloss things over, with a brief, formal meeting between us and exchange of courtesies. Now that we had had those, I hoped Simon would again leave me in peace; no doubt any man would, I thought, catching sight of myself in my mirror.

But he did not.

He must have ridden over many times during that

summer and autumn. I did not always have speech with him, though I would know at once that he had come; for one thing, the children told me. I made a point of keeping to my own place unless sent for; going on with various tasks, teaching the children, mending the frilled shirts, telling them stories, as I often did, to pass the hour after a meal when it is not, as every informed person knows, good for children to run about immediately and grow heated. One way of keeping them still was, I had found, to tell them about Ulysses, whose exploits, though not all of those, I related over most of that year, for he took a long time to return home after the war with Troy. It was inexcusable, to my mind, to pretend, as he must have done, that ten more years were necessary between leaving the defeated Trojans and rejoining that good and, evidently, still desirable Penelope. The various storms and shipwrecks he made his excuse however diverted the Steed children, and I was telling them also about Penelope's web, to encourage the girls in their embroidery, when Simon walked in.

"But the poor old dog," Mary was saying. "Did he not even pat it? After waiting for him all that long time." Her blue eyes regarded Simon indignantly, as though he were Ulysses; he was so familiar a figure by now that his arrival need not even have interrupted the story, except that I made the girls rise at once and perform their curtsies, as I always did.

"Is Melissa here?" said Bertram hopefully.

"No," Simon told him, and the child's face fell. "You will see her soon at Aske, perhaps, if Miss Leah permits it," he told Bertram, and as always when Simon was in presence of the children I had the sensation of conspiracy, though what it was about I could not yet know. I was, with accustoming, somewhat more at ease with Simon himself by now, as I knew he had probably intended; we talked easily and formally enough, when we did so, as any father or guardian might do with any governess. As for my position here in that way, it had begun to trouble me that shortly, as all of the boys would soon be away at school except for the youngest, who did not need me yet, perhaps I was not, or would not presently be, of as much use as I had once been at Steed.

6

THE FOLLOWING MATTER, which must have been in his mind for some time, was revealed to me on one of Simon's subsequent visits. He saw me concerning it himself; he must already have sounded Avice, for she made herself scarce. I feel now as if a long time ought to have passed, but it was still fine weather; Simon was standing by the downstairs window at Steed, looking out on to the lawn where, in the near distance, all the children played together with hoops, dogs and a ball. Their shrill voices, high with excitement, sounded now and again through our talk by the open casement.

It was no longer an astonishment to me to be able to stand talking with Simon here, calmly as though he had been any other acquaintance. He had, I felt, intended that we should progress again to such a degree of friendship, for even this it could already be called; he was a witty, courteous and interesting companion, and I myself knew well, by now, that if one wills it is possible to down all other feeling into the depths of one's mind, subduing it while it is not required, or even if it shall never be so again. So in history there have been many such instances of old lovers remaining friends, whether or not with intervening years of lonely heartbreak between; Louis XV and the Pompadour achieved this, and though I could never have rivalled the physical attractions of that lady I knew that she had also had much wit and knowledge and I could try to emulate that. In fact, I tried as a rule to emulate nothing and no one; he knew me only as myself, and so in spite of everything we were by now again at ease. I can explain this in no other way than that it had already happened.

I was able, without trembling, therefore, to survey his appearance; today as often, he wore riding-dress. He had broadened by this time about the shoulders and neck, as men do in early middle age; he was, if anything, handsomer than he had ever been, with the grey lock of hair at his temple and hair cut in the new short fashion. The easy habit became him, and I felt my heart turn over with a sad, familiar little flutter; how long, in time and experience, was it since I had gone in timidly, that first day of all at Aske, and found Simon in his accounts-office, dressed thus, his whip and gloves by him?

I was the one who had changed most, I knew. I had no illusions about myself and my appearance, a tired middle-aged woman in a drab gown on whom his eyes rested, when they did so at all, with compassion.

"You seem tired, Leah," he said, as if he read my thoughts. "Do they tax you too much here?" He returned his glance to the group down on the lawn, where I perceived, as often on such visits, the flying black curls of Melissa. Robert stood nearby, under one of the elms. He was a tall fair reserved boy, and was not shouting or playing.

"He will not join in games," said Simon, again as if I had spoken; and the glad certainty came to me that this could still be so between us. "He will not royster about as other boys do, and Melissa rules and mocks him, and—" Suddenly he swung around. "Leah," he said, and I knew at once that this was the purpose of his visit, perhaps of many visits, "will you come back again to Aske and help me with them both? Robert's no task, as you can tell, but Melissa—" He smiled, and spread out his hands in a gesture of complete, beguiling helplessness. "I have tried everything; no governess will stay, and the child grows daily wilder and more pert, and will learn nothing from anyone.

Avice has told me of how matters used to be here, with all
the children savage as monkeys, till you came; by now,
you have made useful lieges of them, and a school can do
the rest. You see? I need your help, my dear, more than
Avice does; more perhaps that she ever did, in such a way
though not perhaps others. Will you come back?"

I felt a faintness overcome me, and grasped at the
casement with fingers that had grown inept. I, of all
people, to be asked to deal with Melissa for Simon, and if
he himself could not . . . And the child did not like me. I
murmured something of it, and it was disposed of; nobody
at that time would admit to taking seriously the whims
and pettinesses of a small girl. And all the time, in any
case, I knew that I would agree in the end, and so was lost;
the thought of returning to Aske, of seeing Simon himself
almost daily, of the blossoming of our friendship again,
was so blindingly sweet that I called nothing in question.
As I have said before, I am a fool in such ways.

I turned away, to hide the sudden tears which pricked at
my eyelids; I did not choose that he should know of them.
He might otherwise feel that he must comfort me, a
woman who had long outgrown her attraction for him;
there must be no question of such comfort.

He mistook my silence for continuing refusal and said
suddenly, roughly, "It will not be made embarrassing for
you, Leah. You knew that Prossy had died? There is a
housekeeper now, a good woman; if you prefer, however, I
will dismiss her and you may choose your own. It will
be"—his voice had thickened—"as if you were mistress at
Aske, I promise you. All of us will respect your wishes."
He spoke by now gently, considerately; I was reminded,
poignantly, of the gentle and generous lover of that
long-ago summer in Rome. To down my tears I must
laugh, I knew, and agree. So I did so, but still not facing
him directly so that, standing by the casement as I was, I
could close my eyes as if the sun hurt them, as the same
time smiling valiantly as I spoke.

"Simon, do not make me out an ogre even to the housekeeper. As it will please and aid you, then, I'll come; perhaps only for a little while, should Avice again need me." For this proviso I kept, though I knew well he had already spoken of the whole matter to Avice. Perhaps this was what caused me, after he had left, to go up to my room again and cry. I was not, however, certain on this occasion what I was crying about, except that it was no longer with sorrow.

Avice endured my loss with so little sorrow of her own that it occurred to me to wonder if, perhaps, she felt some slight relief at my departure. Perhaps I had kept her from her easygoing ways, without intending to. The children however expressed much sadness and bought a gift with their own pocket-money, which they pressed on me; it was a candle-bracket, which must have cost a great deal and is very ugly, and I still keep it by me. They also gave me a Honiton lace tucker and three pairs of gloves, and promised to drive over almost every day and see me at Aske. Needless to say they did not do so nearly as frequently; their own concerns, in particular school, swallowed them up, and in any case once one has gone from anywhere there is a place waiting to be filled, and someone will be found to fill it. I had learned this many times already in my life, and I was glad to hear that in a short while Avice discovered a good, diligent woman as governess, who would cope even with Bertram's occasional vagaries in her own way, till it was time for him to go to school also.

So I returned to Aske. It was a statelier return than any hitherto, in Simon's carriage which he sent to fetch me and my gear. The equipage itself was new and shone with jet enamel and gilding, and the coachman also was new and shining in his livery; he tucked a fur rug over my knees when I was settled in my place, as though I had been a

visiting marchioness in midwinter, and whipped up the
matched bays so that we went spanking down the avenue
from Steed, to the mingled delight and tears of the
farewell party on the steps. The miles were so rapidly
eaten up thereafter that it was still early afternoon when
we reached Aske, and the sun standing high above the
crow-steps and chimneys. Everything, I saw, had a sparkling new-washed look, as though lovingly maintained with
soap, paint and mortar. I knew for the first time what
Aske should look like, a cherished lived-in house, even a
beautiful one. The lawns were close-shaven and the pond
glittered in the bright day, showing the dark gliding shapes
of the waterfowl I remembered and other new kinds I did
not, with exotic colourings and head-tufts, and there was a
flower-garden.

Melissa and Robert were waiting for me together on the
steps, hand in hand. I had the impression that they were
being maintained in this unwilling pose by the housekeeper, who waited behind. She was a good stout soul in a
black satin gown, and her name I found was Mrs.
Boothroyd and she came from further north. By the time I
had spoken to her, young Melissa had already jerked her
hand free of Robert's and had shoved it firmly into her
frilled lawn apron, which still had the French pocket,
supposedly for needlework. I had a strong notion that
needlework with Melissa would bring its own problems, as
would most things. Her jet-black eyes were mutinous when
I kissed her, and she kept silent as we all went inside.
There was no sign of Simon, who had tactfully stayed
elsewhere for this reunion; he was, as it happened, away at
the time on a trip to his warehouses.

7

WHAT AM I to say about my life as a governess at Aske?
All the time I was reminded of my youth there, though

less than I had expected of the way in which this had come
to an end, that time I left for Europe with Simon. All of
that was by now however kept carefully by me, as can be
done, in a further place in my mind, where there is still a
little door which locks, and stays shut till I choose to open
it. But there were other things still at Aske, besides Melissa
whom I shall come to presently; and there was still poor
Ann. She had a paid attendant now who can have known
nothing of the days when she was beautiful. Ann was not
beautiful now. She was seldom seen, for they kept her
close, in the little house in the grounds which had been a
lodge no longer used, and Simon had had it made ready
four or five years ago and had furnished it, at the time, for
Ann with some of her own gear out of Aske. But
sometimes she would take the air in the garden, with the
attendant leading her like a child on two long red strings;
they were of leather, fastened about Ann's middle and,
some way off, the attendant held the ends. Sometimes I
would go myself and lead her about in this way, though it
was useless as well as sad, for she did not know me now, or
anyone.

I had been disturbed by that tale I had heard from Prossy
about the children's tormenting of Ann. In her way, I
knew, as though I could see with their eyes, she was a
comical figure and a butt; this I think was why Simon
could no longer bear the sight of her. The bosom of her
gown would still be all stained with food which had dried,
for it was a constant, heartbreaking business to keep her
clean, and her mouth hung open, dribbling saliva. But one
of the tormentors was her own son, and I knew enough
about children in general, and by then about Robert in
particular, to know that his baiting of his poor crazed
mother was less due to cruelty of his own—he was not
cruel—than to a desire to copy Melissa, perhaps outbid her,
even at the cost of his own innate decency and kindness.
For Melissa herself in all ways, at lessons and at play, and

in the affection of Robert's father, outstripped Robert; ordinarily a gentle, considering boy, and moreover two years older than she and, in however unofficial a sense as yet, her affianced husband. For any male creature it would be a galling position; but to chase and torment poor Ann, throw stones and call after her in the woods as I found them doing one day, was not to be endured on this head or any other, and shortly I took young Robert aside, when I had won enough of his confidence in other matters. I told him that his mother and I had been at school together and had been friends all our childhood, and that I had been an attendant at her wedding.

"She was very beautiful on that day, in her white satin gown," I told the boy, whose blue, vague eyes were beginning to focus with some interest and, I perhaps imagined, a slight lessening already of the shame which had lain behind them. "But I think that the time I saw her looking the most beautiful of all was on a day when she had a new pony, and I rode on another behind her, only mine was not as spirited. She had a hat with a blue curled feather and—" I told him the rest and felt tears come at the back of my throat, remembering Ann as she had been. "And that was the day we first met your father, she and I," I finished. "He was standing at the outer gate."

Robert considered the matter for a long time, in his slow way. Then he said, idly, "What colour was the pony?" and I knew I had won, that time, against Melissa.

Robert was not as a rule fond of ponies. At least, he said so, but I noticed that Simon had recently bought Melissa a beautiful little Arab mare, of the Godolphin strain lately come out of France, and too spirited for any other child to ride. The pair, Melissa and Simon, would go off sometimes, she on the little mare and he on his tall bay. That their going was like the wind when they rode out at last on to the high moors I can well believe; I never saw them. That mare was the first of many and for speed, and delicate spirit and fiery quality of eye, she was unequalled until that other came, years later; the black devil with the black ways and fiend's temper, that I will never forget as long as I live and can still unlock the door of memory.

But Robert's idle question now showed that already he thought of his mother differently. I knew well that it was not my own pony on that far-off day at the gate that he asked about, and I answered without hesitation "A chestnut. A beautiful pony, with a white fetlock; she rode it like a princess, I thought at the time."

"Princesses," said Robert with faint scorn. He changed the subject to a more manly one, but I know for a fact that he never did trouble his mother on her wanderings again, for the attendant told me. And when she saw it no longer pleased Robert to try to vie with her in tormenting the poor creature, Melissa forgot about it also, to outward evidence.

Perhaps—I wondered this both at the time and later—it might have been better for Ann's son had his mother not been kept at Aske at all, but elsewhere; it would have made no difference to Ann. But Simon would never have confined the harmless thing in a bedlam, and at the very least we were still nearby and could see that she was not ill-treated, perhaps by some ignorance on the part of the attendant, and that she was given enough food and kept warm.

8

MY RELATIONS WITH Simon in those days at Aske remained as they had latterly become on his Steed visits, easy and friendly; in a way, it was again between us as it had been long ago before, perhaps just before, I had gone down that first day to the accounts-office. I could even, or thought I could, recall our Roman interlude now kindly, as something not to leave bitter afterthoughts but, again, to remember gladly when I should be old: a blowing leaf of dried passion in the wind, no more, but dead leaves can have bright colours. All this was helped by the fact that he was very frequently away from home, and that I generally ate my meals alone or else with the children. Only occasionally was the long, ancient table I remembered from old days, with its black patina on the mediaeval oak, ever used now; sometimes, when Simon's county-acquaintances would call and dine, or business friends from London or the seaport, the heavy silver would be set out, and I would hear them all till late in the night talking and laughing, boisterous a little with wine. But he did small entertaining at Aske.

It had become to him, almost, I thought a cherished toy; almost as I had been once, not to be used for everyday, only to have, to dress grandly and possess, as one chose, but always in solitude. He would often walk, when he was at home, alone about his garden, or through the rooms, any of which might by now have graced a nabob's residence, so fine were they with gewgaws Simon had bought or collected, and the furnishings were once again all new. For a lonely man to occupy such a house, with no prospect of ever assuaging his loneliness save irregularly, was sad, or should have been; but Simon seemed content enough, in particular when his eyes lighted on the two children, and I knew everything in his mind now, including all of Aske, was for Robert and Melissa and for their sons' sons. Melissa meant far more to him now than Robert, being certainly an Aske. I never spoke of such matters to him, but once he opened the subject with me, on an occasion when he had invited me to join him after supper, as I would not come down, and to drink Tokay with him, a fine case of which had been delivered that day from the warehouse at the port. We walked together in the garden afterwards, for it was a summer night; certain pale flowers which do not open till dusk had come out, filling the air with a wistful fragrance. "I often walk here about this hour, or in early morning," he told me. "It is one time when I and the house are alone with one another. I feel now, Leah, as I would have done had my father been able to bring home my mother to Aske, as his bride. It means all things to me; it is all mine, all of Aske; there is no longer a curse on it, despite Ann."

Yet Ann was there; so was Melissa, and the latter's dislike of me had not abated and, though I had never before been defeated by any child, I doubted if it now would. The feeling between us was less that of pupil and governess, less that of child and adult, than between two grown women, two forces, perhaps pulling opposite ways. As had formerly been the case at the Florentine school, each moment now could bring its unexpected, small miseries; I knew they were deliberately inflicted, but again could never say so to anyone; how could a woman my age complain in such a way about a child of Melissa's without giving rise to accusations of incompetence? I should be able, I supposed, to control her better; or at least, however slowly, to win her trust, if not her heart. But I never won either; and after some further petty, unmentionable defeat of the kind, I would find, alone in my room afterwards, that the very presence of poor Ann somewhere at Aske brought me a certain relief, in a way I could not fully explain unless it were for the following reason.

Simon, as I have said, was at this time handsomer than he had ever been, with an added charm the years of worldly experience and contacts in his business, and perhaps with the county, had brought him. He was also, by now, very rich; the later advent of Napoleon Bonaparte, whose embargo on imports of English muslin and the like had brought hardship to certain dealers in such things in these islands, would not affect Simon greatly, for he had had the foresight already to build up a market, as soon as it might be done, with the new States of America as soon as the war there with us was over. This perhaps made Simon unpopular in certain diehard quarters, but it filled his pocket. Otherwise, there was broadmindedness in rural England still, though owing to the close domestic habits of George the Third and his consort it had died out some time before in London for a while, though the pendulum was by now beginning to swing the other way with the emancipation of the Prince of Wales and his brothers, who as is well known were not domestic. This brought me to the part that troubled me. Many a pretty daughter of a county family, perhaps despairing of finding a suitable husband, and her parents too, would have been pleased and honoured had Simon cared to make arrangements to set up such a young lady as his mistress at Aske, to reign over his household, for he could not of course take a wife because of poor Ann. That he did not do this, or at any rate not at Aske, saved my reason; if such a woman had arrived to queen it there, I think it would have broken my heart. Perhaps I have underrated the resilience of this organ. It might be more accurate to say that I should have died, shortly and quite quietly, of grief.

But it did not happen. Ann's presence had given a legend to Aske, and the legend, rightly or wrongly, included Simon himself, the husband who had ill-used and then abandoned her, the Devil of Aske. That this might have enhanced his suit with the young ladies as well as making them shiver—the prospect of reforming any rake, let alone the devil, is always attractive—is probable, but the parents might have looked askance unless the settlement was very handsome. They were not, as far as I know, however, given the opportunity; moreover for any reigning mistress, as for myself, there would have been the problem of Melissa. I had already had enough to do with that young lady to know that she would have made the existence of any other queen of Aske intolerable till such a person left; and although I did not come into the context in such a way, she very nearly made mine intolerable also.

9

THINGS WENT ON in this way, with moments of great contentment and others of sharp misery, and what I should have done in the end I do not know. But one day, as it happened—and in the press of the events that followed I even forget why—Melissa bit me on the hand. It was a quick, vicious, rather disabling bite, and I was so shocked I could scarcely reprimand her: I went later and bathed it and tied it up, and said nothing to anyone, but I was in some pain, and in this state Mrs. Boothroyd the housekeeper found me. She held up her hands.

"Has that she-devil"—the servants had no illusions about Melissa—"bitten you, Miss Leah?" She added that Melissa had done so before, to some of them at Aske, but that they had put up with it, knowing how the master felt about her. This made me feel much worse and almost totally inadequate, and when she announced her intention of going straight to Simon the very minute he came back home (he was away at the time) I begged her not to do so.

"Please, please, Mrs. Boothroyd, it will only cause more trouble," I said. "I can deal with the matter if it is left alone." This was mendacious, as I knew, and the good creature snorted.

"You can't deal with her, Miss Leah, any more than anyone. *He* could, if he had a mind and could ever see daylight for her; he has never laid a finger on her for all her wild ways. Oh, I shall tell him this time, for she's hurt you, which is a different matter; nobody will prevent me."

And tell him she must have done, that and perhaps more, as I knew instantly on Simon's return; he came up to the schoolroom, walked across and picked up my hand and looked at it; the scar was healing by now, but still visible. He said nothing at all and went out again and presently came back with a whip from the stables. Then he turned to Melissa.

"Shall I take my drawers down?" she said pertly

to him; she knew very well what it was all about.

"It does not matter," said Simon grimly.

And he whipped her. I have never seen such a whipping in my life; it was far worse than Peter's, that time long ago when the poor half-witted creature had been held over Jonie Braik's shoulders and flogged to Old Madam's order till he poured blood. Melissa did not bleed; neither did she cry. I watched, horrified and almost fainting; it was like an orgiastic rite of devils, with the man's teeth clenched and the girl's, in a kind of echo of intense will, the same, and her eyes were screwed shut; not a tear came from them, and there was no sound in the room but the whistling whip, and Simon's rasping breaths. He flogged Melissa until even I, the cause of it, sickened and tried to reach him and get hold of his arm; but the whip flailed down between us as though I had not been screaming at him long since to stop, and it was evident he could not hear me, for it went on . . .

In the end it was Melissa who fainted. She rolled over quite suddenly on to the floor and I knelt down at once by her, and adjusted her clothes; I believe the last of the whip caught me. I had remembered by now that her flesh was only a child's, and not a demon's; a child's tender body, used to pampering and rich clothes, and now . . . I was weeping, I recall; I looked up at Simon through a blur of tears. I could not see his face as he stood over me, the whip still in his hand, still breathing hard; presently he laid the thing down.

"You needn't have hurt her so," I heard myself whispering, aware that he did not even know he had also caught me with the tail-end. I hardly yet noticed it myself.

"She hurt you," he said between his teeth, and before he could say more, if he had intended it, Melissa opened her eyes. They fell on me, and held pure hatred. I have never seen such an expression before or since. I recoiled, and she laughed aloud where she lay. I cannot forget it.

"You will not laugh for much longer, my fine madam," said Simon. "I have been lenient with you, but—" and to this overstatement he added one which, even then, flooded me with joy which I would not have believed that I could yet feel, so close to horror. He was arranging to send Melissa to a boarding-school, he said, as it had proved impossible to turn her, by kindness, into an educated or an agreeable person. The latter are not the words Simon used. They are mine.

This made Melissa cry, indeed. She howled like a lost soul, and rolled and lay at Simon's feet like a dog, begging and slavering, entreating him not to send her away; I was reminded, not for the first time, that her blood was three parts foreign. But he turned and left us, for as always, once his mind was determined on any matter he would not change it; and for once, this trait of his brought me great and unashamed relief.

10

SIMON HAD LEFT the choice of Melissa's school to me, and at first I had considered sending her to some other establishment than Miss Fish's. I had no desire to burden my old friend with the problem I knew Melissa to have become, largely, perhaps, by reason of my own failure to bring her on. But I myself knew little of other young ladies' establishments in England, and having written to Fishy for advice on the whole matter, she professed herself quite ready to undertake Melissa, no doubt for my sake. The child could not, I knew well, be in better hands.

She was to travel to London with me, but Simon suggested that Mrs. Boothroyd should accompany us in the carriage, and I would be glad of her assistance. Simon himself had by now gone to the capital with young Robert, who had already been away at school for the whole of one term; this was the reason why he had not been present at the *dénouement* with Melissa, that day in the schoolroom. Robert's school reopened one week before Fishy's, and Simon would meet myself and Mrs. Boothroyd in London; a plan which would, as may be evident, obviate any necessity of my having to stay overnight with Simon alone at some inn, on the return journey. He was always extremely considerate in such ways, and so curious a thing is human nature that I was grateful to him; I had never put myself forward in any way since coming to Aske.

Melissa sat in silence in the coach and, I believe, addressed no single word to Mrs. Boothroyd on the entire journey, and the barest replies to myself. She looked as pretty as paint, in a moss-green redingote cut with a high waist, and double buttons; her dark curls clustered becomingly below her matching bonnet, and she carried a muff. Anyone looking at her through the coach window would have seen only a beautiful, pensive young girl being driven off to school between two dragons, unless they looked more closely at Melissa's eyes. These contained, I declare it, ancient evil. When we came to our first sight of London, a fact of which I informed her when we had reached the last eminence on the Grantham road, she raised them an instant. I had the impression that London meant nothing to her, any more than Sardanapolis had, Palmyra, Babylon and all the cities of the plain. I turned to Mrs. Boothroyd and hearkened instead to that pleasant soul's ecstasies, for she had never been to the capital before, and intended a day's shopping in some of the arcades, after we had met Simon by arrangement so that he, not I, might deposit Melissa personally with Miss Fish.

I waited in the coach while the pair went in. I would have liked to see Fishy myself, but would perhaps call later, after Melissa was settled, if so one could describe it, and had been withdrawn. I was sorry not to be present at the meeting of Fishy and Simon, the initial survey of Melissa, and the consumption of madeira and fruit cake. But I would hear about it all in any case, I knew, from my old friend by letter. Meantime Simon returned, quite shortly, to the carriage saying no more than that everything had gone off very well indeed. I could scarcely credit this; but no doubt Melissa knew when she had met her match, or else foresaw that a stay at Fishy's could be of benefit to her.

I had already offered to go with Mrs. Boothroyd in her search for linen, but Simon had said he had one or two matters to discuss with me. So having left her alone to her shopping, which made her happy, Simon and I drove on together through London, saying very little in the companionable way of two persons who again know one another well.

However it was evident that he had something on his mind, and shortly informed me; Robert's rector, after only a week of the term, had written that Robert was still very backward, did not mix well with the other boys and, he recommended, should spend some further time at home with a tutor before returning. When I heard this I was troubled, though not surprised; it had always seemed to me that Robert was too much withdrawn into himself, living in a separate world. It had taken time and patience to reach him, more than is possible in any school. I blamed myself that I had not perhaps, progressed with Robert in his lessons to a greater extent, as a result of all this, making him handicapped as compared to other boys of his age. A bleak sensation chilled me, like autumn wind on grass; was it possible that what Simon had to say to me now concerned my having to find myself another situation? It was, when all was said, the fate of governesses; and I had after all failed with Robert, as I had failed with Melissa.

I stammered something of all this, and when he did not answer I grew rose. Presently he ordered the coachman to stop and handed me out at the Park, telling the men to go and refresh themselves and the horses and to meet us again there in an hour. He then offered his arm to me, which I took, and together we made our way towards Queen Mary's Serpentine.

I could not by now bear the silence, and heard myself chattering as I always have when tension grows too great; I think I talked about the sheet of water and how King William's wife had been responsible for its presence, or some other instructive matter. He turned and looked down at me, listening gravely, and more than ever I had the conviction that what he had to say finally concerned myself. But all he said, when I gave him leisure, was "Tell me of Queen Mary. As you know, I am not well instructed, except on a limited number of matters."

So I told him everything I knew of that poor queen; that she had been beautiful, plump, and a Stuart, and childless, they said, as a punishment for disowning and supplanting her father; having herself been married young to the unpleasant little Dutchman of whom she later, for some reason, grew fond. Simon asked exhaustive questions and in the end all I myself knew was shaken out and aired; Queen Mary's regency, the Protestant wind, her high lace headdresses and elegant perfumed gloves, and her untimely death from smallpox. Afterwards I said, "Simon, you did not bring me all this way to hear me talk about Queen Mary, who is dead all of a century, or very near. What is the matter you wished to speak to me of?" And I closed my eyes, but made no other sign; if he had to say it, then it must be said. We were standing together by the oddly-shaped water, watching the ducks.

"You know, perhaps," he said, "what I would ask of you, if I could." And at this my heart sank, then rose again. Then he said, "But while Ann lives, I cannot ask you to marry me, Leah, if you would do so."

My senses whirled. I opened my eyes presently and stared at Simon; and saw certain things, in particular how grey his hair had grown, so that with the thick white strand at the temple it might have been powdered now. There were lines about his eyes, and he was thinner; he had, almost, the defeated look of an ageing man. A great rush of tenderness came to me for him. Was it the news about Robert that had caused him to look like this? And then the realisation came, as it had so often done in the course of my dealings with this extraordinary man; far, very far, from wishing now to jettison me, he needed me as much as ever. And this made me, in myself, young again.

He turned now from the contemplation of the water-fowl on the pond, swimming and diving as they always did at home, and asked me roundly if I would come back to him, as his mistress. "I am fashioned so," he said with apology, "that I cannot live like a monk. I never have," and he mentioned briefly, what I had always assumed was the case, that he had had casual mistresses, once or twice keeping some woman in town over the years since I had left him. "But it no longer satisfies me even after a fashion, and I need a steadier flame," he said. "When one is older, there are moreover other things; like being instructed about Queen Mary, or told again, perhaps, even what the—the Romans ate for breakfast. Leah, my dear, if you can forgive what I once was, perhaps still am in ways, I think that, by now, I might be faithful to you, if that is your desire."

Why did I refuse? I loved Simon, as he knew and I knew it; that he should still want me, even on such terms, was far more than the little squab I was, plain and well past thirty, might have expected. But I refused, and without offending him. At least I did not do that. I was still filled with astonishment at the turn things had taken; it had never occurred to me that he still noticed me for myself, other than as the instructress of Robert and Melissa.

It was for Robert, in fact, that I declined; and at first Simon could not see this. He had never, I well knew, given the boy as much attention, let alone pampering, as Melissa herself had h; d. The news from the school had been a disappointment and shock to him, and he tended, I now saw, to think of Robert almost as degenerate, perhaps inheriting a tendency from his mother. This must not be permitted, and I used all my eloquence to convince Simon now, leaving aside the matter of myself, that for Robert to be able to remember his mother as beautiful, with a childhood friend who had been myself, would perhaps draw him back from his secret kingdom, to which he might well retreat for ever if that friend, in the meantime, changed from being his governess to become his father's mistress, his mother's supplanter. This is as I saw it; and far-fetched as it may have seemed, I made it apparent to Simon. He stood watching me till I had done talking, a little sideways smile on his face.

"Do you never," he said afterwards, "consider yourself? Must it always be Robert, perhaps Ann, or the Steed family; never Leah and Simon?" And I gave a slight, non-committal sound like a grunt; I must stay off that dangerous ground.

In the end we temporised, without embarrassment to either of us; if there ever came a time, he said, that Robert no longer needed me, then I might remember that he himself existed. And I said I would remember; how could I forget? But other things might, I knew, happen by then; time stands still for nobody, and I had already had great joy of that meeting, like a flower which suddenly blooms on its stem long after summer is over, and it had thought itself expended.

It gave me pleasure also that Simon still wanted me to remain as Robert's instructress, perhaps with some help from a tutor from the nearby village school, or some young clergyman, to augment his knowledge of certain things young men must know and in which I, perhaps, was not fully proficient. So we settled all these matters amicably before collecting Mrs. Boothroyd, and again returning to Aske. But in the night hours, at the inn where we all stopped on the way, I lay awake for long with the good woman's broad back turned, to the sound of her snoring. Some matter was still not as it should be, and although the glow of pleasure I was in had not yet faded—which of us but likes to know that we are needed, in whatever way, and have attraction of a kind, when we thought we had none?—I was increasingly aware that I had not been perfectly honest with myself, or with Simon. For the matter of Robert could have been overcome, with understanding of the kind I had already and with success applied; during the year which followed we were to grow much closer, and I could draw out his mind to meet mine, and he would become a man, not a retarded schoolboy, in the end, though not as quickly as the others had done at Steed. No, the reason for my having refused to become Simon's mistress at Aske was due, I knew, to one factor, that of Melissa. I was glad that I had said nothing of that to Simon; his affection for her was of a kind which I could not define, nor I think could any pedestrian person have done. And although Melissa was now safely at Fishy's she would return; and the return was what I dreaded, in my heart.

                                    11

OUR ENCOUNTER THAT day at the Serpentine suc-ceeded, quite naturally and easily, to a continuation of our former friendship. I stayed on at Aske with Robert in my charge, for he did not ever return to school; he was not suited to it. Later Simon engaged the tutor, who one year took Robert on a tour of Holland and Germany; at other times he would be at Aske with us, where, more often than formerly now, we all sat at meals together at the long table. Our talk there was pleasant and, on Simon's part, not too critical of his son; he showed in fact great patience

with him, for Robert would always be slow and considering in his replies, although he was not stupid, as in his
childhood one might perhaps have thought. But for all of
that time he had been overshadowed by Melissa.

The boy never said anything on the subject of his
feeling for Melissa, to whom, as he was naturally dutiful
and attentive, he would expect in due course to be
married as had been arranged. Simon had insisted that he
write to her at Miss Fish's school once monthly, and the
letters were so well supervised both at our end and hers
that, no doubt; they meant very little. We saw less of
Melissa in the school holidays than might have been
expected, because the old merchant, Signor Giorgio, had
her to visit him in Italy once or twice, and seemed to
maintain his affection for her.

Finally the year came when Melissa would leave
school. Robert made a suitable escort, I remember, for
her at the evening-assembly to which, since my own day
when it had not yet transpired, all the young ladies were
taken in white gowns, having invited, many of them, a
permissible male escort. There was dancing, of course,
and Melissa, in her new assembly-rig which was of heavy
white silk, stiffly embroidered all over with ears of corn,
stood up with Robert for four figures. Her black hair,
which when it was loose hung down her back past her
knees, was dressed up in ringlets with a Grecian knot,
and the Ceres-motif repeated in silver corn-ears, in a
wreath round her head. She looked like a young bride,
moving up and down the long lines of country-dances
and the quadrille. Seated among the watching dowagers,
sipping ratafia which had been carefully served to us in
our chairs, my eyes followed Robert and Melissa among
the rest, noting that they made a handsome pair, for his
fair Aske looks were a foil for Melissa; and I wondered
how soon Simon would expect then to wed. It was not
too soon to anticipate, by this means, the looked-for
undoubted heir to Aske; Melissa's breasts now were

perfect. And Robert? As I say, I did not know.

Simon had not come to London himself on this occasion, and I saw Miss Fish. She received me in her own sanctum, where there were many fine first editions of the Georgian poets and all of the novels of Richardson, Fielding and other writers. She looked older, though not so much so as I knew she was; she appeared pleased to see me, regretted that I would not stay with her longer, and had very little indeed to say about Melissa. "We have completed the task," she told me, "as far as anyone can. The rest must be seen. Where does she go now; to Aske for her marriage?"

I replied that so far as I knew, Melissa was to return once again to Signor Giorgio, for a final holiday in Rome and at the summer villa he had lately acquired at Albano. He was old now and had made her his heir.

"That will suit everyone," said Miss Fish, nodding wisely. Certainly, I thought, it suited me; Melissa would not, or not for some months yet, be back at Aske.

But when Melissa came home for good, almost a year after the school evening-assembly, I was at a loss for words.

She had always been beautiful. She had been so even as a tiny baby, at Teresita's breast (how much, other than sustaining milk, had she imbibed from Teresita, who had stayed at Aske till she was five? I had never enquired of her), and now surpassed her promise. She wore a gown which could have been purchased nowhere except in Italy, and had I been present I should not have allowed her to do so even there, for it was unsuitable for any lady young or old anywhere, but looked enchanting. It had silver stars on a grey ground, which enabled it to go by the name of walking-dress; it was made of some fairylike, transparent stuff, as light as a letter, and it also had a completely revealing bodice, low at the neck and, in any case, without any lining. The pearly globes shone through, and Melissa's nipples, like small wild strawberries, thrust against the stuff quite visibly. I had opened my mouth to tell her to go upstairs again at once to change the dress and never let me see her in it again, unless she put on an under-bodice or wore a fichu. Not a house in the country, I might have added with truth, would invite her twice to any function in it. But I did not even say the words, and instead shut my mouth and kept quiet. For Simon, who had been out riding with his son, came into the room, Robert behind him; they had neither of them seen Melissa since she had emerged the previous evening, suitably chaperoned and clad, from the London coach. I did not look at Robert; one glance at Simon was enough. He might have been beholding a goddess, and I felt my heart turn over. He said nothing to Melissa, then or later, about the bodice, and neither did I.

It came about first on one of their swift rides together, on the high moors.

I knew that it must happen: perhaps I had always known. I could do nothing to prevent it, and I should have gone away at once, as soon as I was certain, from Aske. I did go to Steed in the end, for a time at least, after things had become intolerable. Looking back now it does not seem that I could have acted differently, or that had I done so it would have altered the course of events. I do not, in such a way, reproach myself; and I could not even, for he was bewitched, reproach Simon. He was at an age of men about which even a governess can know a great deal, for at certain times of their lives they are like small boys again; greedy for what they must have, prepared to tell lies and grab and steal to get it, whatever it may be, and not greatly considering the feelings of others outside the plan. Afterwards they may grow out of it again, or some do; the fever attacks them before old age, upsetting, if they have any, their wives, to whom they are often for the first time unfaithful. If they have no wife they sometimes acquire a young one, or a young mistress, and find madness for a while in pursuit of lost youth; then they tire of it. I do not think that Simon was ever mad, except in this sense and the one to which he had been always prone, namely that arrangements he had himself made must go on, whether or not his own conduct had made them despicable. And for this reason, because he had long ago willed it, he still expected the marriage to take place between Robert and Melissa. That would, indeed, have been abominable; the abomination of desolation. I do not think that in the end I could have let it take place: but, of course, it did not.

Something else did, however. It would happen among the harebells and clover and bedstraw blowing yellow on the high bluff, among the short rough grass the horses cropped while they waited. They would have ridden by already, the pair, at the speed of the wind, then have wheeled, and be walking their horses, and then Melissa would stop and dismount, knotting the reins to a branch and turning away. Then she dropped down, I think, on the sward and lay there, saying nothing and smiling up at him: oh, I know how it was. Then his shadow, then himself, as he seized her; my Simon, my devil and friend, my lover, knowing, as I too did, his own now, the queen of hell; Ashtaroth with the jet-black hair, of old, from Babylon.

Afterwards I saw them come home together, laughing.

12

I DID NOT go to Avice at once, or to Miss Fish or other places I could have done, because of Robert. He likewise, as he let me know much later on, in his indirect way, did not leave until after I had done so; he endured the situation because of me. As, like myself, he had known at once, this was not easy for him. Nothing at Aske was easy now; there was a malefic change in the air.

Yes, Aske changed; subtly, even while we still sat

together at dinner at the long table, making converse of the kind instilled by Mrs. Musgrave long ago. Fishy's sister Carp had died by now; her successor, who had instructed Melissa in the art, was a young widow of connections genteel that one of these was a patroness of Almack's. This was very useful for the school. We discussed the general news of the day, the uneasy peace in France; Melissa would talk of Italy. Her descriptions of the places to which Signor Giorgio had taken her were, many of them, the same Simon and I had known together, in another life. That she knew the heartbreak she must be causing was quite possible; I only smiled, as Simon did, and listened. A new item for us was that the Pretender's German wife had left him long ago, and he had quarrelled with the Pope before that and had gone to live in Florence.

I thought of Florence, and the Villa Fiori. Had Cornelia Fraser and Melissa met in Rome? I did not ask. Cornelia would be married years since. A social accident, or, perhaps, a meeting at midnight, flying on the air, over mountain-ranges? They belonged to the self-same coven. As though she had read my thoughts, Melissa went on smoothly to speak of the Cardinal of York, whose chairs Cornelia's father had once upholstered. He had, she said with admiration, young running footmen, who ran almost daily very fast from Frascati in the heat, all the way to Rome before the Cardinal's horse-drawn carriage travelling at speed. It was a great sight, and everyone waited to cheer the runners and the Cardinal.

Robert, who had been regarding his plate, spoke up now, as he seldom did in presence of Melissa. "That is very cruel," he said in his slow, rather precise voice. "It could not happen in England now, if it ever did; it's worse than bear-baiting. They can burst their hearts in a few years, those footmen, while they are still young." And he got up and then went out. I had told him, long ago when he was a child, about the appalling cruelties there had used to be before Shakespeare and his theatre came, baiting and whipping a blinded, castrated bear in a pit in London south of the river and elsewhere. I had not thought he would remember about the blind bear all these years.

Melissa laughed after Robert had gone; otherwise, there was a silence. I remember the whole episode as one of the few times the boy had showed what he felt about Melissa, and the way we all remained, the three of us, afterwards at the long table finishing breakfast as if nothing had happened, or altered. In a way, it had not; but otherwise I do not know why I remember the episode at all.

But I can remember the black horse. Its name was Suliman. Simon bought it for Melissa at Newmarket. I do not know what it had cost him.

It was a great tall-legged, powerful brute—this word does away with gender although, unlike a lady's ride as a rule, the animal was a stallion. No gelding would have done the things Suliman did when he was wild, like a nightmare; sometimes in his box at night, out of devilment, he would drum with his hooves, so that the whole house was wakened. Even the groom was scared after such nights, and would not go near in the morning, except hesitantly; no one blamed him, for at the beginning he had gone in and had been kicked, and for a week was lame. The only one unafraid was Melissa, and she had never known fear of man or beast. She would open the door, as though nothing had happened, and go into Suliman's box, and run her hand over his neck, and give him sugar; in a little while she would saddle him and ride him out, and for her he was always amenable enough, even though the whites of his eyes still showed; it was like a queen riding. Simon, who would only have bought her so wild a brute at her request, said a thing about it all, unwittingly, one day at breakfast after he and Melissa had come in together from their ride. She preceded him in her habit with her hair all down, and her cheeks red as a rose with the wind; they were smiling at each other.

"You had a fair tussle with him today," said Simon. Melissa laughed aloud, and flung back her black hair.

"I'm used to ride, with the devil above me or under," she said. "It doesn't trouble me either way."

I could hardly believe that I had heard her, or that he endured it. She went over to the side-table and helped herself, then sat down and began to eat her breakfast. They were laughing together, and I pushed my plate away and rose and went out. Ann was being trailed across the lawn by now on her walk and I saw the red leading-strings and the attendant, and wondered again if the latter were quite suitable for Ann. She was strong, and an adequate nurse, but taciturn, and it was known she drank a great deal. Such people are however not easy to find and it was necessary to put up with her, but I tried at least to ensure that the poor creature was not ill-treated in her fits, which sometimes still overcame her. Later I went and sat with Ann myself for a while, and talked at her as one will do with a little child, but there was of course no answer.

I may have coupled them in my mind too soon, the black horse and Ann. But I had to fill it with such things. I had to.

13

I HAVE NOT mentioned Jonie Braik all this while, or that he was, incredibly, still alive at Aske. It had long been a matter of the boy who cried wolf, every time Jonie said he was going to die; no one believed that it would happen, although in the nature of things he could not be expected to last much longer. Nobody reckoned how old he was in actual years; by now he was like an ancient, lichened stone that has stood upright in the wind for more centuries than anyone can remember. I imagine his real age to have been perhaps eighty, knowing the time he had been out with the Pretender, not even then in first youth. It was hard to tell.

He stumped about now with a long stick, that he had cut, bent and shaped under water for himself, like a shepherd's crook; and walked about with it in his hoddens, fancying himself a patriarch, which in his way of course he was. They had great respect for him in the village, almost as though he had been one of Abraham's visiting angels; they would bring great platters of meat and bread to him at the doors, fresh baked that day and still hot, or whatever he asked for. He also ate very well for himself in the servants' hall at Aske, but remained thin as a stick. One day I met him and his supporting crook, when I was on my way to see Ann at her lodge-cottage. He had, evidently, been returning from there himself. I greeted him and went on up the path, remembering, as I had not done for many years, how fond he had used to be of Ann and she of him, and how in her childhood he had flung her up on her pony. It seemed so long since then that, although she was his own daughter, he might well have forgotten her.

But when I called at the lodge the attendant seemed scared. It was the first time I had seen her like this and it was unchancy, for she was a big, muscular creature with a whiskered upper lip like a man's. Looking at her I realised for the first time how little I knew about her; one enquires very little about such people apart from their suitability, and experience of the work. Her name, I knew already, was Janet. Janet told me, when I asked, that Jonie Braik had come, and had stood for a long time in the doorway, which stood open in summer with a guard, and looked at Ann. Then he had said something in the Gaelic, and had nodded once, then made the sign of the cross towards her. This last intrigued me; I had never thought, though perhaps I should have done, that Jonie might at one time have been a Papist. No one else had thought of it either, but that was less surprising; he would have taken, I am sure, any religion which suited everyone at the time, like the Vicar of Bray. But now he had done that strange thing on meeting Ann. "Do you know what it can have been that he said to her?" I asked the attendant, idly and without much hope. I knew in any case that it could have been nothing Ann herself would understand, whether in English or Gaelic. It had certainly not occurred to me that the attendant might follow the latter; I thought she might have guessed something from Jonie's tone as he spoke. But I had forgotten the Highland glens, laid bare with fire and sword in Simon's father's time, so that those who escaped found work later in far places. This woman would have come south in such a way, then or afterwards, for work and food. She looked at me now and I saw that her eyes were slate-grey, as they can often be in the north. She was a big woman, with heavy shoulders and grey-black hair.

"He said," she told me slowly, not as if the matter were wonderful to her, "that he was going soon and that she would be coming after him, and that he would wait for her on the road."

It did not make any sense to me and for the time I forgot it. But Jonie did go, very shortly, seated in his chair outside the cottage, with the hens still scratching about his feet when they came and found him dead there. After that the married coachman moved in with his wife and children, and they cleaned everything up and got rid of the hens and the remaining cats, and buried them somewhere, and Jonie also was buried, in Aske churchyard. I do not know if it would trouble him not to have a priest at his death. I do not know where any of us could have found one for him.

But all that time I was less concerned about Jonie or Ann, for whom no more after all could be done, than about Simon.

It may seem, even on the face of it, that I troubled myself excessively. He was, after all, a man of mature years and well able to look after himself. Whatever our former or, even, our recent association had been, I was a plain, ageing woman so that the whole matter was no uncommon one to outward judgment, resembling only the old, essential law of the jungle and the cave. I was the worn-out mate, pushed without more words into the background shadows, while a younger, luscious wife was borne in at the door in triumph by the hunting male. (I have been following lately, with much interest, what is being read aloud to me here about the discoveries dug up near Dover, which tells us a great deal about the habits of these early people, and I understand a female archaeologist is the leading light in the whole matter.) But it all meant more than that; much, much more to both of us. For Simon still persisted in his arrangements for Robert and Melissa's forthcoming marriage, which he repeatedly stated must be soon.

When he quarrelled with Melissa—they had begun lately to do this, like mating cats, in broad daylight, and would make it up afterwards—he would tease her about it, sometimes in Robert's presence as well, of course, as mine. I was by now as nearly invisible, I daresay, as anyone can be who still in a manner lives and feels; but I had eyes and ears also, and I saw Melissa's wedding-dress. I do not know what happened to it, for she never wore it; it was brought from France, of silk woven to order in Lyons. That was almost the last purchase anyone could make from that country before the revolutionaries overran it; that is, no doubt, why I remember. The one Melissa wore in the end was different, and Mrs. Boothroyd described it to me one day when she came over to Steed, for of course I had left Aske by then . . . As for the other servants, now Jonie had gone none of them said what they thought, or if they thought at all; no doubt they did, and talked also. And the village would talk as well, and then the county; they had been watching everything in their silent, indirect way for a long time, and said nothing openly. But there were few callers now at Aske.

I myself left in the end as a result of one matter, not that it was new, which occurred one day before dawn. I had been to the privy—no other reason, after all, is likely for being out and about at that hour, except one other; and I was returning to my room on the floor below. It happened to be near that place in the corridors where I had once encountered Simon, long ago just after his marriage to Ann, and we had gazed at one another down the long pencilled misty distances made by the perspective of windows, marching in regular file like grenadiers below the roof. Something made me look back over my shoulder now as I had done then, and I saw Melissa, coming back up to her room from Simon's by the further staircase, her nightgown trailing behind her unsubstantially, like a ghost. She saw me at the head of the stairs, where I had already made as if to go down.

"I wouldn't go quite yet, if I were you," she called, "he's sleeping," and laughed in her guttersnipe-fashion, seeing my face and hearing the sound echo, so that the whole house might also hear it. He is sleeping . . . he is not dead but sleepeth . . . he is bewitched, his manhood taken away and drained, sucked into that other flesh by night, a vampire's, a succuba's. That was what I could not, even by the end, forgive Melissa; after all, in ways they were well matched. But by now Simon himself was being coarsened and blurred at the edges, turning, with her expressed contempt as it increased, into a lecher. She had taken my splendid man and used him for her purpose, leaving only where he had been, asleep now, a set of inflamed, demanding genitals. And to insult me was part of the pattern.

That same day I left Aske, for I could endure no more. I arrived at Steed without even taking time to warn Avice, on this occasion. But she would give me houseroom, I knew, till I had found somewhere else to go. I did not know yet where that would be.

14

THE ROOM I had formerly occupied while at Steed was now inhabited by Mary and her two older sisters, and the nursery was a schoolroom and the new governess slept in the old nursery. So Avice told me when, that night, she and I shared the bed she had once slept in with Sir Napier, and still kept to now that she was a widow. It was wide, but I could not forget that I probably lay on the self-same pillow as the squire when, nightly and in fettle from the hunt and his wine, he would turn to Avice to cast a proprietary leg over her. His ghost and I made unlikely bedfellows.

Avice slept soon and I made myself, to drive out other thoughts, continue in recollection of Sir Napier. In this process I was reminded of a story which of its own self would never have filtered to my virginal upstairs chamber, had not Young Napier himself repeated it to me on his fifteenth birthday when he, for that occasion, was flown with wine and had pinched the tavern-maid's bosom at the inn. The legend had it that old Sir Napier, at a certain hour of the night by which the household could set its clocks (the good man's transports were said to last twenty minutes, no more and no less, to allow for an early start to the hunt in the morning) would bellow companionably, so that it could be heard downstairs, "There, my lass, ye are done, ye are done!" and would then lapse promptly into slumber. How much delighted embroidery there was attached to all this I know not, but I found myself now remembering it, rather than some matter of refinement more suitable to my profession if not my years, which were still a great deal less than Sir Napier's. Yes, I knew why I lay there, reminiscing like a bawd; it was to prevent my thinking of what passed at this very minute, in that other wide bed at Aske, the same one wherein I myself had slept with Simon that first night of all long ago, in nunlike slumber against his chest, before we set out together on the journey to Rome to find Melissa.

Next day, a letter was brought me from Simon. It had been written in great haste, and sent over to Steed at once by messenger. Young Robert, it said, had also left Aske, the evening of the day I had done so. He had left without much money or all of his gear, and Simon now asked if the boy was with me or if I had news of him. I had not, but I feared less for Robert than for his father. Simon's son had always a vein of pride in him, known perhaps to nobody but myself, for he seldom drew attention to it: now, as a relief from an intolerable situation I could only approve his conduct, young as he still was. No doubt he would inform his father in due course where he had gone; and so I told Simon in a note, hastily and somewhat coldly written, in time to send back with the servant who had ridden from Aske with his letter.

Simon came himself next day. I was alone when he was announced, for Avice had already arranged to visit somewhere. I was shocked at the sight of him; he looked older, defeated and, I thought, for the first time, ashamed of himself and of what he had done. I realised, never having thought of it very greatly, that he had been fond of Robert in a more personal way than he himself knew and had also wanted—pathetically, now when it was too late—his son to be proud of him.

I sent him away, after refusing to go with him back to Aske. He should have understood that well enough, I told him; how could I go back? In the end, as he still seemed obdurate, we quarrelled; not hotly, as we would once have done, with healing afterwards, but sourly, as the old do, with age in every word and line. I turned my back before he left, which I was sorry for as soon as he had ridden off; as far as I knew, I would not see him again. There was no reason to do so, any more; he had his life as he had made it, and I had mine. To try to pick up its threads, I wrote to Miss Fish; I seemed to do this in every crisis.

She wrote back and said that she had a place for me if I cared to take it, for a little while only; the teacher was ill.

So I went, and then I came back again to Steed, this time by invitation, for something the same cause; Avice's governess, who had not been well for a long time, was now confirmed in a consumption, and could no longer carry out her work. As she had no home to go to, and as Avice was too kindhearted to turn her out of Steed in such a state, she lingered for some months, and later died, a skeleton, I believe, in bed in the former schoolroom or nursery. I no longer took much heed which, I fear. For it was then, at almost the same time, we heard of the death of poor Ann. She had been found drowned that autumn, in the pit above Aske.

15

It had been spoken of, naturally, everywhere the news was received, as a merciful release. Others said they hoped she had not suffered. There was, I believe, a large attendance of the villagers particularly, at the funeral; death once again conferring on Ann the remembered legend of beauty. She had, they say, looked almost beautiful even now, lying in her coffin in Aske great hall for two days, with the mud and leaves washed away from her poor face, and her hair combed loose after being dried. Ann had always had lovely hair.

She had been found lying face down in the pit-water in her nightgown, barefoot and with her cloak round her that was put on for the daily walks when the weather grew colder. It had been late at night when she was first noticed to be missing. The attendant had been down, as she always was regularly on Thursdays, to visit her crony, a woman who lived at the farther end of the village. They would sit together inside the doorway there mostly in silence, having long ago said everything there was to say; drinking Hollands from two cups and staring out of the door at whoever passed. That was the attendant's time off, which

was not strictly kept account of, as she had left Ann safely
enough in her bed. When she returned, the bed was empty,
and the door unbolted from the outside, which meant
someone had come in; who would come after dark to that
poor soul, in such a place? It was hard even to find one's
way, without a lantern. And no lantern-light had been seen
that night from the house; it had been dark, with a late
slim moon.

So they all said; and, of course, blamed Janet the
attendant, who had not troubled to bolt the door as she
said she did, so that the poor creature awoke, saw the
moonlight and wandered out, and up the hill to her death,
not knowing night from day. But Simon gave the
suspected attendant a character, for he was merciful in
such ways; no doubt Janet was able, with it, to find a
situation elsewhere. I heard no more of what became of
her, or how she came to know the Gaelic.

It had still been dark, without any moon till later, that
night it happened. I know it all as though I had been there.

After the attendant had gone—Thursdays, without fail,
and coming back drunk, two hours or more after—when
she had gone, the bolt was drawn back again on Ann's
door. The poor soul was inside, in bed and asleep,
doubtless; but knowing neither night nor day, and hearing
a soft voice calling to say it was time now for her walk,
and she must get up and come, she came. She would be
sleepy and slow, no doubt; for Ann was always slow these
days, even when full awake.

"Come quickly, Aunt Ann. Time for your walk.
Quickly; into these. Now your cloak, to keep warm.
Quickly, Aunt Ann; there is not much time. Quick, quick,
quick, quick."

Quick, out of the door; moving, with the sudden pull of
the reins on her, more boldly than under her own
guidance, when she would knock herself sometimes against
walls. But the reins were tight as they pulled, and too thick

and heavy; where were her red strings she was used to? What had they put on her instead? She began to cry; small, whimpering sounds at first, muffled by the night where nearby, against the dark of the moon, a great, darker shape waited silently. Ann knew what it was; a horse. She smiled a little, dragging up her lip; she was used to horses, had ridden a pony, a chestnut it was, once at the gate when . . . and again the clouds came over and she snuffled and sobbed, frightened now; she even knew why she was frightened. She was afraid of the horse's rider, who had vaulted up onto the horse's back still holding Ann's reins, but not taking Ann; they were moving now, too fast, much too fast for anyone running beside them, so that after a while she would part run, part be dragged along beside the churning hooves, faster, faster, while the encircling reins grew tighter about her body and pulled till they or she might burst. The leaves crackled and crunched under her stumbling, terrified feet, for the ground was not certain, or flat like it was on the lawn; she was shaken and jogged and pulled most cruelly, and somewhere above her someone laughed, and the great hooves pounded.

Shaken and jogged, and dragged along, trotting or being dragged, pulled tighter, a pony, a fat winded pony whose breaths came shorter and shorter. Trot, then canter; faster and faster, through the wood, up the slope, running through brambles which tore like cruel, restraining hands at her clothes and flesh, so that the tearing was like knives, like whips and scorpions, as they jolted on and on.

Above her, that other would laugh now and again. It was a sound she would remember long after other things had gone; a cruel, jeering note of laughter, reminding Ann of the time they had used to come, two of them, and throw stones, and make her try to get away and hide among the brambles so that she was trapped there, held fast by the thorns. Somebody had come and rescued her, those times, but nobody would come now. It was too dark, and she was tired out and torn and had no more breath. On, on. And the devil laughed. On.

"Come on, Aunt Ann. Canter, now. Gallop now, gallop, you fat witless swine, my fine sweating pig, gallop, or I'll whip you. I'll whip you anyhow, Aunt Ann; you know I will. You know me, don't you? Gallop, jump now, jump. Uphill again . . ."

They found her at last down in the pit in the wood next day, and though the brambles had ripped at her there was far more; great weals about her body, as though she had been cut with a whip, but it could be only the brambles, if she had grown frenzied and had run among them. She had pitched face down when she came to the pit-slope, and fallen; that was all, and a great red weal about her middle meant nothing, for she had not been wearing her reins. Had they always been so tight? The attendant should have noticed . . . But they were hanging safe enough, the red reins, back at the lodge; they had not been taken down that night at all. No she had gone out by herself, and lost herself, and fallen over, and drowned at last in four inches of muddy water; poor Ann Aske.

There was a missing saddle-girth in the tackroom at Aske stables and on being asked about it young Miss said it had been broken, and she had let it go one day. She did not know where.

Nobody asked much more, as the release was so merciful. There were, however, certain matters troubling the young groom, who slept above the stables now that the coachman lived in Jonie's cottage. He had, on the night of the death, heard Suliman's hooves drumming, at about three in the morning, in his box, as though some matter troubled him. Young Miss had not come down, for she would be in her bed and asleep; later she said she had heard nothing. The groom had gone himself and looked in at Suliman, using the stable-lantern; he had seen the great horse all flecked with foam, and his eyes staring white as

though he would run mad; the groom hadn't dared to go in
further, to rub the stallion down or see to him, and had
waited for the morning, when Miss came out. Miss had
gone in, of course, and had seen Suliman was all right, and
had led him out for a while, after which he came back as
usual. He hadn't been out at all the night previous, she
said; and she stuck to that, and what could the groom say
otherwise, without losing his place, which he was in danger
of doing anyway? But he often remembered, especially
after the poor body was brought home, seeing that black
horse the way it was that night, and wondering. But there
would have been trouble if anything had been mentioned,
and there was only himself and his word on the matter;
better to say nothing, so in the end he did that. But he
kept his own counsel, about that matter and the missing
girth. If he ever came on *that*, he'd take it straight to the
master, with the tale of where it had been found lying, and
then others could do as they liked. But he searched, and all
of that winter found nothing; there had been high winds
and much drifting over of leaves.

Much later I learned of what happened the night before
the burial.

Simon stood for a long time by the coffin, alone;
presently the village folk would be allowed to come in and
file past, looking at Ann.

He, of course, as the widower, had gone first, alone as
was his duty. But he had spent longer here by now than a
widower need do, unless he is inconsolable and has deeply
loved his wife. Simon had never loved Ann.

There were candles burning now about the coffin-head;
it was open, and the warm light shone on Ann's hair. Her
face had not been too badly disfigured to have them all see
her. There was a bruise on one cheek, and they had of
course closed the eyes.

Ann. She had never, he remembered, meant anything to
him at all, even when he had thought of her as an Aske. In

a way, he still did. She had borne his son; he should have
been more grateful to her. In his way, in being good and
patient at the beginning, and even afterwards, he had done
what he might. And he had seen she was not ill-treated,
until . . .

His mind shied away. It had been an accident, he
thought again; an accident.

The candlelight flickered and he saw Ann's mouth seem
to smile, as if the instant's shadow lifted it. An accident.
She had wandered out, as they said, and lost herself in the
dark wood, and had been torn by brambles, and in the end
had missed her footing and rolled down the steep slope of
the pit and had drowned. An accident. A merciful release.

He became aware now that there was somebody with
him, standing by him, and he did not turn; he had not
heard her come in. Melissa. He made himself turn and look
at her at last, dragging his eyes up from the face of his
dead wife in her coffin. Melissa. She was so very young.
She wore a hooded cloak, dark blue, over her hair and her
eyes, looking full at him, were unreadable, wide and dark.

Melissa. She took him by the hand. "The villagers are
waiting to come in," she said in her clear voice. "Are you
ready?" She was so composed; he envied her. Of course
she could feel nothing about Ann. Of course she—

Melissa lost patience. "Why make pretence of mourning
her any longer?" she said. "You never cared two pins for
her while she was alive; why wait here by her now she's
dead? Come away; they can look, then close the coffin and
bury her, and—"

She had not finished, and he downed the certainty of
what else she might have said. He let her lead him away,
and out of the death-chamber, and upstairs.

Next day, they had Ann's funeral.

Some time later, he asked Melissa if she had ever at any
time ridden Suliman up into the woods. He could not tell
why he had asked her, but remembered doing so, and her

answer. She had raised her thin black brows, a little surprised.

"Up there?" she said. "No; why should I? He'd break a leg, as like as not. He likes the turf, and a good flat run, as you know well."

And she chose that moment to tell him about the coming baby, so that he shelved the other matter.

16

I HAD NOT gone to Ann's funeral.

I was by then back in London, for some cause I forget. I was like a dandelion-clock, with its comings and goings governed by the prevailing wind, but free after a fashion; and I decided not to go back again to Aske and witness the sad trappings, and the horses with black plumes to draw the hearse, and the county mourning-faces. The county would, each separate one, attend the funeral, for they never miss such things; but never one of them had called upon Ann after she became mad, or had helped to lead her about anywhere on the red strings. So I could not join wholeheartedly in their mourning.

Then there was Melissa. I believe Simon married her less than a month after the death. That was when I heard about the second wedding-dress. I was back at Steed again by then and Mrs. Boothroyd came, and when she saw me we fell into each other's arms at once in a way to which I am not greatly given, but she was a good old creature and had been much shocked and mortified, and had given in her own notice.

I had known, of course, without this information, that Melissa must marry Simon soon, or he her. It had been brought to my awareness at a time which seems now to have been before I knew what had happened to Robert, after he had run away that time from Aske; and yet it must have been before he went, in fact; he and I were still under that roof when Melissa told me. I did not see her again until after the marriage. And yet our talk concerned Robert, and some doubt even then that he might marry her. She had laughed; all of those days seem now to be filled with her remembered laughter, not strange or bitter always, not a devil's, but high and excited, the laughter of a young girl who has too many gowns. She said, "Will Robert perhaps not marry me after all, Miss Considine? I think Uncle Simon should." For she still, incredibly, called him that to his face. "I think he should; you know, I'm pregnant by him."

But the little minx was not, though she may have thought she was. It was eleven months after the marriage that her boy was born, the one she called Simon after her husband, as he was by then, and George for the old merchant, who had lately died in Rome and as expected had left Melissa his money.

17

IT WAS GOOD, gregarious Avice, of course, who tried to heal the breach that had arisen; Avice with her love of a good gossip, her kind heart, her innocent weakness—it was that by this time—for sitting down with a pot of tea at all hours, and some seed-cake or a biscuit to nibble at between her meals, which continued large. She had grown immensely fat, and knew everybody and heard everything, and she was concerned about Melissa, whom no doubt she remembered as a little girl kicking up her frilled ankles with a cricket-bat on the front lawn at Steed. "They have," she said to me one day, and it was true, "been married near enough the year now, and no one has called at Aske. She's a young thing, when all's said, younger than Sophia." Sophia was married by now, and expecting her first in a few weeks' time also. "With the baby coming so soon, and in wedlock," Avice said, returning to the subject of Melissa, "it does not seem right or Christian to continue in such a way, and judge our fellows." So with this, and to encourage the rest, she called at Aske, and persuaded me to go with her.

I am too easily persuaded, as I know well; but what right, after all, had I to object to anything, or refuse to oblige Avice who had been so kind to me? I cannot help it, even yet, if it is the way I am made, to try to judge things as evenly and as fairly as I can. It seemed to me, sitting upon the matter like a judge with his wig, that it was good of Avice to call upon Melissa; yet the latter was not grateful, as might at least have been pretended. She sent word down that she was out of sorts, and lying in bed, and could not come down to see callers that day. So the new housekeeper they had found showed Avice and myself into the withdrawing-room, and presently Simon came in and talked with us about everyday things while Avice was refreshed with some tea, and possibly cake as well; I did not notice. I myself took nothing, and neither did Simon. He looked sixty years old, I thought; I knew well it might, on this occasion, again be the last time I should see him, and very probably the last visit I should ever pay to Aske. For I had plans of my own by this time, and stayed behind for a few moments to relate them, while Avice went back and waited outside for me in the carriage.

Simon did not like my plans; but he was glad, by then, to know that I had news from Robert, who was in London. I shall say more of this presently; but as we talked together, Melissa came into the room. Whether she thought that I had gone, or knew that I had not, I cannot say; I had the notion that she might have been standing outside the door for some moments. She did not look like someone who had been out of sorts and in bed; she looked very well, and I felt angry on behalf of Avice, who had troubled to visit her, but was now, perhaps, too old and fat to rate courtesy.

The door opened and framed Melissa as she came in;

Simon had had her painted by that time, by a pupil of Romney's, and the portrait, when I saw it later, looked as Melissa did then. She wore a gown of striped dark blue silk in the newest mode, with a high bodice and straight skirt falling from the artificially raised waist. Her hair was done in the carefully disordered curls then fashionable, and lightly powdered. She carried the unborn child proudly in front of her; from the old wives' tale, which says boys sit well forward, I could tell that it would be a son. She moved flauntingly to where we both waited, Simon and I; I could not tell how much she had heard, from beyond the door, of what did not concern her.

"I did not know that you had come with Lady Steed, Miss Considine, or I might have made an effort to come down," she said with arch sweetness. "Have you had tea?" Her eyes slid towards Simon. The contempt sat openly in them now, and I thought how correct I had been in thinking that he was unhappy. I felt sick with pity and anger, but he spoke mildly enough.

"My dear," he said, "Miss Considine is leaving us shortly to go and stay in London, where she will make her home."

"Indeed? How much we shall miss you," said Melissa in honeyed tones. I said nothing; Simon had in his own way, sealed the matter for himself and me, and we had said our farewells and now there was nothing to do but go. Was it the second or third time I had driven away from Aske, convinced, as on other occasions, that there would be no return? But this time must surely be the last. I did not stay longer watching Simon's torment, but shortly murmured my excuses and rejoined Avice in her carriage, and we drove away.

18

IT IS NOT my purpose to burden this tale with the full story of how I fared in London, other than that I went by arrangement to look after Robert at his lodgings, which were above a shop in Bloomsbury. This entails some explanation of how I had learned of Robert's whereabouts; he had written, shortly after he left Aske, to me at Steed, to say he was well, and in London, but could not give a settled direction meantime. Even this news had been a relief to me, as I had been afraid, at first, that he might have gone to join the army, for which he was not suited.

Shortly after that again he wrote to say that he was working for a bookseller, and later still that he had been left in charge, as the owner was often away. This sounded as if Robert had found his own feet, although friends helped him at the beginning; he told me about it later, when I joined him. He did not ever intend going back to Aske. He did, however, attend his mother's funeral, but only to church and the burial. Afterwards he rode straight back to town.

He had done well enough, I found, in the time since he had left Aske; almost as though now, for the first time free of its shadow and his father's plans for him, he could become a person in his own right. He was not, nor ever would have been, such a person as Simon would have wished him to become; he was timorous, though obstinate when he had made up his mind; kind and dutiful, until outraged as had happened; slow in most matters including anger; and meticulous in his business dealings, a trait which he may have inherited from Simon. I like to think, however, that his neatly kept ledgers, and the love he showed for his growing stock of books, had been partly fostered by myself. It diverted me, a little, to hear, as I did later, Robert advise customers on which book to purchase, and he did some fair amount of reading for himself, though formerly he had not shown any great interest in it. But it was a means of independence for him and as such, he fostered it.

The shop was pleasant, not too dark, rather square than narrow. The remembrance of shops I keep after so long a time seems to consist mainly of their smell; the one in Rome, full of dark bottles slung from their hooks, comes to me yet whenever I smell wine and dust; dust was, again, here in Bloomsbury, admixed with an aroma of paper and leather, reminding one of the library at Aske. I went into the shop sometimes but—here I must digress a little—I soon had concerns of my own, unlikely as such an event may now seem. I had started a school.

I had not intended anything so ambitious. All I had meant to do—if my care of Robert allowed it, which I guessed it might as he was never demanding of my time—was to take a few pupils whom I should possibly acquire by putting up a small card in the bookshop. Persons who frequent such places, and show an interest, say, in purchasing a set of Lawrence Sterne, or the works of James Boswell, are generally in touch with others whose tastes and requirements may be very valuable to such purposes as mine. I had little hope of using my Latin and Greek, which are already well enough taught in schools and are in any case the love of the few, who by themselves pursue them. But it had occurred to me that, with my teaching experience at the Villa Fiori some years before, and my reading since, it should be feasible for me to impart Italian and also French, which of course is a part of every young lady's accomplishments even if she shall never leave these shores. With regard to the young ladies themselves, I had no qualms about my own suitability. It was many years since I had left the Villa Fiori, for reasons which had not been widely known even then; and my appearance now, I reflected sadly, was not such as to rouse doubt or even speculation in any parent, however particular.

So I pinned up, or rather Robert did so for me, a small white card in the bookshop.

The results were gratifying.

Within a week I had three pupils; soon I had more than I could take. I think that having quite genuinely lived

290 The Devil of Aske

abroad, while at the same time remaining an English person, as this latter state perhaps reassures the timid, brought me enquiries: then having met and conversed with me, initially in Robert's rooms above the shop, the enquirer seemed satisfied that I could give them what they wanted for their daughters. In a very short time I was able to consider renting premises of my own, and having found Robert a good housekeeper meantime, I did so; the house I took was in a discreet part of Bloomsbury, which even by that date was almost a continuation of the town itself; and, by the year's end, I was employing two assistants. I was most fortunate in these, and in the range of their attainments. We were able, as a result, to expand our curriculum to include other subjects besides foreign tongues, which however remained the foremost reason for the little school's existence. I could say much more; indeed I could have remained for the rest of my life quite readily, and contentedly, turning into a Miss Fish: that lady was of course delighted to learn of my exploits in such a field, gave me very valuable advice about how to avoid certain pitfalls at the beginning, and came across on frequent invitation to be shown over the school and remark on the girls' progress. I should have been happy, and in the way of being usefully occupied, both physically and mentally, I was so; but sometimes, unbidden in the night hours, there came the thought of that other, once abiding reason for my happiness, and when I think again of that I am glad that I did not after all remain for the rest of my life in Bloomsbury, growing slowing as dry as the dust on an old book, while the years passed.

I had heard, of course, at the proper time, of the safe delivery of Melissa when she gave birth to Simon's son.

How can I describe the passing of time? It was, again now, a matter of trivial things, but how much in our lives is not trivial? How, in any case, are we to assess its relative importance to our own pattern and fate by its effect on

the very stuff of which we are made? My own stuff, if this
is the correct term, toughened and hardened during those
years in London, like the shell of a tortoise; I had to learn
to deal with people and situations that had never come my
way when I was a private person, responsible for no one
but myself and a few children. Now, I had sixteen spirited
young girls to my charge, and knowing from the Villa Fiori
what girls can be like I took full cognisance of the fact
from the beginning. No doubt they thought I was a
dragon. My two assistants were a man and his wife, or
rather—with respect to their relative sizes and occupations—a wife and her man. The woman was English and she
had married a German artist and engraver, Herr Rauch. He
was a fairylike person quite different from the rooted idea
one has of large, omnivorous Germans; *mein Herr* was
dainty, with hands and feet small as a woman's, and a
delicate precision of touch; he was, besides being sensitive,
extremely terrified at first, for he had never taught before.
But his wife, who had many things he lacked and lacked
many things he had, egged him on, and he became a
successful drawing-master with occasional lessons in
German, which was of course an added recommendation
for my school. Moreover, the good little Herr was not
romantic enough in appearance for the pupils to fall in
love with him, and in any case Madame—we did not ever
call her Frau—kept him under her thumb. I am sorry if I
appear to undervalue Madame Rauch, for she was very
useful also, though less sympathetic; she taught English
grammar to the younger pupils (I took the older ones
myself) needlework and deportment, and, the year I left,
the basic essentials of household management. I do not
think that this is a waste of time even for a young lady
who will marry so grandly as never to see the inside of her
own kitchen. Servants, even the major-domos of a ducal
establishment, will have a greater respect for an employer
who has a grasp of certain facts, and are by far less likely to
cheat such a person at every turn. So I informed parents,

who at first had some doubts; in England, a girl must seem totally innocent of all practical ideas before marriage, and afterwards quite suddenly know everything.

I also had visiting masters for music, polite dancing and, if wanted, the enunciation of correct English speech. This to me is another important and neglected facet, and a retired actor taught it. His connections were of course perfectly respectable, and I also had a visiting divine.

One day my little maid came in to announce a gentleman. I thought it was a father I had arranged to see, who wanted me to fit in his daughter at half-term; this would not be easy, for we were already full, and I was pondering the means of telling him so without incurring too much resentment. Then I looked up and saw who my visitor was. It was Simon, with the dust of the journey still on his clothes; he looked haggard and his eyes glittered.

He walked straight over to me and said "Leah, I've killed Melissa. The funeral was yesterday and I've ridden straight down. Will you come back with me now to Aske?"

19

IF ONE IS to go mad, it had better be done with completeness. I found that I did not take time to doubt what he had told me, or even ask about it further. My chief concern, I recall, was lest the thing should have been overheard by anyone in the house; I went to the door, listened for a moment, then called again for the maid, who came. I gave orders that nobody was to be admitted to me on any pretext, that I was not at home to callers (so much for the parent, and whether or not he came I never knew), and that a tray of food was to be made ready and set outside the door, where I myself would collect it. Then I went back to Simon. My first thought had been that he must eat, and secondly that I must listen to him.

He was sitting with his head in his hands now, and raised it as I returned; his face was that of an old man. "Leah, did you understand me?" he asked. "I said that I had killed Melissa. I—I loved her, as you know." He stared at me, as if I could put the whole matter right. I went and sat down by him.

"Who knows of this?" I said. Certain things, no matter how it had all come about, were apparent to me; he was still a free man, and he said they had buried her. That meant—

"No one yet," he said, "as it chanced; but that does not matter. They will know afterwards; I have left a letter in my desk, for Wynmalen." Sir John Wynmalen was the Justice of the Peace, and I began to have a sensation as if not only Simon and I but the world, as we had always known it, were whirling together down into the maelstrom. "What of yourself?" I said, guarding the impulse I had to put my arms around him. He hardly seemed to notice, yet, that I was in the room; yet he had come straight to me, before anyone knew. I did not yet myself know what had happened to Melissa or how she had died.

He told me then, quite calmly, that it did not matter about himself. He would make an end to his life, when all affairs were settled; he had resolved meantime to see me again, possibly Robert. It would not be a hangman's rope for him, he had resolved, but a bullet; he carried the gun always with him. My feelings on hearing this may be imagined; I tried to remonstrate, in any way Simon might now understand. "What does it matter?" he kept saying. "I must die, and that's an end of it. Melissa is dead. It was a retribution, for Ann. She killed Ann that night; I always knew, I think. Yet I let her persuade me and—" He raised his head, surveying the room with lost, wandering eyes; as though he asked himself where he now was.

´ Presently he smiled. "You see how it all fits the pattern?" he told me. "If it had not been for me, for my will regarding the vow I'd made, Ann would have been married, happily no doubt, to some other man long ago, and would have stayed sane and whole. And because I had driven her to become as in the end she was, Melissa killed her. And then I—"

I was silent. It was like the Greeks, one life for another, blood for blood, and the gods on Olympus never sated, placing their silent wagers. "How can you blame yourself wholly, or say what might have happened?" I said. I knew, however, as he did also, that he had been partly to blame; as any of us must be so, for any action taking place in all of our lives which governs and affects other individuals. To escape such a necessity one must live in a high tower on a remote island, seeing no man. I tried to tell Simon this; he hardly heard me.

"How did you kill her?" I said, as nothing else weighed with him. If he could be brought to tell me of the killing of Melissa, I thought, it might ease his mind. I knew that it would not ease mine for him.

There had been the high winds that winter, swirling the papery leaves about the ground even in the sheltered wood; later they settled, sodden, into mould. Long after that Simon himself went up to the coverts, taking the coachman's eldest boy who was twelve now, and a knowing hand with the young growing pheasants, whom he fed carefully each day with sprouted barley. They had inspected the young birds and had then made a detour to avoid the place where Ann's body had been found; nothing had been said, but it was understood that Simon would not go there for himself or look over at it. "I never did that, any more than I saw her as she was, the way they found her there. I told them to have the pit-bottom drained and filled up with earth, and they did."

The boy had however wandered about among the trees. Presently he gave a shout at something he had found, and Simon, who had been walking quickly past the place, turned and caught sight of the child's eager freckled face and his red hair. He was holding something in his hands, salvaged from the garnered heaps of blown beech-leaves from last year, the darkened galaxy which now, with the long dryness, had cracked and again shifted a little, revealing things which had lain a long time beneath. This was such a thing: a shrivelled, almost unrecognisable strip of leather, with the buckle rusted to the colour of the surrounding leaves. "It'll be the girth Joey said was missing from the tackroom," said the child, pleased. He would trail round after the young groom whenever he was not having an eye to the pheasants; he was still uncertain whether he would like to become a stable-hand or else perhaps, if the opportunity came, a gamekeeper.

Later the groom himself brought the girth to Simon, who by that time knew, or had guessed, how it had got there. Perhaps, as he said afterwards, he had always known. Suliman's girth, and he must have been up that time in the woods, though Melissa said he had not; and in that moment everything fell into place in Simon's mind, and it became clear to him what he must do.

He had said nothing of importance to the groom about the girth, bidding him to get rid of it; and it was of no more use. On his way out he paused at the loose-box and saw the great black horse inside; Melissa rode him less often these days. Suliman's eyes were red-rimmed and sullen, like a bull kept captive for too long before being loosed again into the ring. Simon went in to the gun-room and took down a heavy pistol, not one of the light duelling pair he had, and came back. He fired a shot straight into the horse's temple, and watched him fall dead. The great body slid down, limp and inert, without a cry; it twitched once only, then lay still. Simon saw the groom about burial of the carcase and then went into the house.

Melissa was in the withdrawing-room, lying on her sofa. She had grown idle lately and complained a good deal, saying nobody ever called at Aske. She turned her head now as Simon came in; and stayed, for an instant, quite still, seeing his face.

"I heard a shot," she said. "Bats or pigeons?" She put up her hand to conceal a yawn; then the hand stayed, then fell again to her breast. "Neither," Simon told her, "but a black murderer you'll not ride out on again."

"A black—" she rose slowiy, and stood there regarding him, mouth fallen open as though it had been Ann's. "You killed Suliman?" she said in a voice like a child.

"As you and he killed Ann."

"I?" And the hand at her breast pointed, tapped, as if to identify herself. Then she began to laugh. It was for her laughter, he knew later, that he had killed Melissa; perhaps, despite everything, he would have spared her otherwise; but she had never been afraid of anything, himself or a hangman's rope.

"You killed her, the pair of you," he said. "Now *he* has had a quick death and a clean, which is more than you gave to her, that night when you rode Suliman up into the wood. Why did you say you had never done that, Melissa? It was a clumsier lie than is worthy of you." He was advancing towards her now, hands hanging. When he drew near she began to retreat from him; suddenly, she had whisked past and was at the door, turning and spitting like a cornered cat with its lips drawn back. He remembered her afterwards thus, and about her head the black hair wreathing, like Medusa's.

"Yes, I killed the fat fool," she said. "It could have been done long before, couldn't it, quickly and cleanly?" And she mocked him. "We made her canter, Suliman and I, in the woods that night, bouncing and grunting like a great pig; it was long enough since she'd been made to move fast, not since the days we used to chase her for our diversion, Robert and I. She ran, and she cantered, and the rest, did Ann; in the end the girth snapped about her fat body, and she rolled down into the pit. Had I intended that? I'm not certain. But it happened, and I lost the girth.

Why cling to your grotesques? Ann, and the governess, lud!"

She turned and went out of the doorway, and presently retreated up the stairs; the indoor servants were away that day at the Lammas fair, except for the nurse upstairs with the baby. They were alone, he and Melissa, now in Aske, with the sun alternately lighting and forsaking her figure in its pale dress as it ascended, and he followed. Neither moved at speed; it was inevitable that she should retreat, and he should follow, hearing her voice come back to him idly, as though she talked at a card-party or rout.

They climbed to the upper part of the house, and she made as if to go to the child in his nursery, and Simon moved quickly to prevent her; she should not, he was determined, again see the child. He moved crabwise, heading her off to the further stairs, and she fled up them, afraid now that she saw his intention; she would have escaped him, run along the upper passages and hidden herself, or gone for help; he did not know what she would have done. He cornered her at last, at the door which had once led to Peter's rooms; it was locked, on the other side. She stood against it, unable to go further, waiting for him.

"Simon." Her voice had changed now and was honey; when he grasped her by the body he felt it yield, as if her limbs would flow towards his as they had been used to do, when she would have her way; she might have been water. She made no outcry as he picked her up and carried her to the corridor, to a casement; her unresisting weight seemed light, like a child's. It might have been either that she already knew what he would do, or that she did not think he would bring himself to it. He did not ask her, either way, but unfastened the casement. The frame flung outwards on its hasp like a yawning mouth, and he lifted Melissa over; far below, the courtyard stones lay dreaming in sunlight. There was nobody about.

He said to her, "Now go to your master," and flung her

down. He saw the drifting of her dress and heard her cry, and then ran downstairs. When he got out to her the body lay in such a way as to show that its neck was broken, and the brains spilled out pinkly on the stones, and she was dead. He knelt down by her.

"It was the groom who came," he said to me. "All the rest, except for the nurse who was all the time in the child's own rooms, at the other side of the house, were at the fair. He was a solitary creature, that groom; they say he was a son of Jonie's. He looked down and then looked at me and said, 'It's no use troubling yourself, sir, she is dead,' which I knew, of course, and then he said, as if he knew very well what had happened, 'She was in a melancholy for a long time, sir, and hadn't troubled even to take out the horse; it was the best thing to shoot him, as you did, for he was wild, and I'll see him buried. As for the mistress, I saw her myself stand at the window, and then she climbed out; there was no one with her.' And then he went for help, and left me still kneeling by Melissa; I was dazed, I suppose, and had not corrected him or argued with him as to what had happened, although I knew he knew. Why should he do that for me? But no one, as it happens, asked him anything: it was taken for granted by everyone that she'd thrown herself over, and I—I let them bury her, and attended it, and then I came to you."

20

I MADE UP my mind, as early as this, that Simon was not going to die. He was not going to put an end to himself, as he intended, he said, once affairs were wound up and he had seen Robert again. On the face of it, I may have been wrong to set aside not only this course, but the undoubted one of justice. For a man to kill, in cold blood, a young girl, who had been his wife and the mother of his child, by throwing her out of a high window or by any other means, is a crime rightly punishable by death. But no judge could know the things I knew, both of Simon and Melissa, and also of Aske. It moreover seemed, from what he told me, that in the minds of everyone—including no doubt Sir John Wynmalen, who had come to the funeral, as had all the other county-faces who had never called on Melissa, any more than they had ever done on Ann—Melissa's death had joined the procession of the other deaths at Aske; inevitably, in a kind of accepted formula of horror reserved separately for haunted places, whose inhabitants have a curse in their brains and flesh. Nobody, accordingly, would now do more about it until Simon, with the letter for Sir John in his desk, should be found lying, in expiation and failure, in some spinney in a pool of his own blood. And I would not have this. I would not allow it. I might have been talking to a recalcitrant pupil in this way, within myself; I did not yet say it aloud to Simon.

Firstly, I saw that he ate the food from the tray, which the maid at my instruction had already left outside the door. There was a cold pasty with an egg through it, some cut bread and butter and a jug of coffee, which by now had grown cold. I took the coffee and warmed it again on my fire in a skillet I had, and made Simon drink it. Then I broke the pasty into small pieces in my fingers and fed it to him piece by piece, putting it in his mouth as though he had been a little child. After that he was still restless, and would still talk on, and talked for hours, as if for all of his life till then he had had no listener. In the end I got on my hooded cloak, which was grey, and went out with him. I took time to leave a note for Madame Rauch to say that I had been called away, and to ask her to supervise things till I should return. I did not myself know when that would be.

We walked out of my school together, Simon and I, and into the streets of London. It was quiet now, and so late that even the link-boys and pickpockets had gone home.

Here and there was still a lit torch, guttering low in its bracket outside some lord's house whose owner was still out roystering. We walked through the sleeping streets and picked our way over the heaped gutters and refuse, down past Robert's shop which had the shutters closed and not a sound or light above; and in the end came to the river. It was near dawn by then, and we stood together on Westminster Bridge and watched the sun rise. What I felt then was written many years after by a poet, standing on the same spot at the self-same hour; so I will not repeat the sense I also had of the power and glory of the world, and also the power in myself and that I was not going to lose Simon to death. For I was now as strong as Melissa.

But I could not leave him by himself for a moment yet; it was not safe. I stayed with him while he went to his lawyer's, but little was said there; he had made a will already, except that Melissa's money from the old merchant must be made over to her son: then they talked briefly of Simon's investments and of the warehouses, and the news out of France. Then we came downstairs again and found a coach to take us to. Aske; Simon would send for his own horse later. On the way that evening we stopped at an inn, had supper and stayed overnight, and this time there were not three of us. No doubt I may seem a determined woman, holding fast to the hem of a widower's cloak; and so I was. For he had come to me in his trouble, and I knew I had my place with him still, that Melissa had never taken; that night I filled it.

I will say no more of this, except that I can remember what he said when he had found me again, or I had found myself; I think I never knew myself before. He used few words, and only said my name, as though still incredulous that I was again with him; then again and again, each time with a new astonishment. "Why, Leah ... why, Leah, Leah!" And for the first time, perhaps, since it had happened, he no longer thought entirely of what had been left behind by him at Aske. I welcomed this for his own sake also; when we saw, next day, the crow-steps and the towers, it would, I knew, be the testing-time; either he would become again a man who must die, or one who would live. And I would make him live, for himself and for me.

21

TO MAKE A man live who wants to die, to draw him back as it were from the brink of death, the thought of self-infliction, takes more time than a day and a night, or even weeks; I do not know how long it was till I was sure Simon was out of danger. The worst night was I think when I awoke to find him gone, and the bed cold; we had known great tenderness together before I slept, as if, I thought now, knowing him, it had been a farewell. I flung on a shawl and went down to where I knew he might be, the gun-room; I had replaced the pistols there long ago out of his luggage, but I could not lock the door for it had no lock; in any case, Simon would not have let me make of him a prisoner lacking the exercise of his will.

I hurried through the silent dark house with my heart pounding, expecting at any moment to hear the sound of a shot; he might do the thing here, in the house, or outside to avoid wakening me. But he was still in the gun-room; without a light, for the moon flooded in through the windows as it had over our bed, and showed me the wall with the guns, each one pointing wickedly upwards in its place like hell's reeds, thickly, white on blue. He had not taken down any of them. He was standing staring, as he may have been doing for a long time, perhaps not the first, at them on the wall, deciding which to choose; I thanked God for the hesitation he had shown, and displayed none of my own. I went and took him by the hand, as if he had been sleep-walking.

"Simon," I said gently, for one does not waken such

people with harshness, "come back to bed; it is very early in the morning."

He turned and looked down at me, and as so often I saw the light gleam on his hair, which was grey now, and his eyes which glittered strangely. Something which was akin to anger rose in me for myself and him; why should a fate pursue us which was different and harsher than other fates? What had we done to make the gods angry at our birth? I was no longer young, and he—

"Simon, did I ever tell you something that happened to me that time I left you in Rome?" I said. He said nothing and I felt a chill, dread certainty that he would not even hear me, did not remember who I was; the night's cold struck up from the floor, like the tomb. Soon he would die, by his own hand, some other night, if not tonight while I was with him; some hour, perhaps, or moment when I was no longer vigilant, or slept or had for the time being turned my eyes elsewhere. I sighed, and felt very tired. "Simon," I said, and saw the light draught in the room, which came in from the hallway, stir his shirt-sleeves, making their white fullness tremble as though they dressed a corpse, that within them was quite still. "Simon, if you will do this thing how can I prevent it, I who am only a woman who loves you? But as such a woman I carried your child, that time, only it did not live; and now if you will leave me with the memory of that, and of how you made an end to yourself also, what else is there for me?"

He had stirred, and heard me; I felt the flesh change from wood, or stone, to feeling substance again; he turned, and drew a great harsh breath.

"My child?" he said. "You, Leah? You did not tell me; no one told me, when I . . . "

He asked me more of it. Then he gave a great sob and bowed his head down at last on my shoulder, and drew me to him, as if to comfort himself and me. I held him till he had done and knew, without more words, that he would stay with me now; he would stay, and there would be no further need of his death, as an expiation for Melissa's.

He had already said to me once "Leah, I know you are a good woman of business," and the incredulity, almost amusement, in his voice was an index of the general belief of men that we cannot do as they do, and succeed in it entirely by ourselves. "Before I go, you will understand, I want to leave you provided for, and the boys and—" he left the rest of it. "I once bought you a ring in Paris that you would not wear," he reminded me. "Would you—if I were to buy another—wear it now?"

At some time about then, accordingly, we were married. We did not tell many people. About then, or a little later—for although by now he had promised that he would not again leave me, I did not want to abandon him at Aske for many days by himself, with his memories—I wrote to Herr Rauch about the school, which had meantime, in whatever fashion, been going on without me. It would not be possible, I regretted in my letter, for me to return in the foreseeable future, and having considered the matter very carefully I had decided that, while I myself would have preferred to retain a controlling interest, and would in any case always associate myself very closely with the school, I must now look about me at least for an acting head to manage the day-to-day affairs. This person might be salaried, but as an alternative, if he and Madame considered that their interest in such a matter was as great as their industry had always been, I was prepared to let them purchase the school at a price somewhat lower than it might fetch on the open market. I would also help them to buy it.

Needless to say the Rauchs were overjoyed—they had never had much money and the good Herr's engravings, with which he had used formerly to illustrate books sometimes if a publisher would pay him, had hardly by this means kept body and soul together. He would make, by now, an excellent and methodical school-principal, and his manners were those of a polite person and would not alienate parents. On my advice, which I gave very tactfully in order not to offend Madame, they consulted my dear old Miss Fish, over eighty as she now was but still very active and interested in such things. She found a good, wise, cultured woman she already knew of, who had taught for her previously, and was now widowed, and would take an immediate personal interest in the welfare of the girls. The school has flourished and some years after I left, they were able to buy the adjoining house when this fell vacant, and expand their activities and staff. That was as much as I heard before losing touch with them, for I was by then, of course, out of the country.

I have not yet mentioned one other person at Aske; Melissa's son Simon George. When I returned that time with Simon from London, I had not yet seen the child. I went, I remember, up to the nursery in fear and trembling, lest he resemble Melissa and the whole thing start again adversely . . .

But when the nurse, with whom he had been always left, curtsied and drew aside the curtain of his bed for me, there was Simon himself lying there; a little boy with black hair and eyes. The colouring, it is true, was Melissa's, but the boy was not; he was Simon himself, sleeping as he had once done in Big Het's cottage under an old blanket on a pile of twigs. Simon, a baby with no fear in him; and with all his life still to live.

I would see to that, and that he did not suffer anything from which I could save him. For this was my boy, that I had lost after he came over the Lombard plain and up the Alpine passes with me, lying in me below my heart, and I knew him again. This was Mark, with whom I had later parted; now he was found, and I would never lose him again, or let him lose me.

I knelt down at once and put my arms round him, this other Simon. He was awake, and pulled my hair.

22

THERE WAS ONLY one thing more to do. Had it not been for my stern upbringing in notions of right and wrong, of crime and retribution as expressed in Holy Writ, perhaps, it might not have had to happen. But if it had not, I do not think that Simon would ever have been a whole or happy man again, or other than constantly haunted by his own guilt. He had promised me, and I knew he would keep his promise, not to take his own life in punishment for the death of Melissa; but neither he nor I thought that he would emerge scot-free, nor wanted this to be done. We were honest with one another, and he knew how I felt. Gradually, I regained enough of his confidence to make it no longer inadvisable to raise the matter. This happened some weeks after our marriage; it was by then spring at Aske.

That time of the year is overrated in many places, but can be peerless at Aske, turning the gardens and woods into enchanted country, the place where Ann had died all drifted over with aconites and, later, wood-anemones, and in May the bluebells, like a breath blown by a god. We were walking one day, when it was fine, together about the grounds, watching Simon George in the distance with his nurse; he had learned to stagger his first steps, holding on to her hand. By the time the daffodils were out, blowing everywhere in a great pale-yellow carpet, he would be running about to pick the wild bright double flowers with their frilled petals, like a woman's petticoats. The thought of what the years should bring for Simon George at Aske reminded me of the matter I had been thinking of, for some days now, and I fell silent, walking by Simon with

my hand on his arm. I was bareheaded, and wore no cap,
for I liked to feel the sun on my hair. I looked at Simon
and saw that he was no longer watching his son learn to walk.

"You have a stern and thoughtful air, Mrs. Aske," he
said. "It becomes you, and the parting in your hair is
always entirely straight, white, and mathematical, and the
two sides smooth and precise, like an isosceles. The
prospect pleases me," and he returned his gaze to Aske
rather than my parting, for it was also looking its best, as I
have said, in the spring sunshine. My heart reproached me
that I must soon dispel his gay mood, which did not come
often. I said, "Simon, please listen to me; there is
something which I want to suggest, and then you may
think of it further, if you will." For most things, I knew,
had to be put to Simon in this way; like most men, if he
were coerced towards a thing he would take nothing more
to do with it. As it was, he said, "You are my wife, who
orders me," and set his mouth in obstinate fashion, so that
it was necessary to placate him still further. I marvelled
that I, who only a few weeks and months before had been
my own mistress, and accustomed to dictate to everyone
what my wishes were, should now again be subject, as he
knew very well I was, to him in all ways; he knew also who
did the ordering. But all I said to this, and not in words,
was to turn a deep pink, in my old confused fashion, and
stammer as I spoke.

"You know well I do not," I said, colouring more
deeply than ever. "But, a moment ago, you called me Mrs.
Aske. Simon, if your name were not Aske, but again
Carden; if you no longer owned Aske, and there was no
hope of it for your sons or for their sons' sons, and you
were never to see it again, or perhaps hear of it any more;
how would you feel?" He stared at me to see if I were
jesting; and when I did not falter any longer, but held his
gaze, watching the anger die in it and give place at last to a
kind of fear, I knew I had partly won.

"If you were to give up Aske," I said, "would that be a

great   enough   punishment   for   what   befell   Melissa?"

We talked of it, naturally, many times before he agreed to
regard it seriously, or as other than a fool of a woman's
pitiful sop to what he had always called, and with some
cause, my passive Christianity. I had never made any
pretence to continue the good and charitable work of my
parents among the poor, or make a great show in a church
pew regularly, blossoming forth in different bonnets; nor
did I ever mouth, to my girls or to myself, such quotations
from the Scriptures as are commonly invoked to conjure
up hell-fire for the evil and heaven for the good, for I do
not believe in such cut-and-dried distinctions as certain
persons would instil in us. I had always been careful not to
offend anyone by my lack of orthodoxy, but to myself, I
knew, I was at least part pagan, and though the Christian
faith to many replaces all of the older beliefs which went
before, to me it is, or should be, a continuation of them,
perhaps ridding itself of the unworthy parts and holding
on to those worth keeping, like the clarity and logic of
Greek pagan thought. But, in addition to all this, I cannot
discount certain aspects of old, very old beliefs which are
still among all of us, whether we know them for what they
are or not; like not angering or provoking the wrath of the
Almighty, which is the same as it used to be when men in
the early days propitiated the gods before taking almost
any action of their own will. And I had seen, in the pattern
of Simon's fate, the inexorable pursuit of the jealous gods,
who resented his love of Aske and the lifelong war he had
waged, with himself and other factors, to win it forever for
himself and his sons. To propitiate the gods with what he
best loved, I told him, might placate them; and to this, by
then long after, he turned his eyes again to me, and said in
a dry voice, "I do not love Aske best of anything. And if
you think, my darling, that I will act as that elderly
personage did in the Bible, and elsewhere, and impale you
on a stake to propitiate any gods including Jehovah, you

are wrong; but I will give them Aske instead, as you say I must. Did I not tell you the other day that you ordered me?"

It had not happened as swiftly or as easily as that implies, for it was a brutal notion to make him part with Aske, and I knew it. It was, in a way, my home as well at his; but I had never slaved in servitude for Aske, or perjured my soul and body for it. And there was the vow made at his mother's death, and all of the long, wretched marriage to Ann, for its sake; and the marriage to Melissa had been here, with its hours of passion of a kind that I, fashioned as I was, perhaps did not even yet comprehend any more than the other things of darkness. It would have been the expected thing for Simon to have laughed me into silence, and forbidden me to mention the matter again, and then to have gone on brooding till he died. At least that process would have left him the right to walk in Aske always, as one of its ghosts.

Sometimes he would not move or speak for a long time once the thing was planted in his mind, and for a long time he would frighten me by leaving, again, our bed often in the night hours, and walking alone about Aske. I did not follow him again at such times; he must make the decision, whichever it was, alone, and I could do nothing more than I had done already, which might, I almost began to think, have been too much, and he would run mad of melancholy, in the pattern of things as they had always occurred at Aske.

But Simon was made of other stuff, or I would not have loved him. And in the end he came and said to me, "You are right, Leah, and we should sell out this year. Where shall we go then?" And I knew it did not matter to him where we went, and I thought the further away it was, the better, once the sacrifice had been made. He would not endure the sight of other owners about Aske, other men's plants in his garden, the furnishings altered that he had chosen, the portraits taken down and replaced by those of strangers. And it would happen; so almost without thinking I said to him:

"Shall we leave England? Shall we go to America, where I know you and Sam Grover have connections already established in the export-trade, and you could go on with it, and perhaps do much more once you are there in person, and can see for yourself what they need?" For I myself had always wanted to visit that country, because I had had, from the beginning, much sympathy with the colonists there, who had been made to endure indignities out of all proportion to their worth because we had a stupid, stubborn king. Since then there had been the War of Independence, and Simon, as I knew already, had been one of the first traders in England to bridge the gap. I knew we should find a friendly welcome in the new United States; and the speed with which Simon took up this idea pleased and delighted me. He was soon himself again, planning, projecting what do do, where to go, and the ways to do it most profitably. He was already, in the way he had always had, looking ahead instead of back; that was one reason why he had been a misfit at Aske. He had almost, when the time drew near for us to leave, begun to look on it as a charge to be rid of; this was far more than I had dared to hope for in the process of his cure.

It was time to be gone, in any case, from the ghosts about Aske. Chief among these was of course Melissa; Melissa still sliding into Simon's bed, goading him again with her strong young thighs till the devil once more rode above her, while the night passed; and by dawn she lay quite still, below on the stones. And Ann, of course, was another ghost; poor Ann, trailing across the lawn for the length of a moon-beam, the space of a sigh, with the strings about her, and afterwards the smell of stagnant water where she had passed. And Old Madam would be about, hunting for the lost paper to destroy it, her eyes bright and terrible as emeralds, and a whip in her hand for Dorothy, who was long since gone; and Nicholas would be on the stairs with his boots on, and, always, everywhere, Peter. Peter's lost white face at the window, Peter on the stairs again, torturing a cat; these were my own ghosts, and I would remember them; and that ghost also of a little, lost puppy, a cord knotted tight about its neck, betrayed and whimpering. Yes, it was time to leave; we would go where there were few such ghosts yet, few older memories for our race. We would make our own laughter without echoes there, and hear our children's.

For Simon George would sail with us, of course; the sacrifice had included his own loss of Aske. Perhaps, I thought privately, Robert would come later, if he could be induced to try to build up another book-business across the Atlantic. There were men of letters there. And there was another, a thread of life, a hope, of which I will speak later, for now as then there was no time. There was everything to look through and some things to pack; we would take the portrait of Simon's father. There were letters to write and all the lawyers' business, and the finding of a buyer for the house, which by mercy was quick; matters of such a kind, however, bring innumerable pettinesses with them, and I was glad when it was all over, and we could leave Aske. This happened by the summer.

After all the arrangements were made, and our ship would soon sail, the last night before departure, we walked for the last time together about Aske.

It was a still, moonlit night; the grounds and garden, the pillared folly and the pond, with its reeds upthrusting straight like swords, and the birds asleep among them, were silvered over, like a coming of old age to Aske now we were leaving. But it would have its own renewal with whoever came.

We ourselves had known such a renewal. I remembered it, and I knew that now, even with the gables of the house

and its blind, untenanted windows looking down on Simon
for the last time, he was not thinking of Aske any longer,
nor of the past, but of me and of our future. I do not
think that old age had quite come for either of us yet.

But he took my hand, and harked back nevertheless.
"You remember the day I first came back to Aske, Leah?"
he said. "You were a little, determined creature on a white
pony with short legs, behind Ann."

"I remember," I said, glad that he had named Ann
again. It was, in a way, like laying the sad ghost. I no
longer feel that Ann haunts Aske nowadays, though where
she has gone away to I do not know. I added, then, that I
had not been at all determined in those days, but shy. He
smiled. "You were angry with me for not opening the
gate," he said, "and I thought, though I did not know who
you were—"

"You were not thinking of me at all, but of Ann and the
arrangements for your marriage, and the plan for Aske," I
said. "You hardly looked at me, and I thought, rightly,
that you were a great black-avised creature without
manners."

But he shook his head, and told me not to interrupt. "I
was not thinking of Ann," he said. "I looked at her—she
was a showy piece, on the pony, and resembled her
mother, so I knew who she was, and that it would have to
be done as I'd planned. But I looked again at you—I
remember it, Leah—and I thought, even then, that
wherever you were, would be home. I still feel this, and
that Aske may go down the wind now, if we are together; I
care very little by this time."

"My dearest love, what tales you tell me," I answered
him, but my eyes were wet; for had I not also told myself,
much later on in Rome, that night he was in the inn with
me, that that was home, and anywhere else he might be?

Our next home was to be in New York, where Simon had
friends in the import-business. I will say little of that,

though it is not the end but, in ways, the beginning of our
story; all of our lives together there, and the things that
happened, made of us two new people, though not
different people; conditions suited our growth. We grew
rich, or rather Simon did, but that is not so important; the
importance, to me, was that he need no longer conceal, for
social reasons, the fact that he was a knowledgeable
importer of goods and a clever salesman. Some of the
friends he had at one time made in Barbados were met
with again, over the years, and others; Sam Grover came
for a long visit, and so did Robert, and in the end stayed,
as I had hoped.

All this filled me with a kind of incredulous joy, and in
those days I could also watch my daughter. Mine; for at
more than forty years of age, at about the time we set out
on the Atlantic voyage, I knew for certain that I was, once
again, carrying Simon's child. I hardly dared hope that all
would go well; I said nothing, I remember, till we were
four days out to sea, because he would have wanted to
turn back with me; as it was, he scolded me and behaved,
for the rest of the voyage and after landing, as if I were
made of glass, which I had lately discovered I was not.
Self-evaluation they say is a good thing; so, possibly, is
abstinence. I never knew why it was that the baby started
and grew, thrived, was born—the pain then was nothing,
the joy everything, and Simon was away on some
business-trip and had arranged to be back in time for the
birth, but I defeated him, by one week. He would only
have been in the way, as I told him later, when, to my own
amazement, I even found myself able to feed my own
child. I will never forget Simon's expression as he came in
that first time through the door, having arrived with the
horse and himself in a lather, and saw us for the first time
together, Robin suckling me.

We called her Robin although it is a man's name,
because from the beginning, even before her eyelids lost
their birth-swelling, I could see whom she was going to

look like; Simon's father, Robin Aske. It is clear proof, I think, that the slanders spread about at the beginning regarding Big Het were malicious nonsense, thought of by Old Madam and, no doubt, Hester's father. I myself added Maria to the name, in memory of poor old Maria Gore to whom we also owed something. Robin Maria had dark hair, not as dark as Simon's own had been but of the colour of a chestnut-conker, very smooth and straight; I used to cut it short, like a boy's, to save her the weary necessity of curl-papers and hair-ribbons all her childhood. She grew taller than I, and very pretty, and was never bookish; at eighteen years old she was married to a son of one of the former officers in General Washington's army, and now they have children of their own, whose faces I have never seen.

But in my memory I can still see clearly, unlike those blind from birth. I can remember, again, an episode from Robin's childhood, which because I am an old woman I tend to confuse with the nursery-years at Steed, a little; the stories I told Robin were the same as those for Mary and Bertram and Barnabas and Sarah long ago, and they were mostly about the classical heroes, who have always been real to me. I remember once, on an autumn evening in the house where we lived before we found Oaklands, Robin was seated on the firestool in her favourite place, and Simon was at the farther side of the fire smoking his long-stemmed pipe he had lately taken to; he looked very peaceful. I was, not for the first time, finishing the story of Ulysses for Robin, and she listened, but not with her usual rapt attention; I was about to say that if she did not care to listen further it was her bedtime, which it was in any case, but the child herself forestalled me, looking up with a sideways glance of her dark eyes, which are so like her father's and have excellent vision.

"Mama, dearest," she said, in the respectful, pretty manner she still uses, "who, pray, tell me, was the Devil of Aske?"

I do believe that there was silence in the room for a full minute, while the wall-clock ticked. Simon and I did not look at one another. Then I said, with my voice expressionless and under control, as I hope, "Where did you hear of that, Robin?"

"I have no idea, Mama." And she waited, with the bright-eyed look that let me know she would not be satisfied until someone answered her, so I did my best. "He was," I said, "a tall dark personage, very ugly, who appeared at a gate one day at Aske when two young ladies were about to ride through on their ponies."

"Aske is in England, is it not, Mama? Why was he a devil?"

"No doubt because he had not the common manners to open the gate."

Simon spoke up. "He did open it," he said, still drawing at the pipe. He bent forward then and knocked it out deliberately. "A devil, my dear Robin, is anyone who does not act precisely as everyone else does in England, where they are extremely conservative. There are those who still say there that President Washington was a devil. There is no proof, on the other hand, that the devil in some other context is not very often a woman. In point of fact, I know of one instance where this was so. Her name was Lilith."

"Indeed, Papa? Pray tell me of her."

"Robin, it is your bedtime," I said inexorably, looking at the clock on the wall. I did not greatly like the talk, or where it might lead. Our life here was ordinary, solid, prosperous enough; we had put the past behind us. I wanted to shelter my daughter from that as much as could be done; Simon George, who was not present on that occasion, would have to be told, when he was older, that I was not his mother. I had intended that he should know from the beginning, but as he grew, and accepted me, I found that I had not the heart. I closed my eyes, and when I opened them found Simon and Robin regarding one another gravely.

"Please, Mama, just one more story. Papa hardly ever tells stories; permit him to do so this once."

"This woman who was a devil," said Simon, "also lived at Aske, in England, and she was very ugly."

"Are devils always ugly?"

"No; some are very beautiful, and they are the worst. This one, however, was not a devil proper, as they say; she was perhaps a cross between a witch and a fairy. She was tiny, and had her nose forever in a book."

"A magic book?"

"Undoubtedly. With it, she used to cast spells on a poor man, whom she later led by the nose. Every time he thought he had captured her, she would fly farther off, on her witch's wings; over mountain ranges and, once, an ocean. Wherever she went he had to follow; he had no choice."

"What happened?" said Robin relentlessly, adding, "If she was so ugly I don't see why he was unable to free himself, spells or no spells." My daughter is of a practical disposition.

"They all grew old; her ugliness wore off a little. In the end he caught her, and—"

"And then I was born and we all came to New York, and lived happily ever after," said Robin suddenly, and the pair of them burst out laughing. Such things lighten my darkness.

Shortly after that we found our house, which is called Oaklands and is eleven miles out of the city, and there we lived very quietly. The previous owner had built it, shortly before the outbreak of war with England, and had, like Admiral Collingwood, planted English oaks from acorns in the driveway. This pleased me; I had not brought a single acorn, seed or plant from Aske, in order that Simon need never be reminded of it. These oaks would not be an avenue in our time, as we knew, though Robin's children may sit in their shade when they are my age, if they live as long as I have done. But they were oaks from England.

The house has pillars and a portico, in the colonial style, and is not like Aske. One thing that pleased me however for Simon's sake was that it had a staircase, even nobler than that remembered one we left. It ascends from the tiled front hall in a graceful spiral, with gilding on its panels of delicate wrought ironwork. I believe that it was brought from the South, and was fashioned there last century by French craftsmen. It is of a splendour fit for some powdered beauty, descending in hoops and panniers for a ball; for Simon, escorting Robin down it for her wedding, looking like a marquis of the old régime, as I told him afterwards, but my old bones toiling up and down in a plain cap and gown never did it justice. They have done so, in fact, less often this year than last; I have not been very well, and all of the summer have stayed with Robin in her house in town, to be near the physician, which troubles me as I do not like being away too long from Simon where he lies now, under the young growing oaks. I hope to return soon, to the place where we were happy.

If we had indeed parted with Aske in exchange for a few years of ordinary happiness, the gods kept their bargain. I cannot recall anything notable about those years, only small things, showing Simon as, perhaps, he should always have been had circumstances, or his fate, been different. For now that so much stress had departed from our lives they may have seemed plain and dull to others, though not to us; like the time we roasted a pig on the front lawn at Oaklands, for the first Thanksgiving there, and it had snowed, and Robin wore a fur hood and Simon George, who would be eleven then, and Robin stoked the fire with maple-chips. And there was the time shortly after Robert himself came and joined us, and I said we all ought to go to church, and so we went, the men in great shovel hats and I in a Paris bonnet, and we filled up a pew, with the children as well, which made me think for the first time in many years of the day at Aske so long ago, when I had first seen Old Madam and the rest and she had worn a blind-bonnet and carried her ebony cane, and filled me with awe.

And there were the other things; Robin's bringing-out and her young men, and her marriage; and the negro servants we had, who loved Simon for his kindly treatment of them, which granted is common up here, and one old man used to make us a rag rug each year for Christmas, and the last was unfinished when Simon died, and the old man wept at his funeral and said that he had been a saint, which is very far from being known as the Devil of Aske.

There are all those things; and I can remember them, now I am alone. But I do not think Simon was a saint any more than he was a devil. His state, like most people's, depended on his happiness; and he was happy at Oaklands, and so was I.

I do not know whether the gods punished me with blindness, before the end, for my presumption in having rescued Simon from the course of the law or from making an end of himself. Had I not loved Simon it would not have happened; but had I not done so, and had somehow learned of his circumstances, the way in which almost from birth he had to fight for very existence, let alone recognition or riches, and that unaided, I think that I might, even as a judge, have shown mercy. As it was, had I been asked to fling away my sight as a gift to propitiate the dark gods, I would have done so gladly; perhaps I did. After the first beginning, and before he and Grover made things run smoothly again following the 1812 war, I would sit by Simon night after night with a candle, helping with accounts; no doubt it was foolish, but in love one grudges nothing, and he was grateful to me. I always said that if I could see his face to the last, whichever of us died first, this was all I asked for; this was granted to me just before my sight failed. Simon died in bed at seventy-four, a calm and peaceful end for an Aske, and I was with him. By that time there was again a flourishing import-business, he was a respected citizen, and had done much good. I do not think that I acted wrongly in saving him, years before, leaving aside the fact that it made me personally happy.

Yes, we were content together to the end, and one can ask nothing better; for the rest, I do not know any more than anyone else. But if the gods chose later to punish me somewhat by this blindness, it shows they respect the growth of purpose in women. For Helen was never punished by them for her part in the war of Troy, but went back home again with Menelaus to die in due course of old age, as if she were a chattel. For the most part, except for Electra, all the retribution-tales concern men. The gods do not yet take us women as seriously as, very shortly, even they will have to do; since my own youth great advances have been made in the knowledge and education permitted to girls, and I heard, only the other day, of a young woman in a northern state who spoke of wishing to study medicine, whether or not her parents will permit her to do so. I can see no reason why they should not.

Simon George took over the import-business finally, to allow his father to retire with me to Oaklands, and plant his garden. We had worried, or I had, at some point about Simon George, who was wild for some years after he had learned about his parentage; he wanted, I remember, to become a trapper in the north, and for five years went and lived up there among the Indians. But instead of settling down with some squaw in a leather wigwam, and scraping beaver-skins, he fortunately met and married a missionary's daughter and in the end brought her south, where she keeps an eye on him. Robert never married, and never now will; the line of Jonie Braik and Aske has come to an end, for Ann's son died four years ago and I miss him greatly.

But I am still most greatly concerned with my own dear Simon. He died happy, or rather, as I say, content; happiness is too wild a thing to suit anyone but the young, and by then we had long grown together like two gnarled twisted branches springing from quite separate roots. I was with him as he died, and before he went he said, "Leah, if I go now I'll wait for you, or if you take too long I will return for you, when it is time," and I remembered Jonie again and how he made the sign of the cross over Ann, and said something the same to her. So Simon went, and it seems very long now, and I sit here remembering and when she can, Robin comes in and sometimes reads to me, and there are the children. I love them, but they are not as real to me as Simon, whose face is still clear in my mind, as it was that first day at Aske. To have Simon come for me at my new journey's beginning, which must be soon, comforts me. And after that we will surely travel on together.

Note written in the hand of Robin Farquharson, but unsigned, among the papers.

My dear mother, Leah Carden Aske, died here today at a great age in my house in New York, the fourth of October, 1835. She is to be buried beside my father at Oaklands.